About the Author

After a successful career over nearly thirty years in the corporate world, based mostly in London, Andrew Pratt now lives and writes in Prague, Czech Republic.

Head to Head is his second book in the Honza crime series. He is currently writing the third novel.

The first book in the series was published in 2021 – *In the Heart of Prague (Honza Book 1)*.

Head to Head – Honza Book 2

Andrew Pratt

Head to Head – Honza Book 2

Olympia Publishers
London

www.olympiapublishers.com
OLYMPIA PAPERBACK EDITION

A CIP catalogue record for this title is
available from the British Library.

ISBN: 978-1-80074-536-0

This is a work of fiction.
Names, characters, places and incidents originate from the writer's
imagination. Any resemblance to actual persons, living or dead, is
purely coincidental.

First Published in 2022

Olympia Publishers
Tallis House
2 Tallis Street
London
EC4Y 0AB

Printed in Great Britain

Dedication

This book is dedicated to my mum and dad.
Your first visit to Prague was so special to me and is one of my favourite memories.
Thank you for your love and support.

Acknowledgements

Thank you to my dear friends, Nick White and Dominic Jennings, for supporting me through the process of writing this novel. Your guidance, suggestions for improvement and encouragement were invaluable.

Dan Gracie and Paul McCarthy also read through the final draft and, as frequent readers, including crime and mystery novels, they helped me refine the detail of the serious crime investigation. Thank you for your sharp eyes and honest feedback.

Thank you also to Věra Colbecková for reading through the final version, ensuring the story held together and picking up a last few grammatical errors.

My partner, Pavla, remains the inspiration for me coming to Prague and writing this series in the first place. She deserves a medal for her patience and support. Thank you.

1

Karlovy Vary, Czech Republic

Tuesday, 13 April 2010

Their afternoon walking tour had led them through the maze of cobbled streets and colonnades, seemingly transporting them back in time. The landmarks of the famous spa resort were enthralling, the dramatic setting enhanced by the expanse of tree-lined forests banking up the hill behind the historic buildings. Water was everywhere: the river winding through the heart of the town, the bubbling hot streams underground, even in the visitors' excited chatter as they praised the healing powers of the mineral springs.

The Market Colonnade made a strong claim to be Karlovy Vary's centrepiece, the historic architecture of the building and the eminent square beguiling in its charm. Despite Ivana extolling its virtues ahead of their trip, Jonny had not expected the building to be so original and majestic.

"This is bringing it all back to me now," Jonny said, entranced.

"What do you mean?" Ivana replied.

"Well, this experience reminds me of exploring Old Town Square in Prague a month ago. And, look how that turned out."

Ivana snorted, a tinge of impatience evident in her reaction. "Honza, nobody is going to get murdered. This is just a quiet, relaxing trip. Let's just enjoy ourselves."

"You're right." He smiled and took her hand. "After Felix began putting these thoughts about fate into my head, I've started to expect danger around every corner."

Ivana laughed, shaking her head. "Felix Mikeš may be a famous detective, but he talks too much."

He laughed, enjoying the banter. "The Black Cat wouldn't be happy with you saying that."

"The only good thing he did was nickname you Honza. It's perfect, reflects your Czech heritage."

"My mother would certainly be shocked if she was around to see me now. She always called me Jonathan."

"I think she'd approve. You worry too much."

At first glance they appeared to be like any other middle-aged tourists on the square, but on closer inspection, Ivana was the free spirit in their pairing. The vintage velvet jacket worn over a long summer dress with matching long scarf, combined with her long, loose hair gave her a bohemian air. Jonny's choice of clothes was more conservative, reflecting his years of dressing for the job: a simple blue shirt the only colour in an otherwise plain chino and jacket combination.

Sensing the grandness of the setting, he turned slowly in a full circle to take in the full glory of the Market Colonnade. The cobbled street passing the bottom of the square was alive, visitors milling in and out of the souvenir shops or relaxing with a drink at an outside table. The natural spring on the edge of the square provided the accompanying sound of water, softening the scene and complementing the thermal waters simmering under their feet. The Swiss-style white wooden structure of the main feature was framed by the colourful, historic buildings almost floating to impress on the levels above, accessible by the steps up from the

Holy Trinity Column.

Ivana watched Jonny surveying the scene, smiling to herself. "So, Honza, what do you think?"

Jonny shook his head gently, in awe of his surroundings. "I didn't think anything could compete with the centre of Prague. But Karlovy Vary runs it close. It's…"

"It's sometimes hard to describe beauty," she offered when he didn't finish his sentence. "I didn't have words either when I came here first time."

Jonny smiled at her, nodding his head in silent agreement. Ivana took his hand and, raising herself on tiptoes, kissed him gently on the lips.

"What was that for?" he enquired, playfully.

"For showing me the sights again through someone else's eyes. I've been here more times than I can remember, but when you see the reaction of someone seeing it for the first time it brings back the sensations you felt yourself on the first visit."

"I understand completely," Jonny concurred. "I remember showing Charlotte around the London sights when she was small and her eyes were alive in wonder when we stood outside Buckingham Palace. I'll never forget it."

Ivana reached up and kissed him again, this time lingering with her lips on his as she looked deep into his eyes.

Jonny grinned. "This is becoming a little habit of yours, isn't it?"

"Well, it is my birthday trip, and you did say I could do whatever I wanted."

His wide, soft smile conceded defeat immediately.

"I thought," she continued, her eyes twinkling, "we should go into the Market Colonnade to see the natural springs and then have a cocktail in the afternoon sun."

"It's your show, birthday girl."

"Come on, Honza!" She pulled at the sleeve of his casual jacket, smiling to herself, and led him across the square towards the queue formed outside the Market Colonnade.

The last month had been calm and relaxing compared to his full-on introduction to life in Prague. Following the drama of his role in an unexpected murder hunt, dubbed Vražda na Staroměstském náměstí (*The Old Town Square Murder*) by the Czech media, he had smoothly slotted back into tourist mode. Despite being featured in a few newspapers, Jonny had not been recognised anywhere and had been able to continue his exploration of Prague untroubled, ticking off the list of sights he'd originally planned to visit on his three month trip.

Ivana and the regulars at their local pub, Hloupý Honza, had also recommended more interesting places to visit in the city, allowing him to discover parts of Prague not usually explored by visitors led by the conventional guide books. The various urban parks across the city had proved a particular revelation: green spaces steeped in history and hosting famous statues, hidden amongst the growing sprawl of the city.

His return visit to the Petřin Lookup Tower, the scene of his joint effort with Mikeš to accost the murderer, had provided a suitable conclusion to his first detective adventure in Prague. Leaning on the rail of the lower observation deck, looking out over the River Vltava and the city skyline, he'd realised how much solving the case had meant to him. It also seemed to have provided closure on his final, haunting case before he'd taken early retirement from the Metropolitan Police; he no longer had nightmares about feeling guilty for not being able to save the last victim of the notorious serial killer, Bill Sutherland.

Jonny had even built up the courage to visit the area where

his mother may have once lived, before she left for the UK, never to return. He had found only one street in modern-day Prague with the same name as stated on her old residence papers and had walked there full of excitement and trepidation. Walking the unknown and empty street, he'd sensed ghosts from her past watching him. Nothing had happened, of course, no answers had miraculously presented themselves, but the experience served to stoke his interest and strengthen his desire to find out more about his mother's Czech family.

Spending time with Ivana filled his evenings, both exploring the city nightlife and staying in, lounging on the sofa and talking into the early hours. The extensive and varied music scene in Prague in particular had surprised and delighted him, numerous humble but cosy venues showcasing new and developing talents from all music genres. The underground clubs reminded him of what he'd read about the New York Greenwich Village music vibe in the 1960s, music that defined a generation and gave a platform to his beloved Bob Dylan.

Mikeš had also been a constant feature. He was in touch every day, inviting Jonny for coffee, lunch or dinner whenever work allowed, building their friendship and cementing their partnership for future police work. Jonny had learned to accept and enjoy all of Mikeš' eccentricities, valuing his emotional but always insightful views on life and the paths it had to offer. Jonny only drew the line at a foursome dinner: Ivana and him with Mikeš and his ex-wife, Pathologist Ella Králová. Although Mikeš suggested it almost every time they met, Jonny wanted to keep these personal relationships separate. Despite his recent good fortune with relationships, including improved communication with his estranged daughter, Charlotte, he was still intrinsically cautious by nature.

His relationship with Ivana had initially baffled and scared him. After all, Ivana was first and foremost his landlady during his stay in Prague. Whilst he'd been adamant, he didn't want a romantic liaison with all the complications it could bring, their time together had proved so easy and enjoyable. In truth, this was all down to Ivana. She was happy to enjoy life and take each day as it came, not letting the past shape the future. Jonny had never felt so comfortable and was learning to live in the moment. He knew the point would come when some decisions would need to be made about the future, but for now he was content to keep his senses open and enjoy the taste of life.

The trip to Karlovy Vary for Ivana's birthday had been Jonny's idea. Her initial protests were easily overcome, her eyes lighting up in excitement when he showed her the brochure for the spa hotel. She never agreed as such, simply leapt straight to the planning stage, listing all the places she wanted to show him.

Arriving mid-morning, she'd immediately taken him on a strenuous walk up the forest paths out of the small town. The Deer Jump Lookout, the site of a famous Chamois statue, was claimed to be the oldest lookout structure in the town and afforded a birds-eye view of the River Teplá winding its way around the ancient town. After stopping for a quick lunch in a backstreet café, they'd strolled to the Castle Tower. The climb up the inner staircase delivered a breath-taking perspective of the surrounding maze of narrow, cobbled streets.

At the front entrance of the Market Colonnade, they joined the short queue under the pillared arcade. The other visitors were mainly elderly Germans and Russians wanting to take advantage of the healing powers of the mineral waters. Ivana was excited, claiming it her favourite place to visit in Karlovy Vary; they had planned to finish their route here, to enjoy the ancient setting and sample the waters.

Jonny craned his neck to study the architecture as the queue slowly delivered them inside. The colonnade building was beautifully carved from wood, the neoclassical structure created by fabled Viennese architects in the 1880s. The central piece inside was the bronze panel above the vase of the Charles IV Spring, depicting the legend of the discovery of the natural hot spring. He marvelled at the three springs seeping within the colonnade, tasting each in turn: the Charles IV Spring, the Market Spring, and the high-rising fountain of the Lower Castle Spring.

Although Jonny found the springs enlivening, imagining the long journey of the hot water from deep beneath the earth surface, he found the taste far less appetising. His first sip of the mineral waters from their purchased porcelain cup had Ivana laughing at him, the strong taste bringing a grimace to his face. Being polite, he decided to grin and bear it, thinking instead of the alleged health benefits: improved digestion and metabolic function.

With a heavy, lingering taste of minerals in his mouth, his tongue trying to scrape the taste from his inner cheeks, Jonny was quick to remind her of the suggested cocktail when they exited back out into the late afternoon sunshine. They chose an appealing restaurant on the edge of the square, providing lingering views of the Market Colonnade.

Ivana protested but Jonny ordered a bottle of champagne, the tray arriving with local strawberries at the bottom of the flute glasses. He raised his glass and held her gaze as they clinked glasses. "Happy birthday, Ivana."

"Thank you, Honza. And, thank you again for my birthday treat. Na zdraví."

"Na zdraví."

Jonny had a gulp of the champagne, washing the slightly

sweet, bubbly alcohol around his mouth, then quickly took another smaller sip. "That's better," he declared.

Ivana smiled. "Don't forget we have a sauna booked back at the hotel before dinner. Too much alcohol beforehand is not good. If you don't drink some water, you'll end up looking like a prune."

Jonny laughed, placing his glass back on the table. Sensing a break in the conversation, he turned his head away from the table and scanned the restaurant. Seeing what he was doing, Ivana pulled a face at him. He just shrugged his shoulders in acceptance of the inevitable and continued his in-built human radar; the experienced detective was never off-duty, always assessing his surroundings for potential signs of danger. The interior of the restaurant was sparsely occupied; only a few older tourists had stopped for an afternoon beverage. The other customers were on the small terrace: an older couple, probably in their eighties, fit and healthy-looking, but both were resting walking sticks against the frame of their chairs.

"I'm sorry, Ivana. After nearly twenty-five years as a policeman, I'm never going to lose the compulsion to examine my surroundings. It's a natural instinct and I just can't do anything about it." He smiled. "You'll just have to think of me like your bodyguard."

Ivana turned her head, following Jonny's previous scanning operation, and chuckled to herself. "I think we're safe here!" she exclaimed, sarcastically. "The only people in the restaurant are old enough to be great-grandparents."

Jonny remained resolute. "I have been in many situations, like Old Town Square, where everything appears normal and calm. But, then suddenly something unexpected happens and people can be in danger."

Ivana smiled, clearly not wanting to be drawn in further. Although Jonny had only known her for a month, he'd already experienced her lack of patience with the subject.

She raised her flute. "Na zdraví."

Before Jonny could reach for his glass his mobile phone bleeped. He took the phone from his jacket pocket and unlocked it. "It's from Felix," he relayed. "I've had a few missed calls from him this afternoon." Turning to Ivana, he read the message out loud.

"Honza, come quickly. I have the strange feeling a British man living in Prague has been murdered!"

2

Birthday Suit

The view from the second floor dining room of the spa hotel was unblemished; the scene before the dinner guests swept across the lower level of Karlovy Vary. Old streetlights in the streets below provided a subtle yellow illumination, reflecting a bygone age. The Castle Tower stood proud and resplendent amongst the colonnade structures, the three arches on each side of the observation level lit up below the dark roof and spire of the reconstructed Baroque style tower.

The corner table, requested in advance by Jonny for the occasion, was offset by a gold candelabra. Flickering flames from the three long-stemmed candlesticks weaved shapes in the darkened light, glinting off the silver cutlery and the crystal glasses. The position of the secluded table cut them off from other guests as they looked out of the large sash window. Only the waiters interrupted their privacy, politely enquiring about the food and topping up their wine glasses.

Ivana had made a special effort for her birthday dinner, wearing a long black dress with silver straps. Her hair was pinned up, a silver choker necklace and matching dangling earrings setting off her neckline. Jonny's effort was more modest, but he had bought new shirt and trousers.

They had both opted for the soup of the day, as recommended by Ivana: garlic soup, or česnečka, a simple broth made with onions, garlic and potatoes, topped with local hermelín cheese and croutons. Jonny was initially reluctant, expecting an over-powering taste, but the broth was refreshing and subtle in taste, only a hint of garlic evident. He laughed when she told him the soup was the number one hangover cure in the Czech Republic, envisaging the multiple attempts to substantiate the claim.

The main course was easily chosen; the roast duck was an appropriate celebration, a repeat of their first night out together in the Hloupý Honza pub a month ago. The duck was seasoned with caraway seeds and marjoram, a much featured herb on the menu, and served with potato dumplings and red cabbage.

Hungry after their busy day of sightseeing, Jonny finished eating the duck and placed the cutlery together on the empty plate. "Delicious." He took a sip of the German red wine, a Pinot Noir from Baden, and waited for Ivana to finish.

Their walk back from the restaurant earlier in the day had been slow and meandering after the bottle of champagne. Luckily, the town centre was compact, allowing them to see all the main sights by daylight. Jonny had felt like a nap on their return to the hotel, but Ivana had quickly reminded him about the sauna, also making him gulp down plenty of water.

Ivana had giggled when she came out of the bathroom, wearing the hotel's white bath robe. Jonny was standing in the middle of the room in his new swimming trunks, cleverly bought on impulse in Prague only a few days before. Or, so he thought.

"Honza, you do know the sauna rules, don't you?"

"What do you mean?" he'd replied, a perplexed look on his face.

Ivana had laughed again, suddenly realising he was a novice. "Have you ever been to a sauna or steam room before?"

He'd shaken his head slowly, a worried frown developing on his forehead.

"I think you British say that you need to wear your birthday suit."

In slow motion, Jonny had looked down at the slight bulge in the front of his swimming trucks and then back up at Ivana. "You mean naked?"

Ivana had nodded slowly and deliberately, her hand over her mouth to prevent her laughter from bursting out.

"Well, I'm not going," he'd stated flatly, sitting down in the armchair in protest.

Having supressed her amusement, she'd approached Jonny and put her palm gently on his cheek, her favourite gesture. Eventually, he'd lifted his head to hers. "Come on, it'll be fine," she attempted to reassure him. "You've told me lots of times that this is a new phase in your life. This is just another one of life's new experiences."

Jonny had shaken his head, unconvinced and embarrassed, but eventually allowed Ivana to lead him to the lift and downstairs to the spa in the basement. After speaking to the receptionist, she'd led them to the sauna rooms where she'd quickly disrobed, wrapped a towel around her waist and entered the women's sauna after a peck on his cheek. He was left standing alone, glancing towards the men's sauna, not sure what to expect behind the closed, wooden door.

Opening the sauna door tentatively, he'd been immediately faced with two naked men. Both were sitting astride their white towels, leaving nothing to the imagination. Jonny instinctively lowered his gaze and headed for the safety of the corner, muttering "Dobrý den" in greeting. He sat intently watching the clock for the allotted time, the seconds ticking away slower than he could ever remember. The two men left and were replaced by three burly, elderly, Russian men, who brashly walked around without their towels on, splashing water on the hot coals to create more steam. His heart leapt with joy when the time was up, heading off for the cold shower and steam room.

On recounting the story later in their hotel room, Jonny had expected some level of understanding or sympathy. Instead, he'd just received a battery of uncontrollable laughter from Ivana; his relation of events had her in stitches, bent over double in pain.

Whilst Jonny gazed out of the dining room window, privately reflecting on another new life experience, Ivana finished the last of her main course. A waiter came over to their table to collect the plates. "Would you like to see the dessert menu?"

"I think we need a little break," Jonny replied.

"Certainly, sir." The waiter retreated, leaving them alone.

"You were right, that was delicious," Ivana stated. "Mind you, I still think you should have had the local sausages after your sauna experience today."

Jonny turned to look at her, his face breaking into a grin. "Not again!"

"Honza, I swear I haven't laughed like that since I was a teenager."

He gave her a mock, stern look. "Well, I'm glad it made your day. But, if you don't stop teasing me, I might decide against giving you the present I've made."

Ivana clapped her hands together excitedly. "You've *made* something for me? I'm intrigued."

Jonny slipped his hand into his jacket pocket and pulled out a wrapped present – clearly a CD case shape – and handed it over to her.

"Thank you," she said, and leaned over to kiss him on the lips.

"Go on, open it… I just hope you like it."

She slowly peeled back the tightly sealed edges and then, looking towards Jonny with an eager smile, proceeded to tear off the rest of the paper. She turned the CD case over in her hand and read aloud from the handwritten sleeve, *"To Ivana. Happy birthday. These are ten of my favourite Bob Dylan songs, chosen by me for you. Love Honza x."*

Ivana looked at him, stunned, mouth open in shock.

Misunderstanding her silence, Jonny quickly filled the space with explanation. "I wanted to give you something personal. So, I searched through my collection and selected the songs that most made me think of you. The first song is *If Not For You*; it makes me think about what would have happened if I hadn't booked your spare room when I came to Prague. The second song is *Most of the Time* which is mostly about me and how I felt last year. The third song—"

"Honza, stop!" She looked directly at him, reaching across the table for his hand. "I love it. It means so much to me already. But, I want to listen to it myself and form my own relationship with the songs."

"Of course," Jonny apologised, putting his palms up in excited schoolboy innocence. "But, make sure you listen closely to *Love Minus Zero* – it's one of my favourite songs."

"I will. You know I will. Don't worry…" She smiled. "I will tell you all about the songs when I've listened to the whole CD. But, I want you to know that I love it. Thank you."

He leaned back into his chair and let out a relieved, deep breath. "You don't know how worried I was about making the CD. I didn't know if you'd like it."

She reached out and put her hand on his forearm. "I told you, I love it. Relax."

The lights in the restaurant suddenly dimmed and the head waiter waltzed over to their table holding a dessert plate, the small chocolate pudding holding up a burning candle. He placed the plate in front of Ivana on the table, wished her happy birthday, and retreated back to his position at the bar. People at the adjoining table leant over and extended their own wishes whilst an older lady dining alone behind them clapped her hands in celebration.

"Happy birthday," Jonny repeated, nodding towards the flickering candle.

"Thank you, Honza, I've had a lovely day."

She puffed out her cheeks and blew out the candle.

Jonny's mobile phone started ringing and he took it out of his jacket pocket. "It's Felix," he said to Ivana.

"Do you need to take it now?" she said quickly, her eyes pleading with him.

Jonny hesitated, looking between Ivana and the ringing phone. "You know I've been trying to reach him all evening, after that message earlier. He said he'd call as soon as he could, but…" Aware that nothing he said would suffice, his explanation tailed off. He knew he had to take the call. But, he also knew how hard it was for anyone else to fully understand. This situation had repeated itself at numerous times during his career: special events overshadowed by his absence at key points like lighting the cake, or with him lurking in the background on the phone.

He turned slightly in his chair, away from Ivana, and took the call. "Felix?"

"Honza, I'm sorry," Mikeš began. "I wanted to call you back earlier, but we're flooded with new serious crime investigations.

Marek and Lucie are doing a great job, but we are short of officers at the moment and I'm finding it hard to prioritise all the searches and interviews we need to conduct. Plus—"

"Felix, I'm sorry to interrupt, but I need to be quick. I'm having dinner with Ivana. It's her birthday today."

"That's great, my friend. We must have dinner all together soon, us two with Ivana and Ella—"

"Yes, we will at some point. But, Felix, what was this message about earlier? Has a British man been murdered in Prague?"

"Well, a British man who's lived in Prague for over ten years has just disappeared."

"A missing person!" Jonny exclaimed, a tinge of anger developing.

"Well, that's what we thought initially," Mikeš started explaining. "His wife reported him missing this morning. They live apart now, but she was contacted by his office because he hadn't turned up to work for two days. Marek has started investigating, but it is very suspicious. The last time we know of anyone being in contact with him was on Friday. Nobody seems to have seen him at all over the weekend."

Jonny tutted, turning quickly to check on Ivana, who was looking glumly out of the restaurant window.

"But, you need more than that to jump to the conclusion he's been murdered."

"Yes, I know. But, there's something very odd about this case. Can you come to the office in the morning? I'd like to go through what we have with you."

"That's not so easy, Felix. I'm in Karlovy Vary."

"Very nice." Mikeš paused. "Tomorrow afternoon then?"

"Yes, okay. We're driving back tomorrow morning. I'll call

you, but I'm not sure what time we'll be back in Prague."

"Okay, my friend. Have a nice evening and say happy birthday to Ivana from me."

Jonny finished the call, discreetly putting his mobile back into his pocket, and turned back to Ivana. She was still staring forlornly at the view from the dining room.

"Felix says happy birthday," he relayed, smiling.

Ivana turned to him, her face showing no emotion. "Honza, is this what it's like being in a relationship with a police detective?"

3

Love is the Key

Wednesday, 14 April

The conversation in the car on the drive back to Prague was strained. Jonny's attempts to start discussions were met with polite but distant responses, Ivana rarely starting a conversation. They settled into a mutual silence: she focused on the driving, carefully manoeuvring the Audi through the country roads out of Karlovy Vary and onto the highway back to Prague, whilst Jonny watched the forest through the passenger window.

There hadn't been an argument the previous evening, not even any harsh words. However, the jubilation at the birthday dinner and the present opening was lost, somehow fizzling out not to return. Jonny had tried to restore the high spirits by recalling the humorous events of the day and raising another celebratory toast, but neither had worked. Ivana was responsive, answering his questions, returning his toasts positively and also smiling at his tales. But, something in the celebratory mood had gone astray during the telephone call with Mikeš. When they had retired after a nightcap, she'd dressed for bed quickly, yawning her excuses after a tiring day, and was soon asleep.

Jonny had been in this position before, more times than he cared to remember. People close to him knew he cared passionately about bringing criminals to justice, something they liked and respected about him. But somehow, they eventually drew the conclusion that his work was more important to him than they were. Obviously, he would protest, attempting to make good the situation, but he could never seem to recapture the mood before the job started to impinge on the relationship. This had proved the case for loved ones, including his daughter and some friends. Whilst he knew he wasn't innocent, it was never intentional. The nature of being a high profile police detective meant he had to be available twenty-four hours a day; he could get an emergency call at any time, even in the middle of the night. Sometimes the emergencies came at inopportune times, maybe during a celebration or family time. Many of these could have waited, but how was he to know? He always saw clearly what the other person sensed when this happened; it was in their eyes. The feeling of being insignificant.

As they passed through Krušovice, the town famous for the Royal Brewery started in the 1500s, Jonny reflected on his own journey since arriving in Prague. He'd had no intention of any adventures, just a relaxing break before deciding on his new challenge. The historic city clearly had different ideas and had placed him under its spell, pulling him into a murder hunt and setting off a string of events that had questioned his thinking and approach to a number of personal matters. Everything had seemed to be for a reason. Now the murder had been solved, and life had settled down somewhat, he found himself still connected to the police, albeit in a different capacity than before and in a different city. He resolved to somehow find the right balance; to stay committed to his work but to manage personal relationships better. If romance didn't blossom between Ivana and him it could not be due to something as slight as this misunderstanding.

He was so deep in thought, he didn't register Ivana asking

him a question.

"Honza, when is Charlotte coming to visit you?" she repeated.

"Well, in the end it wasn't a good idea during the Easter holidays. She had too much school work. So, instead, we've agreed she'll come over for a few days when she finishes her exams in the summer."

"That sounds sensible. You might even have found out some information about your Czech family by then. It would be exciting to share with her."

"Yes. I'm meeting Barbora tomorrow," Jonny stated. "It'll be interesting to see what your friend is able to find out."

"She has worked in the government department for registrations for a long time. If there are any records remaining about your mother or her family, Barbora will find it." She smiled as she drove. "She's an expert in this area."

"Ivana…" Jonny started. "I want to apologise for ruining your birthday celebration last night. I know you weren't happy I took the call from Felix during dinner."

She stalled in thought, clearly wanting to choose her words carefully. After a long pause she started to talk with eyes on the road ahead, hands firmly on the steering wheel.

"Honza, I had a really good time. Thank you for taking me to Karlovy Vary for my birthday. Really. It was a lovely gesture." She hesitated, mouth slightly open. "I am not really the best person to talk about relationships because my track record is poor. I have had two serious relationships and both of them failed. Sadly, the timing was also bad because I have no children to show for them. For this reason, I set my expectations with new relationships intentionally low on purpose. All that really matters in my opinion is to enjoy our time together. But…" She delayed again, glancing quickly across at him. "But, sometimes it feels like you have to be available around the clock. It's not something I'm used to, or want, if I'm honest. I don't want to feel like I have to compete with your job. Does that make sense?"

"Yes, it does," he replied softly, head down. "And, it is something I want to change."

Jonny turned to look across at her side profile as she drove, her hair tied back but loose strands falling down across her cheek. He slowly reached over and, with his index finger, moved the escaped hair back behind her ear.

"Now, do something useful and reach across to my bag on the back seat," she said, smiling. "I want to listen to the special CD you made me for my birthday. But no commentary, please – I want to listen to the music."

Jonny leaned behind and found the CD. Just as he was taking the disc out of the case his mobile phone started ringing. Looking at the screen, he saw Mikeš was calling him again. He impulsively muted the call and returned the phone discreetly to his jacket pocket, not looking at Ivana. He carefully entered the disc into the mouth of the CD player and moments later the low-key guitar intro of *If Not For You* started to play. Jonny relaxed, settling back into his seat, and listened to the Bob Dylan songs that had framed the most recent episode of his life.

***

After quickly dropping his overnight bag back in his rented attic room, Jonny picked up his iPod and headphones and set off to the Prague city centre. Listening to some of his favourite music in the car had soothed his anxiety about the success of the trip, Ivana humming along as she drove the final stage of the journey.

Dylan's music had been a constant companion during his life, often the yardstick for accomplishments and tragic moments, some songs forever attached to key events. Clearly, this was never going to change. As he walked the short distance to the Náměstí Míru metro station, he plugged in his headphones and turned up his jacket collar to combat the changeable April weather.

The journey to Prague Old Town was still a relatively new experience but had already become important to him. It signified his new independence, living and working in a foreign city. The short commute also led him to his place of work, where he was already admired and respected.

His involvement in police investigations had been minimal since the Neil Robson murder in Old Town Square, but Mikeš had used the lull to integrate him into the Serious Crime and Homicide Team. Jonny had used the time to orientate himself, becoming familiar with the local policies and procedures in the handbook, even making suggestions for improvement. Mikeš had also used him to review the evidence on some local cases and provide training and mentoring services to key staff. The language was still a barrier but he was working hard to learn, even enrolling in a Czech beginner's course that met two afternoons a week. Overall, he was satisfied with his new role. It was not the same as when he was captain of his own ship in the Metropolitan Police, but he knew he'd needed a change before being burnt out completely. Being a consultant to the Czech Police was providing him with a new challenge, learning experiences, and also new friends.

As Jonny walked from the Staroměstská metro station and entered the café, Mikeš was already sitting in their favourite corner with a coffee. Although well groomed, his eccentric dress sense always drew attention and had taken Jonny some time to get used to. Mikeš was wearing his usual immaculately-pressed, tweed three-piece suit, paired with an orange paisley shirt and tie combination. His wide-brimmed hat and black cane were resting on a spare chair.

Knowing that Jonny needed to establish some roots of his own in Prague, Mikeš had encouraged Jonny to choose the venue for their daytime catch-ups and the café had soon become their favourite meeting place. Their other favourite haunt was the Černá kočka (*Black Cat*) pub, the place for a beer after a long day, or just a place for Mikeš to hide when he was heavily in demand.

The café owner, Luka, made good coffee – an essential requirement for both of them – and provided breakfast and simple working lunches. Although small, the café was thriving, becoming renowned for the delicious Croatian sweets, ranging from cherry strudel to krofne, Croatian doughnuts: boozy and non-alcoholic versions. Both being non-Czechs living in Prague, Jonny and Luka had a shared bond which was developing into friendship with Jonny's almost daily visits to the café.

Luka smiled seeing Jonny enter. "Ahoj, Honza. Good trip to the spa town?"

"Yes, thanks," Jonny replied, waving across at Mikeš who was impatiently consulting his pocket watch.

"I'll bring your coffee over in a minute," Luka stated. "The Black Cat is eagerly waiting for you."

"Thanks, Luka."

Mikeš stood up as Jonny approached. His profile was of a much younger man: his slim, wiry frame conveying vitality and his eyes shining brightly. Only the thinning hair and facial lines gave hint that he was closing in on retirement age.

"Ahoj, my friend. I've missed you," Mikeš boomed out.

"Ahoj, Felix. How are you?"

They shook hands vigorously, as was their ritual. Mikeš patted the seat next to him so loudly that other customers in the café turned to see the source of the noise.

Jonny composed himself and sat down. He loved Mikeš' energy but had learned it was better for both of them if he remained calmer to counter-balance their conversation. The times he had become animated himself, the mix with Mikeš' vitality had become almost toxic, with no room to breathe.

"So, did Ivana enjoy her birthday trip?" Mikeš questioned, his voice carrying around the small space.

"Yes, I think so."

"You think so!" Mikeš laughed loudly.

"Well, as you already know, I'm not the world's leading expert in relationships. It was fun, but Ivana and I are taking it slow... Getting to know each other."

"We are so different," Mikeš chuckled, "but I suppose that's one of the reasons we get on so well."

"Yes, probably—"

"When I met Ella my whole world started spinning," Mikeš continued, unabated. "I couldn't eat, I couldn't sleep. I could only think of her... and she was driving me wild. Honza, I knew it was love straight away."

"I know, Felix. You have told me the story many times."

"Yes, yes, Honza. My point is that when you know, you know. Do you understand what I'm saying?" Mikeš gave Jonny a knowing look, searching his eyes.

"Two things, Felix," Jonny retorted. "Firstly, we are very different people."

"Yes, agreed," accepted Mikeš.

"And secondly," Jonny continued. "Look at you and Ella. It hasn't been easy for both of you. Whilst you still love her dearly, you have to live apart."

"Good point, Honza," Mikeš acknowledged. "But, I wouldn't change anything. Love is the key to a happy life."

Jonny looked directly at his friend and laughed quietly, warm affection in his eyes.

"What?" Mikeš looked confused.

"Nothing. You just have this great ability to make me smile. Thank you."

Mikeš was not to be distracted. "Bring Ivana to dinner with Ella and me. We can all look out at the Charles Bridge from our favourite restaurant. I will know from her reaction whether she loves you. It's as simple as that."

Jonny sighed. "Maybe I don't want it to be as simple."

"Nonsense!"

"Let's take a rain check for now. I'll think about it."

"What?" Mikeš shook his head in exasperation. "Why are you British so obsessed with the rain?"

Jonny laughed, louder this time, feeling comfortable once more. Mikeš always managed to have this effect on him, even if they were heartily disagreeing.

"Felix," Jonny started, deciding to change the subject, "tell me about this missing person and why you think it might be murder."

"No way, my friend. All these missing and dead people can wait. Before we go to the police station, I want to hear about everything you did in Karlovy Vary." Mikeš put his arm around Jonny's shoulder and pulled him in, an impish grin on his face.

4

Missing Person

Inside a police station was where Jonny had always felt at his most comfortable. The style and layout of the buildings he'd worked in had changed over the years, but he had always settled comfortably into the environment easily, performing the job he seemed to have been made for – catching criminals.

His new station was relatively modern inside, housed within an old, historic building in Prague 1, close to Old Town Square. The basement was dedicated to the evidence room and reference material, including the police handbook and training materials. The holding cells were securely housed on the ground floor, behind the reception area. The detective team and uniform officers worked across the first and second floors, which were open plan with glass-fronted meeting rooms. The upper floors were dedicated to interview rooms, used for questioning suspects and witnesses connected with serious crime or homicide cases.

Jonny knew he could work anywhere, from a luxury office to a Portakabin – his surroundings didn't matter to him. His last office building in London had been cutting edge in modern design but lacked warmth: floor to ceiling glass frontage and decorated in a grey-silver theme throughout. It was all a far cry from his first station, a warren of dour, box-shaped offices and connecting corridors, the only constants being the smoky atmosphere, metal filing cabinets and stacks of live files on desks.

It was the criminal investigations that framed his existence and his fellow police officers who provided the lifeblood. The staff on his team had changed over the years, with promotions and transfers to other departments, but the ethics and culture of law enforcement had always prevailed. Mikeš' detective team and supporting uniform officers had the same core principles, working together to maintain law and order in the face of the risks on the job.

Chief Sergeant Marek Boukal and Sergeant Lucie Dvořáková were the pillars of Mikeš' team: the former was his sidekick and deputy, the latter responsible for the uniform officers and organisation of administrative duties. Jonny had first met them on the Old Town Square Murder case and continued to work with them in his loosely defined consultant role. Mikeš had also asked Jonny to set up a mentor programme for Boukal, the framework for which had been sketched out but not yet started.

Jonny's arrival was greeted with the same warm hospitality as his first visit to the station, with shouts of "Ahoj, Honza!" He had gone out of his way to meet everyone working at the station, from the night porter to the uniform officers nearing retirement, and this had added to the endearment. Although he had to apologise for his poor Czech, they always found a way to get by using broken English and hand signals. Jonny's friendship with the most celebrated detective in the Czech Republic ensured he had celebrity status.

Boukal and Dvořáková were waiting as Jonny and Mikeš walked towards the Incident Room on the first floor. Boukal was upstanding and full of smiles, a respectful and promising detective in his mid-thirties. His attire was, as usual, a poor contrast to his demeanour: his suit was scruffy and ill-fitting, his shirt poorly ironed with the collar slightly yellowing at the neck, his tie poorly arranged. Next to him, Dvořáková was impeccably dressed, her uniform pressed and fitting to perfection. She wore her blonde hair tied up in a short ponytail as her police hat was not needed inside the station.

"Ahoj, Honza. Did you enjoy Karlovy Vary?" Dvořáková asked as they entered the office.

"Yes thanks, Lucie," Jonny replied. "It was a great trip. The setting of the town was stunning. I was taken aback by how beautiful it was."

Boukal stepped forward to shake Jonny's hand, nodding his head in reserved recognition.

"I go there with my girlfriends once a year for a weekend of pampering," Dvořáková continued. "We especially love the spa treatments."

Mikeš cleared his throat in mock hilarity, intended to raise interested glances from Boukal and Dvořáková. "Don't mention the sauna to Honza – it's a sensitive subject."

Jonny gave Mikeš a cold stare, then smiled sheepishly at Boukal and Dvořáková. His cheeks reddened slightly, but he kept his own counsel.

Boukal provided a much-needed diversion. "I have prepared one of the whiteboards with all the information we have about the Corbet case. Shall I take you both through it?"

"Excellent idea, Marek," boomed Mikeš, slapping Jonny on the back.

The main Incident Room whiteboard had been devoted to a higher profile case that Jonny was not aware of. Boukal lifted up a smaller board and stood it up on a table, leaning against the wall. It was sparsely populated with only one photo in the centre, just a few handwritten names and arrows to and from the centrepiece. After taking their seats, Boukal stood, marker pen in hand, and summarised the case.

"The central police department received a telephone call yesterday, Tuesday morning, at 11.27 a.m. to report Alex Corbet missing. He is British but has residency in the Czech Republic having been living and working here in Prague for twelve years. He is married to Helena Corbetová, a Czech resident, although they are living apart having recently separated. Helena placed the call to the main switchboard."

"Corbetová?" Jonny looked puzzled.

"It's normal for the wife to take the man's surname, but then add a gender adjective," Boukal explained. "Very often 'ová' is added, but it changes based upon the surname. The unmarried daughters also take this changed surname."

"Yes, I remember now," Jonny said. "What job does Alex have?"

"He is a software engineer," Boukal clarified. "He works in the IT Department of a large, multi-national finance company in Chodov."

"Chodov is in Prague 4," Mikeš added. "There is an industrial park and a large shopping mall. Many international companies also have offices there. Sometimes it feels like you're not in Prague when walking around Chodov. It's very cosmopolitan with a large mix of languages being spoken."

"I haven't been there," Jonny replied, "but I've noticed the Chodov metro station on the C Line."

"Alex Corbet's boss, Torsten Lindberg, was the first person to raise the alarm by calling his wife," Boukal continued. "I have spoken to him over the phone and he confirmed that Alex was in work as normal last week. But, he didn't turn up for work on Monday or Tuesday and didn't even call in or leave a message.

They tried contacting him, but there was no reply. His boss said Alex was very diligent, hardly ever taking a day off sick, and in addition they have an important, new system going live next week and Alex was leading the project."

"So, why did his wife call the police?" Jonny questioned. "I thought you said they were separated."

"I've also spoken to Helena Corbetová by phone. She told me she'd tried to contact Alex over the weekend because he was supposed to be taking their young children out on Sunday. It was a prior arrangement; he takes the children out one day most weekends. But, he didn't turn up on Sunday as agreed, and he didn't return her calls or messages. The last time she spoke to Alex was on Friday when they confirmed the details for Sunday. She told me she was concerned because it was unlike him regarding the children, but then his office also called her Tuesday. It seems she was the only other contact they had for him in his HR file. When Alex's boss recounted his story to her, she realised it was serious and decided to report the situation to us."

"Makes sense," Jonny acknowledged. "But, we still need to dig into the relationship between Alex and Helena."

"Unfortunately, I haven't been able to interview anyone in person yet," Boukal reported. "There has been too much going on here with all the other open cases. One of Lucie's uniform officers did visit Helena Corbetová and took a short statement after we received the call."

"Honza, we've been almost overrun with new cases in the last few days," Mikeš explained. "I don't know what's happened. It seems like the local people have gone crazy with the improved weather."

"No problem," Jonny reassured him. "You have me on contract so I'm here to help. Anyway, I like to be busy."

"Excellent!" Mikeš bellowed. "We should hopefully have more resources available in a few days as we close some of the minor investigations. Marek can be your main contact during the early stages of the inquiry. We can take it from there once we have a clearer understanding of the situation."

"The only thing I have had time for so far is to visit Alex Corbet's apartment," Boukal explained. "We had to make sure he wasn't there, alive or dead. I looked around, but there was nothing obvious. The apartment was mostly tidy apart from the dirty dishes in the sink. We also spoke to the neighbours, mainly retired residents. Nobody had seen him in the past few days, but one told us they know he'd had a female visitor a few times recently because they'd seen them together on the stairs. We are just starting to check his social media, but at this stage there don't appear to be any postings to indicate he was planning something out of character, like suicide."

"Because the missing person is British, I believe it would be good for you, Honza, to lead the investigation," Mikeš reasoned. "As you know, I strongly believe that an understanding of the culture and language really helps improve the chances of solving these types of cases."

"Sure, I'll take the lead for the time being," Jonny concurred. "And I agree with you, it helps to understand more about the native culture. But…"

"What is it?" prompted Mikeš.

"I'm not sure I understand why you believe it could be a serious crime, maybe even murder," Jonny stated flatly.

Boukal cleared his throat and prepared to explain his rationale, all eyes on him. "Well, in my opinion there are three reasons why Alex Corbet's disappearance is suspicious. Firstly, his wife told me he's a conscientious father and so it is out of character for him to miss seeing his children at the weekend. Secondly, he was leading an important project at work and would be unlikely to miss the key implementation phase. Finally, nothing in his apartment looked out of place, and there is no note or explanation for his absence. It's as if he has vanished into thin air."

Jonny nodded at Boukal in respect, a proud smile on his face. "Marek, my question was a test and you passed it with flying colours. Your summary was spot on. You have quickly identified the key points and presented them clearly and succinctly. Congratulations."

"Thank you, Honza," Boukal murmured, pleased but slightly uneasy with the open praise.

"Yes, yes, excellent presentation, Marek," Mikeš approved. "But, what is all this 'thin air' and 'flying colours'? Are we still speaking English?"

"Don't worry, Felix. I'll explain later." Jonny laughed. "The main thing is that Marek is improving his insight skills after our initial work together. I know this is only a missing person case at this stage, but he is already starting to think like a criminal. This is vital for successful detective work."

"I agree, very important," stated Mikeš. "Honza, you are an excellent teacher."

"Not really. Marek learns fast. We haven't really started the mentor programme yet, but he is picking up important points from our informal chats. We just need to take him to the shops to get him some new clothes so he looks like a top detective as well."

"Bravo!" Mikeš roared, clapping his hands together in glee.

All eyes were again on Boukal, his cheeks now reddening in embarrassment.

Sensing an opportunity to save the blushes of her colleague, Dvořáková started to update the senior detective team with progress on the case. "I have started an investigation file and inside is the statement taken from Helena Corbetová, as well as Marek's notes. The file also contains a simple timeline of Alex Corbet's last known whereabouts."

"I also requested Alex Corbet's telephone records yesterday," Boukal added, regaining his composure. "It's often the most important information in a missing person case, so I made the request as soon as the disappearance was reported. The phone number is from a Czech mobile provider so we should have the results back soon, maybe even this afternoon."

"Excellent," Jonny stated, full of admiration. "It seems to me we should start by visiting Helena Corbetová and finding out more background information about her husband, their relationship and the last time she saw Alex."

5

State of Mind

Jonny followed Boukal out to the back of the police station, into the car park. He jumped into the passenger seat of the black Skoda Superb without thinking, still reflecting on Boukal's improved analytical and presentation skills at the briefing. Boukal suddenly roared up the engine, slammed the car into reverse and swung the car out of the parking lot in one slick manoeuvre. Jonny was initially jerked forward, and then thumped back into his seat as Boukal changed gear and set off down the street at full speed.

Although he'd spent a lot of time with Boukal over the past few weeks, he'd forgotten about the stress of being a passenger in a car with him; blotted from his memory was probably a better way to express it. Boukal had initially been reserved when first driving Jonny about the city at the start of his stay, assured and proficient behind the wheel but always driving at a reasonable, legal speed. Later, during the Old Town Square Murder case, Boukal had transformed into an ultra-speedy driver – his skills honed as a junior racing car champion, Jonny later found out.

The journey was a bit of a blur. Boukal cut corners with minimal effort, remaining calm and composed throughout, steering the car alongside the River Vltava past the National Theatre. Jonny's left hand firmly gripped the hanging strap as he tracked the route through half-closed eyes. A strategic red traffic light provided a much needed breather. The pause allowed him time to study the famous Dancing House, its curved façade having an almost hypnotic effect, whilst also giving the impression that the building was going to come crashing down at any minute. He had taken a tour up the relatively recent building, providing great views across the river towards the castle, but he still had to visit the top floor restaurant.

His train of thought was shattered as Boukal tore away from the lights, leaving the traffic standing behind him. Approaching the dignified Vyšehrad fortified castle, Boukal veered left away from the river and, after sharp left and right turns, parked the car smoothly in a side street.

Boukal calmly unclipped his seat belt and looked across at Jonny. "Are you okay?"

The loudest noise in Jonny's head was his own heavy breathing.

"Yes," he managed, removing his fingers from the hanging strap. "But only just. Don't the police ever stop you for speeding?"

Boukal laughed. "Honza, we *are* the police!"

"What I mean is, don't they even attempt to pull you over? After all, the car is unmarked, the same as any black Skoda Superb in Prague."

"The traffic police are used to me by now, but I was stopped a few times when I started driving Felix around. Now, they're scared to stop me."

Jonny shook his head slowly. "I must remember to walk next time."

He was still trying to compose himself as Boukal hopped out of the car. The residential street in Prague 2, close to the river, was quiet and tranquil: the only noise came from a group of teenage children returning home from school and a few mothers talking to each other as they pushed buggies with their younger children. The scene was idyllic, a cool freshness coming from the water less than one hundred metres away. It was hard to believe the city centre of Prague was less than thirty minutes on foot.

Boukal led them to an apartment building and stepped forward to press the entrance buzzer, speaking Czech into the intercom speaker. After waiting for a couple of minutes, the large, heavy door was opened by a smartly dressed, buxom woman in her fifties with pristine permed hair and makeup.

"Dobrý den, Chief Sergeant Marek Boukal," Boukal introduced himself. "Are you Mrs Corbetová?"

"No, no," she smiled, shaking her head. "I am Helena's mother, Daniela Nováková." She beckoned them into the hallway, shaking their hands. Her phrasing and intonation was almost perfect, slightly posh to Jonny's ear.

"I am sorry for the wait," she added. "The intercom system is temperamental and due to be fixed soon. At the moment, we have to walk down to let guests in."

"Hello, I am Jonathan Fox. I am a consultant working with the Czech Police. I didn't expect you to speak such good English."

"I spent many years in England when I was younger. That's where I met my first husband, Derek. Actually both my daughters were born in the UK before we came back to the Czech Republic."

"I am impressed," Jonny added. "Your English is excellent, better than most British people."

Daniela smiled at the compliment.

As they all entered the lift and Daniela turned her back to press the button, Jonny exchanged a look of surprise with Boukal

– Daniela Nováková was not what he'd expected.

On the third floor they were immediately engulfed by noise coming down the short corridor. "I'm sorry, the two young children are quite boisterous," Daniela explained. "Very noisy, but great fun."

Daniela led them through the open apartment door and the noise stopped immediately, one child grabbing his grandmother's dress and the other heading off at speed towards the end of the hall. Jonny smiled to himself, remembering Charlotte at a similar age, creating dents in the plasterwork as she dashed around the house quicker than he was able to fill them in.

The apartment gave visitors an impression of wealth and sophistication, despite visible childproof locks. The paintwork in the hall had recently been renewed and the wallpaper was a deep plum colour embossed with gold flowers. Everything Jonny could see was maintained to a high standard and was cleaner than most residences without children.

In the living room, a slight but pretty woman got up from the sofa to greet them, introducing herself as Helena Corbetová. Her shoulder-length, light brown hair had been prepared as if for a night out, her makeup subtle but professional-looking, and her nails had been newly manicured. She wore a knee-length dress and shoes, like her mother. Jonny guessed they had been out for lunch.

The main room was also expertly decorated, reflecting the immaculate mother and daughter: an expensive rug was the centrepiece of the wooden floor, and the room was surrounded by polished cabinets, a gold tipped mirror above the fire feature and a lush three-piece suite. After introductions, Helena asked her mother to take the children into the kitchen and indicated for Jonny and Boukal to sit in the armchairs.

"I love them to bits, but sometimes you can't hear yourself speak," she explained.

"How old are they?" Jonny enquired politely after the introductions were completed.

"Emilie is five now, just started kindergarten. Tomaš is just two and a real handful. Mummy comes to help me most days."

"I hope you don't mind us speaking in English," Boukal said, "but because Alex is British, we have asked Mr Fox to help on the investigation."

Helena nodded in consent. "Either language is fine with me."

"Thank you," Jonny replied.

"We have a brief statement from you yesterday, taken after you reported Alex missing," Boukal summarised. "But, it would be very helpful for both of us to hear it again in your own words."

"Well, there is not much more to say really," Helena started. "I last spoke to Alex on Friday. He called me during the day, when he was at work, to ask if he could pick the children up on Sunday a little later than we'd agreed."

"Did he say why?" Jonny probed.

"No, he didn't, but…" Helena stopped, instead sighing heavily.

Jonny leaned forward in his chair. "I know this is difficult for you, but it would be useful if you could tell us more. Sometimes the smallest details can help lead us to what has happened. It seems like something serious has happened to Alex and we want to find out what it is."

Helena looked down, her eyes welling up. She took a tissue from the box on the side table and dabbed gently at her eyes. "I'm sorry, it's all very upsetting. Alex only moved out at the end of last year and it looks like he'd already started a new relationship. It's not fair on me, or the children…" She dabbed her eyes again.

"Do you know the name of the person he was having a relationship with?" Jonny asked.

"I don't know her personally. Her name is Tanya. She is American and works at the same company as Alex. He started seeing her before we had even separated." She sighed heavily. "I can't believe he told me such lies."

"Have you heard anything more about their relationship?" Jonny explored. "Maybe where she lives, or if they had any plans for a trip somewhere?"

Helena shook her head slowly. "No. I asked Alex, but he would never tell me anything. He just said it was none of my business. I think I have a right to know, after all we are still married. I drew the line at my children meeting her so early after we had separated, so I insisted that he could only pick up the children at the weekend, usually Sunday, and take them out rather than going back to his apartment."

"I understand, very sensible," Jonny offered. "We will contact her ourselves."

"Do you know Tanya's surname?" Boukal asked, scribbling in his notebook.

Helena shook her head. "Sorry, no. Alex wouldn't tell me. I suppose I could have found out, but I didn't have the energy or the inclination."

"And, sorry to ask more difficult questions," Jonny continued, "but why did your marriage have difficulties? It might help us understand more about Alex."

"We were arguing all the time," Helena confessed. "I have found it difficult since the children were born, but Mummy has been great. She lives just outside Prague but comes in most days to help. Alex always complained about being smothered and ended up going out a lot in the evenings to escape. That was his story anyway. He ended up being out more than he was in, drinking too much. It just led to even more arguments. Plus, as I've said, it was clear he was having an affair last year."

"But, you haven't started divorce proceedings yet?" Jonny followed up.

"No," Helena answered, dabbing her eyes again. "It just seemed too early."

"Do you have any reason to worry about his state of mind?" Jonny asked. "I know from personal experience that relationship breakdowns are very stressful. Even if someone seems fine, they are probably suffering inside with the stress and hurt."

Helena's eyes widened. "Oh no, please don't say that."

"Mrs Corbetová, I am not saying anything," Jonny clarified quickly. "You must understand that we need to look at every possibility. Please think, can you remember Alex acting strangely or saying anything odd over the past few weeks?"

Helena paused to think. "I'm sorry, no. I don't remember anything strange, but to be honest we weren't really talking very much. It was very strained between us. Maybe..."

"Yes?" Jonny encouraged her.

"Maybe you should speak to George. They are close friends. If Alex opened up to anyone it would be him. Sorry, I should explain, George and Zuzana are good friends of ours. They have a daughter the same age as Emilie. Our separation has been very difficult on them as well because we used to spend a lot of time together as families."

"Can we please have George's mobile number?" Boukal asked.

Helena checked her phone and read out the telephone number.

"Thank you." Boukal paused to make a note. "It would be

useful if we could talk about the weekend in more detail. Can you please take us through the sequence of events?"

"I had no reason to contact Alex on Saturday, but I called him on Sunday when he was thirty minutes late. I then called him three or four more times that day and also sent him some messages. I must admit, a couple of the messages later on Sunday were a bit angry. I'd made arrangements to meet Zuzana in the afternoon and had to cancel. Also, Emilie was very upset because she was looking forward to seeing her dad." Helena paused to compose herself. "On Monday I tried again, but nothing. I called George, but he also got no response. He even went around to Alex's apartment in the evening but got no reply when he rang the buzzer. We were all starting to get a bit concerned when I received a call from Alex's boss, Torsten, on Tuesday morning. He was worried because Alex hadn't turned up for work on Monday and Tuesday. That's when I decided to call the police and report the situation."

"Thank you, you did the right thing," Boukal acknowledged.

Helena dabbed her eyes again and blew her nose.

"I think we're nearly done," Jonny stated, looking at Boukal for confirmation. "Just one more question. Is there somewhere that Alex would usually go on a Friday night? Somewhere he'd often go at the end of the working week?"

"Yes," Helena confirmed, her eyes brightening. "There is a pub called Červený lev which he used to go to a lot. Most of the customers are ex-pats and they have events like pub quizzes. Often, they have live music on a Friday. The pub is close to I. P. Pavlova, not far from here."

"I know it," Boukal confirmed.

"Thank you very much, Mrs Corbetová, that has been very useful," Jonny stated with a smile. "Hopefully, we will find out soon what has happened to Alex. I'm not sure how long it will take, but we will definitely update you tomorrow. In the meantime, try not to worry and look after your children."

"Thank you, Mr Fox," Helena replied with a weak smile.

6

Warning Message

Rejecting Boukal's offer of a lift, Jonny opted for the less stressful option of travelling on foot. Alex Corbet's new apartment was still in Prague 2, east of the river and just over one kilometre in a northerly direction towards the city centre. Whilst Jonny stood checking the directions on his smartphone, Boukal jumped back into the car with a parting shot of, "Beat you there," a wide grin on his face.

Jonny decided to take his time. After all, it wasn't as if they were on a murder hunt, chasing a killer. He knew from experience a missing person case could lead to a variety of different outcomes: an unfortunate accident under the influence of alcohol, a nervous breakdown, suicide, even a kidnapping. At this stage, there was no evidence to suggest foul play and Alex Corbet could very well turn up in a day or so rubbing a bump on his head and claiming memory loss after a binge weekend.

This was an unexplored part of Prague 2 for Jonny. Although he'd trekked further out of the centre following the river, he hadn't yet visited the Vyšehrad fort and its grounds, including the cemetery that contained the remains of many famous Czechs such as the composers Antonín Dvořák and Bedřich Smetana, and painter Alphonse Mucha.

Walking with his head held high to take in the grand architecture at almost every corner of this historic city, he walked along the main road Vyšehradská that lead uphill, away from the castle. As the trams travelled past him in both directions, he followed the high wall surrounding the hospital complex. The only break in the wall was provided for the entrance steps up to the Church of St. Jan Nepomucky at Skalka. Jonny crossed the busy street to get a better view of the two tall, elegant steeples flanking the central entrance, the gold star gleaming above the tall, arched window in the lowering, late afternoon sun.

Rounding the bend in the road, the space opened up. The expanse of the Karlovo Náměstí square stood before him, one of the largest squares in the world according to his research. He had walked through the square before, enjoying the contrast between twisting paths through the lawns and trees, and the surrounding hubbub of city life. The square was one of the main transport hubs in the city centre, with tram lines and main roads crossing at ground level and a busy underground metro station.

The apartment was on the opposite side of the square so Jonny took a winding diagonal route across the green space, the sun warming his face. He crossed at the traffic lights, taking the first left and then an immediate right, and found himself in the correct street. Up ahead, he could see Boukal leaning on the door of the unmarked, black police car, a pleased look on his face.

"What took you so long, Honza?" Boukal asked cheekily.

"About two hundred years of Czech history," Jonny retorted. "You should slow down sometimes and look around. You don't know how lucky you are to work amongst such history."

Boukal's face dropped, his mouth open slightly.

"No time to waste, Marek," Jonny continued briskly. "Which building is it?"

Boukal pointed across the street and rummaged around in his pocket, fishing out the correct set of keys. "We have a warrant to search Alex Corbet's apartment now he has been officially registered as a missing person. The landlord has provided us with a set of keys for easy access."

Leading the way, Boukal opened the large, wooden building door and took the concrete stairs up to the second floor. "No lift, I'm afraid."

"I had a quick look around yesterday," Boukal explained, opening the apartment door and handing Jonny a pair of plastic gloves. "The apartment should be exactly as I first found it. I was careful not to touch anything."

"The security here is poor," Jonny noted, pointing to the door lock. "This lock mechanism could be easily forced. And, the lock on the main entrance door wasn't much better."

"The landlord told me that most of the people living here are students."

"That doesn't make it right, though."

Jonny stepped inside the studio apartment and scanned the space. Apart from an internal door to the bathroom, everything else was housed within a rectangular room less than forty square metres. Only one window provided light, facing out onto the street. Next to the window was a small table and chair, strewn with a few books, stationery and an odd collection of items, including a bicycle pump. Facing the table was a wardrobe with a single door next to a pull-down studio bed folded up, flush to the wall. An old sofa broke up the room, facing a flat screen TV fitted to the wall to save space. The darker end of the apartment was allocated to a small kitchen unit: two cupboards and matching drawers, a fridge, sink and a small oven with two hobs on the work surface. The apartment was painted white with pale red curtains, all intended to provide the sense of more space. But, whatever the colour scheme, the room was drab and cramped. He couldn't imagine anyone spending a lot of time here by choice.

Jonny peered into the bathroom. There was only enough room for a shower unit, a sink, toilet and one cabinet on the wall. The only way to move around without banging his arms was to turn around on the spot.

Out of the bathroom, he stood in the middle of the studio apartment with a confused look on his face. "I know Alex and Helena have only separated recently, but I wasn't expecting his new apartment to be this small and miserable," he stated. "I got the impression he had a good job."

"Well, rental prices in Prague are going up," Boukal explained. "Maybe this was just temporary until he worked out the financial situation with Helena."

"Maybe, Marek. You could be right. It's just…"

"What are you thinking, Honza?"

"It's just that Helena Corbetová and the children are living in a luxurious apartment. Helena and her mother were all dressed up today, as if they'd been out for an expensive lunch. Alex by comparison is living in this small, poky apartment. If he was the conscientious father Helena told you he was, he surely would have at least wanted to get an apartment his children could come and visit, maybe even stay overnight."

"I did notice the difference in living standards," Boukal confirmed. "But, there could be a simple explanation. It is early in their separation and the children are very young. Maybe he was hoping for a reconciliation. The landlord told me the lease was initially for only six months. He may have just taken the first apartment that was close and also easy for his work."

"I hadn't thought of that," Jonny confessed.

"To get to Chodov on the metro, he would just have to walk to the station at Muzeum or I. P. Pavlova. It is only seven or eight stops on the C Line, probably less than thirty minutes."

Jonny nodded in recognition. "Let's have a look around."

He started in the kitchen area, slowly and deliberately opening cupboards and drawers, noting only plates, cutlery, packet soups and tinned food, then the fridge, and finally looking through the debris on top of the work space. It didn't look like Alex Corbet ate there much at all, probably preferring to eat in the office canteen or get take-away food.

Boukal's mobile phone rang and he quickly answered, mouthing "Felix" to Jonny. After taking instructions from his boss, speaking in Czech, he turned to Jonny. "I need to get back to the station. We have a potential suspect to interview on another case. Will you be okay here on your own?"

"Of course," Jonny confirmed. "Leave me the set of keys just in case."

Boukal threw the small bunch of keys to Jonny and left the apartment quickly. "See you later, Honza."

Jonny now had peace and quiet, which, despite his efforts to be a team player, was always how he preferred it. This was partly because of his insular personality, but also due to the way history had panned out; most of his breakthroughs in high profile cases had been when he was alone, able to let his instinct lead him without distractions.

After his inspection of the small kitchen area, Jonny searched the grubby-looking sofa. Despite being well past its best years, he sat down and leafed through the newspapers and magazines on the glass coffee table. Recognising a UK music magazine from the previous month, he paused to flick to the new album reviews. He realised that since arriving in Prague he'd gone without British TV, newspapers and magazines. Some of it he knew he'd be happy not to return to, only needing to check the news online when he wanted. Music was more important to him, though, and coming across the magazine made him realise he needed to make more of an effort to keep up to date.

He stood up and lowered the studio bed down from the wall, taking care with the squeaking brackets, and pulling out the legs to safely rest the frame and mattress. Thankfully, the bed linen at least looked recently washed. He turned over the pillow and duvet and made his first discovery. Along with the men's sleepwear were a women's t-shirt and a pair of black knickers. So, a woman had stayed in this apartment fairly frequently, or had arrived Friday and was possibly staying the weekend. Probably Tanya. Jonny took a couple of photos with his phone before closing it up, flush to the wall.

Next to the wardrobe, laying on the floor, were two bags. The first was a small, black rucksack which on first impression looked like Alex Corbet's work bag. Inside was a laptop as well as a notebook and loose papers. Jonny placed the rucksack on the table for further inspection later. The other bag was a woman's designer handbag containing only a change of underwear, a tightly rolled women's t-shirt and some makeup. He searched in the zips and pockets but found nothing other than an eyeliner pencil and lip balm. For the record, he took a couple of photos of the bag from different angles.

The wardrobe offered nothing interesting: only men's clothes were either hanging up or lying on shelves, shoes and trainers lined up on the bottom with some sports bags. He searched the pockets of a couple of smart jackets but found nothing but loose change and a pen.

Next, he went and sat at the table. The room was so simple and bare; nothing gave an impression of the life that was lived in the place. The walls and the flat surfaces were bare: no framed pictures, no notes stuck up as reminders, and, most surprisingly, no photos of the Corbet children. Jonny knew he just had to look deeper – sometimes people didn't want to put their past lives on show, either to lessen the hurt or prevent someone else seeing.

First, he worked his way through all the items on the table: a small pile of books, a couple of DVD cases, a small pile of computer discs with handwritten labels, phone and laptop chargers, a block of post-it notes, some pens and, strangely, the bike pump he'd noticed earlier. The items revealed nothing so he lifted up the small, black rucksack and emptied the contents carefully onto the table. He opened the laptop but it was password locked, as expected, so he closed it again. Sifting through the items, there appeared to be nothing to raise suspicion, only the notebook and loose papers. Jonny noted the front and back bike lights in the front pocket of the rucksack and made a mental note to find out where Alex Corbet kept his bike, one possibility being that he'd been involved in an accident.

The notebook seemed to be solely for Alex Corbet's work: daily to-do lists and notes, as well as scribbled thoughts on IT system design points and planning. Not being technically minded, Jonny didn't understand much; it was like reading in a different language. The loose papers were mainly printed emails from work and what looked like an unpaid bill. Jonny's Czech wasn't proficient enough to understand the subject of the letter, but it seemed IT-related. Turning to the next page he froze. It was an unlined A4 piece of printer paper with a clear warning message handwritten in large, capital letters.

LEAVE HER ALONE!
I'M WARNING YOU

Jonny opened the notebook and compared the handwritten notes with the warning message – it didn't look like Alex Corbet's handwriting. Using his mobile phone he took photos of the note, both from a height to capture the complete paper and also close-ups of the writing.

The last paper in the wad was also intriguing. It was roughly A5 size, but was uneven in shape, having been torn from a notepad. The paper had just a handwritten name on it with a Czech telephone number underneath. Jonny opened the browser on his smartphone and typed in the name written.

JUDr. Pavel Rosický

Jonny nodded his head slowly, now interested – the contact details for a solicitor. Another search revealed that JUDr stands for Juris Utriusque Doctor, or Doctor of Law in English. Finally, a lead to follow up. Alex Corbet could simply have been searching for a solicitor to discuss his current separation with Helena, but Jonny knew that asking simple questions in cases like this often led to less than obvious, sometimes even surprising, answers. He checked the handwriting against the notebook and the warning note; to his untrained but experienced eye, none of them seem to be written by the same hand.

He tried to call Mikeš but there was no answer. Deciding his search of the apartment was complete, he took a photo of the solicitor's details and then made notes on separate post-its and attached them to the two interesting, handwritten pages. Carefully he returned the laptop, notebook and loose papers to the rucksack, in the same order he'd found them, and placed the bag back on the chair.

As he was locking the apartment door, a young man in his

mid-twenties was striding up the stairs. "Dobrý den. Mluvíte anglicky?" Jonny asked.

The man stopped. "Hi. Yes, I do speak English. I'm a foreign student studying in Prague."

"That's great because my Czech is still poor. Sorry, my name is Jonathan Fox and I'm a consultant with the Czech Police." He showed his police badge. "Do you know Alex Corbet, the man who lives in this apartment?"

"I only know him to say hello to. We pass on the stairs like this sometimes."

"No problem," Jonny reassured him. "I think Alex has a bike. Do you know where he keeps it?"

"Yes, actually, I do. Every apartment has a small storage space in the basement. I put some stuff in my storage area over the weekend and saw his bike there."

"Do you have the key on you? Would you mind showing me quickly?"

Jonny followed the man down to the basement. The small storage areas were made from wood trellis floor to ceiling, allowing sight of the items stored inside, with lockable doors. The bike was there, as described, standing upright on its back wheel.

"The storage areas aren't very secure, but they're useful for bulky items," the man explained. "I use mine for storing my ski gear."

"Thank you," Jonny replied, mentally crossing one possible outcome off the list.

7

The Red Lion

The Červený lev pub was on a corner plot, set amongst a collection of cafés, wine bars and restaurants in a residential area of Prague 2, less than five minutes' walk from the I. P. Pavlova metro station. The exterior of the pub stood out from the other, more traditional, Czech hostelries, the frontage designed in the style of a traditional British pub to attract the ex-pat community and tourists.

Jonny had not realised the symbolism of the pub name when Helena Corbetová had first mentioned it. He knew 'červená' was Czech for 'red', having already covered colours in the early syllabus of his beginner's language course, but 'lev' was an unknown word to him. The sign hanging above the bar entrance was instantly recognisable: the classic red lion symbol outlined in gold on a black background with gold lettering – this was the Czech version of *The Red Lion*.

As he walked into the pub, past customers drinking and smoking in the front beer garden, all he could hear were English accents. The native English speakers were mixed with slanted accents of customers from other countries better able to speak English and mix with other ex-pats rather than learn Czech. The English pub theme was enhanced by the old fashioned British pub signs dotted around the bar.

Jonny had avoided these type of pubs so far during his time

in Prague. He'd even managed to escape the lure of watching British football in a sports bar. It wasn't because he had anything against these communities; he wanted to experience local customs rather than drinking British or pan-European beer and reminiscing about "back home". Now he was curious, and an element of nostalgia was creeping up on him.

The stroll from Alex Corbet's apartment had taken less than ten minutes so, whilst not next door, the pub was certainly local. The walk was not, in truth, Jonny's favourite route in the city. Firstly, it was uphill, the incline steeper than it looked. Far worse, however, was the need to cross two main roads – the noise and fumes from three lanes of traffic in both directions seemed wrong so close to the city centre. He loved the steeped history and cosmopolitan style of the city centre, in Prague 1, and the more relaxing, residential area in Prague 2. But, the major roads separating the two quarters were an aberration to be avoided; he had to come to learn why locals preferred to dissect it by tram or metro. It was, so far, the only aspect of Prague he would change if he had a magic wand, improving walking and cycling routes at the same time.

By the time he'd reached I. P. Pavlova his mood had improved, strolling through the farmer's market on the Tylovo Náměstí square. The stalls were closing up for the evening, but he still had time to interrupt a stallholder packing away and buy a bottle of local Medovina. The homemade honey-based alcoholic drink was bought for Ivana. Maybe they could share a drink together later that evening.

Jonny strode to the bar, showed his police badge, and asked to speak to the manager. The barmaid politely asked him to wait and went through the door behind the bar. The short but stocky, fair-haired manager finally emerged, looking slightly flustered at the police presence, and ushered Jonny over to a quiet table in the corner.

"Hello, my name is Jonathan Fox. I'm a consultant with the Czech Police."

"You must be the guy who helped solve the murder in Old Town Square last month," the manager stated with a strong Irish accent, shaking Jonny's hand vigorously.

Jonny was caught off-guard. "Well, I was involved, yes..." he stammered, not sure how much he should say.

"Anyway, I'm pleased to meet you. My name is Niall Byrne. I'm the manager here."

"Pleased to meet you, Niall," Jonny replied. "You have a nice pub here."

"Thanks a lot. We have a small but loyal group of regulars, all missing home to some extent. The sports coverage with English commentary is a big pull for ex-pats."

Jonny nodded, noting the multiple TV screens positioned around the pub.

"I want to ask a few questions about Alex Corbet," he explained. "I understand he comes in here regularly. Can you remember the last time you saw him?"

"Is he in trouble?"

"No, not at all. We are just trying to track him down."

"Right," Niall muttered to himself, thinking. "The trouble is that when you are working in a pub all the nights tend to merge into one. I don't recall Alex coming in for the last few nights. But, he was definitely in here Friday night. He had a young lass with him, caused a bit of a stir."

"A bit of a stir?" Jonny repeated, intrigued.

"Yes, everyone knows he's recently separated from Helena – you can't keep anything secret around here. But, this was the first time we'd seen this woman and she was very pretty. Everyone wanted to know who she was, but Alex kept himself to himself. He just sat over in the corner with her all night."

Jonny wrote in his notepad as the manager got up from his seat and approached the tall barmaid cleaning glasses behind the bar. The young woman followed Niall back to the corner table. "Mr Fox, this is Leanne," Niall introduced Jonny and he shook her hand.

"Leanne," Niall continued, "when was the last time you saw Alex Corbet? The police are trying to locate his whereabouts."

Jonny gestured for her to sit down. Niall also sat down, choosing a position where he could keep an eye on the bar.

"The last time he was here was Friday, I think," Leanne started. "Mind you, I didn't work on Monday evening. On Friday, he came in with a new girlfriend. Everyone was talking about it after they left and also over the weekend. Some of the regulars know Alex quite well and tried contacting him to find out who she was, but nobody got a reply. I don't know all the story, but I overheard a few of them talking about it on Sunday evening."

"We have a group chat for regulars, mostly about the weekly pub quiz," Niall added. "Alex is usually quite active on it. But, I don't think he's posted anything since last week. Let me check."

"Are you sure the woman was Alex's girlfriend?" Jonny asked Leanne whilst Niall checked his phone.

Leanne paused for a moment. "I don't think I saw them kissing, but they were sitting very close together. My guess is they'd probably met quite recently. New love, you know?"

"Yes, I was right," Niall confirmed. "Alex's last post on the group chat was last Thursday. There's usually quite a lot of banter after the pub quiz on Thursday nights."

"And what time did Alex leave the pub on Friday evening?"

Jonny asked.

"It couldn't have been long before closing time," Niall stated. "Between eleven p.m. and midnight, I'd say."

"Could you describe the woman he was with?"

Niall turned to Leanne.

"She was average height, slim figure with medium length, light brown hair," she explained. "She was very pretty and well dressed. I didn't speak to her but she didn't look Czech to me. More Russian, maybe."

"And would you be able to give us a more detailed description of her, and also what Alex was wearing, if we needed it?"

"Yes, of course."

Niall got up from the table. "Excuse me," he said, heading to the bar to serve a customer waving at him from a nearby table.

Jonny turned back to Leanne. "Are you studying here? You sound American?"

"Yes," she confirmed. "But, actually I'm Canadian, from Montreal."

Jonny nodded. "Last question. Did Alex ever come to the pub with another lady? An American lady called Tanya?"

"No, I don't think so. I don't remember him in here with any other woman."

"Sorry about that," Niall said, returning to the table. "Thirsty customers during Happy Hour!"

"No problem at all," Jonny reassured him. "I just asked Leanne if she remembers Alex coming to the pub with another woman during the past few months."

Niall shook his head firmly. "I've been manager here for two years and I haven't seen Alex with any woman other than Helena. Apart from Friday night, of course. That's why it caused such a stir. Usually Alex comes in with his friend, George Webb. They used to come in with their wives, but it all stopped when Alex and Helena separated. Alex and George are the mainstays of one of the pub quiz teams. Actually, usually the winning team."

"Excellent, thank you. That's all the questions I have for now."

"Would you like a beer whilst you're here?" Niall enquired tentatively. "On the house, of course."

Jonny checked his watch – six fifteen p.m. Tempting. It was effectively the end of the working day and he fancied a beer. The day felt long and drawn-out, especially with the emotional aftermath from Karlovy Vary. And, he suddenly felt hungry, not having eaten much since the hotel breakfast.

He glanced up at the specials board. "I'll have fish and chips and a Czech beer," he ordered. "But, I'll pay for it."

"Coming up," Niall approved, shaking Jonny's hand. "And don't forget our pub quiz. It's good fun."

"Maybe," Jonny muttered, grimacing in mock horror at the suggestion. Niall and Leanne laughed and returned to the bar.

Jonny was scanning the pseudo-British style pub, reflecting on the reason for his first guilty reversion back to British food since his arrival in Prague, when the bar entrance door burst open. Mikeš flamboyantly led the way, his cane tapping its way into the bar space, Boukal following behind at a respectful distance.

"Honza!" Mikeš shouted, spotting Jonny sitting in the corner. All the pub customers turned from their conversations to see the source of the commotion.

As Mikeš walked past the bar he nodded to Niall. "We'll have three of whatever he's ordered," he said, indicating towards Jonny. "But, make one of the beers non-alcoholic. We have a driver."

"Ano, Pane Mikeš."

Jonny stood up to greet his arriving colleagues. "Felix, does everybody know who you are?"

"Pretty much," Mikeš confirmed, smiling. He took off his hat and hung it up on a hook on the wall, resting his cane against the back of his chair.

"How did you find me?" Jonny asked.

"Ah, that was Marek's hunch." Mikeš laughed to himself. "Honza, you seem to forget we are also detectives." He whacked Jonny on the back in his usual, slapstick fashion.

Sensing an opening in the conversation, Boukal explained the purpose for the intrusion. "The information from the mobile phone providers has come back. We now have a list of calls to and from Alex Corbet's mobile phone which we still need to analyse. There are limited messages because he probably used an application, but we can check these also. But, more interesting at this stage, is the last confirmed signal from the phone. It was located in the same position from about midnight on Friday night until Monday afternoon when the signal stopped."

"Maybe he lost his phone on Friday night," Jonny suggested. "The phone battery would have died after a few days without charging."

"Now we have your interest!" Mikeš laughed.

"And," Boukal added, "the last location of the phone is in Prague 2, close to his apartment and on the route back from this pub."

"Interesting," Jonny declared. "Well, once we've had our fish and chips we can go and take a look. Who knows, we might be able to locate the mobile phone and solve the mystery of what has happened to Alex Corbet."

"Fish and chips," stated Boukal, a quizzical look on his face. "I've not had that before."

"I love fish and chips," roared Mikeš. "With lots of salt and vinegar!"

8

Roadworks

It was a tough choice for Jonny: get back in the car with Boukal at the wheel or walk the relatively short distance back towards Alex Corbet's apartment. In the end, the car option swung it; the benefit of staying together and hopefully quickly solving the mystery of the missing mobile phone outweighed the need to stretch his legs after the food and beer. He was looking forward to finishing as soon as he could and returning to see Ivana, armed with the Medovina, before the evening was over.

Once they were over the busy main roads cutting across the city, the route to Alex Corbet's apartment was a maze of one-way, cobbled streets through a residential area. The street they were looking for in Prague 2, Hluboká, was approximately two hundred and fifty metres before the apartment; a side street connecting to the main road running down to the river.

Jonny had become used to the labyrinth of one-way streets in Prague's residential areas. Ivana's apartment was situated in a similar warren, further east but still in Prague 2. The start of their journey to Karlovy Vary had taken an age as she negotiated the succession of turns to zigzag around the smaller streets before joining a main road heading out of the city.

Boukal parked the car in one of the few free kerbside spaces. The street was approximately seventy metres long and running slightly downhill from the entrance to a T-junction at the bottom.

Cars were parked on both sides of the street, facing down the incline, providing room for only one vehicle to pass through the middle. The street was shielded from the main roads by tall buildings so the traffic was only a muted background noise. Visibility was poor in the gathering darkness, only three pairs of old streetlights, positioned at matching intervals on both sides of the street, providing a dull, yellowy light.

Mikeš led the way up the slight rise to the street entrance – the best vantage point to survey the scene. Boukal took a map out of his jacket pocket and turned it around in his hand to orientate it with their exact position. Checking the markings for the phone signal, he pointed down the street. "According to this map, the last signal from Alex Corbet's mobile phone was somewhere about thirty metres down the stretch of pavement on this side of the street."

They walked down the street, calculating the distance with their steps. At the mutually agreed spot, they turned to look at each other, all confused – there was nothing around them that could obviously be hiding a mobile phone. The street was flanked both sides by terraced residential buildings, the large entrance doors the only exit points off the wide pavements: there were no garage entrances or side entrances from the street. At intervals of approximately seven or eight metres stood tall trees in bloom, rising above the cars parked at the kerb. Each tree had a latticed metal grille on top of the soil around its base, surrounded by cubed stones tapped together to create the cobbled effect on the pavement. The footpath was otherwise without feature; there were no small gardens, no low-level window boxes and no waste bins.

"Are you sure this is the right street, Marek?" Mikeš asked.

Boukal paused to reassess the map. "Yes, this is definitely

the correct location the company gave me."

Jonny took his time to assess his surroundings before delivering his verdict. "The only possibilities I can see are that the phone is down one of the street drains, buried around one of the trees, or maybe it was in a car that was parked in the same place on this side of the street from late Friday until Monday afternoon."

Whilst Mikeš took a phone call, Jonny and Boukal worked together to check the drains. Boukal held a torch to provide visibility in the fading light whilst Jonny used a small broken branch from an overhanging tree to poke around the dirt and leaves in the top of the drains. Finding nothing, they returned to the central point of the pavement, close to where Mikeš was circling, still deep in conversation on his mobile.

"I suppose it's possible someone found the phone after a few days," Jonny offered.

"Yes, that's true," Boukal acknowledged. "We had some rain over the weekend which may have dislodged it from its position if it was stuck. The phone signal has not come back on since Monday afternoon, but I suppose someone may have found it and swapped the SIM card."

"What about the cars?" Jonny proposed. "Is there any way of checking the positions of the cars from Friday evening to Monday afternoon?"

"We would have to check manually," Boukal confirmed. "I can note down all the car registrations in the street and we can contact the owners to ask where they were parked over the weekend. But, it's not going to be a quick or an easy job."

"At the moment, I don't see any other option," Jonny stated. "There is nowhere else along this street that a mobile phone could have been stored for three or four days, whether lost or thrown away. Have a look through the car windows as well, you never know."

Boukal took out his notepad and proceeded to work his way up the street, writing down the registration number of each parked vehicle. Jonny could see him checking the number plates on the front and back, as well as peering through the driver's window with the aid of the light from the torch.

With Mikeš still talking earnestly on the phone, Jonny decided to walk to the bottom of the street. He stepped slowly, almost shuffling, searching for anything out of the ordinary. As he moved down the street, he checked again in the drains. Around each tree base he studied the metal grille and earth underneath, moving the soil with the stick to check if anything was concealed beneath the surface. The grilles around the trees were all intact and there were no loose stones on the pavement. There were traces of sand across the top of and in between the small, cubed stones, but otherwise nothing unexpected. The pavement also seemed clean, as if it had been washed recently. He crossed the street and studied the opposite pavement, noting the same sand spread loosely on the surface.

Reaching the T-junction at the end of the street, he turned, perplexed. There were no stray boxes or rubbish containers on the pavement, and no potted plants outside the building entrances. They had also checked all the drains and the areas around the trees. A thought came to him about dustbins and he made a mental note to ask Boukal to check what days the rubbish bins, including recycling, were put out for collection. But, this was a long shot; the bins in the city were usually locked away behind the main building entrances and were only put out on the pavement on collection days and then only for a few hours.

What did catch his eye was not in the street Hluboká, but

rather the two streets it led into. The T-junction at the bottom of the street provided for turns left and right, both into one-way streets, common in these type of residential areas: left for the main road, right for an additional web of residential streets. The striking feature was the chaotic scene caused by the ongoing roadworks. Looking around, all he could see were holes in the pavement. All four corners of the T-junction were dug up, exposing open trenches. New plastic tubing was either already in place at the bottom of the trench or in the process of being laid, the uncut tubing and thick wires sticking up into the air. The trenches ran the length of all four pavements either side of the junction.

He walked around the junction, watching out for passing cars, peering down the holes in the pavement. The trenches were dug to a depth of approximately one metre, some with new tubing resting at the bottom, others empty. The pavements were inaccessible as metal fencing had been erected to guide pedestrians past the obstacles. Metal grilles had been laid over exposed trenches, allowing residents access to their apartments.

At intervals along the street, larger metal fencing had been erected to store the building materials. The fences prevented cars parking in the space and protected the soil dug up, piles of the small, cubed stones, as well as heaps of newly delivered sand.

Jonny bent down to study the profile of a dug trench. The stones at the top edge were embedded in a thick layer of sand, about ten centimetres deep, sitting on top of a soil layer extending down to the bottom of the trench. He felt the sand, rubbing it between his forefinger and thumb – coarse building sand, not easy for the rain to wash away.

Totally engrossed in his analysis of the scene, Jonny didn't notice Mikeš and Boukal approaching.

"Honza, what on earth are you doing?" Mikeš enquired, jokily.

Ignoring the query, Jonny fired off a question of his own. "Felix, why are these pavements being dug up?"

Mikeš peered down one of the trenches. "It's not water pipes, not deep enough. It's either new electrical lines or, more likely, fibre optic cables. The Prague streets are always being dug up. People here just get used to it – the cycle never seems to stop."

"And, how does the building contractor manage the process?"

"Well, it never seems a very well managed process, to be honest," Mikeš scoffed. "But, I suppose they have a plan of the streets, and they progress by digging one up, laying the new pipes or cables, filling it back in and then moving on to the next street."

"How do they fit back the small stones to make the pavement?"

"I can explain that," Boukal interrupted, "because they recently dug up my street. They fill in the trenches and then put down a layer of sand on top of the earth, tapping in the stones to create the cobbled pavement effect. They have a hammer machine to compress the stones into place, to keep them secure."

"That's right," Mikeš confirmed. "It's a slow job."

Jonny nodded his acknowledgment and began to walk back up the street. Mikeš and Boukal looked at each other, bemused, but followed behind him.

He stopped halfway up the street, near their starting point, as indicated by the map. He first used his shoe to brush the loose sand on top of the stones, then bent down and felt the texture of the sand. "It's the same sand," he said.

"Honza, I don't understand," Mikeš stated, a confused look

on his face. "What about the sand?"

"On the two connecting streets, where the trenches are open, there's a pile of newly delivered sand. The same coarse sand is on this pavement. It is also on the pavement across the street. It looks to me like the stones on both sides of this street have been recently replaced."

Mikeš carefully looked up and down the street, following the blurred path of loose sand on top of the pavement stones. "Yes, Honza, I think that could be right. We could easily check with the building contractor. But, why is it relevant?"

"Well, if they are digging up the next street now, there must be a good possibility that last week this street had open trenches down the length of the pavement. Maybe the building contractor filled the trenches on Monday and then the stones were relaid to form the pavement."

"That all sounds perfectly possible," Mikeš confirmed.

Jonny looked Mikeš directly in the eyes, pointing at the walkway leading up the street. "I think there is a very strong possibility that Alex Corbet is buried in the trench somewhere under this pavement... along with his mobile phone."

9

Head to Head

Everything happened so fast once Mikeš accepted Jonny's argument. Initially, it had seemed hard to believe, but the logic and timing, combined with the lack of alternative theories, brought them to a single consensus. Confirmation of the work schedule from the building contractors – corroborating Jonny's suspicion that the pavement had been open the previous Friday evening – only added to the belief.

Knowing the upheaval that would result from the decision, and the supporting manpower required, Mikeš had wanted one final walk-through of the evidence. Standing on the street, under the darkening sky, they tested their collective supposition; to make sure the decision could be defended, if later challenged by Mikeš' commanding officer. Jonny's summation that a man, and a non-Czech citizen, had possibly been lying dead in a trench under the pavement for nearly five days had sealed the deal and Mikeš made the call.

Within an hour the street was sealed off and diversions set-up. Dvořáková had been first to arrive with a small team of uniform officers. A police cordon was established at both ends of the street, a tent erected around and over the suspected area of pavement, and owners of cars parked on the street were contacted. A police lorry carrying a power generator had been mobilised for the portable lighting rig needed for digging to continue during the hours of darkness.

The police operation had caused quite a commotion. A crowd had gathered at both ends of the street, held back by the cordon, the locals keen to find out what was happening. The residents had the best vantage point; many people had opened their windows wide to watch the drama unfold. Aware of people filming the action on their smartphones, Mikeš had requested a larger tent to house all the attending police officers as well as the men starting to dig up the pavement. Word had reached the TV news stations, and a reporter was reporting live on the ongoing drama from the edge of the cordon. The paparazzi were also in attendance, easily identified by their long camera lenses.

Three hours later, Jonny and Mikeš were standing inside the long, plastic, blue tent drinking take-away coffees. Everyone was nervous, the atmosphere thick with tension. The operation had been proceeding for nearly two hours and nothing had been found. The position and depth of the trench had been gained from the building contractor and two separate police teams were digging, moving in opposite directions up and down the street, away from the central position on the map provided by the mobile phone operator.

Mikeš was especially twitchy, agitated by the lack of progress. Jonny had become used to the nervous tapping of his cane from their time together. But as time progressed with no news, Mikeš had moved on to pacing up and down, kicking stones around and humming an unrecognisable tune.

"Felix, go back to the station," Jonny said for the umpteenth time. "I can cover it here."

"No, no," Mikeš insisted. "This operation is too high profile now. I need to be here. Anyway, Marek is back at the station so he can oversee all the other ongoing cases. He'll phone if anything important comes up."

Dvořáková walked over to Mikeš. "Sir, how long do you want the digging to continue tonight?" she asked, breaching the previously unspoken but highly sensitive subject.

Mikeš looked to Jonny, appealing for some words of wisdom.

"I'm sorry to ask, sir," she added quickly, in defence of her question. "It's just that I need to plan the deployment of my officers. It is ten p.m. already."

"Yes, I am aware," Mikeš snapped.

Jonny felt for Mikeš, having been in his position many times before. Being the detective in charge could be a lonely position. The decision to dig up a city street was a big one, especially late at night. The consequences of not finding anything were significant; the longer it went on without results, the greater the pressure.

Understanding his influence in nudging Mikeš towards the decision to dig up the pavement, Jonny decided to try to ease the growing tension by putting forward a practical solution. "It would seem sensible to me to dig up this side of the street and then maybe finish for the night. If we have checked the full length of the pavement and found nothing, we should revisit the situation again tomorrow morning and proceed to dig the other side."

Mikeš mumbled his assent, hardly audible, frustrated with the situation.

Dvořáková glanced at Jonny for guidance. He nodded back discreetly, indicating she should follow his suggested way forward.

A whirl of activity amongst the policemen digging up the slope was followed by a loud gasp of horror. One of the men turned, shovel in hand, and shouted. "Pane, něco jsme našli!"

"They've found something!" Mikeš shouted, running over to the dig site.

When Jonny and Dvořáková arrived by Mikeš' side, he was standing transfixed, staring into the open trench. The diggers moved aside to provide more room. Jonny looked down and sighed heavily at the scene before him. Dvořáková gasped. Dark, plastic sheeting was showing through the cleared soil. The sheeting was pulled tight and underneath, pushing up against the plastic, was the clear imprint of a human face.

One of the policemen brushed off the remaining loose earth and slowly pulled back the sheeting. The forehead was visible first, the pale skin bright against the surrounding dark soil. As the sheet was pulled back fully, the face of a dead, young woman was exposed.

Mikeš took his hat off and held it to his chest in respect. "Well, I didn't expect that, I…"

"And, unfortunately," Jonny added calmly, "I think we will find Alex Corbet buried either underneath her or further along the trench."

"Lucie, please call Dr Králová," Mikeš instructed. "Tell her it's an emergency."

"Yes, sir."

***

Three hours later, past one a.m. the exhumation was still in progress. Dr Králová and her forensics team had assumed control, taking care to unearth the bodies and preserve evidence. The dug soil was kept separate for later laboratory analysis.

The only update provided to Mikeš during the operation was

to confirm that a second dead body – male – had also been found buried under plastic sheeting. In addition, the two victims' personal belongings had been found, including two mobile phones.

Jonny and Mikeš had initially retired to a local bar to rest and find sustenance, Boukal joining them once his duties at the station were completed for the evening. Mikeš' phone had been red hot, briefing his seniors and organising resources over the coming days for what was now his top priority case. The stress of whether his big call would prove correct had dissipated, replaced with concern about how to manage the balance of an increasing workload. Jonny had heard his own name mentioned when Mikeš was briefing his commanding officer by phone but was content to remain out of the limelight and let his friend be congratulated for an inspired piece of detective work.

Whilst Mikeš was engaged, Jonny had borrowed the map from Boukal and plotted the known locations: Helena Corbetová's apartment, her dead husband's new apartment, the location of the exhumation, and finally the Červený lev pub. Once mapped out, even Boukal had to admit the irregular triangle around the site of the burial was uncanny and worthy of further consideration.

The conversation veered from idea to theory, although it was agreed that nothing could be concluded until Králová provided at least an early indication of the cause of death. The victims were naturally assumed to be Alex Corbet and his new, unidentified girlfriend, known to have left the pub near closing time the previous Friday and probably walking back to his apartment. Jonny's first thought was to acknowledge the possibility they could easily have been intercepted by Helena Corbetová or her mother, or both together, however unlikely the scenario appeared to be.

They were last to leave the café when it closed, keen to delay leaving the warmth of the inside for the cold of the external crime scene. With nothing to do, they hung around outside the plastic tent, bored but knowing they could not leave their positions at such a critical time.

The crowds at the police cordon had thinned, but some local residents were still watching out of their apartment windows. The TV crew were still in position, providing regular updates on the twenty-four-hour news channel. Mikeš was receiving regular updates on the news bulletins, enthusiastically relaying the information to Jonny and Boukal, pleased to at least have something to do. Mikeš took glee in imparting the incorrect or distorted information being reported, his disdain for the media clearly deep-rooted.

Králová eventually called them all into the tent. With her forensics team still working industriously behind her, bent over the trenches in their white body suits, masks and gloves, she stood at the side of the trench next to the two bodies. "It is clearly very late so I will make this update brief. We can follow up in the morning, as required, and again after I have finished the autopsies tomorrow afternoon."

Mikeš, Jonny and Boukal stood like naughty, tired schoolboys in front of the headmistress, only able to nod their agreement in unison.

"The male subject is, as we thought, Alex Corbet, according to the ID we've found in his wallet. The female subject also had ID in her purse. Her name is Yulia Ivanova and she seems to be a Russian national. Both their personal belongings seem untouched: Alex Corbet still has his wallet and watch, and Yulia Ivanova is still wearing her jewellery and her handbag was buried next to her. And, as you know already, we've found two mobile phones. We will obviously still need to check them all thoroughly for DNA and fingerprints."

Králová paused to check the notes on her small pad before continuing. Her late-night audience remained captivated.

"Both victims died from injuries to the head. Yulia Ivanova looks to have been hit on the back of her head with a blunt instrument – a hard, possibly metal, object. The attack on Alex Corbet was almost certainly carried out with the same murder weapon but looks to have been more frenzied because he has received numerous impacts to his head and face. At this point, it is impossible to tell you exactly how many or which one was fatal."

Mikeš started the questions. "And, Ella, do you know the time—"

"Yes, Felix, the important question," she declared, reasserting her control. "How long have they been buried in the trench? Well, at this point I can only say definitely more than two days, but also probably less than a week. I will confirm a more accurate time of death for the two deceased tomorrow once I've completed my full forensic examinations."

"The approximate timing fits with what we know," Jonny admitted. "We believe Alex Corbet and the woman he was with left the pub last Friday between eleven p.m. and midnight. I'm sure we'll be able to track them because they would have walked through I. P. Pavlova on their way back to his apartment. That's a busy part of Prague 2, so they must have been caught on CCTV somewhere."

"That's assuming they were going back to his apartment," Boukal interjected.

"Quite right, Marek, we don't know for sure," Jonny

acknowledged.

A tired silence descended, everyone processing the information.

"Ella," Jonny continued, "I have one last question. Were the bodies thrown into the trenches or placed in carefully?"

Mikeš turned to Jonny, surprised at the question.

"We've only seen the woman's face," Jonny explained, "but it didn't appear to be a rushed job. Her body, from what I saw, appeared to have been laid out with some care."

"Very perceptive, Honza," Králová commented. "I was surprised once we had dug around both of them. The bodies have been carefully placed next to each other, in a head to head position. Their heads were almost touching, their bodies laid out away from each other, with their arms folded across their chests. I'm not sure what to make of it, really. It could be whoever did this was following a ritual, or maybe it was just done out of respect. Either way, the murderer or murderers didn't just hit them and throw them into the ditch. No, they have laid them out carefully, covered them with plastic sheeting, and probably a layer of soil so they wouldn't be seen, before the trench was re-filled later."

"Very strange," Mikeš uttered, shaking his head in disbelief.

An eerie silence descended. The late hour and gruesome details were taking their toll on everyone's enthusiasm.

"I will make sure photos of the bodies and details of all the personal belongings are made available for your morning briefing," Králová confirmed. "And, Felix?"

Mikeš turned to his ex-wife, a brightness still in his facial features for her.

"We are going to be here another couple of hours, at least. Given the late hour, I think we'll need to cancel the dinner we have planned for tomorrow night." She looked at her watch. "Actually, tonight now."

Mikeš' face dropped.

Sensing the disappointment, Jonny placed a hand on Mikeš' shoulder. "Let's all go home, it's been a long day."

10

Just Experience

Thursday, 15 April

Despite not getting back to his rented room until two thirty a.m. Jonny set his alarm early. The missing person case was now a murder investigation and he knew that progress during the next twenty-four hours was going to be crucial. They'd already lost five days from when the bodies were supposedly buried and during this time the killer could have absconded or tried to cover their tracks.

There was a lot of ground to catch up, including finding out about Yulia Ivanova. With limited information, the permutations of potential murderer and motive were almost non-existent. All he knew so far was that Alex Corbet's wife, Helena Corbetová, and her mother, Daniela Nováková, had a clear issue with his behaviour over the past months, including the alleged affair with a woman named Tanya. But perhaps Alex was the innocent party, caught up in an outstanding quarrel related to his new girlfriend's life.

Not having clarity on the motive for the murders, Jonny also had the dreaded fear that the murderer may kill again if not caught soon. This had always been his worst nightmare, often keeping him awake all night; it was also the reason for the personal anxiety over his last case before he retired from the

Metropolitan Police. Solving the Old Town Square Murder had provided some redemption, and he'd slept well since, but he had tossed and turned last night, unable to settle, feeling the same stress and tension returning. He hated lagging behind the killer, chasing shadows, getting no closer to finding the reasons why someone had resorted to murder. It was his nature, and probably the reason he made such a good detective, but he knew he wouldn't be able to rest until he was making progress towards the truth.

The short car journey from the burial site back to Náměstí Míru in the early hours had been subdued, the late hour taking its toll on their concentration. Despite Jonny's hunch about the burial under the pavement proving correct, Mikeš was clearly fretting about how to allocate police resources to the increased caseload. They had agreed to reconvene for an early meeting, seven thirty a.m. at the station, hoping some rest and fresh eyes would provide new inspiration.

Ivana had been asleep when he returned late and so he'd climbed the stairs to his attic room carefully, not wanting to make too much noise and disturb her. The early alarm meant he also did not see her in the morning. She'd been understanding when he'd called her earlier the previous evening, responding with excitement about the Medovina, but her reply to his later message had been terse, only confirming she'd seen the police operation reported on the local TV news. Annoyingly, he had also lost the bottle somewhere during the drawn-out wait for the exhumation to be completed.

The early morning metro was crowded as usual, the Czech people starting work early so they could finish early. He was surprised to see many older people travelling before seven a.m. and wondered where they were going. Maybe it was just a capital city that never slept. He made a mental note to ask Mikeš sometime.

Luka didn't open his café until seven thirty a.m. but because Jonny had sent a message early he was waiting at the door with a take-away coffee and a croissant.

"Pay me later, Honza," was Luka's parting remark, seeing him in a rush.

"Thanks Luka, I'm sure I'll be in with Felix today anyway," he replied, waving as he strode purposefully off down the street Kaprova, in the direction of Old Town Square.

The sun was already coming up, peeping from behind the steeples of the famous Gothic church, The Church of Our Lady before Týn. Walking across the cobble stones of the famous square with the rising sun was his favourite pastime in Prague, the expanse of space providing the perfect setting. He felt lucky to be able to follow these steps every day on his way to work, to bask in the glory of the history all around him. Although he wasn't one for morbid thoughts, he knew this stroll would ideally be his dying wish; his last journey, probably in a wheelchair wrapped in lots of blankets and pushed by his daughter, Charlotte.

The square always seemed to do this, taking him away to some far off imagined land. The thoughts often featured his daughter, recalling past events or imagining the future, and he knew it only happened because he felt truly at peace in the space. He was so looking forward to showing Charlotte around Prague, wanting to see the city through her eyes all over again. But first he had to solve a murder, to bring the perpetrator to justice and repay the faith the Czech Police, and especially Mikeš, had shown in him.

Entering the Incident Room, Jonny saw Boukal writing up

the Corbet/Ivanova case on the main whiteboard on the wall; the high profile of the double murder case, supported by the extensive coverage in the media, had promoted it to top spot in the serious crime portfolio. The lonely photo of Alex Corbet as a missing person had been joined by a photo of Yulia Ivanova. The photos were surrounded by scribbled arrows indicating known relationships and possible timings. There were also a lot of question marks, never a good sign on a murder investigation, and a clear indicator of the hard work ahead. Jonny smiled proudly nonetheless, pleased to see greater urgency and clarity to Boukal's methods since he had started to work with him. There was as yet no improvement in Boukal's appearance; the late night and early morning had not helped, his suit looking so crumpled from the back he could have slept in it.

"Dobré ráno, Honza," Boukal greeted him. "I'm updating the Murder Board with what we know about the case. Lucie is printing off the photos of the evidence you found yesterday at Alex Corbet's apartment."

"No problem," Jonny replied, taking a seat and sipping his coffee. "And where's Felix?"

"He's answering emails and he's not very happy about it," Boukal explained. "After the TV coverage last night, everyone seems to have written to congratulate him and ask what leads we have on the case. We've been here since six thirty a.m."

"It's the part of the job I always hated." Jonny shook his head in sympathy. "Poor Felix."

Dvořáková walked into the office with a small pile of papers. "Good morning, Honza."

In sharp contrast to Boukal, her uniform was immaculately ironed as usual and she looked fresh, as if she'd gone home early the day before rather than working all night with minimal sleep.

"Ahoj, Lucie."

She sat down next to him, putting the A4 prints of the photos on the table. "Honza…" she started cautiously.

"Yes," he replied, swallowing his bite of croissant. "What is it?"

"How did you know the bodies could be buried under the pavement? I've been going over it all night, and it seems a big jump from a simple missing person case. I'm keen to understand how you worked it out."

"Well, it would be easy to claim I'm a genius, but sadly it's not the case," he confessed. "It is all about experience. I had a similar case in the UK involving a new bridge being built over a motorway. The victim liked to walk his dog in the surrounding fields every evening. After he disappeared, his wife showed us the route he walked. We were not getting anywhere with the case so I revisited the walking route and saw the builders constructing the bridge. Something made me check their schedule over the past week and I noticed they had laid the concrete foundations for the bridge the day after the missing person was reported. Digging up the new concrete was a big job, but we found him and his dog at the bottom. The murder was committed by his business partner, some feud over the finances. This case, with Alex Corbet initially reported missing, was different, but the evidence framed the limited options and then I saw the roadworks underway further down the street. The sand was the key. It led me to believe the pavement had been relaid recently." He faltered, lost for an explanation. "It's just experience, not magic. The more serious crimes you are part of, the more you start to think like a criminal."

Boukal had finished preparing the board and stood awestruck, watching Jonny finish the story. "Well, I was there last night and I thought it was magic," he exclaimed.

"Thank you, Honza," Dvořáková stated, respectfully. "That is so helpful. I want to learn as much as possible."

Mikeš rushed into the room, a burst of energy with whirling arms. He appeared flustered, slightly red in the face, matching the pink shirt and tie combination chosen to complement his usual immaculate, three-piece pressed tweed suit for the day ahead.

"Why can't we go back to old fashioned policing?" he shouted into the air, immediately claiming the centre of attention. "Emails to answer, texts to reply to, and online reports to fill in for everything you do. It drives me mad!"

Mikeš flopped into a chair the other side of Jonny, his shoulders collapsed, and looked at his pocket watch. "And, it's only seven thirty a.m. in the morning!"

Jonny laughed softly, putting his hand on his friend's shoulder. "Don't worry, Felix, we'll just have to use Marek and Lucie's youth to help us through this. They are very competent."

"I know, Honza," Mikeš replied, forcing a smile. He slowly looked around the room at his colleagues. "Yes, I have a great team and we will get through this. I don't know how, but we will manage it. Now, where are we with this double murder investigation?"

Jonny smiled, pleased to see Mikeš returning quickly to his normal self. When they had first started to work together, Jonny had found Mikeš' mood swings hard to handle, not sure whether to try to cajole him back to his usual self or just leave him to stew. Through experience, he now knew to just wait and within a short time Mikeš would be back to his joyful, flamboyant best.

Boukal took centre stage, pointing at the photos on the board. "The missing person case has now turned into a double

91

murder, the victims being Alex Corbet and Yulia Ivanova. We know about Alex Corbet from the initial missing person case. Yulia Ivanova was a Russian national, working here in the Czech Republic under a visa. She worked for an office design company based in Brno; the business card in her purse states her role as Sales Executive."

"What was she doing in Prague?" Mikeš barked.

"Sir, we don't know yet," Boukal replied. "But, we do know the registered address on her visa is in Hradec Králové. We are in contact with the local police and they are checking the address."

"Yesterday, I spoke to the manager of the Červený lev pub," Jonny started. "He told me that Alex and a lady fitting Yulia's description left the pub on Friday evening near the end of the evening, between eleven p.m. and midnight. The barmaid at the pub confirmed the information. It seems it might have been a first or early date because they sat alone together in the corner all evening. Alex was a regular there, well known, but for some reason he didn't introduce her to any one."

"I have already organised for my officers to check the CCTV cameras between the pub and the spot where they were found buried," Dvořáková confirmed. "Now we have a photo of Yulia Ivanova, we will also check with the pub staff to confirm if she was the woman with Alex Corbet."

"Great work, Lucie," Jonny encouraged. "When I went to Alex Corbet's apartment yesterday, I found a ladies' overnight bag and also some sleepwear in the bed. This makes me think she perhaps had already stayed with Alex on Thursday night. Either that or she had stayed with him before."

Dvořáková handed around the A4-sized prints of the studio bed and bag photos taken by Jonny the day before.

"We will need somebody to formally identify her body," Mikeš stated.

Boukal wrote a reminder on the whiteboard and pointed towards the timeline. "Alex's wife, Helena Corbetová, told us yesterday she thought he was having a relationship with someone before they separated at the end of last year."

"Yes, but she was convinced it was an American woman called Tanya," Jonny corrected him. "Whereas Yulia is Russian. Also, the manager of the pub was adamant yesterday he had not seen Alex Corbet in the pub with any woman since he and Helena had separated. Yulia seems to have been the first woman he has taken to the pub, so it was significant."

"That's strange," Mikeš commented.

"To tell you the truth, the whole set-up between Alex and Helena seems strange to me," Jonny added. "I know any separation is tough, but the disparity between their living conditions was stark. Helena is still living in their luxurious apartment whilst Alex's accommodation was of a really poor standard, like a student apartment. We definitely need to ask Helena some more questions."

"And remind me of the other evidence you spotted yesterday at his apartment," Mikeš encouraged.

"The first was a handwritten note warning him to stay away from a woman," Jonny clarified.

Dvořáková handed around the A4 print of the warning note.

"LEAVE HER ALONE! I'M WARNING YOU" Mikeš read aloud, giving Jonny a quizzical look.

"At this stage we cannot be clear who sent it to Alex Corbet," Jonny clarified. "Obviously, Helena was jealous about another woman, but it seems she may have had the wrong information. We need to find and interview Tanya to get the truth."

"I will organise the interview," Boukal confirmed. "She supposedly works at the same company as Alex did. I think we should also interview Alex's boss, Torsten Lindberg. I have spoken to him briefly on the phone, but I think we should talk to him face-to-face."

"I agree," Jonny concurred. "The other possibility is that the warning note is something to do with Yulia. It could be a jealous ex-partner. At the moment, we know nothing about her. We need to find out about her and her life quickly, because she could be the missing piece in this puzzle."

Dvořáková handed around the final A4 print.

"The other note I found amongst Alex Corbet's belongings was handwritten contact details of a solicitor in Prague," Jonny explained.

"A solicitor?" Mikeš stated quizzically.

"Yes," Jonny confirmed. "It could be quite innocent, but the note was not written by Alex Corbet. Someone else had written the contact details for him. Last night, before going to bed I left a voicemail at the office of the solicitor, Pavel Rosický. His office is on Wenceslas Square. I'm hoping to be able to visit him today."

"Yes, I know him," Mikeš confirmed. "He is a well-known and high profile solicitor."

"I will phone the office again," Dvořáková offered. "I'll book a meeting for you."

"Thank you, Lucie." Jonny said. "The first job of the day though is to break the bad news to Helena Corbetová."

"I will come with you," Boukal confirmed.

"At this stage, I would like to keep the identity of Yulia Ivanova to ourselves if we can," Jonny ventured. "I know we have to confirm a double murder to the media, but it would be helpful to hold back the information about Yulia for as long as possible. It may prove useful in the interviews, especially with Alex's family."

"I have already authorised the press release," Mikeš confirmed. "It only states that two bodies have been found, presumed murdered, and that the identities of the bodies have not yet been confirmed. But, we will be under pressure to release the victim's names once their bodies have been formally identified."

"That should give us enough time," Jonny declared.

Mikeš nodded solemnly, looking around at everyone in the room. "This is going to be a tough case. Honza's inspired talent helped us discover the bodies yesterday, but finding the killer or killers is going to stretch us to the limit. It is important we all work together and use our collective detective skills. I know we can do it but remember to question everything and follow every lead. Now, let's rock n' roll, team. We have a murder investigation to solve."

11

Family Friend

Breaking the bad news to close relatives that one of their family had been found murdered was without doubt the worst part of the job. Autopsies were a close second for Jonny, but nothing was worse than seeing someone break down completely in front of you. Some senior detectives he'd worked with in the past had tried to avoid the emotional turmoil, sending one of their team instead, but he saw it as his moral obligation. There was also the benefit of seeing the immediate reactions in person; the slightest, unexpected facial clues from the spouse or a close family member could lead to a new line of enquiry.

Standing outside the building, Jonny felt the dread creep up on him. Based on the one brief meeting with Helena Corbetová, he was convinced she still loved her husband. Even though their marriage had clearly been under strain, and with the lingering accusation of adultery, her affection for him did not seem to have diminished.

Boukal stepped forward to press the buzzer, introducing himself over the speaker system. Thankfully, the intercom system worked this time, the door clicking open. Jonny was pleased he'd be able to tell Helena the news in the sanctity of her own apartment. They travelled up in the lift along with the female police officer organised by Dvořáková, accompanying them to provide support and early counselling to the bereaved. The short journey seemed to take an age.

When Helena opened the door, her hand lifted immediately to her mouth when she saw the collection of police officers. The next few minutes were a blur. Jonny stepped forward to catch Helena as her knees buckled underneath her and guided her to the sofa in the living room. The female officer gathered up the children and ushered them into their bedroom, asking to be shown their favourite toys. Boukal displayed unexpected domestic skills, making a mug of black tea with sugar and bringing it through for Helena.

Helena sat alone in the middle of the large sofa, opposite Jonny, on one of the armchairs. She looked fragile amongst the plumped-up cushions, head slightly down as she dabbed her eyes with a tissue.

"Mrs Corbetová," Jonny started gently. "I think you already know why we are here again so quickly. I am so sorry to be the person to tell you this, but we believe we found Alex's body last night. And, sadly, we believe he has been murdered."

Helena's body shook uncontrollably as she wailed, covering her face with the palms of her hands.

Jonny waited patiently. His subtle nod gave Boukal the silent instruction to allow her space. The sound of the children could be heard from the adjoining bedroom, enjoying themselves and totally oblivious to the gravity of the situation.

"Mrs Corbetová, would you like some tea?" Boukal offered after a few minutes. "I've put some sugar in it for you. It really helps when you've had a shock like this."

Helena sat unmoved, only shaking her hanging head of hair in refusal.

After waiting a respectful few minutes, Jonny attempted to restart the dialogue. "Can we call your mother?" he asked. "I think it would be a good idea to have someone else around at this time."

She blew her nose, trying to compose herself. "Mummy is already on her way," she finally mumbled. "She comes every day. She usually arrives after I drop Emilie off at kindergarten. I was about to leave…"

"I suggest you don't worry about that today," Jonny reassured her. "Our officer can stay with you to help for as long as you need. She is distracting the children at the moment. They are all in the bedroom."

She nodded her understanding. "Are you sure it is Alex?" she pleaded.

"Well, we found Alex's ID on the body," Jonny explained. "However, we will still need you to formally identify the body later. Or, maybe your mother could do it."

Helena started crying again, her head bent over her lap in despair. Jonny and Boukal gave her time to recover her composure.

"Was it the police operation on TV last night?" she finally asked.

"Yes," Jonny confirmed.

"What happened to him?"

"At this point, we are not disclosing this information to any one," Jonny added. "I know you might think this is wrong, but this is a murder investigation now. In our experience, the less information we share at this early stage the greater chance we have of catching the murderer. And, I think we all want that."

Helena paused to consider the response, wiping the flowing tears from her eyes. "On the TV news, they reported that the police were digging up the street."

"I'm sorry, but I cannot say any more at this stage. I am just going to have to ask you to trust us at the moment."

The silence was broken by the sound of a key turning in the front door. Jonny stood up and met Daniela Nováková in the hallway. She peered over his shoulder, into the living room.

"Mrs Nováková, we were just talking to your daughter. Sadly, we have bad news. Last night we found what we believe is her husband's body."

Daniela froze, her normal composed demeanour replaced with a shocked expression. She looked past Jonny, into the living room, seeing her daughter crying on the sofa. The distressing sight clearly hardened her resolve and she quickly recovered her usual calm, collected appearance. "They were separated," Daniela stated bluntly.

"I think they were still married, though," Jonny gently corrected her, watching her reaction intently.

"Yes," she bristled, "maybe on paper. But he had moved out. He left her and the children."

"Mummy!" Helena shouted from the living room, seemingly familiar with the reasoning but wanting the argument to stop.

Daniela quickly took off her coat, placed it on the side of the sofa with her handbag, and sat down, pulling her daughter close in a consoling embrace.

Jonny sat down again, waiting for mother and daughter to collect themselves.

"Where are the children?" Daniela asked sharply.

"They are in the bedroom with one of our female officers," Boukal reassured her. "They are in safe hands; she is trained for these situations."

"What right have you got to come in here unannounced?" she erupted in response. "Look what you have done to my daughter, she's a gibbering wreck. You barge in here and bring her to tears without anyone to support her. Who is this female officer? We don't even know how qualified she is to look after children, especially at a time like this."

Jonny let the emotion go unchecked – he had heard a lot worse in his time. This was probably the most stressful situation anyone could face. In the past, he'd been sworn at, spat at, pushed and threatened. And, it was almost always a relative unable to accept the news or reacting to the distress caused to the distraught spouse or close family member.

"Mrs Nováková, I understand this is an upsetting situation for everyone, including you. But, we came to tell Mrs Corbetová the sad news about her husband as soon as we could. This is standard police practice, and the correct thing to do in my opinion. I think you would be angry if we didn't come straight away."

Jonny left the alternative floating in the air between them, allowing the severity of the situation to sink in, before continuing. "We need to act quickly because the early stages of this investigation are of utmost importance to successfully finding who did this to Alex."

"I fully appreciate that," Daniela replied, now calm and composed. "But you will also appreciate that my daughter and my grandchildren are my priority right now. Certainly more important than finding out who killed Alex."

Helena had been sobbing, but she suddenly reacted, pulling herself away from her mother's arms. "Mummy! You can't say that."

Daniela responded by pulling her daughter close, smothering her. "You know I am right, darling. We must protect the children."

Jonny noticed Boukal watching Daniela too closely. "Chief

Sergeant Boukal," Jonny began, trying to distract him. "What arrangements do we need to make to formally identify the body?"

Before Boukal could answer, Daniela jumped in. "I will do it. I want my daughter and grandchildren to remain here. I don't want them under any more stress than is necessary."

"I can take you straight from here in the car," Boukal offered, "or arrange for you to be picked up later."

"Later please," she requested. "Maybe around midday. I need to organise for my husband to come over before I leave."

"And who is your husband, Mrs Nováková?" Jonny seized on the opening, phrasing the question lightly.

"Jakub Novák," she replied sternly in return.

"Thank you. And, will he be travelling here from outside Prague?"

"No, he dropped me off just now," she snapped. "He runs an antique shop in Prague 1, in the old town, but he usually doesn't open until ten a.m. or sometimes later."

"Makes sense," Jonny acknowledged, appeasing her to keep the atmosphere calm.

"Mrs Nováková," Boukal intervened, "may I suggest you call me when your husband arrives, and I can drive you to the hospital and then return you back here. I will leave my card on the side table."

Jonny cleared his throat, keen to take back the initiative. "Mrs Corbetová and Mrs Nováková, I appreciate this is a very difficult time, but we will need to interview you both today. It is vitally important we understand as much as possible about the background regarding Alex and the family—"

"You surely can't believe we had anything to do with this!" Daniela erupted.

Jonny put his palms out to pacify her. "Mrs Nováková, I am

not saying either of you are suspects. But, we must ask you some questions to understand more about Alex's state of mind, his friends, and his work. I appreciate you will not know everything about Alex's recent life, but any small detail might help us. It could be the difference between finding out who did this or letting them get away with it. The small details are so important in fact that we would like to tape the interviews. It allows us to revisit the interviews later if we miss something. We can either conduct them here or down the station—"

"Any interviews must be here," Daniela asserted, coldly, interrupting him again.

"Understood," he retorted. "We will come back after Chief Sergeant Boukal has taken you to the hospital. But, please, the interviews must be individual, with the children out of the room. We will also need to take DNA and fingerprint samples from you in order to eliminate you from our enquiries."

Daniela ignored Jonny's comments, squeezing her daughter and kissing her on top of the head.

"And, Mrs Corbetová?" Jonny continued unabated, looking directly at Helena.

He waited until Helena lifted her head to look across the room at him.

"This emotional time might stimulate some memories you might have forgotten. Maybe something odd happening to Alex when he was living here. Or, something you know happened to him recently. If you do get any memories like this could you please write them down on a piece of paper so we can discuss them later. The more you can tell us about him, the better chance we have of catching whoever did this to him."

Helena nodded.

"Thank you," Jonny stated, smiling kindly. "We will show

ourselves out."

Jonny and Boukal rose from their seats and turned towards the living room door. Prompted by a sudden recollection, Jonny turned back to face mother and daughter sitting on the sofa.

"Sorry, one last thing. When I was looking around Alex's apartment yesterday, I found this handwritten note in the black rucksack I believe he used for work. Do you know anything about it?"

He took out his mobile phone and found the image of the handwritten solicitor's details in his phone gallery. He held the phone out to Helena. She wiped her eyes to look more closely at the photo.

"Yes, that's my handwriting," she confirmed. "I gave it to him. Pavel Rosický is our solicitor."

"No," Daniela said firmly. "Pavel is a family friend and *our* solicitor, not Alex's."

"Mummy, don't be like that. Pavel acted for both Alex and I when we bought this apartment. Alex asked me for his contact details and I wrote them down for him. He had as much right as me to speak to Pavel."

Daniela snorted her disagreement and shook her head.

"Thank you," Jonny confirmed, "that is very helpful."

12

The Golden Voice

Having received an urgent call from Mikeš about another ongoing case, Boukal headed back to the police station. Jonny decamped to a local coffee bar, keen to reflect on Daniela Nováková's reaction and plan his day ahead in order to maximise the benefit to the murder investigation. Having ordered a caffe latte and sat down in a quiet area, he took out his mobile phone and called Dvořáková.

"Ahoj, Lucie."

"Ahoj, Honza."

"I'm just calling to check in and to ask about the meeting with the solicitor, Pavel Rosický."

"Where are you?"

"I've just stopped for a coffee. Marek and I have just seen Helena Corbetová. She was naturally very upset, but her mother's reaction was strange."

"How?"

"Well, she was naturally protective of her daughter and grandchildren, but it came across as overpowering, almost intimidating at times. She was also very quick to be negative about Alex Corbet."

"What's your next step?" Dvořáková enquired, showing her continued interest in his methods.

"I really need to see the solicitor as soon as possible. I want to understand why Alex wanted to see him."

"I've just called them and was about to send you a message. You have an appointment at eleven a.m."

"Excellent, thanks."

"Honza, there's something else you need to know. Alex Corbet's apartment was broken into last night."

"What!" Jonny exclaimed loudly, attracting the glances of other customers.

"Yes, Josef Liška has called in, he's over at the apartment now."

"Josef?" Jonny questioned, confused. "What's he doing there?"

"Well, as you know, Josef prefers the sanctity of the evidence room in the basement. But, Felix has asked him to organise the evidence from the apartment because we are so short of resources."

"Thanks Lucie. I'm going to head over there now."

"Good luck, Honza."

Jonny walked over to the serving desk and asked the barista to change his order to a take-away. With coffee in hand, he swiftly walked out of the coffee bar and turned in the direction of Alex Corbet's apartment.

Usually he would stroll around Prague, lifting his head as he walked, hoping to encounter a previously unnoticed feature of the historic city. This day was different – time was of the essence. He strode to Karlovo Náměstí square, his head swirling with thoughts about the unlikely coincidence of Alex Corbet's apartment being broken into the same night his dead body was discovered. Instead of taking his favoured walk through the winding paths, he skirted the square and took the more direct route up the busy, main road Ječná. At the next junction he turned left, cutting across another main road, pleased with his improving orientation within the city.

Nearing the building, his thoughts turned to Ivana. He stopped and quickly wrote her a message.

Sorry I missed you last night. I was also out early. It's going to be a tough couple of days! I'll send you a message later. Honza x

His mobile phone bleeped before he even had the opportunity to put it back in his jacket pocket.

No problem. But don't forget you are seeing Barbora at 14.00. I don't want to let her down. She is a good friend and busy at work.

Jonny looked at his watch, trying to mentally synchronise all the activities for the day. He knew this was a big test. It would be a major issue for Ivana if he missed the appointment she'd booked for him to trace his family tree in the Czech Republic. Even though he had clear intentions to improve the balance between his personal life and police work, a mistake as significant as not making the planned meeting, or just being late, would probably be terminal for their relationship.

Forcing himself to focus back on the murder case, he walked the last few steps to the building and opened the main entrance door with the keys he still had in his possession. He held the door open as an elderly Czech lady carrying a bag of food shopping followed him into the building. They exchanged greetings and she started to ascend the stairs with caution. Whilst she seemed fit for her age, probably well into her seventies, he could see the pain in her hips and knees through the movement of her body. Although he felt it was wrong that a person of her age had to live in a badly maintained building without a lift, he somehow intrinsically knew she'd been through much worse in her life.

Even if she was offered a ground floor apartment with easy access somewhere else, she would probably refuse to leave the apartment that had been her life for fifty years or more.

Turning his attention back to the door, he carefully studied the locking system. It was a simple Yale-type lock, inadequate for the purposes of securing a main entrance. Once forced open, the whole building would be accessible via the stairs. The lock appeared to have been repaired recently, the screw fixings into fresh wooden holes looking new. Jonny reprimanded himself for not paying more attention when he had visited the day before, but it was only a missing person case at that point.

Jonny turned at the noise of footsteps and saw the same young man who had showed him Alex Corbet's bicycle stored in the basement.

"Hello again," Jonny opened the conversation.

"Good morning. I'm just off to uni."

"It's okay." Jonny laughed. "I won't make you late. I just have a simple question for you. Do you know if this door lock was broken last night?"

"Yes, it was," he replied. "I came home late last night, after drinks with friends, and the door was slightly open. The door would still close, but the lock wasn't secure. I sent a message to the landlord before I went to sleep."

"Thank you, that's very useful."

"Mind you," the man continued, "the security in this place is terrible. I've complained to the landlord a few times, but what can you do?"

"You didn't see anyone suspicious hanging about when you returned last night?" Jonny enquired.

"No, sorry."

"No problem. Have a good day."

"Bye," the man said, walking out onto the pavement.

After securing the lock as best he could, Jonny stepped purposefully up the wide, concrete staircase to the second floor, his heart beating a little faster when he reached the apartment. The door was slightly ajar and secured with police tape to prevent anyone crossing the threshold.

He pushed the door open gently, peering over the tape, to see inside the studio apartment. Liška was standing in the kitchen area, clipboard and pen in his plastic-gloved hands, his back turned away from the entrance. His heavy frame and rotund figure, packed into his tight police uniform, made him the dominant object in the space, the studio apartment seeming even smaller in his presence.

"Josef!" Jonny shouted out.

Liška didn't react. He continued his shuffling steps around the tiny kitchen area, opening cupboards and drawers, making notes of the items on his clipboard, oblivious to any activity behind him. Jonny could also sense a slight rhythm to his colleague's shuffle, his backside and hips moving subtly to an indiscernible beat. Jonny broke into a smile when he spotted an old fashioned set of headphones across the top of Josef's head, the cushioned speakers tight to his ears. The headphones led to a 1980s-style portable cassette player clipped to Liška's waistband.

"Josef," Jonny shouted again, knocking loudly on the apartment door and waving his other arm in an animated fashion.

Distracted by the motion in the corner of his vision, Liška turned and saw Jonny.

"Honza," he shouted, smiling widely and lowering the headphones. "Good to see you. Come in."

Jonny unpeeled the police tape from one side of the door

frame and stepped into the apartment, resealing the tape behind him. "Ahoj, Josef, you looked like you were almost dancing there."

"Very funny." Josef laughed loudly. "You only wobble when you're as big as me!"

"What classical musical favourite are you listening to today?" Jonny asked.

"You'll be shocked to hear this, but it's not classical. Usually, as you know, I have my quality CD player in the evidence room. But, when Felix asked me to help out, I grabbed the only portable music system I have." He pointed down to the cassette player hugging his waist. "I don't think I've used it for twenty years."

"I'm impressed it's still working." Jonny laughed.

"The cassette I found inside is a compilation of Karel Gott's greatest hits. I didn't even remember I had it. But, you know, I'm really enjoying it. He is crowned the Golden Voice of Prague and the people here love him."

"I know," Jonny agreed. "When Ivana turns the radio on, it always seems to be a Karel Gott song playing."

"Do you know, it has now been five years since I was out in the field," Liška confessed. "It's quite a shock to the system after being hidden in the basement of the police station for all these years."

"It's good to see you in action," Jonny concurred.

"I've only just started the inventory and afterwards I plan to box up Alex Corbet's personal belongings so they can be taken back to the station."

"I had a look around yesterday," Jonny informed him. "I found a couple of items in the rucksack. When Lucie told me the apartment had been broken into, I thought I'd best come and check everything was still in order. What happened to the door?"

Josef moved slowly over to the door and using his pen, pointed around the lock system. "The lock is really bad quality. Whoever broke in would not have had to struggle. They probably used something like a credit card and then just had to push to force the lock mechanism open. Lucie is organising for forensics to come over later, but I understand they are very busy with the burial site. Finding it was inspired by the way, Felix told me all about it."

"Thanks, Josef. But, as you know, sometimes you just have a hunch."

"I call it good old fashioned police work."

"I hope you don't mind, Josef, but I need to get on. We've got a busy schedule today and I need to get away. Yesterday, I found some interesting personal items belonging to Alex Corbet. I just want to check they're still here."

"Be my guest, Honza," Liška encouraged, handing Jonny a pair of plastic gloves.

Moving across to the studio bed, Jonny lowered the bed frame and mattress to the floor. He checked under the duvet and saw the men's and women's bedclothes in the same place he'd found them the day before. After raising the bed up, he next checked the women's designer travel bag – the contents seemed untouched.

Turning to look at the table on the opposite wall, he carefully studied the positioning of all the objects. The variety of personal items on top of the table seemed unchanged, Jonny remembering how he had replaced each book and DVD case. Then he saw the rucksack. He instinctively knew something wasn't right. He replayed his memories from the last visit, each iteration showing him leaving the black rucksack on the chair. Now, the rucksack was on the floor, leaning against one of the table legs.

"Josef," Jonny shouted, "did you move this rucksack?"

Liška shook his head. "I've only just started in the kitchen. I haven't touched anything down that end of the room yet."

Jonny cautiously moved to the table, lifted up the rucksack and placed it on top of the surface. Sitting down on the chair, he searched the contents. The laptop was there still and seemed intact. The notebook was also there, and flicking through he recognised many of the pages, nothing appearing to have been changed or torn out. Next, he turned to the wad of loose papers. On top was the A5 sized paper, post-it note attached, with the handwritten solicitor's contact details. The next item was the notice for the unpaid bill. Jonny froze, immediately knowing the order was wrong; the warning note, handwritten on plain printer paper, and the attached post-it note were missing. He remembered how he'd attached the post-it notes to the A5 paper and also the warning note, before placing both on the top of the loose papers. He sifted through all the loose papers, also searching through the inside of the rucksack, but he couldn't find it – the warning note was gone!

"Josef," he called out, "one of the key items of evidence has been stolen."

13

Smooth Operator

Mikeš was running late. Jonny didn't mind; he'd never been a stickler for timekeeping. This was especially true in Prague where he always found something new and interesting to occupy his spare moments. But the same rules didn't seem to apply when he was late himself: Mikeš always took umbrage and made a big show, shaking his head and tapping his pocket watch impatiently.

Jonny had phoned Mikeš as soon as he'd discovered that evidence had been stolen from Alex Corbet's apartment. Having got on top of his paperwork and reviewed the other ongoing investigations, Mikeš had insisted on catching up over coffee and joining Jonny for the meeting with the solicitor, Pavel Rosický.

Standing at the midpoint on Wenceslas Square, Jonny had time to stand and observe the buzz of the city. The main square of Prague's new town provided a modern mix of business, retail and tourism, all attracting bustling people. Only the tourists eating al fresco on the wide pathways appeared relaxed, the business people and shoppers hurrying to their next destination.

The classic, red trams cut across the middle of the square. Jonny had travelled on all three tram designs in service: the most modern, bullet style tram, even providing air conditioning and a free wireless network. He preferred the history of the oldest design tram in service and was always secretly pleased when one arrived at his stop; the ride was more rustic and bumpier, but the nostalgic sensation of being taken back in time more than made up for it. The journey on one of these trams always started him thinking about whether his mother had travelled on the same tram before she had abruptly left for the UK. He knew it was unlikely, not even being sure if this design of tram was in service then, but it provided an imagined connection between him, her and Prague that always warmed his heart.

Other people around Jonny, including waiting tram passengers, saw Mikeš before he did. The eye-catching wide brim hat and whirl of the cane were always noticed first, but the stares lingered when they saw his striking dress attire. Mikeš attracted attention wherever he went.

Seeing Jonny, Mikeš lifted his cane in salute, booming out "Honza!" for all to hear.

"Late again, Felix!" Jonny smirked.

"It's all these people in the way," Mikeš responded. "Walking in central Prague is a nightmare sometimes. That's why I usually get Marek to drive me around."

Jonny chuckled. Mikeš would never admit it was his fault.

Mikeš waved his cane, directing them towards the entrance to a passage, Pasáž Rokoko. "Follow me, Honza."

Jonny was already familiar with most of the famous passages in the new town. The passages were like arcades, full of cafés, wine bars and an array of specialist shops. Pasáž Rokoko was perhaps the most famous, housing two music venues and a traditional cinema. The centre of the passage was dominated by a hanging statue of King Wenceslas sitting astride an upside down dead battle horse. He had stood underneath the impressive, parody sculpture a number of times, the subject oddly captivating but with no definitive meaning.

Mikeš led Jonny up the concrete steps next to the statue and into an old, traditional café, the interior dominated by a wooden, carved ceiling and tiled walls. Mikeš was instantly recognised by the elderly head waiter, dressed in an old-style white tuxedo, who showed them to a corner table overlooking the centre of the passageway through the expansive viewing gallery.

After ordering coffee, Mikeš leaned in towards Jonny, lowering his voice. "Honza, this murder investigation is starting to worry me."

"I know what you mean," Jonny concurred. "Nothing so far seems to have been normal."

"Unfortunately, it is also now very high profile. The TV news coverage last night made sure of that."

"Felix, all we can do is follow the leads. But, you're right, we are going to have to carefully prioritise which ones we dedicate resources to in the next few days."

"Ano," Mikeš agreed, unintentionally slipping into Czech, his thoughts elsewhere.

"There is something not quite right about the relationship between Alex Corbet and his wife, Helena," Jonny stated. "Her mother, Daniela, is protecting something. We need to make progress in this meeting with the solicitor, and also when interviewing Helena and Daniela later. It could be vital to solving the case quickly."

"The key to the case is probably finding out who broke in and stole the evidence from Alex Corbet's apartment." Mikeš sighed.

"I think you're right, Felix. We have to presume at this stage that whoever stole the warning note also wrote it and sent it to Alex in the first place."

"I agree," Mikeš declared quietly. "There must be a good chance they are also the killer, or at least involved in some way."

"I was thinking the same thing. It is either a massive coincidence, which I'd find hard to believe, or they saw the news coverage on TV and then decided to break into Alex's apartment and get back the evidence."

"The timing is odd though." Mikeš scratched his head in frustration. "Why would they wait until last night to retrieve the note? If we are right, and Alex Corbet and Yulia Ivanova were murdered last Friday, they would have had five days to get the note back."

"Maybe it's as simple as they forgot about it," Jonny ventured.

"I suppose so," Mikeš acknowledged, distracted by his thoughts, his voice still unusually subdued.

The coffee arrived. The head waiter placed the cups and saucers on the table with a flourish and backed away respectfully. "Pane Mikeš."

"I still haven't met anyone who doesn't know you," Jonny stated for amusement, chuckling to himself.

Mikeš didn't notice or react to the intended humour.

"I have asked Lucie to send some uniform officers to check with residents around both Alex Corbet's apartment and also in the street where the bodies were found," Mikeš stated. "I want to know if there was anyone suspicious hanging around. The trouble is we don't have many spare officers with all these other cases. I think we need to get lucky."

Mikeš' concentrated stare remained fixed on the floating milk foam on top of his coffee.

Jonny reached across the table and patted his friend's forearm with his hand. "We will solve this case, Felix." Jonny smiled, encouragingly. "You and I have a one hundred per cent record together and just being short of resources is not going to stop us."

Mikeš smiled weakly. "I hope you're right, Honza."

"By the way," Mikeš continued after sipping his coffee, "Marek is picking us up at eleven forty-five a.m. to take us to Chodov. He's tracked down the mysterious Tanya. We have interviews booked with her and Alex Corbet's boss, who I understand was also a friend of his."

A concerned look crossed Jonny's face.

"What is it, Honza?"

"I have a personal appointment," Jonny explained. "I need to be back to Náměstí Míru by two p.m."

"Can't you rearrange it? We have a lot to do today. This case is important."

Jonny hesitated, the pros and cons of the situation milling around his thoughts, mixed with the anticipation of Ivana's likely reaction. He didn't believe the meeting with Barbora, Ivana's friend, would take long: introductions, background on his mother and presentation of the limited documents he still had from her past in Prague. He just knew that he couldn't miss it.

"No, Felix," Jonny asserted. "I'm sorry, but I can't change it. And, I must be there on time."

Mikeš didn't argue but was clearly disappointed.

Jonny couldn't help feeling guilty, but on balance he knew it was the right call. The reason for the guilt was that he hadn't been totally truthful and told Mikeš what the meeting was for.

***

The solicitor's offices were not what Jonny had been expecting. It reminded him of the feeling when entering Helena Corbetová's apartment: plush and luxurious. The décor was gold themed, expensive embossed wallpaper framing the quality leather sofa and armchairs. The French bookcase housed Czech first edition books and the coffee table carried all the current lifestyle magazines, from luxury cars to yachts.

"Pavel Rosický is one of the top lawyers in Prague," Mikeš explained, seeing Jonny totting up the value of the lavish reception area.

A stylish, suited man entered reception, his presence immediately filling the room. He moved slowly but with bearing and poise, movements gained from years of experience in the courtroom. His attire was impeccable: a three-piece city suit complemented by a spotty, silk tie with matching handkerchief tucked into his jacket pocket. The greying hair was slicked back, his skin glinting from regular moisturising. Jonny knew the type – a smooth operator. Different city, different language, but intrinsically the same DNA. Someone who would defend a serial killer with a smile on his face and no hint of shame. The sort of person Jonny couldn't stand.

Mikeš stood up and greeted Rosický like old friends, talking animatedly in Czech.

"Apologies," Mikeš said, turning to Jonny. "Pavel, please let me introduce Jonathan Fox."

Rosický gave Jonny a knowing smile. "I've heard a lot about you, Mr Fox. Your reputation precedes you."

Jonny looked at Mikeš momentarily, unsure how to respond.

"I understand your role in solving the Old Town Square Murder was inspired," Rosický continued. "You make quite a team with the Black Cat here."

"Thank you," Jonny responded. "I am pleased to meet you."

Rosický led them through to his office, offering Jonny and Mikeš the antique wooden chairs as he walked behind his imposing carved, teak desk. He arched his fingers, elbows on the arms of his desk chair, and looked across the wide gap at his guests. His delivery was slow, firmly in control. "So, gentlemen, how can I help you?"

Jonny felt all eyes on him, comparable to an initiation ceremony for acceptance into Prague aristocracy. "Mr Rosický," he began, "we are here to ask you about Alex Corbet."

"Please call me Pavel," he responded, smiling smugly. "Yes, a terrible business. Very sad."

"So, you know what happened to him?" Jonny looked confused.

"Well, not exact details obviously. Daniela Nováková telephoned me earlier."

"Why did she call you?"

"The family have been very good clients of mine for many years." Rosický opened his arms warmly in goodwill. "I think it was the right decision to inform their solicitor immediately, don't you?"

Jonny hesitated, silently assessing the situation.

"Of course," Mikeš confirmed.

Rosický smiled and returned his hands to the arched position under his chin.

"But, wasn't Alex Corbet also a client of yours?" Jonny pushed on.

"Yes, of course. I acted for him and his wife, Helena, on a number of matters."

"Such as?"

"When they bought their apartment we undertook the conveyancing," Rosický stated flatly. "Of course, Daniela provided a substantial part of the deposit."

"What percentage?"

"Fifty percent."

"And, Alex provided the other half?"

"Yes," Rosický replied after a delay, during which he looked across at Mikeš quizzically. "But, I do not see the relevance of this."

"Pavel, we are just trying to get some background information on Alex Corbet," Mikeš explained. "This is a serious crime – Alex and another woman have been murdered."

Rosický looked between Jonny and Mikeš, a beaming, false smile on his face. "Gentlemen, of course I will help. But, you must understand my first priority is to my clients."

"Including Alex Corbet," Jonny responded quickly, his tone firm.

"Indeed, Mr Fox." Rosický leaned forward in his chair, planting the palms of his hand imposingly on the desk in front of him.

"As we are talking specifically about Alex Corbet," Jonny continued, "can you confirm for us what other matters you acted on for him?"

"Helena and Alex made a joint will. We hold the legal documentation here."

"And, can you divulge what happens in the event of Alex's death?"

"I'm sorry, that is covered by client confidentiality," Rosický stated, producing another wide, false smile. "The details relating to the distribution of Alex Corbet's estate will be dealt with when the death certificate is obtained, and when I have had confirmation from my client, Helena Corbetová. You will need a warrant to get access to the information before this time."

"And, did Alex Corbet call you recently?" Jonny asked, changing tack.

"Yes, he did. He also came to see me last week."

"What did he want to see you about?"

Rosický again glanced across at Mikeš, his frown declaring surprise at the line of questioning. "I'm sorry," Rosický finally replied, "but without a warrant I cannot tell you any more."

Silence descended, the atmosphere in the room tense and the questioning having come to a halt. Mikeš looked towards Jonny, expecting him to continue with further questions.

Jonny rose to his feet abruptly and extended his hand. "Mr Rosický, thank you very much for your time. You have been most helpful."

Jonny turned and walked out of the office, leaving Mikeš looking flustered and Rosický smiling to himself.

14

Interviews – Alex Corbet's Workplace

The following are transcripts of the recorded interviews conducted on the afternoon of Thursday, 15 April 2010. The interviews were held at the offices of Alex Corbet's employer in Prague 4.

Present at the interviews were Chief Warrant Officer Felix Mikeš (FM), Chief Sergeant Marek Boukal (MB) and Consultant Jonathan Fox (JF).

The interviews were conducted in English, in agreement with both interviewees.

Torsten Lindberg (TL)

MB: Interview commenced at 12.20. Please state your name for the record.

TL: Torsten Lindberg.

MB: Thank you for seeing us at short notice and for arranging a meeting room to speak privately to you.

TL: I want to help in any way I can.

MB: Also, thank you for agreeing for us to tape this interview. It is useful in case we need to go back to the interview at a later date. Taping also enables us to translate the interview into Czech for the investigation file.

TL: No problem.

MB: For the purposes of the tape, we have already explained to Mr Lindberg that a body, which we believe to be Alex Corbet, was found last night. We also believe at this point that he was murdered.

TL: The media are reporting that two bodies were found.

MB: We can confirm that this information is correct, but unfortunately we cannot divulge any further information about the investigation at this stage.

JF: Mr Lindberg—

TL: Please call me Torsten.

JF: Okay, Torsten. Can you please tell us the nature of your relationship with Alex Corbet?

TL: I am Swedish and joined the company six years ago, initially working in the Gothenburg office. I transferred to the Prague office four years ago. The office here is bigger with more career opportunities.

JF: And, Alex was already working here when you transferred?

TL: Yes. He has been with the company for about ten years. I'd have to check his HR record to be sure of his length of service.

MB: Our sergeant phoned through earlier and they confirmed he started in September 2003. So, he has worked here for seven and a half years.

TL: Right, not as long as I thought.

JF: And, your relationship with Alex?

TL: Oh right, yes. I am, sorry… was, his manager. My role is Software Development Manager. I have a team of eighteen staff, both developing internal systems and liaising with third-party development companies. Alex's role was Technical Architect, responsible for the strategic design of all the systems. He had to make sure all systems met the group's company standards, and in particular integrated correctly with each other.

JF: Did he always work for you?

TL: No. We were at the same level when I joined. I was Head of Systems Development and I managed the team of in-house developers. Alex and I had to work closely together because my team were developing software to his designs. Because of this we built a close working relationship. I would say we were also friends.

JF: How did he end up working for you?

TL: The previous Software Development Manager left the company and his position was advertised internally. Alex and I both went for the job, but I got it. He was disappointed, but I had all the experience of managing people, whereas his role was technical and hence quite isolated.

JF: Did Alex bear any grudge towards you about losing out on the promotion?

TL: He wasn't happy when the decision was announced, but after a short while we were back to normal. Our business and personal relationship were always good.

JF: When was your promotion?

TL: August 2009.

JF: So, only nine months ago?

TL: Yes.

JF: How often did you see Alex socially?

TL: More recently we mostly met up near work, either at lunchtimes or for a quick drink after work. I live in Chodov so it makes more sense than travelling into the city centre.

JF: And, did you meet more before the promotion?

TL: Yes, I suppose so. But, he'd also had a difficult time recently because of his separation.

JF: So, the change is not to do with the aftermath of your promotion ahead of Alex?

TL: I don't think so. We got on well, shared mutual interests; we both liked American Football. Alex was a nice guy and I liked to think I helped him through his difficult separation with Helena (Corbetová). Although he didn't confide much in me, I was at least there to talk about other things.

JF: I'm sure he appreciated that. Did the stress of the separation affect his work at all?

TL: To be truthful, he had been quite distracted at times recently and it had affected the quality of his work. We had a serious live system problem about six weeks ago. It happened soon after the new version of a major system went live. Thankfully, we solved it relatively quickly, without any serious damage, but it was due to an oversight in the system design which was Alex's responsibility.

JF: How did Alex take it when you raised it with him?

TL: He didn't accept it and fought back, blaming the new Head of Systems Development, my replacement. I sorted it out pretty quickly, but there was still some resentment between them in some of the recent meetings.

JF: Was anything serious said between them? Or perhaps a fight?

TL: No, nothing like that. I made sure it stayed professional, just business. It was sorted out quickly, within the department.

JF: What did Alex say to you about his separation from Helena?

TL: He didn't say a lot really, he was quite secretive about it. Whenever he did say anything, he always blamed Helena's mother.

JF: Anything specific?

TL: No, not really. He just said he felt he was in a marriage with two women.

JF: And, do you think Alex was hoping for a reconciliation with Helena?

TL: At the start, yes. But, recently he seemed to be giving up hope of it ever happening.

MB: Did you ever meet Helena?

TL: Only a few times. Alex would make excuses for her, always saying she was tired with the children. But, my wife and I went to the pub quiz at their local pub—

MB: The Červený lev pub?

TL: Yes. We went a few times. To tell you the truth, it's not really my sort of thing. Alex and his friend, George (Webb), are really competitive and won every time we were there. But, the atmosphere wasn't very relaxing. My wife didn't really want to go any more.

MB: And, you never went out for a meal as a foursome?

TL: No. As I said, Alex was very protective of Helena and always said she was tired.

FM: Do you know Tanya Murray?

TL: Yes, she works in Marketing.

FM: Have you ever seen Alex and Tanya together?

TL: I do remember seeing them having lunch together in the canteen a few times.

JF: Did they work closely together?

TL: No, not really. But, there are over two hundred and fifty staff working in this building and it's easy to bump into people when going to the ground floor for a coffee or getting lunch.

JF: So, you didn't think anything unusual about it before?

TL: No. But…

JF: Yes?

TL: A few people were gossiping about them. Someone said they saw them kissing at the Christmas party and then the rumour started.

JF: Did you ask him about it?

TL: Yes, I did. He just said she was a nice woman, but not his type.

JF: Did you believe him?

TL: Yes. In a company like this there are always rumours going around, and most of them end up not being true.

JF: So, the rumour died away?

TL: Yes, it did. I can't remember the last time I heard it mentioned. It must be well over a month ago.

FM: Do you know this woman?

MB: For the purposes of the tape, Mr Felix Mikeš is now showing Mr Torsten Lindberg a photo of a woman (Yulia Ivanova).

TL: I recognise her, but I don't know her name.

FM: Please explain.

TL: I've seen her around the office. [Pause] Yes, I think she is working for the office designers. Our company hired them to review the office layout to make it more modern: open plan desks, breakout areas, etc. I've only seen her walking around the office making drawings and taking measurements.

MB: This matches with what we have been told. She works for an office design company based in Brno.

TL: Is she the other person you found?

MB: I am sorry, we cannot divulge that information at this stage.

TL: No problem. Yes, so, two of the six floors in the building have already been refitted. They look good. I think they are planning the next phase of the rollout soon, including our floor.

JF: When was the last time you saw her?

[Pause]

TL: I can't be sure, but she was definitely in the office towards the end of last week.

JF: Did you ever see her with Alex? Or did he ever mention her?

126

TL: No, I don't even know her name.

FM: Do you know of anybody else who had a grudge against Alex?

TL: No, he was popular here.

MB: And, finally, Mr Lindberg, can you tell us where you were on Friday evening and Saturday morning? Please understand we have to ask everyone this question.

TL: No problem. I went for a drink after work with people from the office. It's the pub just outside the shopping mall here. Many people from different departments go there for a drink on a Friday. It gets very busy. I arrived home late after the pub closed, sometime just after midnight, and stayed in all Saturday morning.

MB: Can any one vouch for you?

TL: My wife was at home with me from when I returned home.

MB: Thank you. Mr Lindberg, the information you have provided has been very helpful. We may come back to you with more questions, depending on what we find out over the next few days. Interview terminated at 12.45.

Tanya Murray (TM)

MB: Interview commenced at 12.52. Please state your name for the record.

TM: Tanya Murray.

MB: I hope you don't mind, but we need to tape this interview so we can translate it into Czech for the investigation file. You are not under any suspicion, we just want to get some background information for a police investigation.

TM: Fine.

MB: For the purposes of the tape, prior to this interview we explained to Ms Murray that a body, which we believe to be Alex

Corbet, was found murdered last night.

JF: Ms Murray, is it okay if I call you Tanya?

[Pause]

TM: Yes, of course. Sorry, this is very upsetting for me.

JF: And, you work in Marketing?

TM: Yes, I joined about one year ago. I am a Marketing Assistant, helping to put together promotional material for our corporate clients.

JF: Thank you. Can you tell me the nature of your relationship with Alex?

TM: We were friends.

JF: So, you didn't work together?

TM: No.

JF: When was the last time you saw him?

TM: On Thursday. We had lunch together in the canteen.

JF: Did you meet him often?

TM: A couple of times a week, mostly here at work. Sometimes we'd grab a coffee or drink after work.

MB: We found Alex's mobile phone and are still processing the information on it. But, on an initial look, there appear to be quite a lot of messages between you and Alex. And, some of them are quite flirtatious.

[Pause]

JF: Tanya?

TM: Sorry, this is all my fault.

JF: What is?

TM: How this looks.

JF: Why don't you take your time and just explain. We are not here to judge people's lives, we only want to find out who did this terrible thing to Alex.

TM: Alex was a lovely guy. Who could do this to him?

[Pause]

JF: Tanya?

TM: The truth is I really liked Alex. What I mean is that I was really attracted to him. I'd seen him around the office, even said hello to him a few times. Then someone told me he was having problems with his wife. I suppose you could say I hatched a plan to get close to him.

[Pause]

JF: Please go on.

TM: I found ways to bump into him and show him how much I liked him. One lunchtime, I timed it perfectly and stood next to him in the lunch queue at the canteen. We started talking and he asked me if I wanted to sit with him. Over the coming weeks, he opened up to me about his marriage and how it was breaking down. I listened and gave him some advice, but really I was more interested in getting him to like me.

JF: That is very honest of you, Tanya. Have you ever been on a night out or a date with Alex?

TM: No. But, I wanted him to ask me out. I finished a bad relationship about a year ago and was looking for someone kind, like Alex. He was such a nice man.

JF: Can you clarify the approximate dates of these events.

TM: We started meeting regularly for coffee or lunch in October.

JF: But, Alex didn't separate with his wife until late November.

TM: Yes, but their relationship wasn't good for a while before then. He sometimes slept over at a friend's house when they were arguing.

JF: Which friend?

TM: He only ever told me about George (Webb).

JF: This is a bit delicate, but we understand there were rumours going around the office that you and Alex were getting together.

Someone saw you kissing at the Christmas party.

TM: That was my fault as well. I had too many glasses of wine at the party and we were talking... [Pause] Well, I sort of pulled him into a corner and kissed him. It wasn't very discreet.

JF: What did Alex do?

TM: He was a real gentleman about it. When we spoke later he told me he liked me a lot, but it was not the right time for him. I decided to step back a bit and play the long game, hoping he would eventually ask me out. I told him how much I liked him, I made my feelings very clear.

JF: Have you ever met Alex's wife?

TM: No. I've never met any of his family or friends. Outside of the company, of course.

JF: Why do you suppose his wife thought that Alex was having an affair with you?

TM: I don't know. I suppose she might have seen the messages between us. They weren't explicit, but a few were probably quite suggestive. I was just trying to get him interested in me.

MB: Whilst we've been talking, I've just been checking the messages between you and Alex. There are messages up to Thursday lunchtime last week, but then no messages after that. Can you explain why?

[Pause]

JF: Tanya?

TM: When we met for lunch on Thursday, he told me he had met a woman he really liked. I think he wanted me to be pleased for him, but I was really disappointed.

JF: Did Alex say who she was?

TM: No. I asked him, but he wouldn't tell me. I think I acted rather badly. I left him sitting at the table and went back to my desk. I was upset.

JF: Thank you again for being honest with us.

FM: Do you know this woman?

MB: For the purposes of the tape, Mr Felix Mikeš is now showing Ms Tanya Murray a photo of a woman (Yulia Ivanova).

TM: No, I don't recognise her. Who is she?

FM: It doesn't matter.

TM: Is it Alex's new girlfriend... the woman he liked?

JF: Tanya, this is a murder investigation. I'm sure you can understand that we can't divulge any potentially sensitive information at this stage.

MB: Ms Murray, can you please tell us where you were on Friday evening and Saturday morning? This is just a routine question we have to ask everyone.

TM: I stayed in on Friday night, I was feeling a bit sorry for myself. I was alone, but I did have a video call with my parents. On Saturday morning, I went to the supermarket quite early, about nine, but then went straight back to my apartment. I was at home for the rest of the day until I went out with friends in the evening.

MB: Thank you. Can you please provide us with evidence of your video call log on Friday evening?

TM: Yes, sure. I called them at about 20.00 for just over an hour, I think.

JF: By the way, where are you from?

TM: Michigan in the US.

JF: Nice. Do you have family here?

TM: No.

MB: Thank you, Ms Murray. If we have any more questions we will be in contact with you over the next few days. Interview terminated at 13.17.

15

Family Tree

For once, Jonny had been glad of Boukal's fast, slick driving skills. It had been 1.38 p.m. exactly when they'd finally left Chodov, a heavy shower of April rain putting another obstacle in the path of his promise to Ivana. Checking his watch every few minutes, he didn't believe they would be able to make it through the Prague traffic in time, even when they quickly joined the dual carriageway heading towards the city centre. Waiting an inordinately long time at some roadworks whilst a lorry emptied its load, he was tempted to ask for the blue light and siren to be turned on. Progress was smooth, however, once this hurdle had been overcome, Boukal needing no encouragement to switch lanes incessantly to overtake slower cars. Jonny hopped out at the Náměstí Míru square with just three minutes to spare before his appointment.

The visit to Alex Corbet's workplace had been necessary, but hadn't delivered any new, clear leads. Tanya Murray's story seemed genuine, plus it was hard to believe she had committed a double murder. The pleasantries with Torsten Lindberg and a few other senior staff after the interviews had confirmed Jonny's growing impression that Alex was well-liked and popular amongst his peers. The new incumbent in the role of Head of System Development, Torsten's old position, was glowing in praise for the support Alex had given her since starting her new job and showed no animosity towards her colleague.

A search of Alex's desk had also provided nothing. The company's clear desk policy had clearly been taken on board fully; the few papers and stationery items stored in the desk drawers. When Jonny had asked whether the desk had been touched recently, Torsten confirmed that nobody had even sat at it during working hours since Monday. Jonny had been pleased to see a photo of the Corbet children pinned to the small noticeboard atop the desk, proving that Alex did think about his children. The photo notably did not include Helena.

The HR Manager had minded the police visit from arrival to exit, offering the company's full support in the murder investigation. Access was granted to Alex Corbet's HR file in exchange for the correct police documentation, and a contact within IT Support was established for Boukal to contact about Alex's laptop. She had also confirmed that Yulia Ivanova was working for the office designers and had visited the company's offices on numerous occasions, full details having already been provided by email to Dvořáková. The only time the HR Manager became flustered was when Jonny requested handwriting samples from Tanya Murray and all of Torsten Lindberg's IT Department. Startled by the request, she agreed to check the company position first and then undertake the task herself, rather than cause an unnecessary disturbance within the working environment.

Relieved he was going to be on time for the meeting, Jonny strode purposefully across the Náměstí Míru square towards the imposing government building. The remnants of the earlier shower still lingered in the air as he entered the old building and headed for reception. He was so intent on checking the time, he mistakenly flashed his police badge at the receptionist. After an earnest apology, he quickly corrected himself and stated his purpose in broken Czech and by using the universal English word of 'meeting'.

Seated in a calm, if airless, reception area, Jonny smiled contently to himself. *This balancing act of personal and work life isn't as easy as it looks.* His shoulders started to relax as he settled in the armchair to enjoy one of his favourite pastimes of people watching. The individuals crossing through reception were expressionless; only their formal attire hinted that they worked for a government facility.

His musings were interrupted by the approach of a tall, elegant woman, looking every bit the government official in her smart, dark jacket and skirt. Her shoulder length brown hair framed a face of warm features, her smiling green-grey eyes and wide mouth only offset by a slightly pointed nose. The pinch on the bridge of her nose only added to the studious, authoritative aura of an expert in her field.

"Mr Fox?"

Jonny stood and shook her offered hand. "Yes, Jonathan Fox."

"Good to meet you. My name is Barbora Haseková."

"Thank you for meeting me. I understand you are very busy."

Barbora indicated towards the lift and they walked across the marble tiled floor.

"Ivana told me I should call you Honza," she stated.

"Yes." He laughed. "It's a long story, but I'm getting used to my Czech nickname now."

"Ivana did brief me," she explained, smiling, as they walked into the open lift. "I understand you've made quite a splash since arriving in Prague."

"I don't know about that," he replied. "I came to Prague for an easy, relaxing break, but it seems that trouble has a way of following me around."

"Ivana told me that as well," she added, leading the way out of the lift and down the corridor.

The meeting room reminded him of his schooldays. Behind the wood-effect door, the tables and chairs were basic and the walls painted a universal, plain beige. He was, however, pleased to see coffee and biscuits laid out on the table, realising he hadn't eaten since breakfast.

Barbora put on her glasses and poured them both a coffee, positioning the plate of biscuits closer to him. She opened her folder on the desk and took out a pen, writing Jonny's full name at the top of a new page.

"So, Honza, it would be really helpful to me if you could explain in your own words about your family, especially your mother. And, also what you are looking to achieve through this process."

Jonny smiled to himself, revelling in the irony of being interviewed himself, sandwiched between interviews with Alex Corbet's work colleagues and, next up, his wife and mother-in-law. He took a sip of his coffee and devoured a biscuit as he considered where to begin.

"To tell you the truth, Barbora, I was initially hesitant about looking into my Czech family background. My mother came to the UK in the early 1960s. Despite my questions as I grew up, she never wanted to talk about her past. I know absolutely nothing about her family or what happened to her in Prague. I've never seen any photos and I didn't hear her discussing her family – it was as if her past hadn't happened. When I became old enough to understand better, I concluded she'd wanted to leave something behind. So, I decided to respect her decision and leave it in the past. Now it is too late to ask her. She died a few years ago."

"So, what changed your mind?"

"It was not one specific thing," he stumbled. "Prague just seemed to open up so much for me personally, in such a short time. It felt like a destiny of some sort. I've only been here for one month, but it already feels like my second home. I don't know how long I will be here, but I feel happy and fulfilled in Prague. I still respect my mother's decision, however I want to conduct this search for *me*. If I have cousins, maybe even aunts and uncles, I would like to know about them before it is too late."

"Well, the good news is you've passed my first test."

Jonny looked confused.

"I want people to look for their lost families for positive reasons," she continued. "I get real satisfaction out of reuniting people with relatives they didn't know they had. However, I will not help people find family if their reasons are not genuine."

"You are completely right," he agreed.

"Two more questions," she started. "Firstly, how far back into your family tree are you looking to go? It's fairly simple when you think about it, but with this process we need to go backwards. The further back you want to go the longer it will take."

"I hadn't really thought about it," Jonny admitted. "To be honest, all I'm interested in at this stage is my mother's parents, any siblings she had and then any cousins I have."

"And lastly, I assume you are happy to accept bad news as well as good news?"

Jonny paused to think, the notion of really bad news not having dawned on him before.

"I'm sorry to be blunt, but someone in your family could have committed a serious crime," Barbora explained. "Or maybe a family scandal? Given what you've told me about your mother, I suppose there must be a possibility of some significant event having happened before she left for the UK."

"From my perspective," he stated calmly, "any information you find that can help explain what happened to my mother in Prague would be helpful."

Barbora wrote some notes on her pad and then looked up, smiling. "Right, let's get started. What documentation do you have?"

Jonny pulled an envelope out of his jacket pocket and carefully removed two papers, placing them on the table between them. "It is quite sad, but these are all I have from her Prague past," Jonny apologised. "The first is an expired passport. The second is an old, residence document, stamped as 1958, when she was eighteen. Both documents confirm her full name as Anežka Vašeková. Also, the address on the residence document is Moskevská 15, Praha."

"May I?"

Jonny nodded hesitantly, realising it was the first time anyone other than himself had handled his mother's documents.

She carefully lifted each document in turn from the table, unfolding the old paper and studying all sides, making notes on her pad.

"These documents do not look like much," she started, "but they are actually the most important. Sometimes people come to me and only have a memory of names and dates, maybe as told to them in family tales. I feel quite optimistic we will be able to find out some information about your family. But, and this is really important, it does depend on whether the information was

137

recorded correctly. For example, and I am not saying this is the case with your family, but if a young woman had a child out of wedlock this can be very difficult to trace. The linear nature of the registration is often broken and the information on birth certificates and census records can be wrong or conflicting."

"I understand," he confirmed, dabbing the corner of his eye. "Thank you."

"This can be a very emotional process," Barbora continued, showing empathy. "Shall I explain what I will do after this meeting?"

"Yes, please."

"I will first be checking the census records, as you call them, because they are the most popular documents in tracing family history. The census data in the Czech Republic is different to what you will know; it's actually mixed in with a land archive. But, importantly, we can get to the same information."

Jonny nodded, totally absorbed in her words.

"Next, I will check the birth, marriage and death records. My only caveat here is that death certificates can be unreliable. We have had situations before where the information provided on the deceased's behalf has been either incorrect or complete lies."

"This is amazing," Jonny exclaimed.

"Finally, I will search local stories. By this I mean: old newspaper cuttings, including personal stories and obituaries. Not all are online, but sometimes we can get lucky."

"I can only just about use my smartphone," he confessed, looking dazed. "This sounds like a different world."

Barbora laughed.

"I would like to finish with a word of caution, though," she began. "The Czech Republic has undergone a lot of border and rule changes. In the majority of cases I can find some family history. But, there are occasions where I get stuck. And if I hit a dead end, it can be difficult to pick up the trail again."

Jonny nodded.

"You have to remember that the Czech Republic is a country in Central Europe bordering Poland, Germany, Austria, and Slovakia. It includes the three historical territories of Bohemia, Moravia, and Czech Silesia. From 1918 to 1993, it was the western part of Czechoslovakia. After the Second World War, the country was under communist rule until 1989. Also, in 1990 many streets were renamed to reflect the democratic changes. Streets named after Marxist politicians or historical events linked to the Communist movement were changed back to their former names or renamed." She paused. "I'm sorry for all the potential negatives, but I want to be upfront with you. I suppose I'm just trying to dampen your expectations, with the hope of exceeding them."

"If you find any information at all I will be pleased," Jonny stated. "I've learnt so much in the last hour. It has been fascinating."

"Do you mind if I take photocopies of these documents?" she asked.

"Of course not," Jonny confirmed. "But, I have a question in return."

"Yes?" Barbora answered, looking intrigued.

"Do you mind if I take you and Ivana to dinner as a thank you?" he asked. "I would like to regardless of what you find out about my family. I just know my mother would want it."

"That would be lovely, Honza. Thank you."

16

Interviews – Helena Corbetová and Daniela Nováková

The following are transcripts of the recorded interviews conducted on the afternoon of Thursday, 15 April 2010. The interviews were held at the home of Helena Corbetová in Prague 2.

Present at the interview were Chief Warrant Officer Felix Mikeš (FM), Chief Sergeant Marek Boukal (MB), Consultant Jonathan Fox (JF) and the family solicitor, Pavel Rosický (PR).

The interviews were conducted in English, in agreement with both interviewees.

Helena Corbetová (HC)

MB: Interview commenced at 15.35. Please state your name for the record.
HC: Helena Corbetová.
MB: We understand this is a difficult day for you, so thank you for talking to us so early after the terrible news about your husband, Alex Corbet. We would like to make it clear you are not under suspicion at all, but we need some background on your relationship with Alex and any information you have on his life since you separated late last year. We will also have to ask you routine questions about where you were last weekend so we can

eliminate you from our enquiries.

PR: Helena, if you are unsure of any details, or need a break at any time, we can stop the interview. Also, are you sure you are happy for the interview to be conducted in English?

HC: Pavel, I am fine. Please don't worry. I want to help the police as much as I can.

JF: Mrs Corbetová—

HC: Helena, please.

JF: Helena, could you tell us briefly how you and Alex met?

PR: I don't think this is relevant.

HC: Pavel, please, there is no problem. [Pause] Mr Fox, we met eight years ago. It was very romantic, but Alex always was. I was in a restaurant with some girlfriends on New Year's Eve when the waiter brought over a bottle of champagne and some glasses. When we asked, the waiter told us the man at a nearby table had sent it over. Alex was the true gentleman and came over to the table and introduced himself. He told us the champagne was because our laughter was lighting up the place. That's exactly what he said. Being smooth, he'd also ordered an extra glass for him and so we toasted the New Year. His friends joined us eventually and we had a wonderful evening. I could tell he was interested in me and he finally managed to move to the seat next to me. We talked and talked, and then went outside for the fireworks. It was cold and snow was falling, so Alex gave me his Dr Who scarf, as he used to call it. We went back inside the restaurant for more drinks and afterwards he walked me home. At my apartment, I took off his scarf to give back to him, but he insisted I keep it in exchange for dinner later that week.

JF: That is a lovely story.

HC: Yes. Alex was a true romantic, always writing me lovely letters. We got married the following year, again on New Year's

Eve. It was an unusual date to choose, many people were surprised, but it was such a lovely day and meant so much to us.

JF: When did you move to this apartment?

HC: We rented for a while whilst we saved up and bought this apartment together five years ago.

JF: And, you both own the apartment?

HC: Yes, fifty-fifty. Alex provided half the deposit, Mummy provided the rest. She has been so helpful. I was a librarian so my salary was never very high, certainly not enough for buying an apartment near the city centre.

JF: Then you had your lovely children.

HC: Yes, they are my world.

JF: Excuse me for saying this, but it comes across clearly you still have great affection for Alex. Even when we spoke yesterday, when Alex was still a missing person, your love for him was obvious. So, how did your marriage end up in difficulty?

PR: Helena, please remember you don't need to answer these questions if you don't want to.

HC: I do, Pavel, I owe it to Alex. [Pause] Mr Fox, it is very difficult to explain, like any relationship, I suppose. We were happy for a few years, but I found it difficult when the children were born. I had to stop work, it was all too much for me. Mummy has been amazing, helping out almost every day. But, I suppose the relationship between Alex and I suffered as a result.

JF: Why did he move out?

HC: We were arguing all the time. Alex wasn't happy that Mummy was here so much and he was worried about money.

JF: Why? I thought he had a good job.

HC: He did. But, he didn't get the promotion he thought he deserved. Money was tight. Alex said we were spending more than his salary every month.

142

JF: And were you?

HC: I don't know.

JF: I don't mean to be rude, but why don't you know?

HC: Alex used to manage the finances. Mummy is helping me do it now.

JF: Right. And, is the tight money situation the reason why Alex took such a small apartment after moving out?

HC: I don't know. I've never seen the apartment. He chose it himself.

JF: Helena, can I ask you about the will you prepared with Alex—

PR: Mr Fox, we have already covered this. I am only prepared to let my client talk about their joint will when you have a warrant for the information. And, I suppose you don't have it yet.

[Pause]

JF: Helena, we are only trying to get to the truth.

HC: Mr Fox, I will follow Pavel's advice on this matter. But, I can assure you there is nothing funny in the document. It was a simple will for a husband and wife with children.

JF: Thank you.

[Pause]

JF: This afternoon we visited Alex's company offices in Chodov. We interviewed his boss, Torsten Lindberg, who I believe you know.

HC: Yes, I've met him a few times.

JF: Torsten told us Alex had been under a lot of stress and it had started to affect his work.

HC: I'm sorry, Mr Fox, but I don't know. Alex wouldn't really talk to me after he moved out. All I know is he continued to give me money every month and also see the children at the times we had agreed. That is, until last Sunday…

JF: We also tracked down the Tanya (Murray) you mentioned and we interviewed her.

HC: Did she admit to having an affair with Alex?

JF: On the contrary. She was very honest and told us she liked him, but she said Alex did not return her interest. She said they have never been together in a relationship.

HC: You can believe what you want, Mr Fox. I saw the messages from her to Alex, and also—

PR: Mr Fox, unless you have a specific question, I suggest we move on.

JF: I would really like Helena to finish what she was about to say.

PR: Let's move on. You can see how distressing this is for her.

[Pause]

MB: Mrs Corbetová, can you please take us through your movements last Friday. As I explained earlier, this is solely for the record, to eliminate you from our enquiries.

HC: On Friday morning I took Emilie (Helena's daughter) to kindergarten as normal and then dropped Tomaš (Helena's son) at the child carer. Mummy arrived late morning and we went to the centre for lunch with friends. After lunch we stopped at our favourite shop and I bought a new dress. We picked the children up later and came back home. We stayed at home all evening, cooked dinner, until Mummy left later in the evening.

MB: Do you remember what time she left?

HC: Sorry, I don't, but it was late. Near midnight, probably.

JF: Is this a usual routine, Helena?

HC: I get lonely and upset in the evenings when I'm on my own. They often stay until I'm ready to go to bed.

JF: I understand. I assume your mother's husband, Jakub Novák, also comes here after work?

HC: Yes, that's right.

MB: And, what were your movements on Saturday morning?

HC: Let me think. [Pause] Yes, we stayed in during the morning until Mummy arrived. Then Emilie had a friend's birthday party to go to. Mummy and I had a coffee with Tomaš in a nearby café whilst we waited before we returned home.

MB: Thank you.

JF: When we spoke yesterday, you briefly explained about your friends, George (Webb) and Zuzana (Webbová). Can you give us a bit of background to the friendship?

PR: How is this relevant?

JF: We are keen to gather useful background information.

[Pause]

HC: I met Zuzana in the birthing classes when I was pregnant with Emilie. She also had a girl, Anna (George & Zuzana's daughter), in the same week as Emilie was born. By pure coincidence, her husband was British. George and Alex knew each other from the pub but weren't friends. Because of the children we became close families, spending a lot of time together, mostly around each other's apartments.

JF: Did it become difficult when you and Alex were having problems?

HC: Yes, it did. Zuzana was a great support for me, still is. George tried talking to Alex, but it didn't help. Our time all together used to be so much fun, but it became strained.

JF: We understand Alex used to stay over at their house sometimes.

HC: Yes, he did. It was usually after he'd had too much to drink. I didn't mind because I thought talking to George, even Zuzana, might help him.

FM: Did Alex ever have a falling out with any one? Maybe you remember an argument in the recent past?

HC: I was thinking about this after Mr Fox spoke to me this morning. There was an argument with a Dutch man at the pub about six months ago. His name was Johan, I think. I would recognise him, but I've only ever met him a couple of times to say hello to.

FM: What was the argument about?

HC: Alex accused him of cheating at the pub quiz and they argued about it on and off for a few weeks. I don't know any more, but I remember it got quite heated. You'd best speak to George.

FM: Thank you.

JF: Helena, do you recognise this handwriting?

MB: For the purposes of the tape, Mr Jonathan Fox is showing Mrs Helena Corbetová a photo of a handwritten note.

PR: Can you please explain what this note is?

JF: I am not able to divulge this information at such a delicate part of the investigation.

HC: No, I don't recognise the handwriting. Did someone send it to Alex?

JF: I am sorry, I cannot say right now. But, thank you for looking at it.

PR: If you want to present any further evidence to my client, I want you to first explain what it is and the reason for your questions. I do not want my client distressed or risk her answering the question incorrectly.

FM: Pavel, it is a note we found as part of our investigation. We do not yet know ourselves how it fits in if it does at all. For this reason, I believe we have every right to ask your client these questions.

JF: Finally, can you please provide us with a sample of your handwriting. I know you didn't write this note, but we need the sample for our files so we can eliminate you from our enquiries. Chief Sergeant Boukal will collect the sample after this interview.

HC: No problem.

JF: I have no further questions at this stage. However, Helena, whilst we have been talking I've noticed you have some bruises on your arm. Did you fall over?

PR: How is this relevant?

JF: I'm sorry, I was just concerned.

PR: If you have no further questions, I suggest we terminate this interview immediately.

MB: Mrs Corbetová, thank you for your time and for answering our questions. Interview terminated at 16.03.

Daniela Nováková (DN)

MB: Interview commenced at 16.10. Please state your name for the record.

DN: Daniela Nováková.

MB: I will repeat briefly what we have already explained to your daughter, Helena Corbetová. Neither of you are under any suspicion at all. We just need your help to understand what might have happened to Alex Corbet. We also need to ask you routine questions about your movements last weekend so we can eliminate you from our enquiries.

JF: Mrs Nováková, the main reason we need your help is because Alex was living away from your daughter for about four months before this happened. Any information you can give us could be invaluable in finding who killed him. And, I can assure you, we will be very discreet.

MB: Are you happy to conduct the interview in English?

DN: As you wish.

JF: Can I ask what you thought of Alex?

PR: Daniela, please do not answer such a general question. Mr Fox, be more specific.

JF: I would like to understand more about the marriage between your daughter, Helena, and Alex. Was he a good husband?

PR: Mr Fox—

DN: Pavel, it's fine. Mr Fox, I will give you some background information, but I can assure you my family had nothing to do with what happened to Alex. It was his choice to be living away from the marital home, leaving his wife on her own.

JF: I understand.

[Pause]

DN: Alex was very charming. He swept my daughter off her feet. But, he was not a good husband in my opinion. Both my first husband in the UK, and Jakub (Novák) more recently, have provided for me and my family. Alex talked a good game, but he never delivered. They were always short of money, he did not get the promotion he promised and he spent too much money drinking with his friends at the pub. Do I need to go on?

JF: So you stepped in to help them out?

DN: Of course I helped. I am not going to let my daughter and grandchildren suffer because he could not provide for his family.

JF: And, did it cause problems between Alex and Helena?

DN: That is not my concern. They needed help and I gave it. Alex should have been man enough to provide for his family or accept help graciously.

JF: Talking to Helena it seems money was tight. Were you supportive when Alex wanted to cut the amount of money they were spending every month?

PR: What sort of question is that, Mr Fox?

DN: Mr Fox, you can make whatever subtle accusations you want. My daughter deserves the best. If Alex could not provide it, I would. I cannot do anything about Alex's ability to provide for his wife and family. Tell me, why should Helena not have a new pair of shoes just because he could not afford it?

JF: Was there a specific event that caused Alex to move out?

DN: If there was, I am not aware of it.

JF: Can I ask why you spend so much time at Helena's apartment? Do you have other children?

DN: My other daughter lives and works in London. She has a good career. Helena lives here, in Prague, and I am happy to help her as much as she needs me.

JF: I understand.

PR: Mr Fox, I think this is enough background. Do you have some specific questions for my client?

JF: When we met yesterday, you indicated you came back to the Czech Republic with your daughters after your first husband died.

PR: That is not a specific question, Mr Fox.

DN: Pavel, I will answer. Let's get this over with, although I have no idea what the relevance is. Mr Fox, my first husband, Derek (surname unknown), died in a car accident. My daughters were both less than ten years old so I came home with them. Both daughters were educated here, but my eldest, Kristýna (surname unknown), decided to go to university in London and stayed there. I met Jakub when they were both in their late teens and he has been a tremendous father-figure. See, Mr Fox, no mystery, just a normal family situation, albeit with a tragedy at the beginning.

JF: Thank you.

MB: Mrs Nováková, can you please tell us your movements on

Friday and Saturday morning. As I explained earlier, this is solely for the record, to eliminate you from our enquiries.

DN: Jakub dropped me off here about ten on Friday and later Helena and I went for lunch and some shopping. We picked up the children and came back to the apartment. Jakub came to the apartment after work and we stayed in until we left together about midnight.

JF: And none of you left the apartment in the evening?

DN: No.

MB: And on Saturday morning?

DN: Jakub had some business at an antiques fair early morning so I got here a bit later, maybe midday. Then Helena and I took Emilie to a birthday party in the afternoon. Is that enough for you? Maybe you want to talk to Jakub as well...

MB: No, that will not be necessary. Thank you for the information.

JF: One last thing, would you mind providing a handwriting sample please. As I explained earlier today, this is purely to eliminate you from our enquiries. Chief Sergeant Boukal will provide the pen and paper after this interview.

DN: This is all very odd, but if you insist.

MB: Thank you, Mrs Nováková. If we have any more questions we will be in contact with you over the next few days. Interview terminated at 16.32.

17

Dead Weight

The whirlwind afternoon continued with a visit to the mortuary and Jonny was feeling the pace. He wanted to take some time alone with a coffee and something heartier than biscuits, but Mikeš had insisted that they push on; their appointment with Dr Králová was booked for five p.m.

It wasn't just the physical pace of the day Jonny was worried about; he'd gone hungry before and he knew he could do it again, it simply being a case of mind over matter. More worrying was that the speed with which they were being forced to gather information may result in a vital piece of evidence being missed. He knew they were in catch-up mode, over five days behind an organised murderer, but missing an unintended word or a vital sign now would only be self-defeating, leaving them further behind.

At times like these he needed time to himself – time to just sit and ponder, assimilating all the information his senses had received. Not just what people had said in interviews, but also the way they had said it: body language, slight changes in intonation of voice, distancing language used to avoid directly answering a question, and even facial expressions. The latter had become a specialism of his in the Metropolitan Police; analysing taped interviews with potential suspects in slow motion to watch for one of seven micro-expressions. Many detectives could easily spot the shifty eyes or shaking leg of an interviewee when answering a difficult question, but the micro-expressions of contempt, anger or disgust were natural and fleeting, being almost impossible to hide, but also making them hard to distinguish in real time.

Jonny had developed great affection for Mikeš and the way he managed his team, but sometimes the fast pace and old policing methods risked going around in circles. He had already developed the knack of disappearing, hiding away from his friend and boss (of sorts), to allow himself space to think. Right now, he felt this need stronger than ever, sensing that Helena Corbetová and her ferociously protective mother were trying to tell him something, even if they didn't intend to.

Marching down the echoing corridors of the hospital with Mikeš towards the mortuary entrance, however, wasn't the right time to try to escape. He first had to concentrate hard to survive the post mortems. His inherent dread of blood and dead bodies came only a close second to the emotional turmoil of telling people a loved one had been found dead, believed murdered. Behind the morgue doors was a world he often tried to block out: bright lights, gleaming surfaces, the array of scalpels and saws, as well as the clinical smell of formaldehyde nagging at the back of the throat. And, of course, the lifeless bodies. He shuddered when he thought of the waxed, pale skin, the closed eyes and the hand-stitching up the length of the torso. He would have happily accepted a comprehensive report and some photos, but knew it wasn't what was expected from a senior detective.

Králová was waiting for them, ready to deliver her verdict. Jonny had been to dinner with her and Mikeš, seen her in action at the crime scene the previous evening, but she seemed most at home in the morgue wearing her white pathologist's coat. She looked tired, dark circles forming under the eyes, her usual energy subdued by the tough schedule over the past twenty-four hours.

"Felix, are you ever going to be on time?" she started accusingly.

Mikeš pulled out his pocket watch, appearing confused. Jonny looked up at the clock on the wall. It was 5.05 p.m.; they were less than five minutes late. Jonny smiled to himself, now understanding where Mikeš got his abhorrence for bad timekeeping from.

Králová turned to Jonny, looking for an ally. "He's always on time when we go out for dinner, or to a classical concert. But he's always late for an autopsy. What do you make of that, Honza?"

Jonny shrugged his shoulders, knowing not to meddle in the emotional politics between Mikeš and his ex-wife. The complicated situation of being divorced but still seemingly dating, as well as working closely together, could only be understood by the two people involved. All he knew was that they still loved each other and Králová was firmly in charge.

Getting no response from Jonny, she turned her attention back to her ex-husband. "Felix, I don't want you going into a sulk just because I cancelled our dinner tonight," she started to lecture. "I didn't get home until three a.m. after completing all the paperwork, and I was back in here at nine a.m. to begin the autopsies—"

"My dear," Mikeš interrupted her gently, walking to her side and putting his arm around her shoulders. "Of course I am disappointed. Going out to dinner with you is my favourite pleasure in life. But, I completely understand. We will reorganise dinner for when this investigation is closed and life is more back to normal."

Králová looked up at Mikeš, bending into his love. He kissed her softly on the top of her head. "And, perhaps Honza will finally agree to join us for dinner with Ivana," Mikeš continued. "I don't know how many times I'm going to have to ask."

Jonny rolled his eyes, feeling two pairs of scheming eyes now piercing into him. Even in a stressful scenario, and feeling tired, they were still colluding against him.

"Maybe," he mumbled reluctantly. "But, can we go through the autopsy results now, please? Because I'm starting to feel like a gooseberry here."

"A gooseberry?" Mikeš and Králová almost sang in harmony, confused looks on their faces.

"I'll explain later," he retorted impatiently.

Králová picked up her clipboard and moved between the two metal examination tables, dramatically pulling back the medical sheets. Jonny shook his head in despondency. He always felt strong empathy with the people who had lost their lives. In fact, it was the biggest driver in his quest as a detective – to bring the perpetrators to justice. Even though he had never met these people alive, he felt he was starting to know, maybe even like, Alex Corbet through the missing person search. There was also the possibility that, despite Alex's complicated marital situation, new love had been cut off before it had had the chance to bloom.

"The two deceased are Alex Corbet and Yulia Ivanova, as we assumed last night," Králová began. "We have checked with the UK and Russian authorities and all the data on record matches with the information we have. The body of Alex Corbet was also formally identified this afternoon by Mrs Daniela Nováková. My only caveat at this stage is we haven't been able to match DNA samples; it seems neither of them had DNA on record here or in their home countries."

"I suppose that helps a bit," Mikeš stated. "We've also found no police records for either of them here in the Czech Republic. I was initially thinking Yulia might have been trying to entrap Alex in some way, for bribery or something similar."

"No," Jonny stated firmly. "All the signs are that this was a mutual attraction from when they met at Alex's office. But, we definitely need to find out more information about her."

"As I explained briefly last night, both the victims suffered head wounds," Králová restarted. "The single impact to the back of her head killed Yulia Ivanova. The impact was deep, depressing the back of her skull. I thought initially she was hit with something like a metal pipe because of the sharp edges. But, actually the murder weapon was a medium-sized mallet, about thirty centimetres long, with a metal head."

Jonny and Mikeš looked at each other, both amazed and impressed.

"I would like to say this was some inspired guesswork from me," she continued, firmly in control, "but the mallet was buried underneath her. The murderer must have thrown it into the trench before he laid her body out. The blood on it matches hers, but sadly there are no fingerprints or detectable DNA on it."

"A mallet!" Mikeš exclaimed. "It's not an obvious murder weapon to carry around."

"If the murderer threw the mallet into the trench, they must have been pretty sure there was nothing on it that could lead back to them," Jonny surmised. "Which leads me to believe they were definitely prepared, possibly also waiting with gloves on. Therefore, definitely a premeditated murder."

"Alex Corbet was also hit by the same mallet," Králová continued. "His blood is all over it. But, whereas Yulia's single wound was clean and fatal, he was hit numerous times in the face and to the side of the head. Each impact was hard, the result of a furious attack, but the one that killed him was near the temple. The skull was smashed badly, causing a bleed on the brain. He would have collapsed almost immediately."

"So, Alex probably fought back?" Jonny proposed.

"My guess, yes," Králová confirmed. "He has scratches on his hands and also bruises on his forearms where he has probably tried to stop the blows coming towards him. He also has a bad laceration on his chin where a wayward blow missed its target. He's a bit of a mess as you can see."

"Were there any other items buried with them, anything that might provide a DNA sample of the person who did this?" Jonny enquired.

"No stray items of clothing, or anything like that," Králová stated. "There also weren't any fingerprints or DNA on their mobile phones, or other personal possessions. But, we have found some fibre samples on the victim's clothes. I'm not promising anything but we are examining them now. The problem is that the fibres could have already been in the soil before the trenches were filled in. Plus, you must remember they have been buried underground for nearly a week."

"What are these marks around the torso?" Mikeš asked, pointing to Alex Corbet's waist.

"A good spot, Felix," she acknowledged. "Yulia also has similar marks, but not so pronounced. I studied the skin and body tissue around the marks closely and I believe they are the result of a strong hand grip. But, interestingly, the area around the mark is not bruised on either body. This means the marks must have been made after death. My conclusion is that both bodies were moved. Because Alex is heavier, the marks on his body are more pronounced because of the extra effort required to carry or drag him. The person who moved him would have had to grip or squeeze him harder – a dead weight is heavy."

"So, they were not murdered in the street where they were buried?" Jonny stated, looking surprised.

"I don't think so," she asserted. "The fatal impacts, as well as the wild attack on Alex Corbet, would have resulted in a lot of blood. Having completed my analysis of the soil samples we took from the burial site there does not appear to be enough blood. I also went back to the crime scene today to check. In my estimation, they were killed somewhere else and then moved later, to be buried in the open trenches."

"This case is getting crazier by the hour," Mikeš blurted out, shaking his head in exasperation.

Jonny looked down, running a hand through his hair and concentrating hard. He instinctively knew this information was vital. Moving dead bodies, especially manually, was difficult and, from his extensive experience, the part of the crime where mistakes could be made. They needed to find where Alex Corbet and Yulia Ivanova were killed.

"So," he started slowly, keen to get the story right. "Yulia was probably attacked first: one planned, fatal blow to the back of the head to knock her over and disarm her, probably killing her instantaneously. The assailant then attacks Alex: a frenzied attack with blows raining down on him. The attack is too quick and wild. Alex cannot fight back, but tries to prevent the hammer blows, resulting in damage to his face, hands and arms. The attack has almost certainly happened around midnight on Friday evening, but the murderer conceals the bodies until the early hours of Saturday morning. The murderer drags their dead bodies to the street, which is currently undergoing maintenance work, where he buries them in the open trench before covering them over with plastic sheeting and a layer of soil."

"Sounds logical," Mikeš agreed.

"But, why kill them like that?" Jonny asked, the rhetorical question hanging in the air. "It was well planned and personal… But, was it about *him*, or *her*? Or *both* of them?"

"Unfortunately, I cannot help you with that," Králová responded. "I also cannot be exact about the time they were buried. Due to the decomposition, I estimate both bodies were buried together in the trench sometime Friday evening or Saturday morning. I know this doesn't really help you much."

"And, what's your view on the positioning of the bodies?" Jonny asked.

"I knew you'd ask that," she answered. "If we assume the two victims were killed elsewhere and moved, the murderer or murderers would have had more time. But, it still doesn't explain why the dead bodies were arranged so carefully. They were laid out in a head to head position, eyelids closed, their arms crossed, and the bodies stretched out straight like they were asleep on their backs. It was the neatest crime scene I think I have ever seen. It reminded me of a monument, created carefully in memory of the victims."

"A burial chamber?" Jonny offered.

"I don't know all the English words," she replied, "but it sounds about right. The state of the burial site suggests to me either a neat and tidy mind or some remorse. Unless of course, there is some ritual here, but that's almost impossible for me to determine at this stage."

Jonny was silent in concentration, a frown across his brow.

"Thank you, Ella," Mikeš stated, smiling warmly. "Try to get a good night's sleep. I think Honza and I need to go back to base to review these findings and try to make a plan. At the moment, this case is running away from us."

"There are just a couple of other findings from the autopsies," Králová replied swiftly.

Jonny looked towards her, full of concentration.

"Firstly, they shared a pizza together earlier on Friday evening," she continued. "The contents of their stomachs were almost identical. Maybe they went somewhere to eat before going to the pub? Also, the alcohol level in their blood was high, probably five or six drinks each."

"We'll check the restaurants close to their apartment and on the route to the pub," Mikeš offered.

"Their reactions would have been delayed after drinking," Jonny stated.

"They also had sexual intercourse a few hours before they died," she added. "And, finally, Yulia had lost a baby six to twelve months ago. Unfortunately, I cannot tell you whether it was a natural miscarriage or planned, but she definitely had a cervical procedure."

18

On Your Toes

The atmosphere in the Incident Room was subdued. Jonny sat slumped at a desk, flicking through the printed records from Alex Corbet's mobile phone. Boukal looked tired, standing at the Murder Board, half-heartedly updating the information gained from the interviews and the day's discovery. The only energy was coming from Dvořáková, busily sorting out the case files: unclipping arch file folders and inserting documents at pace, double checking to ensure the correct chronological order.

Mikeš approached the Incident Room and stopped theatrically at the open door. He scanned the room slowly, scrutinising the studious scene before him, a concentrated frown on his face. Only Boukal noticed his boss, nervously trying to gain eye contact with the others. Jonny and Dvořáková remained engrossed in their respective tasks, heads down and oblivious to Mikeš' arrival.

After Boukal's subtle cough made no difference, Mikeš started to clap his hands slowly and dramatically to evoke a reaction. Jonny and Dvořáková looked up, startled by the loud noise. Having gained the attention of everybody in the room, Mikeš stopped clapping. He closed the door behind him to ensure privacy and stepped purposefully into the middle of the room ready to make an important point.

"My senior detective team is a reflection of me. Everybody

respects us, either through seniority or rank, and looks to us for leadership. This is especially true when times are hard, like now, when we are under pressure with many cases to investigate. Our people are our best resource…" He swept his arm across the glass-fronted meeting room, indicating the detective team working away in the open plan office. "But, they need leadership. We will not solve any serious crime investigations by sitting in a quiet room with our heads buried in folders of information. To succeed we need to be leading from the front, inspiring our staff."

Mikeš continued standing, a serious expression on his face, slowly scanning the faces in the room. Boukal and Dvořáková nodded respectfully, demonstrating their unspoken understanding. The drama hung heavy in the air, the next move unclear.

Jonny loved this aspect of Mikeš' character, leading from the front with panache, even if he didn't know which direction he was going in. Jonny, by contrast, was prone to introversion when the pressure was on, keen to crawl into a quiet corner and reflect. Many people had already remarked that their styles were naturally complementary, bringing out the best in each other, despite only having worked together for a few weeks. Jonny could suddenly see it clearly for the first time – Mikeš was like the police partner, maybe even brother, he'd never had. He smiled at the realisation, feeling a warm glow inside.

Jonny stood up and walked slowly and deliberately towards Mikeš. He extended his hand and Mikeš accepted, shaking firmly. Turning to look at Boukal and Dvořáková, it was Jonny's turn to make a speech. "In my many years in the police, I have worked for a wide selection of senior officers. Some were very good." He glanced across at Mikeš. "I am pleased to say that Felix Mikeš may be the best of them. Felix, you are exactly right and I apologise on behalf of all of us. This case has got us in a bit of a knot at present, but…" He paused to collect the right words. "But, with strong leadership and positive attitudes, I am convinced we will catch this murderer."

Mikeš beamed his usual smile at Jonny. Relieved to have avoided any confrontation, Boukal and Dvořáková joined in with vocal agreements. Mikeš again clapped his hands, this time excitedly, and gestured for Jonny to sit down. Show over!

"Marek, take us through all we have so far on this double murder investigation," Mikeš boomed.

As Boukal glanced at the whiteboard, mentally preparing his summary of the evidence, Mikeš leaned in towards Jonny. "Phew," he whispered. "Honza, I thought you were going to resign when you stood up and walked over to me."

It was Jonny's turn to laugh loudly, also returning Mikeš' usual gesture of slapping his friend on the back. "It's good to keep you on your toes," Jonny said between bursts of laughter.

"Toes?" Mikeš questioned, looking confused with the slang.

Boukal glanced between Jonny and Mikeš, unsure of his next action.

"Marek, I think you should just start," Jonny added, still chuckling to himself.

"Right," Boukal began, shuffling nervously from foot to foot. "Alex Corbet and Yulia Ivanova were killed and buried sometime on late Friday night or early Saturday morning. The murder weapon is confirmed as a mallet with a metal head and was found buried with them. I have checked with the building contractors who are laying the fibre optic cables and they have confirmed a mallet matching the description of the murder weapon was stolen from the crew last week. They didn't report it initially because they thought it had just been lost."

"The builders use the mallets to re-lay the small stones to create the cobbled effect on the pavements," Mikeš explained.

"When did the builders notice the mallet was missing?" Jonny asked.

"Only on Monday," Boukal confirmed. "This was the day they started re-laying the pavement. The work to lay the new cables for the length of the street was finished on Friday before the weekend. Also, one of the workmen remembers losing his fluorescent vest on Friday. They have lots of spare vests in the van so he didn't report it at the time. He says he came back from buying a sandwich at lunchtime and the jacket was gone."

"And, what about the plastic sheeting?"

"They told me they have some, but hardly ever use it," Boukal explained. "I sent them photos of the plastic sheeting we found at the crime scene, but it does not match with what they carry in stock."

"So," Jonny started, suddenly enthused, "this is looking more and more like a premeditated murder. What I mean is that it was clearly planned in advance. The murderer steals a workmen's vest and a mallet, knowing the street is being dug up and the trenches will be open Friday night and over the weekend. They bring along their own plastic sheeting so they can cover the bodies quickly and stop them being exposed if it rains. A lot of planning has gone into this. Didn't the building contractor notice anything when they were refilling the trenches on Monday?"

"I asked them about that," Boukal assured his audience. "They said refilling the trenches was the first job on Monday morning. However, most of the workmen had moved to the next street to start digging the new trenches. Only a small team was left to fill in the trenches and then re-lay the pavement stones, but nobody noticed anything unusual. They told me they use a small digger to move the soil back into the trenches and then a machine to flatten the surface before laying the stones."

"I bet the murderer knew this as well." Jonny shook his head in disgust. "They must have watched the building contractors because they knew their schedule."

Dvořáková used the opening to present her findings. "The CCTV search is ongoing, but nothing yet. We have identified the right time slot on last week's recordings and they are being reviewed now. Uniform officers have also undertaken a house-to-house search along the streets where the bodies were found and where Alex Corbet lived. Unfortunately, most people were out at work so we'll repeat the exercise again this evening. I've also extended the search to the next few streets, heading towards the Červený lev pub, just in case someone saw the victims being followed when they walked from the pub."

"The murderer is probably a man," Jonny stated. "To have killed two people and then moved the bodies into the open trenches would take strength. Not impossible for a woman, but less likely."

"A professional killer?" Mikeš suggested.

"I doubt it, but obviously we need to keep an open mind," Jonny replied quickly. "A professional hit is usually clean with less or no effort to hide the bodies. The professional killer is only interested in hiding their own identity, not leaving any traces behind. This murder feels personal. It was certainly not a random robbery because we know the victim's personal belongings, including watches, mobile phones and wallets, were buried with the bodies."

"But, why would the killer go to all the trouble of burying the bodies like that?" Mikeš submitted. "Whilst they don't seem to have made a mistake, it was an elaborate plan that could easily have gone wrong."

Jonny put his finger to his lip, deep in thought. The room waited for his deliberation. "In my opinion," he finally proclaimed, "the murderer either needed the time before the bodies were found. Maybe to plan their getaway. Or…"

"Yes," Mikeš encouraged.

"Or," Jonny continued, his tone solemn, "the murderer is watching us and enjoying seeing the bodies being found."

"Sick!" Mikeš exclaimed.

"Lucie," Jonny asked, "can you contact the TV companies and ask for copies of their news coverage of the police operation last night. There is a possibility that he, or she, was in the crowd at the end of the street watching us. Or, maybe they were watching from an overlooking building."

"Yes, Honza."

"Maybe…" Boukal started but paused.

"What are you thinking, Marek?" Jonny encouraged.

"Well, if the killer stole the fluorescent vest from the building contractor, maybe he used it as a disguise on Friday night. He could have worn it to check the trenches and nobody would have questioned him. Also, he could have been wearing it later when he jumped Alex Corbet and Yulia Ivanova."

"Great thinking," Jonny replied, burning with a sense of pride.

"Yes, excellent work, Marek," Mikeš echoed.

"Lucie," Jonny continued, "can you brief your uniform officers to ask the local residents if any one saw a person in a fluorescent workmen's vest late on Friday night. But, it would have been late, well after the builders finished work, probably after nine p.m. We also need to check the CCTV for someone wearing such a vest."

"Will do," Dvořáková confirmed. "I'll get a photo of the vest from the building contractors and circulate it."

"The other thing we need to focus on," he continued, his mind in full flow, "is finding the place where Alex Corbet and Yulia Ivanova were killed. It will probably be somewhere close to the street where they were found but concealed from the pavement."

"I'll brief the officers conducting the house-to-house search to look along the streets," she replied, scribbling notes on her pad.

Realising a connection, Jonny turned to Mikeš. "Some of the fibres that Ella found buried with the bodies could have been from the workmen's fluorescent vest. We need to advise her. It might help her in the search for any DNA if she knows what she's looking for."

"I will inform her immediately after this meeting," Mikeš confirmed.

"Also," Jonny added, his mind whirling with thoughts, "the workmen's vest wasn't buried with the victims. We should inform the uniform officers doing the search tonight because somebody might have seen it. It's also probably worth checking all the rubbish bins that haven't been emptied."

Boukal stopped making notes on the whiteboard. "But, if the killer has planned everything so meticulously, I doubt they'd just throw the vest away."

"Probably right," Jonny murmured, "but the plan couldn't be perfect. They are sure to have made one mistake – our job is to find it. Brief your officers anyway, Lucie, there's no harm in asking the question."

"Leave it to me," Dvořáková confirmed.

"What did you make of the interviews today?" Mikeš asked, changing tack.

"There is clearly something that Daniela Nováková is protecting," Jonny stated. "Something to do with her daughter. It's still hard to imagine them involved in the murder, but we need to dig deeper; it may be connected to Alex's murder. Their solicitor, Pavel Rosický, knows the situation and is helping to cover it up. He was protecting Helena at every opportunity in the interviews, even preventing her from answering some questions."

"Yes, I noticed that," Mikeš remarked.

"And, he's a thoroughly horrible man," Jonny declared. "A real slimeball."

Mikeš, Boukal and Dvořáková looked at each other, clearly none of them understanding the reference, but appreciating it wasn't a compliment.

"Not many people in this city like Pavel Rosický," Mikeš added in support.

"I was thinking of going to visit the friends, George and Zuzana, after this meeting," Jonny stated. "Maybe they can provide some revealing background information because Alex used to stay with them last year when he and Helena were having difficulties. If this murder was because of Alex, we need to find the motive."

"I think Marek and I are going to be stuck here at the station for a few hours," Mikeš explained, sighing. "We have loads of open cases to review and reports to complete."

"Don't worry, I can go alone," Jonny assured him.

"I'll phone ahead so they know you are coming," Dvořáková added.

"Could you also print me out headshot photos of Tanya Murray and Torsten Lindberg," Jonny requested. "I want to see if George or Zuzana recognise them. Tanya and Torsten both claim not to have seen Alex Corbet outside of Chodov recently. Maybe one of them is lying."

"No problem," Dvořáková confirmed.

"One other thing I noticed," Jonny added. "I was just working through Alex Corbet's phone records. There are a variety of calls and messages to Czech numbers which we will need to check out, but none looked suspicious on first review. The messages from Tanya stopped Thursday lunchtime, as we discussed with her in the interview. One pattern I did notice, however, is that over the week before he disappeared, Alex called a UK number on five occasions. It's a landline number in London, not a mobile. I have the number so I'll give it a call."

Mikeš turned to Dvořáková. "Lucie, what background information did you find out about Yulia Ivanova?"

"She shared an apartment in Hradec Králové with a friend, Svetlana Lebedev. The local police have spoken to her. They were close friends and came to the Czech Republic from Russia together a few years ago. They were previously living in Brno, and only moved to Hradec Králové three months ago. Svetlana told the local police they moved because Yulia was being threatened by a previous boyfriend. That is all I know at this stage, I'm still waiting for the written report."

"That's interesting," Jonny pondered. "Maybe this has got more to do with Yulia than Alex. We do know she was pregnant before she moved away from Brno. Maybe we should go to interview Yulia's friend in person? Where is this town, Hradec Králové?"

Mikeš frowned. "Can't we just wait for the report from the local police? It may contain everything we need?"

Sensing an opportunity, Dvořáková stepped forward. "Sir, I could drive Honza there early in the morning. It is less than an hour in the car from Prague. We could see Yulia's flatmate at eight a.m. and be back here by nine thirty a.m."

Mikeš wiped his palm across his face, clearly feeling the pressure. Jonny could see him mentally weighing up the conflicting options: rewarding Dvořáková's enthusiasm and aiding her development, against losing her at the hub of his team for a few hours at a critical time. "Oh, all right," he blurted out, keen to agree before he changed his mind. "I hope you find something. We need some luck."

19

Starry Sky

Sat in the quiet corner of the café, Jonny was relieved to finally be on his own – no disturbances now. He craved time to himself on any normal day, but the urge to disappear was much stronger when he was working; he needed space to untangle the evidence on an open case. The constant whirl of everyday noise and distractions in the police station made the task almost impossible.

Luka arrived with the food Jonny had ordered on arrival: seafood risotto, the special of the day. "Busy day?"

"You know, sometimes I wished I'd stayed retired," Jonny offered. "The quiet life is appealing."

"I know you don't mean that," Luka replied, smiling. "Anyway, Felix would be lost without you. Whether you like it or not, you two are joined at the hip. The detective duo – Honza and The Black Cat."

Jonny laughed heartily, knowing Luka was right.

"Dobrou chut'," Luka added, before backing away to the counter to serve a newly arrived group of customers.

Jonny tucked into the food with gusto; he hadn't realised how ravenous he was. After finishing the food and drinking the rest of his coffee, he felt invigorated. But he knew he didn't have time to relax; he needed to use the quiet time positively, to find a way to push the boundaries of the evidence gathered so far.

He pulled out his old police notepad and studied the points

he'd made so far on the investigation. The last page of notes listed the details of the calls made by Alex Corbet in the week before he was murdered. The first task was to discover the identity of the person or company in the UK that Alex had called five times in that week. Jonny dialled the London landline number from his mobile phone and after a few rings the call went to voicemail.

"Hello, you are through to the voicemail of Kristýna Davies, Litigation Executive at Hudson Reynolds. I am not available right now, but please leave a short message and I will call you back as soon as I can."

Kristýna? Jonny flicked back a few pages in his notepad – Kristýna was the name of Daniela Nováková's eldest daughter, now living in London. Was it the same person? If so, why would Alex have called his sister-in-law on her work number before he was murdered? He smiled to himself, realising he now had a new lead as well as something with which to put pressure on Daniela Nováková.

Jonny turned back to the page of notes on the phone records. The messages that had most caught his attention were in the group chat named 'Red Lion Pub Quiz'. The name was interesting in itself – the ex-pats having taken back the traditional British pub name – but it was the vitriol of some of the messages that had stuck out.

Johan: You're a smuck and I'm gonna take you down!
Alex: Just try fatty!
George: Death Stars rule ☺
Johan: Dead Stars would be a better name
Alex: Fuck you!
Johan: You're a dead man walking
Pieter: I can help with that J!

Jonny closed his notepad, no clearer on the true nature of the banter. He knew the younger generations used some of the messaging applications for crass mockery, accepting the spiteful language without concern or worry about retaliation. He also remembered the manager of the Červený lev pub telling him the group chat about the pub quiz was active. Could it contain hidden messages about what had transpired in real life?

***

Realising the day was in danger of escaping him, Jonny finished his second coffee and left the café. Luka wanted to talk, but he fled with the excuse of being late for an interview and the promise of popping by the next day for a longer chat.

George and Zuzana Webb also lived in Prague 2, on a well-known street called Londýnská, not far from the Náměstí Míru square. It was a quiet suburban street, trees lining both pavements, popular with moneyed ex-pats of almost all nationalities for their residence in Prague, whether permanent or temporary. Jonny knew the area, having walked down the street on numerous occasions, enjoying the eclectic mix of shops: a herbalist, independent coffee shop, a vegan restaurant and, of course, Czech pubs.

Feeling the effects of the day in his legs, he decided to take the metro. He knew the next couple of days were going to be equally testing and he wanted to preserve his energy and be alert for the last interview of the day.

The Staroměstská metro station was busy, tourists returning from day trips to Old Town Square or across Charles Bridge to the castle. The crowd and the accompanying excitable chatter thinned out as the metro left the centre, first stopping at Můstek, under the bottom half of Wenceslas Square, proceeding through the Muzeum station towards Náměstí Míru. The journey was short, only three stops, but the difference in the relaxed feel of the suburb compared to the hustle and bustle of the city centre was notable and welcome.

Ascending the metro station steps into the dwindling light, he noticed the rain had cleared to leave a cloudless, starry sky. Having been used to so much cloud and rain in the UK, he'd been surprised by how often the skies were clear above Prague. The resulting nights were often cold, but it was worth it for the prize of what felt like someone leaving the top of the observatory open. Jonny walked into the middle of the cobbled square and craned his neck upwards. The expanse of the large plaza in front of the church provided the perfect position to stand and gaze skyward, the city's old, yellowy streetlights providing a dull background colour that did not compete with the twinkling stars. Although stargazing was better late at night, he could already make out some of the closer constellations getting ready for their night-time vigil over the city.

Caught in the moment, Jonny suddenly realised he was in danger of being late for his agreed seven thirty p.m. arrival, as organised by Dvořáková. He walked at pace to Londýnská and found the correct building. Whilst waiting for the intercom buzzer to be answered, he calculated the walk back to Ivana's apartment would be less than five minutes. He hoped she would have the evening free so they could spend some time together.

George Webb welcomed him at the apartment door and showed him into the living room. His wife, Zuzana, joined them soon after putting their young daughter to bed. They sat closely together on the sofa, his large frame and receding hairline contrasting with her slim figure and shoulder-length, highlighted hair.

"Thank you very much for seeing me so late," Jonny opened. "Sadly, this is now a murder investigation so I'm trying to get as much background information as I can on Alex's life."

"No problem," Zuzana assured him. "Despite what has happened between Alex and Helena, he was still a good friend of both of us. We want to help in any way we can."

"Can I start by asking what jobs both of you do? It just helps paint a picture for me."

"I am a management consultant with one of the big four consultancy firms," George began. "I am also based in Chodov, like Alex was, but I travel around Europe quite a lot."

"I worked in HR in the same company," Zuzana added, "but gave up work when Anna was born."

Jonny opened his mouth to thank them, but before he could say anything George quickly continued with his narrative. "It's strange. I'd seen Alex around so many times, either in Chodov or down the pub, but despite both being British we'd never talked. We only really got to know each other when Zuzana met Helena at pre-natal classes."

"Yes, Helena mentioned it," Jonny replied. "Was Alex happy in his job recently?"

George exchanged a look with Zuzana before answering. "Alex loved his job. He used to bore us silly with his IT technical talk. It was funny because none of us, including Helena, could understand what he was talking about. But…"

"Was he less happy recently?" Jonny suggested, sensing the hesitation.

"Yes," George admitted. "When he was passed over for the

174

promotion, he started to become disillusioned. At first, we just thought he was bitter because—"

"Torsten Lindberg?" Jonny offered.

"Yes, Torsten," George concurred. "According to Alex, Torsten made a number of bad system development decisions in his previous role and tried to blame it on Alex. There was one serious problem, something about a live system. Alex had an email trail which showed that Torsten had signed off the system design changes which caused the issue."

"That's interesting," Jonny stated. "When we interviewed him, Torsten implied the error was more to do with his replacement and Alex. He also said the matter had been resolved."

"I don't think that is right," George replied quickly.

"What was Alex planning to do about it?" Jonny enquired.

"Alex sought our opinion on a few occasions," George explained. "He was especially keen on Zuzana's view because of her HR experience. Torsten was under pressure from his senior management to apportion blame and give out a disciplinary, but he knew Alex had the email trail showing the source of the bad decision making."

Jonny waited, sensing George would continue.

"It came to an impasse, I suppose. Torsten was trying to encourage Alex to take the disciplinary for the team, but Alex was having none of it and wanted to fight back. The communication completely broke down between them. Torsten even came looking for Alex at the pub quiz last week—"

"Last Thursday?" Jonny interrupted, looking surprised.

"Yes. He came to the pub, but Alex didn't want to talk to him. Alex said that Torsten had been pestering him over recent weeks to meet up and resolve the situation."

"And, I suppose that was the last you heard about the matter," Jonny suggested.

"Yes," George confirmed. "I messaged Alex over the weekend, and then went to his apartment on Monday after Helena called us. But, the last I saw or heard from him was last Thursday at the quiz."

"What was Alex like?" Jonny posed.

Again, the glance between husband and wife.

"From my perspective," George started, "Alex was a top guy. Really honest."

"We really liked him and Helena," Zuzana added sincerely.

"So, why do you think their marriage had problems?" Jonny asked. "You must have a unique perspective because firstly, Zuzana, you are close friends with Helena, and, secondly, I understand Alex used to stay overnight with you sometimes."

"As I have already said, Mr Fox, we really liked both of them," Zuzana answered. "We tried everything to keep them talking about their problems. We even thought they might get back together at one point, but sadly it didn't happen."

"And what about the impact of Helena's mother on their relationship?"

"I couldn't really say what the problem was," Zuzana replied.

"I am sorry to press you, but is it 'couldn't say' or 'won't say'?" Jonny pressed.

"Mr Fox," George took over, "as Zuzana has just said, we were friends of both of them. We tried not to take sides, but we desperately wanted them to get back together because our families were close. Unfortunately, it just didn't happen."

"Thank you," Jonny continued. "Helena believes Alex was having an affair with a lady called Tanya at work. I've

176

interviewed Tanya and she is adamant they were not seeing each other, although, by her own admission, she wanted it to happen. What did Alex tell you about her and did you ever see them together?"

"This is the only part of the story that makes me angry." George sighed heavily. "I talked to Alex for hours about this. I also asked him directly about her on numerous occasions. He always gave me the same story; that there was nothing going on between him and this lady, Tanya. And, I believed him. Neither of us know why Helena was so convinced."

"Zuzana?" Jonny referred the question.

"I only know what George has just told you," she added. "It was the one part of their separation I didn't understand and still don't. Every time I tried to talk to Helena about it, she just clammed up. She said she'd seen some messages between Alex and Tanya but would never elaborate."

"And, so I assume you never saw Alex together with Tanya," Jonny pressed.

"No," George confirmed. "I don't even know what she looks like."

Jonny pulled the headshot of Tanya Murray out of his jacket pocket and showed it to George and Zuzana.

"No, I've never seen her before," George confirmed.

Zuzana shook her head. "Sorry."

"But…" George started, before hesitating.

"Yes?"

"Well, I haven't been to the pub since the quiz last Thursday night," George continued, "but, on Friday night, I received messages from friends who were there to say Alex had arrived with a new woman. They said they were sitting closely together, like boyfriend and girlfriend. That's the other reason I was trying to contact him over the weekend. But, as you know already, he didn't respond to my messages."

"Yes, we do know about this," Jonny explained, "and we are following up on the matter."

Jonny flicked through his notepad, checking he'd covered every angle. "Oh yes." He looked up at George and Zuzana. "Alex received a handwritten note. I found it in his work bag. The note was written in capitals and was warning him to stay away from someone. Did Alex mention anything about this to you?"

"Yes," George confirmed. "He showed it to me when we were at the pub quiz last Thursday. In truth, he was very confused about it. I asked him who it was about and he said he didn't know. Obviously, I didn't know then he was seeing anyone else, but maybe it was to do with the woman he was with on Friday night."

"Yes, that is very possible," Jonny concurred. "Did he say when he received it?"

George paused and scratched his head, trying to recall the conversation. "Sorry, I don't remember if he said. He did imply he'd received it only recently. My guess would be in the few days before the pub quiz... Yes, sometime that week."

"Thank you, that is very helpful. I'm sorry to ask this but we need a handwriting sample from all the people who knew Alex. Also, for the record, can I ask where you were on Friday night and Saturday morning?"

"We stayed in Friday night and ordered a take-away delivery," Zuzana explained. "I think George popped out for a paper on Saturday morning, but apart from that we were in until we took Anna to a friend's birthday party around lunchtime. We met Helena and her mother there because Emilie was going to the same party."

"Thank you."

"I'm sorry to be rude," George started, "but is this interview going to take much longer? It's just that the pub quiz starts at eight thirty p.m."

Jonny looked at his watch quickly, working out what day it was. It was Thursday, he suddenly realised, the day of the Červený lev pub quiz. It had completely slipped his mind in the chaotic schedule. "I'm surprised the quiz is still going ahead after the terrible news," he commented.

"It is what Alex would have wanted," George answered firmly. "He loved the pub quiz. Besides, we are holding tonight's quiz in honour of Alex. It was Niall's idea. Everyone is going to be there."

Jonny raised his eyebrows, taken aback, but not sure what to say in response.

"You should come along," George continued. "Our team is one short now."

The next few minutes were a blur, Jonny finding himself cajoled into attending by George's enthusiasm and the realisation he would have the opportunity to observe and talk to the characters from the group chat. As he stood by the apartment door, waiting for George and having said goodbye to Zuzana, he took out his mobile phone and sent a message to Ivana.

Hi, sorry I've not been in contact. Crazy day! Do you fancy going to a pub quiz?

20

The Tie-Breaker

Ivana's reaction had shocked Jonny. Whereas he loathed these types of events, reminding him of the torturous nights of bingo and quizzes he was forced to attend with his mother on their annual summer visits to holiday camps, Ivana had been delighted by the idea of a pub quiz and agreed to meet him in twenty minutes.

When she arrived at the pub, she was in an excitable mood. She wore a casual blouse and jeans, her hair worn down for the evening. Jonny whisked her across to the table hosting the Deadly Stars, introducing her to the other team members he'd only just met himself. Her demeanour changed immediately when, after accepting the beer he'd bought for her in advance, she recognised the photos of Alex Corbet posted on the walls all around the bar.

"Honza, this is work, isn't it?" she snapped. "I recognise the photo of the murdered man from the TV."

"I'm sorry, I didn't get the chance to explain," he confessed. "I need to talk briefly to a couple of people here, but I can do it between quiz rounds. We will be together on the pub quiz team for almost all the evening. George and his friends seem nice. We might even win."

Ivana sighed, clearly not convinced.

"Please, Ivana," he pleaded. "It'll be a fun night."

She sighed again, less heavily this time. After looking him directly in the eyes, trying to read him, she turned and started talking to the only other woman on the quiz team.

If he hadn't realised it before, he now knew how tricky it was going to be to manage the balance between work and play. He sincerely wanted to spend time with Ivana, but this high profile case was also demanding his attention. He cursed himself for not thinking it through properly, but silently vowed to stay positive and make the evening a success.

The earlier walk to the pub close to I. P. Pavlova had allowed Jonny time to extract some background information on the pub quiz from George. The quiz had started small, eight years before, attended by only a few quiz enthusiasts. But, under Niall's stewardship, it had grown into one of the most popular weekly events amongst the ex-pat community. Almost all the tables were booked in advance and a paid quizmaster was now in charge of proceedings, allowing Niall and his staff to concentrate on serving food and drinks to the clientele. In short, it was the busiest night of the week in the Červený lev pub.

George's explanation about the group chat banter was understandable, albeit still a little disturbing. The leaders of the regular teams, including the Deadly Stars and the Pig Heads, had taken on personas not dissimilar to sci-fi characters, launching intentionally provocative attacks at the other teams. When Jonny had mentioned the dispute between Alex and Johan, George had just shrugged his shoulders, explaining that it happened sometimes, but ultimately was not taken seriously, nor was it long-lasting. George had agreed to introduce him to Johan and Pieter between rounds but asked respectfully for any interviews not to overshadow the quiz.

The loud pub noise was hushed by the quizmaster who

opened proceedings and invited George forward to the microphone.

"Ladies and gentlemen," George started solemnly. "Our great friend, Alex Corbet, was tragically killed a few days ago. I am sure you will all join me in passing our sympathy to his wife, Helena, and their two children. Tonight's quiz is in honour of Alex. He will, of course, be up there watching to make sure nobody is cheating. So, let's make this the cleanest, best pub quiz ever at The Red Lion."

The pub erupted in respectful applause.

"Before I hand back to the quizmaster," George continued, "I would like to invite up Detective Chief Inspector Jonathan Fox to say a few words."

Jonny was shocked by the unexpected announcement and tried waving at George to stop him. George, however, was totally engrossed in his task of addressing the lively crowd and did not see Jonny's hand gestures.

"DCI Fox, or Honza, as I believe he now likes to be known, is working as a consultant with the Czech Police," George continued. "Please listen to him and help if you can. Thank you."

All eyes were now on Jonny. He stepped forward to the microphone, turning to catch Ivana's blank stare across the table and only able to shrug his shoulders in muted response.

"Thank you, George," he began, microphone in hand. "This is really quite simple. You will have come to this pub many times and you know Alex Corbet. If you saw anything unusual at all last Thursday night, the evening of the last quiz, or last Friday, I would appreciate if you could speak to me. Alex was here both nights. We also know he was with a woman on Friday. Maybe you saw one or both of them talking to someone you didn't recognise, or you saw someone following them when they left the pub. Any small, unusual detail could be vital and help us solve this case. Thank you for listening and I hope everyone has a wonderful evening."

As Jonny walked back to his table, Niall handed him two new beers. "I thought you weren't a fan of pub quizzes," Niall joked, grinning.

"I'm not!" Jonny exclaimed, taking the beers.

Niall laughed and returned behind the bar.

Back at the table, Jonny squeezed into the seat next to Ivana and handed her the beer. "Ivana, I'm sorry, I didn't know George was going to—"

She put her finger up to Jonny's lip, preventing him from finishing his apology. "Honza, it's fine. I understand. I was a bit annoyed when I arrived, but I'm fine now. Let's just have a nice evening. Na zdraví."

"Na zdraví," he responded. They clinked glasses, looking directly into each other's eyes, and sipped their beers.

"By the way," she continued, a twinkle in her eye, "you look very sexy when you have a microphone in your hand, speaking to an audience."

Jonny looked at her, prepared for the following joke. When he was sure she was being serious, he burst out laughing, almost spitting out his mouthful of beer.

The first half of the quiz passed quickly, only the last round before the interval becoming boisterous as the alcohol consumption started to slow down the delivery of the questions. Ivana became totally engrossed in the competition, helping the team work their way to the right answers. In truth, the existing team members were almost professionals in comparison to the new arrivals, seeming as if they swatted up on general knowledge in their spare time. Jonny was only pleased to see Ivana was having a good time and, despite his initial reticence, he found himself also enjoying the evening.

A few people had approached Jonny during the intervals between rounds, responding to his request to come forward. No new information was forthcoming, only repeated descriptions of the other woman in the pub with Alex the previous Friday. Some also came to ask questions, but Jonny politely but firmly sent them away. Seeing the difficult situation he was in, Ivana held his hand under the table and gave him a proud smile.

At the interval, the pub seemed to come alive, people moving around to stretch legs, talk to other friends or visit the restrooms. George had organised for Jonny to talk to Johan and Pieter in the opposite corner of the pub, around the only table kept permanently reserved by Niall.

"Close match," Johan opened, shaking Jonny's hand.

"I understand from George that the rivalry between your Pig Heads team and Alex's Deadly Stars was quite intense," Jonny stated.

"Yes, but it was always good-natured."

"Really?" Jonny questioned. "I thought you and Alex nearly fell out over an accusation of cheating."

Johan sighed and shook his head. "One time last year, Alex got really upset because he lost on the last question. He was convinced we'd cheated. There were a lot of insults thrown around, but it was nothing really. We sorted it out over a beer a few weeks later."

"It was nothing," Pieter added. "Our combined love of the pub quiz was always stronger than individual rivalries."

"I've had a look at the group chat and the language is quite strong," Jonny noted.

"I know how it looks," Johan responded, "but it's just fun.

Niall stoked up the rivalry initially, probably trying to fuel interest in people coming to the quiz. Now, the banter is almost as much fun to some people as the quiz itself."

"Alex and George won last week so it's again level between the teams," Pieter added. "It's quite a rivalry. We're all going to miss Alex a lot – it won't be the same without him."

"Did Niall have a lot of interaction with Alex about the quiz?" Jonny asked.

"Yes, I suppose so," Johan responded. "Alex was the pro amongst us. He was involved in pub quizzes going back to his university days back in the UK. I think he helped Niall set up the quiz in the first place."

"Thank you for talking to me," Jonny said. "Enjoy the rest of your evening."

"We will if we win!" Johan exclaimed, laughing loudly.

The second half of the quiz could only be described as manic. Jonny was amazed how competitive the teams were; people who seemed naturally quiet came alive. Ivana seemed to thrive on the energy, her voice becoming louder with each quiz question.

The quizmaster took the microphone and asked for quiet three times before the noise dropped enough for him to be heard. "Ladies and gentlemen… and of course, Johan," he began, to rehearsed laughter. "I have finished adding up the scores and I'm delighted to say we have another exciting draw. The lead has gone backwards and forwards tonight between the Pig Heads and the Deadly Stars, but they have both finished on eighty-six points from a possible one hundred. As is customary, we have one tie-breaker question, selected in advance by me."

A hush descended on the pub.

"Here is the question," the quizmaster continued, leaving a

pause to create tension. "We all know Bob Dylan's real name is Robert Zimmerman. But, where was he born and in what year?"

Jonny chuckled to himself. Could this really be happening? The only subject he was proficient in, other than policing, was Bob Dylan. And here was a question so close to his heart, asking for some basic facts that he would never be able to forget even if he tried.

The Deadly Stars' team members put their heads together in a huddle, all talking excitedly. The focus was so intense none of them heard Ivana speak. "Honza knows everything about Bob Dylan," she repeated, rapping on the table with her knuckles.

The team turned in unison to look across at Jonny. "Honza, do you know the answer?" George asked calmly.

"Duluth, Minnesota, 1941," Jonny responded calmly, keeping his voice low.

The words had hardly come out of Jonny's mouth before Ivana planted a big kiss on his lips. The whole team responded by cheering and punching the air in delight.

George and Johan went to the quizmaster and handed in their team's answer.

"I am pleased to say we have a clear winner," the quizmaster began. "Both teams got 1941 correctly, but the only team to get Duluth, Minnesota, and hence our clear winners tonight, are the Deadly Stars!"

The pub went berserk, people screaming and shouting in a combination of joy and despair. Jonny and Ivana found themselves in a team scrum, bouncing up and down in celebration, George overcome with emotion and crying in the middle.

***

The walk home was slow and meandering, Ivana's exuberance slowing their progress as she told everyone they met, in Czech and English, that Jonny was the hero and had won the famous pub quiz. Passers-by smiled in solidarity but continued swiftly on their way.

He was just happy the evening had been a triumph; after the less than promising start, he could not have written the script better. Despite not really advancing the investigation, the real reason for him attending the pub quiz had not stopped Ivana enjoying herself.

"Honza, we won!" she shouted again.

Jonny pulled her close and kissed her passionately. "Come on, let's get you home."

Ivana held onto his arm tightly, steadying her stagger, her head leaning into his shoulder. At the Náměstí Míru square, she dragged him to a stop and they both looked up at the sky in wonder. The stars were shining brightly in the midnight darkness, not a cloud in sight, just the fog of their breath hanging in the cold air.

"I forgot to ask you," she started. "How was your meeting with Barbora?"

"It was fascinating and quite emotional. Barbora is a lovely lady and clearly an expert in the search for lost families. She explained everything so well. To think I am so close to knowing if I still have family here in Prague... It's exciting and quite scary at the same time. Thank you so much for helping me."

He paused to point up at a shining star. "Ivana, there is your star."

She followed the direction of his pointed finger to see a bright, shining star to the north-east of the city.

"It is *your* star," he continued, "because it's shining the brightest in the sky right now."

She turned to look up at him lovingly. His head remained unmoved, looking upwards to the night sky above. She leaned heavily into his body and kissed his neck.

The sudden movement of a dark figure behind them caught Jonny's attention. He swivelled his neck to see the man hurrying along a path at the bottom of the square, about ten metres away from them. He wore a dark coat and a trilby hat.

"I'm sure I saw that man earlier," Jonny murmured. "He was waiting outside the pub, on the other side of the street. And... yes, I saw him earlier tonight when I was walking to meet George and Zuzana."

"Honza, please," she pleaded with him.

"I'm serious," he stated flatly. "I think he's following us."

Ivana laughed and thumped his chest playfully. "You just have a vivid imagination. Why would anyone want to be following us at nearly midnight on a Thursday night? I mean—"

"Come on." He grabbed her arm and pulled her across the square, in the direction of Ivana's apartment.

Ivana began to say something, but Jonny, now fully focused and in the zone, put his finger to his lips. They walked down a street away from the square, turned left, their usual way, but then turned right quickly, away from the apartment. At the next corner, Jonny stopped abruptly, pulling Ivana into a garage doorway.

"Honza?" she muttered impatiently.

"Ivana, just trust me, please."

They waited for five minutes, Jonny checking down the street every thirty seconds or so. Eventually, the dark, hatted figure appeared at the end of the street, looking around him as if lost. Jonny slowly guided Ivana's head so she could see, careful not to reveal their position.

"You were right," she gasped, softly, "it's the same man."

"I know. But, why is he following me?"

Jonny checked again and the man was still there, pacing around the corner of the street.

"Don't worry, it will be okay." He pulled her close. "Let's wait until he disappears and then we can go home."

21

Man of her Dreams

Friday, 16 April

Still feeling the effects of the late and disturbing evening, Jonny met Dvořáková early at the Náměstí Míru square. Although he'd felt sure the person stalking him wasn't dangerous, he didn't want to risk escalating the situation by being picked up outside the apartment. To be certain he wasn't being followed, he'd left the building in the opposite direction, head down and jacket collar up against the lingering, overnight rain. He walked a big lap of the residential streets, using techniques he'd learned in detective training, eventually doubling back to the square from a small side street.

"Dobré ráno, Honza," Dvořáková greeted him brightly, as he opened the car door and jumped into the passenger seat.

"Ahoj, Lucie. Dobré ráno."

As he settled in his seat, brushing the pools of rain off the shoulder of his jacket, he looked across at his driver for the day. Dressed in her usual uniform, her brightness beamed back at him, no hint at the long evening she'd probably worked the night before.

"Lucie, how do you always look so fresh?"

"I think it's more to do with your age, Honza," she answered cheekily. "I bet you worked every hour you could when you were in your twenties, like me, and could survive on only a few hours' sleep."

Jonny chuckled to himself, knowing she was unequivocally right. The break between taking early retirement from the Metropolitan Police and being dragged into the role of consultant with the Czech Police had been refreshing, helping to repair his mental health and prepare him for his future challenges. But, it hadn't helped his fitness levels at all. He'd already begun to feel the pace in his last years working in London, but it was worse now; a sound night's sleep was imperative to feeling good and being on top of his game. This day was going to be another tough one, but he was determined to power on and match his younger colleagues.

"By the way," Dvořáková added, "Marek told me you like a caffe latte and croissant so I stopped on the way here."

Jonny looked down at the central column between the front seats and shook his head in wonderment. "I'm not even going to ask where you got these so early in the morning," he replied. "But, thank you. You may have literally just saved my life."

"Marek said you might say that as well."

Without waiting for a reply, Dvořáková put the unmarked police car in gear and sped off. Jonny didn't reply, knowing it wasn't expected or needed, but smiled to himself, feeling the warmness of family he'd missed for a long time. He knew it would be hard to explain exactly what he felt, but somehow he'd been enticed into the fabric of a group of people in this foreign city that wanted and needed him – and Mikeš was the head of the family. He had his daughter, Charlotte, but otherwise his life in the UK had been without close family, not even a father figure, for a few years.

The coffee started to work, helping him feel better than when his alarm had started beeping at the unearthly hour of five forty-five a.m. His first reaction then had been to groan audibly and nestle close to Ivana's warm body. Already lamenting the late night and one too many Czech beers, he'd slowly prised open his eyes and forced himself out of bed and into the shower.

Ivana had naturally been upset that someone suspicious was following them, needing to talk it through and understand the possible reasons why. Knowing it was all about him, Jonny had tried to calm her and encourage her to go about her normal business in the coming days. His only caveat, to which she agreed without argument, was for her to send him regular messages to let him know where she was. The whole process had taken time, including a last drink before bed to calm the nerves, resulting in only four hours' sleep.

Although Jonny had been in the police force for nearly twenty-five years, the previous night had been the first time in his career he'd been followed. Now he knew what it felt like – an odd sensation, an invasion of privacy enough to put anyone on tenterhooks. Having rationalised the situation, his only conclusion was that someone wanted to know what he knew about the case. He certainly couldn't believe the murderer would follow him, even if they did perversely enjoy revelling in the crime; the risk of revealing their identity would be too high.

After only ten minutes driving they were pounding down the clear highway, the heavy traffic travelling in the opposite direction towards Prague. The traffic signs showing ninety kilometres to Hradec Králové. Jonny had finished his coffee and croissant, starting to feel some life returning to his foggy head and lacklustre limbs.

"Ivana and I were followed back from the pub last night," Jonny said.

"Really?" she replied, shooting a shocked look at him.

"Yes, it was strange. He wasn't particularly threatening, but he was definitely tracking me. He obviously wants to know something about me or this case. It certainly spooked Ivana, that's for sure."

"Did you get a good look at him?"

"It was dark and he was wearing a hat, so I couldn't see his face. His outfit was classic: a dark mac and a hat – it was like something from the movies. He's either worked in the police or security… or watches too many detective films."

Dvořáková chuckled, her eyes fixed on the two lane road ahead. "I can ask Felix for an officer to stay with Ivana, but as you know—"

"No, it's fine, Lucie, but thanks," he interrupted. "I've briefed her on the precautions she needs to take. I think it is quite innocent, he probably just wants information. The question is for what or whom?"

"We had a few breakthroughs last night," she offered, changing tact.

"Yes?" He was alert and interested now.

"We haven't finished reviewing all the CCTV from the surrounding streets, but we've confirmed the route that Alex Corbet and Yulia Ivanova took, both going to the pub and leaving it, by tracing their mobile phone signals. On one camera along the route back, we've found recording of a man with two small dogs approaching them at 11.27 p.m. The man seems to know Alex and they appear to argue for a few minutes. There is no physical contact, but they are pointing and gesticulating at each other. I've printed a few still images. They're in the folder on the back seat."

Jonny reached back and found the prints. He studied them

closely, the grainy quality of the image providing few clues to the man's identity. "I don't recognise him," he finally stated.

"The detective team have gone back through the portfolio of people we have spoken to in connection with the case, including those on the house-to-house search, but none match the profile of the man in the photos."

"The dogs should be a giveaway. They look like a small-sized breed, maybe a Shih Tzu. One is very dark, maybe black, and the other is white and greyish." Jonny paused in thought. "I wonder who he is, and what issue he had with Alex?"

"Also," she continued, pleased to report new information. "We've located the Italian restaurant where Alex and Yulia ate before going to the pub. You can watch the tape later, but it doesn't reveal much we don't already know. They arrived at seven p.m. and left at approximately eight thirty p.m. But, the restaurant CCTV does show them holding hands across the table both before and after their meal. They seemed very happy."

"New love," Jonny remarked, thinking of Ivana. "I wonder if these murders were driven by jealousy."

"And, lastly," she added, "I ran—"

"You have been busy, Lucie. I'm impressed."

"Well, it's probably nothing," she qualified. "I decided to run a search on our police database of all the people involved in the case, and Tanya Murray's name came up."

"How?"

"Last July, she called the central police line regarding a potential harassment report. There is not much information on the call log. She told the officer who took the call she was being followed. The officer asked some questions and explained what would happen if she decided to file a complaint. Tanya Murray didn't leave any specific details of the alleged harassment, and there is no name mentioned. There was no follow up to the call and there are also no further reports on record, so I can only assume the situation must have resolved itself."

"She mentioned a bad relationship during the interview."

"I thought you should know." She shrugged.

"Quite right, excellent work." Jonny paused in thought. "There seem to be lots of fragments of information or evidence hanging in the air, but nothing to bind them together. We need to get lucky, and quickly. Let's hope Yulia's friend can shed some light on the start of her relationship with Alex."

***

Coming off the highway in good time, Dvořáková followed the satellite navigation system into the town of Hradec Králové. The traffic they encountered was heavier than when leaving Prague due to it now being the rush hour. They skirted the old town, the Czech renaissance architecture reminiscent of Prague, then took them through a multitude of backstreets lined with unappealing low-level blocks of flats. Ivana had warned him that many of the larger towns in the Czech Republic were an amalgamation of the aesthetic and a concrete maze, and here he was experiencing it close up for the first time.

Pulling up outside a block in dire need of some love and a makeover, Dvořáková double-checked the address and led them to the main entrance door. After announcing themselves over the intercom system, they walked up the concrete stairwell to the top floor.

The inside of the building was as undesirable as the outside indicated: the stairs were cracked in many places, the walls were grey, unpainted plaster, and graffiti had been sprayed throughout.

Svetlana Lebedev greeted them at the apartment door, her dour appearance matching her habitat. She wore an old but comfortable tracksuit, understandable for the early hour, but the pulled back, unkempt hair and downturned mouth gave the distinct impression of tiredness and general displeasure with life.

She led them to a small table in the kitchen. "I'm sorry, the apartment is very small. Yulia and I had a room each so the only shared space is the kitchen."

"No problem," Dvořáková replied, smiling warmly. "Thank you for seeing us so early. Are you comfortable speaking in English?"

"Yes, my English is still better than my Czech," she confessed. "I only speak Russian at work and so I am learning very slowly."

"I understand you and Yulia moved to the Czech Republic together?" Jonny started.

"Yes, we come from a small town in Russia. There was not much chance of getting work so we moved to Brno two years ago."

"And, you both found work?"

"Yes. Yulia had good qualifications and spoke English well, so she got a job easily. I had to take a cleaning job, but eventually got a better job through the Russian community there."

"We understand Yulia's job took her around the country as an office designer?"

"Not initially. She worked in the office in Brno for a year, but they soon realised how clever she was and gave her a chance."

"Can I ask why you moved to Hradec Králové?" Jonny enquired.

Svetlana sighed heavily. "The Russian community is small.

Yulia and I used to mostly stay in and save our money, but sometimes we would go to a popular, local Russian restaurant in Brno. She was very pretty and was always being asked out by the men there. Eventually, one man persuaded her and they started a relationship. He was good-looking and charming, but I told her from the beginning he was a bad man. I know the type from Russia. He expects you to do and say everything he tells you. If not, he hits you!"

"Is that what happened?"

"Yes. After one month she came home with a bruise. Then it was two bruises. I hate these men, they just want to control you."

Svetlana wiped away the tears with a tissue.

"So, you decided to move?" Jonny continued.

"It was my idea," she asserted. "I could see it was going to end very badly. I found another job here and told her we should move. She was already travelling all over the Czech Republic, but mostly to Prague, so it didn't matter where she lived. But, it had to be secret; her boyfriend could not know. These men follow women and keep trying to control them."

"What is his name?"

"Mikhail Antonov," she answered, venom in her voice. "He is based in Brno but works mostly in Prague and stays there at weekends. He's involved in some bad business. I don't know what, but definitely bad business."

"Do you have his mobile number?" Dvořáková interjected.

"Yes." Svetlana checked her phone and showed the number to Dvořáková, who wrote it in her notebook.

"Do you know where we will find him?" Jonny asked.

"I only know he works at a club in Prague called 'Passion.'"

"Thank you, that's helpful," he replied. "And, did Yulia have any trouble from him since you moved here?"

"No, I don't think so. Yulia was always worried, especially because she was working in Prague, but she hadn't seen him. He was calling her and sending her lots of messages during the first month, but then he stopped."

"When was the last time you saw Yulia?" Dvořáková asked.

"It was Thursday evening. She stayed in Prague on Wednesday night but came back to see me because she was planning to stay in Prague over the weekend."

"With Alex?"

"Yes."

"And, we understand you reported her missing to the police here in Hradec Králové?" Dvořáková queried.

"Yes, that's right," Svetlana confirmed. "It was strange she didn't reply to my messages over the weekend, but I just assumed she was having a good time. But, I knew something was wrong when I didn't hear from her on Monday."

"We also understand Yulia had recently lost a baby," Dvořáková stated.

Svetlana stared hard back at Dvořáková, then across the table at Jonny. "How do you know about that?"

"The pathologist who examined her body confirmed she had either lost a baby or had a termination," Dvořáková answered gently.

"In the week she found out she was pregnant, he had hit her badly – she had a lot of bruises. We talked it through and she wanted a termination. Maybe it was fate because she lost the baby anyway a few days later. It was sad, but probably the best thing. And, then she met Alex…"

"When did they meet?" Jonny asked.

"It was only in March, about three weeks ago."

"And, when did she lose the baby?" he followed up.

"It was in December last year. We moved here in January."

"When was the last time Yulia saw Mikhail?"

"I've already told you," Svetlana replied firmly. "She hadn't seen him since we moved here. She would have told me if she did."

"As far as you know, was Yulia in contact with anyone else in the Czech Republic? Perhaps a friend at work, or another man who was interested in her?"

"No. She knew a few women from the head office in Brno, but she kept her work and business life separate. She just wanted to develop a good career."

"Final question," Jonny stated. "Were there any problems with Yulia's family?"

Svetlana shook her head. "They are a good family, living a simple life. Yulia sent money home to her parents when she could, but there were no problems."

"Okay, thank you."

Svetlana took a new tissue from the box on the kitchen table.

"Do you think Mikhail killed Yulia?" she asked after composing herself.

"I'm sorry, we don't know yet," Jonny confirmed.

"I never met Alex," Svetlana confirmed, "but Yulia was so excited when she met him. I only hope she was happy at the end."

"Based on everything we know, I believe she was happy," Jonny answered.

"I remember her saying to me she'd met the man of her dreams," Svetlana reflected, breaking down into floods of tears.

22

Man's Best Friends

In order to maximise the use of time and fulfil their promise to Mikeš, Jonny and Dvořáková had jumped straight into the car and headed back to Prague. The gamble had paid off; the reducing traffic after the rush hour had allowed Dvořáková to put her foot down and they were approaching the city centre by nine thirty a.m.

Although meeting Svetlana Lebedev hadn't provided any brand new revelations regarding Yulia Ivanova, the background information on Mikhail Antonov and the context of his relationship with her had been invaluable; the violent relationship and pregnancy provided a possible motive, and his phone number and work location meant they could find him without delay.

A quick search of Yulia's bedroom had unveiled nothing surprising, but Jonny did find a scan photo from the miscarried pregnancy as well as doctor's letters following the operation. Svetlana had agreed for Jonny to borrow them as evidence, promising to return them at a later date. He wasn't an expert in medical matters, but he knew the doctor's contact details would help Dr Králová get to the truth about how the pregnancy ended, maybe even who the father was.

"I suppose the next step is to find Mikhail Antonov," Dvořáková said as they were speeding along the highway.

"Yes. Will you liaise with Marek?"

"Sure. Leave it with me. It'll be my first job when I get back to the station, assuming of course I don't get pulled into some urgent task."

Jonny laughed, remembering the desperate feeling of not being able to manage his own workload. Criminal investigations sounded easy; follow the leads and you discover the identity of the criminal and the motive for the crime – just like the TV shows. But real life puts obstacles in the way, the most common being the distractions of other cases. It was never linear – the interferences only served to distract attention and swallow time. He often imagined how powerful and efficient the police would be if one dedicated detective team could work each case without interruptions, but he knew this ideal would never be realised.

"The piece of information I most want to know," Jonny stated, "is whether Mikhail Antonov knew that Yulia was pregnant."

"You think it might be the key to the case?"

"I don't know. Looking at the dates on the scan and the doctor's letters, it seems Yulia was no more than ten or eleven weeks into her pregnancy when she lost the baby. But, maybe her boyfriend guessed; sometimes people can tell from changes in the body. Yulia might even have told him in a happy moment."

"I saw how scared Svetlana was when I asked her about Yulia's pregnancy."

"Yes, exactly," he concurred. "I was also surprised the boyfriend stopped contacting Yulia so easily after they moved away from Brno. If he is the bad character Svetlana says he is, I would have thought he'd try every avenue to track her down. And, if he knew about the pregnancy, it's hard to believe he'd leave her alone. Unless…"

"What?"

"Unless he did know everything and put together a plan to make her and her new boyfriend pay."

"There's a definite motive," she acknowledged.

"By the way, Lucie, I really liked the way you slipped the question about Yulia's pregnancy subtly into the conversation with Svetlana. It was perfect and got such a pure facial reaction. You are going to make a top detective."

Dvořáková looked across at him, unable to hide the pride in her smile. "Thank you, Honza. That means so much to me."

***

As they weaved through the inner city streets towards the centre, Jonny called Mikeš to announce their timely return and agree the day's schedule. Another interview with Torsten Lindberg was confirmed based upon the information provided by George Webb. Mikeš was also excited by the discovery of Mikhail Antonov's identity and contact details. Having agreed to meet Mikeš at Luka's café, Jonny stated he was first going to see Helena Corbetová and her mother.

Hopping out of the car near I. P. Pavlova, he immediately felt the effects of nearly three hours in the car. The overcast, showery weather wasn't helping; his back and legs ached from the humid air. He decided to address the creaks in his body the only way he knew how, setting off at pace on a power walk towards Helena's apartment.

The rolling hills across the middle of this famous city never failed to amaze him. As he cut his way down the slope towards the River Vltava, he had a view to the castle on the opposing hill, the dense, low-hanging cloud and the showery rain creating a dark and imposing image.

Jonny had attempted to call Kristýna Davies twice whilst in the car, but both calls had gone straight to voicemail. Knowing he ideally needed more ammunition to unsettle Daniela Nováková, he took out his mobile and tried again. He came to an abrupt stop in the small backstreet when the call was answered.

"Kristýna Davies."

"Hello, Ms Davies. My name is Jonathan Fox. I am a consultant working with the Czech Police."

A pause was followed by a tentative reply. "Hello, Mr Fox."

"Have you heard the terrible news about Alex Corbet?"

The line went silent.

"Ms Davies, I am sorry for the unannounced call, but there is currently no way to come to visit you in person; I am in Prague and you are in London."

"How did you get my number?"

"Alex Corbet was found dead, believed murdered, earlier this week. We have been, as you would expect, reviewing his belongings and also his mobile phone records."

"And?"

"Alex Corbet called your work number five times last week, between Monday fifth April and Thursday eighth April. We believe he was murdered on the Friday or the Saturday."

"I am sorry, but why are you telling me this? Are you implying that I am some way involved in his murder?"

"Ms Davies, this is a murder investigation. I have at this stage only a couple of simple questions for you. I am also not implying you are directly involved in any way. However, Alex called you five times in a similar number of days before he was murdered. And yours was the only non-Czech number he called in this period. I'm sure you can see that I need to clarify the position. So, if you will allow me to ask my questions, it will take just a few minutes of your time. However, if you are not willing—"

"What do you want to know?"

"Are you Alex Corbet's sister-in-law?"

"I suppose strictly, the answer is yes. But, since Alex left Helena, I don't respect the relationship between us any longer."

"I understand. Were you acting in a legal capacity for Alex?"

"No."

"So, why did he call you on five occasions last week?"

"He wanted to ask me some questions."

"About your sister?"

"Yes."

"Can I ask you to elaborate? It would really help our enquiries, putting some context to what was happening in Alex's life in the last few weeks."

"Mr Fox, this whole situation was Alex's fault. Nobody else's. He left Helena and the children, was having an affair with another woman, and—"

"Ms Davies—"

"I'm sorry, Mr Fox, that is all I can tell you. I have another meeting now so we will have to leave the matter there. Goodbye."

The call disconnected before he could phrase his next sentence. He smiled to himself, the conversation having gone almost exactly as he'd expected. Kristýna Davies was clearly assuming the family position, almost certainly directed by her mother. The only surprise to him was the blatant accusation of the affair against her brother-in-law. What evidence did the mother and her daughters have, he thought, to hold such a firm position when the information he'd gained suggested otherwise?

Timing it to perfection, Jonny arrived at Helena Corbetová's apartment less than two minutes later; not enough time for Kristýna Davies to call her mother or her sister. He couldn't be sure Daniela Nováková would have yet arrived, but knew she would imminently, assuming she followed the same schedule outlined during the interviews.

Helena was surprised to hear his voice when he announced himself over the intercom. She buzzed him into the building after a short, silent pause, probably used for a whispered consultation with her mother.

Jonny knew there was a risk Daniela Nováková would prevent any discussion at all, insisting their solicitor be present. But, he also knew Helena was keen to assist in getting to the truth, to find out who killed the man she still loved. On balance, he felt the risk was worth taking. The natural reaction on Daniela's face when he asked questions about her older daughter would tell him more than a hundred stifled answers to staged questions in formal interviews.

Daniela was waiting for him by the open apartment door when he reached the third floor.

"Dobrý den, Mrs Nováková," he opened brightly.

"Why are you bothering us again? My daughter is very upset."

"Mrs Nováková, some new information has just come to light and I need to ask you both about it."

"I really think I should call Pavel Rosický." Daniela stood firm, holding the door.

"Mrs Nováková, you and your daughter are not under any suspicion in the murder of Alex Corbet. But I need your help with the new information I have uncovered."

Jonny saw Helena walking briskly into the hall from the living room. "Mummy, let Mr Fox in. He is only trying to help...

Please."

After a few moments' silent consideration, her eyes boring holes into him, Daniela released the door and reluctantly beckoned Jonny in. "But, only five minutes, Mr Fox. My daughter is very tired."

"Thank you."

Jonny sat in the armchair indicated and waited whilst mother and daughter settled on the large sofa. He knew he was going to be asked to leave very quickly, so had his words carefully prepared.

"Helena, I have just spoken to your sister."

"Mr Fox!" Daniela roared. "Are you trying to persecute my family? I want you to leave. Now!"

Jonny turned to Helena with a warm, encouraging smile. "Helena, your husband called your sister five times last week. He called twice on Monday fifth April—"

"Mr Fox!"

"He called once more on both Tuesday sixth and Wednesday seventh, and then finally again on Thursday eighth. The initial calls were very short, but Alex spoke to Kristýna for over five minutes on the last two occasions."

Daniela was standing up now, but Jonny refused to move, his gaze fixed on Helena.

"Helena," Jonny persisted, "what did Alex want to talk to your sister about? It could really help us find who killed him—"

"Mr Fox," Daniela shouted loudly. "If you do not leave the apartment this very minute, I will be making a formal complaint against you."

Jonny slowly rose from his seat, all the time looking kindly towards Helena, attempting to silently convey his compassion.

Helena stayed in the living room as Daniela led him to the

apartment door. As they entered the hall, the mechanical sound of the door lock could be heard, turning from the outside. The door was opened by a stocky man with greying hair, impeccably attired in an olive linen suit, cream shirt and orange patterned tie, finished with a pair of dark brown brogues.

"Mr Fox was just leaving," Daniela stated bluntly, pulling the door fully open.

"Jonathan Fox." Jonny held out his hand in greeting.

"Jakub Novák," the man replied, shaking the outstretched hand.

Jonny looked down to see two small dogs circling his feet, both excitedly jumping up on their leads, keen to get further inside the apartment. He reached into his jacket pocket and pulled out the printed still photo from the CCTV recording, quickly comparing it to the scene before him. Man's best friends: one black dog, one white and grey dog, both Shih Tzu breed.

"Mr Novák, I think we need to interview you at the police station."

23

The Stand-off

Even the gloomy weather couldn't stop Jonny smiling all the way to the café. He couldn't stand someone taking an unnecessarily stoic position, which not just imposed on others, but also prevented a criminal investigation from running its course. Daniela Nováková was protecting people close to her, which was understandable on one level, but she was also impeding the search for the truth.

When he had identified Jakub Novák and his dogs from the CCTV image, Novák had accepted his fate with dignity; he'd not tried to reason, in fact he didn't present any argument against the request for a formal interview at the police station. Daniela, by comparison, became apoplectic. Her role as family guardian was threatened and she fought back, unable to accept the assertion that any member of her family could be involved in what had happened to Alex Corbet.

Jonny had simply asked that everyone take their seats, requesting calm, whilst he called Boukal. A police car had arrived within twenty minutes, Jakub Novák was whisked away to the station, leaving his faithful dogs in the care of his wife and step-daughter. Daniela's frantic calls to Pavel Rosický had only served to create a lot of noise and distraction but hadn't changed the course of events.

Whilst strolling along, enjoying his small but emphatic win, he sent another message to check-up on Ivana.

Hi. Are you okay? Any sightings of our mystery stalker? x

Although she had agreed to send him regular updates, he had pre-empted these with messages of his own. It was unusual for him to send so many, but he felt responsible and couldn't shake it off even if he wanted to – the welfare of those close to him would always be his number one priority.

Ivana's reply arrived just as he was entering the café.

Honza, that's five messages today already! Thank you for caring, but I am a big girl and can look after myself. See you later x

He smiled to himself, stepping into the café, greeting Luka and waving to Mikeš already seated at their usual table. Whilst Ivana would never give up her independence – the fiercely contested freedom to live her life the way she wanted – he also knew she was secretly enjoying him showing so much care. He just needed to know when to back off.

Mikeš looked as dapper as ever, wearing a purple shirt and tie combination to contrast his tweed suit. He laughed heartily, matching the exuberance of his dress sense, when Jonny conveyed the unexpected events of the meeting with Daniela Nováková. Despite their differences in character and style, their approach to policing was underpinned by their shared belief in honesty and justice.

"Honza, where is Jakub Novák now?"

"He's stewing in an interview room, waiting for us. Marek has the key."

Mikeš laughed again, enjoying the irony.

"But, what is this 'stewing?'"

"Felix, we need to start a book of English slang for you."

They both laughed.

"Do you really believe Jakub Novák had anything to do with the double murders?" Mikeš asked.

"I really don't know," Jonny replied, considering the option properly for the first time. "This case is wide open at the moment, anyone could have done it. There is definitely a family secret surrounding Helena. Maybe we just got lucky."

Luka approached the table with their ordered coffees. "You two seem very happy today."

"This man here," Mikeš began, indicating Jonny, "is a top detective. Certainly, the best I have ever worked with. He just seems to sense where to go next on a big case."

"Felix, we haven't solved anything yet," Jonny corrected him.

Mikeš smiled. "Yes, but we will, my friend, we will."

Luka hurried back to the counter and returned with a piece of paper in his hand. "Seeing as you are both in such a good mood, here is your unpaid bill for the last three weeks." Mikeš' face dropped. Jonny could only smirk at the perfect timing, reaching into his back pocket for his wallet and pulling out some Czech Koruna notes.

After a brief talk over their coffees, the relaxing calm before the next storm, Jonny brought the conversation back to the business of the day. "So, we have the interview with Jakub Novák next. Then Torsten Lindberg?"

"Yes. Marek has organised for Torsten to come to the police station for two thirty p.m."

"And, what about Mikhail Antonov?" Jonny questioned.

"I phoned him. He's on his way to Prague for work over the weekend. We will meet him at the club he works at later this afternoon."

"Passion?"

"Yes," Mikeš confirmed. "It was strange though, he seemed quite keen to talk to us."

Jonny lifted his coffee cup, gazing out of the café window onto the street. Cars and pedestrians passed by, the raindrops on the glass obscuring the images.

"At least we're starting to make some progress," he mused. "Hang on…"

"What is it, Honza?"

Jonny quickly turned his gaze away from the window, lowering his head to look down at the table. Careful to keep his eyes lowered, he scanned the café to see if any customers were watching them, then whispered to Mikeš. "Felix, the man that was following Ivana and me last night is on the opposite side of the street."

"Where?" Mikeš immediately craned his neck in an exaggerated fashion, pushing himself up in his seat to look around one of the wooden frames dividing the café's front glass window.

"Felix, sit down!" Jonny gasped. "Don't make it obvious, he'll see you."

Mikeš instantly twisted his head back to look directly at Jonny, their eyes locked in understanding, and lowered himself back into his chair. With careful moves, Mikeš leaned back into his cushioned seat to give himself a wider field of vision, and, appearing to look in a different direction, studied the scene across the street.

"I can't see his face because he's too far away," Mikeš started his analysis. "He's wearing a dark grey coat, like a mackintosh. Black hat, like mine, but not as wide. Quite tall, upright physique."

"That's him," Jonny confirmed, looking down. "What's he

doing?"

"He's leaning against a wall, smoking a cigarette. He's not directly opposite the café, one shop across. It doesn't look like he knows you are here. It's more like he is waiting for you to appear."

"So, he knows this is our regular meeting place," Jonny stated. "He's waiting to pick me up so he can follow me for the rest of the day."

Mikeš changed the angle of his head, making it appear as if he and Jonny were having a normal conversation. "Honza, go to the restrooms. Walk round the tables at the front of the café so he can see you. I will then be able to observe his reaction."

Jonny rose from his seat, made a fake hand gesture to Mikeš, and walked around the tables slowly, exaggerating his movements to draw the attention of anyone watching. He walked towards the counter, stood in front of the glass-fronted entrance door, and ordered two more coffees.

"Honza, you don't need to come over to order," Luka said, looking confused.

Jonny, his back to the door, raised an index finger to his lip, requesting silence and complicity, then proceeded to the restrooms. Thinking it was a game, well used to the duo's eccentric behaviour, Luka just shook his head and continued on with his duties.

"What did he do?" Jonny asked when back in his seat.

"He first saw you when you were standing at the counter. He quickly put out his cigarette and retreated to the left. He's now out of sight, probably waiting for you to come out of the café. But, he definitely recognised you. His demeanour changed as soon as he saw you."

Jonny took a sip of their newly delivered coffees. "We need

to agree a location where the entrances are concealed," Jonny proposed. "I can then lead him on a merry dance and you can approach us discreetly from the opposite direction. Somewhere we can trap him, somewhere with no escape."

Mikeš rubbed his chin, deep in thought. "I know," he finally exclaimed. "Týnská."

"Where?"

"You know where it is, Honza, but maybe you don't remember the name of the street. On Old Town Square, take the pedestrian exit off the square to the left of the Gothic church—"

"Yes, I know the plaza through there. There's an Irish bar and a few restaurants."

"Exactly. But, don't go through the arched entrance to the plaza. Instead, just before it takes the small street to the left, called Týnská. You go through a walkway under an old building overhead. The street is narrow with no exits, but it connects through to the main road behind the square. If I leave first, I can hide behind the archway and then follow him down Týnská after you have both passed through. If you stop and turn after thirty metres or so, we will have him trapped. And, he won't be expecting it."

After synchronising their watches, Mikeš left the café first, turning right to take the long route and avoid unnecessary interest.

Jonny finished his coffee, giving Mikeš a five minute head start.

"What was that about earlier?" Luka quizzed Jonny when he was leaving the café.

"I'm sorry, I can't talk now," Jonny replied, "but hopefully we'll have a funny story to tell you tomorrow." He quickly exited the café, leaving Luka looking bewildered.

Outside, he stopped on the pavement to check his phone and glance at his watch, keen to give the impression of being preoccupied. He then set off on the pre-agreed route towards Old Town Square. Careful not to look behind him or show any sign of being followed, he joined the throng of tourists heading towards the square. Acting as he usually would, he stopped on the square to scan the exquisite architecture, as he did every day. Hordes of visitors were swelling around the astronomical clock, ready for the hourly chime, the only difference to a normal sightseeing day being the abundance of umbrellas and plastic macs in the crowd due to the inclement weather.

After faking a quick phone call, he set off directly across the square, attempting to look like he had a destination in mind. On Týn, the cobbled street closed in, only a few small bars and restaurants breaking up the monotony of doorways leading to small businesses. He showed no hesitation at the archway, leaning left into Týnská, under the overhanging building, into the narrow, cobbled backstreet. There was no way to check the man was behind him, but that was the beauty of the plan. Not slowing his pace, he appeared as if he was using the street as a shortcut, connecting through to the main road running behind.

Týnská was empty, only a few pedestrians visible in the distance. The backstreet housed mostly specialist, second-hand hobby or antique shops, only attracting collectors in search of a bargain or tourists wanting to enjoy a quiet walk down memory lane.

After walking twenty paces down the middle of the narrow street, Jonny heard footsteps behind him. The echo of leather soles on stone was clear and distinctive. Keen not to give the game away, he kept his focus on the street straight ahead. The steps behind him continued to match his own: left, right, left, right.

Jonny stopped and abruptly turned on his heel. The hatted stranger in the long coat stopped as well, lowering his head so the brim of his hat covered his face. The man smoothly adjusted his body position, appearing to have been drawn to the window of an antique book shop. Moving close-up to the glass window, he nonchalantly studied the shop window display.

Jonny saw Mikeš enter the street, through the passageway under the building. Mikeš stopped, blocking any exit with his feet planted wide and braced with his cane between his two hands. The plan had worked to perfection – the unknown man was trapped.

"Dobrý den," Jonny shouted.

The man ignored him, continuing to study the books through the glass. He looked like a book enthusiast, no hint at all that he'd just been caught red-handed following someone. At that instant, Jonny knew he was a professional; the moves so smooth from years of experience, perfect for not drawing attention to himself and achieving anonymity in a crowd of people.

"Dobrý den," Jonny shouted again.

No reaction.

"Dobrý den!" This time the greeting was shouted by Mikeš from behind the man.

The stranger's composure was broken. Not expecting the call from behind, he quickly turned away from the shop window, jerking his head sideways to look back towards the passageway.

The stand-off was complete. The man, face still concealed by the hat, looked towards Mikeš. Then he turned his head slowly to gaze at Jonny, clearly contemplating his options. Mikeš was grinning, cat-like, enjoying the drama.

Jonny proceeded to slowly walk towards the stranger – slow,

steady steps forward. But, instead of facing him as he approached, the man twisted around to face Mikeš. With smooth movements, he slowly raised his hand and tipped his hat in respect at the famous Czech detective.

"Ahoj, Felix. Jak se máš?"

24

Second-Rate Hack

The tension had dissipated immediately once Mikeš had recognised his ex-colleague. Jonny didn't understand the Czech spoken in their greeting, as they shook hands vigorously, but relaxed knowing the mystery of why he'd been trailed would be revealed in time.

Seeing Jonny looking bemused, Mikeš led the introductions. "Honza, this is Petr Řepka. He used to work for me – one of my best detectives."

Řepka removed his hat and extended his hand in greeting. He was of a similar age to Mikeš, close to or just post-retirement; his deep-lined face, tired eyes and thinning hairline told the story of a hard fought police career with some troubled times. His blood tinged eyeballs and rosy cheeks hinted at an excessive drinking habit.

"Why are you called Honza?" Řepka asked.

"That was Felix's fault," Jonny explained. "My name is Jonathan Fox, but he christened me Honza within thirty minutes of meeting me."

"Sounds likes Felix." Řepka laughed. "Anyway, great to meet you. Felix was my favourite boss. Working with him was so enjoyable. The old days in the police were fun, but everything's changed now."

"Top guy," Mikeš added to support the claim, slapping

Řepka on the shoulder. Jonny knew Mikeš well enough already to trust his judgement about people, but something didn't feel quite right. Mikeš' brief but telling glance at him told Jonny all he needed to know – another promising career ruined by the booze.

Jonny knew the type. Whisky was the police officer's traditional tipple of choice, a bottle often hidden away at the back of the drawer. The new approach to policing had challenged this old fashioned approach head-on in the 1990s, and Jonny himself had faced a difficult but worthwhile choice. He could remember clearly the day his boss, also his commanding officer at the time, had brought out two crystal glasses and a bottle of malt whisky for a mid-afternoon meeting. He had been so tempted, but ultimately refused, asking for a glass of water instead. The months after had been difficult, feeling shunned from group discussions. But, he'd been proved right; within a year he'd been promoted to a higher rank and his commanding officer and other old-school colleagues, unwilling to ditch their old habits, had been forced into early retirement.

Even Jonny's Czech was good enough to translate Řepka's suggestion of decamping to a local pub to explain the situation. Seeing the time was only eleven thirty a.m. Mikeš wisely guided his ex-colleague towards the police station where they could talk over a sobering cup of coffee. Jonny followed discreetly behind, allowing the old friends to catch up. He knew Mikeš would tell him the full story later, but he already expected a tale of indiscretion; a misjudgement forcing Řepka to resign and take the closest, but ultimately unsatisfying, career of a second-rate hack, running around the city following people and producing lurid shots of unfaithful spouses.

Back at the station, Mikeš guided Řepka directly up the stairs once they were past reception. On the second floor, he showed Řepka into a free interview room at the end of the corridor. Despite Mikeš' attempt at confidentiality, avoiding walking through the detective team in the open plan office, Řepka had still been recognised by a few of the older officers whose careers had spanned the past few decades.

Seated in the room with coffees on the table, Mikeš set the tone for the meeting. "Petr, I've decided we'll start this with an off-the-record chat."

Mikeš turned to Jonny. "Is that acceptable to you, Honza?"

"Yes," Jonny concurred. "But, if something comes out of the conversation which has an influence on the case, we will need to make it formal: either a statement or a recorded interview."

"There won't be," Řepka assured them.

"We'll be the judge of that," Jonny asserted. "We have a double murder to solve."

"I respect what you say," Řepka stated for the record. "But, I was just undertaking a job somebody had paid me to do."

"And, Petr, I assume you are happy to talk in English?" Mikeš asked. "It will help Honza."

Řepka nodded, taking a sip of his coffee.

Jonny's initial judgement was that Řepka was once suave and debonair, from a privileged background, quite the ladies' man. He had probably found life easy, always able to use his charm or someone he knew to get him out of a tight spot. Mikeš had only had time to whisper two rushed words to Jonny on the stairs, "sexual harassment" being clear enough and fitting with the profile. Řepka had probably tried it on with a young, female witness or a member of staff, expecting to get away with it as he had many times before. But, instead the changing times had imprisoned him in a complaint, disciplinary case and then dismissal or forced resignation – a hard fall and the end of a promising career. And, if first impressions were to be believed, the harsh lesson had not altered his carefree approach to life.

"Can you please tell us about the job you were undertaking and who hired you?" Jonny began.

"Of course I will tell you, but normally the information you want would be covered by client confidentiality," Řepka replied. "I need your word that you will not reveal me as your source. If word gets out that I've provided the police with information without consulting my client first, there's a big likelihood I'll never work in this city again."

"You have my word," Mikeš assured him. "If we need to formalise this, I will organise a warrant to protect you. More paperwork, but I will do it."

"Děkuju." Řepka paused to take another sip of his beverage, clearly forming the story in his head. "I do a lot of work for solicitors, as you probably expect. Usually my role is to catch people in the act, so to speak, to provide evidence to smooth divorce petitions or settle post-divorce monetary disagreements. One of my best clients—"

"Who?" Jonny pressed.

"Pavel Rosický."

Jonny and Mikeš shared an interested look.

"He's a sleazebag in my opinion," Řepka continued, "but he pays well. He contacted me back in February and gave me a job to find out information about Alex Corbet."

"What did he want to know?" Jonny probed.

"I'm getting to that, hang on." Řepka took another sip. "Alex and his wife, Helena, had separated late last year. I was told there had initially been the chance of a reconciliation, but the relationship broke down completely when Alex started talking about filing for custody of the children."

"Custody?" Jonny looked amazed. "He lived in a dump."

"Yes, I know. I was surprised as well. I asked more questions to get some background for the case, but Helena's mother, Daniela, was adamant that I didn't need to know anything more. I just had to get some dirt on Alex so they could use it to block any move by him or have it up their sleeve to use later in defence of any legal action he took."

"You're a good investigator, Petr." Mikeš prepared the ground. "What was your instinct telling you?"

"I don't know the cause of the marital problem, but I got the strong feeling there was some disagreement about Helena. The mother was protecting her and it caused an issue with Alex. The strange part was that the mother was in a big rush to get information on Alex. Rosický was putting me under pressure, but I couldn't work out why."

"Can you explain the work you did and what you found out?" Jonny encouraged.

"Initially, I just followed Alex: from his apartment to work, sometimes out at lunchtimes, back home, maybe out meeting friends. And, of course, to the pub quiz. I tracked him for two weeks but discovered nothing untoward. He didn't seem to have another girlfriend and he never brought anyone back to his apartment. I also attended the pub quiz once, but Alex wasn't interested in any other woman there, only the quiz itself. Changing tack, I started rifling through his rubbish. I waited to try to catch him putting a bag of rubbish in the trolley bin on the day the bins were being collected. I even got inside his building one time to rifle through the rubbish bins. Again, nothing. Finally, I started to talk to his friends at work and also at the pub close to the office. This is what led me to Tanya Murray."

"What did you find out?" Mikeš urged.

"I was having a cigarette outside the pub where many of the staff go for a drink on Friday evenings. One guy was quite drunk and started talking; it didn't take much to open him up. The rumour going around the company was that Alex and Tanya Murray were starting a relationship, having kissed at the Christmas party. It was the luck I needed. The next week or so were focused on finding out about Tanya and getting some photos. But, all I could get were shots of them having lunch together in the company canteen. I thought I was onto something when they left the office together one day, but they just went for a drink local to the office. She was always quite tactile, putting her hands on him a lot, but Alex didn't reciprocate. No kiss, no night out in the centre of Prague, no nights of passion. Nothing."

"All this match what Tanya told us," Jonny reconfirmed to Mikeš.

"I showed the photos of Alex and Tanya together to Rosický and Daniela Nováková. I also explained that, from what I had observed, there was no ongoing relationship between them. Daniela wouldn't listen to me, though. She took the news of the rumour and the photos as confirmation of an affair and pushed me to find out something incriminating about the two of them. Over the following days, I traced Tanya as much as I could, and kept following Alex and poking around. But, if there was any evidence of a relationship or a previous affair, I couldn't find it."

"Was Helena with you when you presented the information you'd found to Pavel Rosický?" Jonny asked.

"No. The meetings were always at Rosický's office, and Daniela Nováková was the only other person present."

"So, that's why Helena was so convinced Alex was having an affair with Tanya Murray," Jonny stated. "Daniela convinced her daughter about the affair, trying to turn her against Alex. It was all part of Daniela's plan to split them up forever."

"I had started to give up," Řepka continued, "but Rosický was still paying me. So, I went to Alex's office last Friday and saw him leaving with a different young woman, someone I hadn't seen before. I knew straight away there was something between them. It was the smiles they were exchanging as they walked, the anticipation of what was to come. Once you've seen it before, you recognise it instantly. I followed them all the way to Alex's apartment, then to a restaurant, before they went to the Červený lev pub."

"Petr, why didn't you come forward with this information before?" Mikeš asked, exasperated at his former colleague's behaviour.

"Because I didn't see anything," Řepka pleaded. "I went into the pub across the street to wait. I bumped into some old mates and completely lost track of the time, had too many whiskies. By the time I came out they had left the Červený lev pub. It was just before midnight, maybe eleven forty-five p.m. or eleven fifty p.m. I went into the pub to check, but they were starting to close up; Alex and the woman had definitely gone. I hurried off in the direction of Alex's apartment but didn't see them. In fact, I saw nobody suspicious, just a few drunk people. And, then I saw the news..."

"Have you briefed Daniela Nováková yet?" Jonny queried.

"No. I wanted to be sure of my facts. All I had were a few photos of the young woman with Alex. I don't even know her name. I went back to the pub over the weekend and discreetly asked a few people, but nobody knew who she was. Plus, you haven't yet released her name to the media." Řepka paused. "I suppose..."

"Yes?" Mikeš encouraged.

"I suppose I saw the opportunity to make a name for myself. I thought if I could find out who she was before the press released it, Rosický would be impressed and maybe it would lead to more work for me."

"So, you followed me to try to find out her identity?" Jonny clarified.

"Yes. In hindsight, it was a stupid plan. Especially with your reputation."

Jonny ignored the compliment, pondering the situation and his next move. "When you hurried back to Alex's apartment, did you see any building contractors? Someone wearing a fluorescent vest?"

Řepka finished his coffee, taking time to reflect. "Yes, I did. I remember seeing a building contractor on the way to Alex Corbet's apartment. It was quite late so I remember thinking it was a bit odd."

"That's very interesting," Jonny stated, glancing at Mikeš.

"He was quite tall and well-built, but I didn't see his face," Řepka continued. "Under the fluorescent vest he was wearing a black, plain jacket and had a black cap on. He walked past me as I rushed to the apartment."

"Did you see anything else suspicious?" Jonny questioned firmly. "Maybe blood on the floor? Even someone laying on the floor?"

"No, nothing," Řepka confirmed. "I would have come straight to the police if I'd seen anything like that."

"My friend," Mikeš began solemnly, "I believe we now need to make this a formal statement. We need a detailed description of the man. We also need the location of where you believe you saw this workman. And, we need all the photos and notes you have from last Friday. I will prepare the police documentation to cover you as the source of the information and I will not share it with Pavel Rosický unless I am forced to."

"I understand. Thank you."

The room went silent in contemplation.

"There's one more thing," Řepka added, the others watching him intently across the table. "Whilst I have been doing this work, I've had the strong sense I was being followed myself. I never caught anyone, and it wasn't every day, but I had a strong feeling about it. Like Honza, I think an experienced policeman knows if they are being followed."

"Why would someone follow you?" Mikeš asked.

"I've thought about it myself. The only conclusion I came to was that someone wanted to find out the same information I was looking for." Řepka shrugged his shoulders in defeat, demonstrating he was out of information.

Jonny and Mikeš rose from their chairs.

"One of my younger detectives will come in soon, to get a statement and collect the other details we need," Mikeš stated, opening the door.

Jonny stopped at the door. He turned to face Řepka, who was still seated at the interview table, looking lonely and tired. "By the way, we know that the young woman had stayed at Alex's apartment before last Friday. You must have missed her."

"What can I say?" Řepka replied slowly. "It must have been one of my heavier nights."

25

Interview – Jakub Novák

The following is the transcript of the recorded interview conducted on the afternoon of Friday, sixteenth April 2010.

Present at the interview were Chief Warrant Officer Felix Mikeš (FM), Chief Sergeant Marek Boukal (MB), Consultant Jonathan Fox (JF) and the family solicitor, Pavel Rosický (PR).

The interviews were conducted in Czech at the request of the interviewee. This version of the transcript has been translated into English.

JF attended the interview in his role as consultant to the Czech Police. Because he does not speak fluent Czech, the interview was stopped a few times whilst the questions and/or answers were translated into English for him by FM. These parts of the interview are indicated for clarity.

MB: Interview commenced at 12.56. Please state your name for the record.

JN: Jakub Novák.

MB: Mr Novák, thank you for agreeing to come into the police station promptly. As Mr Jonathan Fox informed you when you met this morning at the apartment of Helena Corbetová, you have been identified on the CCTV recordings last Friday, ninth April 2010, meeting Alex Corbet on the street near to the point where he was subsequently found murdered.

PR: Before we begin, I would like to have it clarified if you are raising any charges against my client. If so, you should clearly outline what they are now, before we continue further.

FM: As you well know, Pavel, we have found some evidence that needs to be explained. At this point, we just want to ask Mr Novák some questions to explain his role in what we have found. This is a perfectly normal process, certainly in such a serious matter as a murder investigation. A double murder, in fact. Depending on his answers, and our further investigations, we may charge your client. If we do, you will be the first person to hear about it.

MB: Can we start by asking you to explain your movements last Friday evening, ninth April?

JN: I closed up the shop about 19.00 and drove to Helena's apartment in Prague 2. My wife, Daniela (Nováková), was there, as well as Helena and her two children. We had a quiet evening: dinner followed by watching the TV. Daniela is very dedicated to her family and has been spending a lot of time at the apartment, supporting her daughter through a difficult time. We often stay the whole evening, but usually leave by 23.00. On this evening, Helena was more upset than normal and Daniela wanted to stay later, until Helena went to bed. When Daniela told me, I decided to take the dogs out for a walk.

MB: For the purposes of the tape, I am now showing Mr Jakub Novák numerous still photos taken from the CCTV recording on the route from the Červený lev pub to Alex's apartment. The photos show various points in a five-minute exchange, starting at 23.27, between Mr Novák and Alex. The identity of the woman in the photos has been confirmed by the police; she spent all evening with Alex.

PR: Can you please clarify the identity of the woman?

FM: No. We can confirm that the woman was found murdered with Alex. However, her body is still to be formally identified so we cannot release her name yet.

MB: Mr Novák, can you explain in detail exactly where you walked on leaving Helena's apartment, up until you met with Alex and the woman?

PR: My client would like to make it clear from the outset that he did not plan, nor have any intention, of meeting Alex Corbet on the walk.

FM: Mr Novák?

JN: I have no particular route for walking my dogs when we are staying at Helena's apartment. I do, however, know the area of Prague 2 reasonably well now. We usually just start walking, turning left or right as I wish, roughly walking in a rectangular shape, eventually bringing us back to the apartment. The same was true last Friday.

MB: Just to clarify, when you say 'we' or 'us,' you are referring just to you and your dogs?

JN: Correct. I always walk the dogs alone. [Pause] On the evening in question, we left the apartment at about 23.15.

MB: Are you sure about the time?

JN: Yes. We had just finished watching a TV programme that finished at 23.00. I expected Daniela and I would leave then, but Helena was very upset. The dogs needed to go out and I needed to stretch my legs, so I suggested I go for a walk whilst Daniela sorted out the situation. By the time I put my coat and shoes on, got the dogs ready, it must have been about 23.15, give or take a couple of minutes.

MB: Thank you.

JN: I remember we turned left, staying to the backstreets. Going right leads to the main road and there are often drunk people around on Friday or Saturday evening. The dogs don't like it. I chose a route around the quieter streets, not having anywhere particular in mind, only to get back to the apartment in about thirty minutes. The dogs don't like going out for long in the winter months, but they like a longer walk when the evening temperature is not too cold.

MB: Did you meet or notice anyone else on the walk, before you met Alex and the woman?

JN: If I remember right, we only met a gentleman I see often, maybe a couple of times a week. He also has a small dog, a Maltese variety, and the dogs all get on well. I stopped and talked to him.

MB: Do you know the man's name?

JN: Sorry, no. But, I can give you the name of the streets I usually see him in?

MB: That would be helpful to corroborate your story.

JN: But, other than this gentleman, I don't remember seeing anyone. Certainly not anyone I know or recognise. [Pause] Anyway, we were walking down the street Polní, nearly halfway through the walk. At the end of the street we bumped into Alex. And, as you say, he was with a woman whom I did not recognise.

MB: To clarify, for the purposes of the tape, the street Polní meets Sadová on the one-way road system. A right turn further down Sadová leads into the street Hluboká, where the murdered bodies were found. The distance between where the bodies were found and the point where Mr Novák met Alex and the woman is approximately two hundred metres.

PR: If you have a question for my client, ask it. But, please refrain from insinuating my client is linked in any way to the murders. I have already made it clear my client has nothing to do with the murders of Alex Corbet and the woman.

MB: Mr Novák, can you please take us through exactly what you remember of the conversation with Alex, from the initial greeting up until when you both departed the scene.

JN: It was dark, and my eyesight is not what it was, but my dogs were the first to recognise Alex. They always loved him, he was very attentive to them. The dogs started barking and we all stopped at the same time. After he stroked the dogs, we politely asked how each other was and he asked about my business. But, then the conversation stalled. I was expecting him to introduce the woman, but he didn't. She seemed a little embarrassed.

MB: Were you talking in English?

JN: Yes. Alex's Czech was passable, but we'd always talked in English.

MB: What happened next?

JN: Alex asked how Helena was, but to be honest I didn't like the tone of his question. He had obviously had a few drinks and he seemed to be implying something about my wife.

MB: What did he say?

JN: I cannot remember how he phrased the question, but he was questioning if Helena was bearing up under the strain of having to deal with her mother.

MB: What did you do?

JN: I got angry with him. I told him the situation was all his own fault: having the affair, leaving his wife and children, blaming my wife for everything, and then making a claim for the children.

FM: For the purposes of the tape, I will now take a few moments to consult with my consultant, Jonathan Fox.

[There was a short pause in the interview whilst FM briefed JF in English. A brief inaudible conversation followed.]

FM: Mr Novák, can you please confirm what you said to Alex Corbet about his claim on his children?

PR: This is highly irregular, and not relevant to this interview. Mr Fox should know better.

FM: Pavel, I asked the question, not Mr Fox. I would like an answer.

PR: How can you justify wanting to know this level of detail? My client cannot remember every word he said in a meeting on the street nearly a week ago now. He has already told you the subject headings of what he said.

[There was a short pause in the interview whilst FM briefed JF in English. An inaudible conversation followed lasting two minutes.]

FM: Mr Novák, you mentioned four subject headings, as Mr Rosický has labelled them, you raised with Alex Corbet when you got angry. The first was 'having the affair' – we know Helena believes this. The second was 'leaving his wife and children' – this is a fact. The third was 'blaming my wife for everything' – this is clearly a matter of conjecture we are not interested in at this stage. The fourth was 'making a claim for the children'. This last one has never been mentioned before by anyone in the family, in either formal interviews or informal conversations. So I repeat, Mr Novák, what did you say to Alex Corbet about his claim on his children?

PR: Jakub, I would advise you to say very little, or nothing, in response to this line of questioning.

[Long pause]

JN: All I know is what my wife has told me. Alex Corbet had threatened to claim for custody of the children and it was making

Helena and my wife both very upset.

FM: Why did Alex Corbet threaten this?

PR: That's enough. My client does not need to provide his opinion on why Alex Corbet did or said something. Move on.

[Long pause]

MB: What was Alex's reaction when you got angry and made these statements?

JN: He got angry himself and said some very bad things about my wife.

MB: What was your response?

JN: We both raised our voices, drowning each other out. The dogs started barking as well. The situation was going to get out of hand so I pulled back the dogs and returned up the street we had come from.

MB: What did the woman do during your exchange with Alex Corbet?

JN: She didn't say anything at all. She looked quite shocked.

MB: Did you follow the same route back to Helena's apartment?

JN: Approximately. I may have taken a slightly shorter route rather than follow the exact same streets.

MB: What time did you get back to the apartment?

JN: I don't recall exactly, but probably between 23.45 and 23.50. I walked quite fast back because I was still angry.

MB: Were Helena and your wife still at the apartment?

JN: Yes. Helena was in bed. My wife was tidying up the living room. We departed in the car about fifteen minutes later.

MB: So, about 00.05 or 00.10.

JN: Yes.

FM: And, what was your wife's reaction to your altercation with Alex Corbet?

JN: I did not tell her.

FM: Why not?

JN: She was very upset already. I realised that my actions, especially getting angry with Alex, were not appropriate. Nothing had happened other than a heated exchange of words, so I decided to keep it to myself.

MB: On your walk, both from and back to the apartment, did you see anyone suspicious?

JN: No, not that I remember.

MB: Did you see any of these people? For the purposes of the tape, I am showing Mr Novák a series of headshots of people we are interested to talk to in connection with the case.

[Pause]

JN: No, I do not remember seeing any of these people.

FM: Do you remember seeing any building contractors still working? Maybe a workman in a fluorescent vest completing some unfinished work?

JN: Yes, I did see a building contractor walking down the street. I remember the vest. I didn't think anything of it at the time because I know some of the streets in the area are undergoing work. Actually, thinking about it, maybe there was more than one contractor.

FM: Would you be able to give us a description of the person or persons you saw?

JN: I will try, but, as I said earlier, my eyesight is not great. I wear glasses at work and for watching television, but not when I am out walking the dogs.

MB: Mr Novák, after this interview we would like you to sit with one of our detectives and plot the route you took on the walk. We would also like you to give us as much information as you can remember about the building contractor or contractors you saw. Finally, we will need to take fingerprint and DNA samples. This is to rule you out of our enquiries, by comparing against evidence we have already gathered.

JN: That is fine.

FM: Pavel, we know from the CCTV recording that your client did not come into contact with Alex Corbet during the meeting on the street. My expectation is therefore that your client's DNA will not be found on the dead bodies. If this proves incorrect, we will definitely have further questions for your client.

PR: Felix, with due respect, my client has already voluntarily told you that Alex Corbet stroked both of his dogs. Seeing as Mr Novák will have been in regular contact with his dogs before the meeting you mention, I think it is highly likely his DNA will be found on Alex Corbet's body and also possibly on the woman's body.

[Pause]

MB: Thank you, Mr Novák. If we have any more questions we will be in contact with you over the next few days. Interview terminated at 13.37.

26

The Burden of a Detective

Mikeš stormed into the Incident Room, Jonny trailing behind him. Instead of sitting down, Mikeš continued pacing around, swinging his arms around in anguish and accidently knocking an empty mug off the table. Jonny stepped tentatively into the room and closed the door, keeping a safe distance from the whirlwind before him. He had not been able to understand the last exchange with Pavel Rosický during the interview, but Mikeš' blurted summary whilst descending the station's inner stairwell had been sufficient for him to understand his friend's rage.

There was no doubting it; Rosický was a good lawyer, even by the high legal standards Jonny had experienced in London. He was nevertheless also extremely annoying, his slick manner and whiny voice enough to get under any one's skin. His false smile at the end of each sentence also seemed to suggest anyone present was honoured to witness his wise words. Jonny didn't suffer fools gladly and was loathed to grant such a privilege to a man like Rosický.

Jonny couldn't stand it when talented people focused their skills and made money from the criminal world. It went against everything he believed in. He knew everyone had the right to a defence, being innocent until proven guilty, but people like Rosický got rich and built a prominent reputation by putting layer upon layer of obstruction in the way of justice. It was the permanent burden of a detective – only wanting simple answers to simple questions, but instead finding legal hindrances at every turn.

The only detail that Jonny and Rosický agreed on was Jakub Novák's innocence. Jonny's lack of involvement in the interview had allowed him to study Novák's body language and facial impressions, but nothing came across as either conceited or false. Likewise, Novák had answered questions directly – when allowed by his solicitor – rather than trying to evade the responsibility of explaining the reality of what had happened.

"That man is impossible," Mikeš thundered.

"Very true. But, he's probably right."

"What do you mean, Honza?"

"Well, I find it very hard to believe Jakub Novák was directly involved in the murder of Alex Corbet and Yulia Ivanova. Or, his wife, Daniela. And, definitely not Helena."

Mikeš huffed and puffed, still pacing the room, his frustrated anger impossible for him to hide.

"There is definitely motive there," Jonny continued, unabated. "Something significant has happened, enough to ruin a marriage and force Alex to raise the contentious subject of custody of their children. And, whatever it is has got Daniela worried enough to have him followed. But, would she organise for him to be murdered? No, I can't see it."

"So, we should let Jakub Novák go?" Mikeš asked, fearing his own rhetorical question.

"I don't think we could hold him even if we wanted to – Rosický would make sure of it."

"We are getting nowhere on this case," Mikeš retorted, banging the table.

"Felix, sit down," Jonny encouraged. "Let's wait for Marek

and Lucie, and then go through everything we have on the case. The murderer must have made a mistake. We've just got to find it."

Still riled and snarling like an imprisoned animal, Mikeš stood at the glass walls of the Incident Room, looking out into the open plan office. Any of the detective team watching the unfolding drama were quick to lower their gaze to their computer screens or paperwork, not wanting to be caught staring at the big boss.

"Where's Katka?" Mikeš pouted. "I'm starving."

As if on cue, Dvořáková came walking around the corner of the L-shaped office floor, carrying a pile of folders, followed earnestly by Katka. Mikeš was delighted, a wide smile breaking out on his face. Boukal could be seen about ten metres behind, scampering to catch up and not face accusations of being late for the meeting.

Katka was wearing her standard housecoat, slowly pushing her faithful trolley laden with refreshments: a flask of coffee, water, plates of sandwiches and fruit. "Ahoj, Felix. Ahoj, Honza." Katka beamed her normal, warm greeting. She wheeled the trolley into the room and diligently moved the food and drinks onto a table at the side of the meeting room.

"You really are my saviour, young Katka," Mikeš hollered, putting his arm around her and pulling her close. She smiled in return, understanding nothing of the spoken English other than the mention of her name. Shrugging her shoulders, she waved goodbye and wheeled her trolley out of the room and back across the floor.

"What a woman," Mikeš remarked. "She must be about seventy-five. Incredible for her age."

Boukal looked hungrily at the food but stood back

respectfully, allowing Mikeš and Jonny to load their plates. Boukal took a plate, ready to tuck in himself, when Mikeš clapped his hands to start the meeting. "Marek, let's get going. Take us all through where we are on this case."

Looking forlornly at the sandwiches, Boukal picked up the marker pen and stood in front of his audience at the Murder Board as they ate. "Right," he began, "Jakub Novák is now with one of the detectives providing all the information you requested in the interview."

"Be sure to get the DNA over to Dr Králová straight away," Mikeš stated. "She left me a message to say she's found some fibres with identifiable DNA buried with the victims. Her next task is to check the DNA she's found against the database and all the samples we've taken during the investigation. The fibres were in the surrounding soil so may not be connected, but if any matches with one of our potential suspects it will be hard for them to refute the evidence."

"Apart from the dogs," Jonny joked.

Mikeš shook his head, despondently. "Move on, Marek… Please."

Sensing a lull in the presentation, Dvořáková handed around a wad of papers, at the same time discreetly sliding a loaded plate of sandwiches across the table to Boukal. "The CCTV analysis has been completed for now," she began. "We all know about Jakub Novák, I only need to check his appearances on camera match with what he told you in the interview."

"I can give you the timings after this meeting," Boukal confirmed.

"The big news," she continued proudly, "is that we've found images of a building contractor on the CCTV around the assumed time of the murders. The same workman appears on a number of

CCTV cameras, and he fits with the description given to us by Petr Řepka: he is wearing a black jacket, black jeans, and a black cap, with a fluorescent vest over his jacket. Unfortunately, we haven't found an image good enough to clearly see his face, but he definitely seems to be Caucasian."

"Good to see Řepka's memory is still working enough," Jonny declared. "Maybe we have a breakthrough – a bit of luck at last."

"I am pleased for Petr," Mikeš said. "Honza, I know following you wasn't justified, but maybe he has unintentionally really helped with the investigation."

Jonny puckered his lip, unconvinced by the claim that one good deed might right a wrong. In his opinion, people should take full responsibility for all their decisions, an error of judgement and a good act being unrelated. But, Řepka wasn't his concern; he would probably never even see him again.

"We've also located recordings on the CCTV of Petr Řepka hurrying down the streets at the times he gave us," Dvořáková continued. "He walks all the way to Alex Corbet's apartment and then finally gives up and leaves. There are, however, no recognisable images of Torsten Lindberg on the CCTV for the evening. Unless, of course, he's the man posing as the building contractor."

"It could be him," Jonny suggested. "He is quite tall, but probably slimmer than the workman on the CCTV. I know we haven't met Mikhail Antonov yet, but do we know what he looks like?"

"We've checked his social media and there are a couple of photos in your pack," she answered. "He looks tall and broad, probably works out. But, it's hard to tell exactly how tall he is from the limited photos we have."

Silence descended as everyone looked between the photos of Torsten Lindberg and Mikhail Antonov, searching for clues to the identity of the building contractor, and presumed murderer.

"Jakub Novák didn't recognise the headshots of Petr Řepka or Torsten Lindberg in the interview," Mikeš stated. "Lucie, can you also check to see if he recognises the headshot of Mikhail Antonov."

"Yes, sir."

"Have you established the route the workman took?" Jonny asked.

"Yes, the route is also in your pack," Dvořáková replied. "You will see from a few of the photos that he walks around, looking like he is checking the trenches and the cabling. But, the CCTV is patchy and doesn't cover every angle of the streets. We can see Alex Corbet and Yulia Ivanova approaching, but then they disappear. The last sighting of them is 11.47 p.m., after meeting Jakub Novák, and they do not appear on the tape again. The workmen do appear before and then again after, the last sighting of him being twelve fifteen a.m. But, the workman and the murder victims are never seen together on CCTV, nor are there any images that look remotely like bodies being moved."

"The murderer must have either studied the position of the CCTV cameras or had inside knowledge," Jonny mumbled.

"This feels more and more like a professional job," Mikeš added.

Murmurings filled the room, even though Boukal had a mouth full of food; it was hard to disagree.

"The house-to-house search has unfortunately revealed nothing yet," Dvořáková proceeded, "although we only had a limited number of officers available last night. Nobody they spoke to remembers seeing a building contractor walking around the streets late at night, nor recalls seeing a discarded fluorescent vest. The officers also searched all around the burial site, approximately one hundred metres in each direction, and haven't found anywhere that could be used for storing the dead bodies. They also found no obvious traces of blood on the surrounding streets, although it has rained heavily a few times in the week since last Friday."

"That is odd," Mikeš stated loudly. "Where could they have been killed?"

"Yes, I agree," Jonny concurred. "I might take a look myself after we've been to see Mikhail Antonov." He paused to think. "Lucie, could you map out all the CCTV sightings for me. I'd like to know where on the nearby streets the workman and the victims are spotted and exactly what times."

"It will take an hour or so, but no problem."

"Thanks, Lucie," Jonny replied. "I know resource is tight at the moment but following the meetings with Torsten Lindberg and Mikhail Antonov we might also need to check the CCTV for the days before Friday. Maybe one of them can be spotted doing reconnaissance work in the days before the murders took place."

"It will take a lot of resources and we are quite stretched," Dvořáková declared.

Mikeš sighed loudly, leaving the open request hanging in the air.

"On a slightly different subject," Dvořáková continued, "Yulia Ivanova's body has now been formally identified. Her friend, Svetlana Lebedev, didn't want to do it, so her boss travelled up from his office base in Brno. We are making contact with the family in Russia, but I think we should now release her identity to the media."

"I've already approved a press release," Mikeš confirmed.

"Just let the Media Team know."

"Can you hold it back until five p.m.?" Jonny asked. "I don't want Mikhail Antonov to know before we speak to him."

"Sure, leave it with me," she agreed.

Boukal had finished eating and was scribbling the updates on the whiteboard. "We've checked all the handwriting samples," he informed his seated audience. "The warning note Alex Corbet received, the one that was also stolen, was written in capital letters so it is hard to match. The external graphologist we use unfortunately cannot find anything to link any of the samples with the photo Honza took."

"Who provided handwriting samples?" Mikeš asked.

"Helena Corbetová and her mother," Boukal confirmed. "Also, George and Zuzana, Tanya Murray, and all the staff in Alex's IT Department have provided a sample, including Torsten Lindberg. Plus, now we also have the handwriting of Jakub Novák from the form he filled in when he was booked in at the police station earlier."

Mikeš sighed heavily and shook his head.

"There is only one more bit of information from me," Boukal added quickly. "Alex Corbet's parents are flying to Prague tomorrow. We obviously had to inform them, with the help of the UK Police. The mother was initially distraught and collapsed; Alex was their only child. But, I found out about an hour ago that they are getting the early flight tomorrow morning."

"We should talk to them," Jonny stated. "I'm still not sure how it all fits together, but they will hopefully be able to give us more information about the background to Alex and Helena's marriage."

"Right, anything else?" Mikeš asked.

Jonny paused, and flicked through his notepad, looking for

the relevant page. "Yes," he said to himself, before turning to address Mikeš. "I think we should also raise a warrant for Pavel Rosický to give us all the information he has about Alex Corbet, including a copy of the joint will he shared with Helena. I'm sure Rosický will try to resist the warrant because Helena and her mother are also his clients, but we could ask for redacted copies of the will and his client notes. I'm sure the courts will agree to the request because of the seriousness of the crime and the fact that Alex went to see Rosický in the week before he was murdered. It might not tell us much, especially about the custody of the children, but it's worth a try. It will also cause Rosický a lot of stress."

Mikeš' mood suddenly changed, a wide grin spreading across his face. "Honza, you're a genius. I love the idea!"

27

Interview 2 – Torsten Lindberg

The following is the transcript of the recorded interview conducted on the afternoon of Friday, sixteenth April 2010.

Present at the interview were Chief Warrant Officer Felix Mikeš (FM), Chief Sergeant Marek Boukal (MB) and Consultant Jonathan Fox (JF).

MB: Interview commenced at 14.37. Please state your name for the record.

TL: Torsten Lindberg. Can I ask why I have been asked in for another interview? I had absolutely nothing to do with Alex Corbet's murder. You should be looking at other people, not—

FM: Mr Lindberg, please calm down.

TL: Well, people at work, including my senior management, now think I had something to do with it.

FM: Calm down first. Then we will explain.

[Long pause]

MB: Let me start again. We have asked you to come in today because we have uncovered new evidence. We need to ask you some questions because this evidence appears to contradict what you told us in the interview yesterday.

TL: What evidence?

MB: We will come to that. Before we do, I want to state for the record that you are not being charged with any offence at this time. These questions are to establish the truth and, hopefully, to eliminate you from our enquiries. You are fully entitled to legal representation at any time. If you want a state-appointed solicitor we can arrange this.

TL: I understand, but why wasn't I told about this new evidence before the interview?

MB: Mr Lindberg, we have no obligation to tell you about the evidence beforehand. The purpose of this interview, as I have already stated, is to ask you some questions about what we have found and establish the true facts.

JF: Torsten... sorry, is it still okay to use your first name?

TL: Yes.

JF: Thanks. Torsten, I would like to start by asking you to first clarify what you told us yesterday—

TL: Clarify what? I told you everything yesterday.

JF: Please let me finish. We know you were Alex's boss from September last year when you were successful with the promotion. You have already told us you and Alex had a close working relationship but were also friends. You had even met his wife, although not many times. I would like you to tell us again when and where you have met with Alex since the start of this year?

TL: I told you yesterday, I met with Alex regularly. Obviously, he now works for me and so we had lots of meetings in an official business capacity. These were almost daily and always in the office. But, I also considered us to be friends, and so occasionally we met socially, either in the canteen for a coffee or lunch, or sometimes outside the office.

JF: Where did you meet outside of the office?

TL: Only local to the office, in Chodov. There's a coffee bar in the shopping centre. Or, sometimes for a beer after work at the local pub which people from the office go to. I haven't met him anywhere else for a long time.

JF: How many times did you meet Alex this year at either the coffee bar or pub?

TL: I don't know. Not many.

JF: Can you be more specific?

TL: I'm sorry, I can't remember exactly. Not many, maybe two or three times.

[Pause]

JF: Let's move on. In the process of this investigation we have spoken with many people, as you would expect. One of these people has told us you came into the centre of Prague last Thursday, the night before Alex disappeared. On this night, you were seen going into the Červený lev pub in Prague 2 before the pub quiz and you spoke to Alex. The witness claims you asked to speak to him alone, but Alex refused.

TL: So what?

JF: Torsten, this is a serious matter. We are investigating a murder. I would suggest you are not so flippant in your responses.

[Pause]

JF: In the interview yesterday, I asked you how often you met Alex socially. Your answer, and I quote, was 'More recently we mostly met up near work, either at lunchtimes or for a quick drink after work. I live in Chodov so it makes more sense than travelling into the city centre'.

[Pause]

JF: The witness also told us you had asked Alex to meet you outside of work on numerous occasions over the past few weeks. The actual word they used was 'pestered'.

TL: What evidence do you have?

JF: I am asking the questions, Torsten. Did you travel to the city centre to try to talk to Alex last week, on the evening of Thursday, eighth April?

TL: Yes, but I didn't meet with him.

JF: You went into the Červený lev pub and spoke to him?

TL: Yes, but we didn't sit down and talk. I asked him a question, he didn't want to talk, so I left the pub.

JF: You are playing a game of words with me, Torsten. If you don't start helping with this investigation, we will consider charging you with obstructing the course of justice.

FM: Mr Lindberg, we have had a busy couple of days on this investigation. You are annoying me now. If you do not start answering our questions honestly, I will suggest charges are brought against you.

[Long pause]

JF: Torsten, do we have your agreement? [Pause] If you are innocent, prove it by helping us with our enquiries.

TL: [inaudible]

MB: Mr Lindberg, can you repeat what you just said for the tape.

TL: I said, yes.

JF: Do you want to know what I think, Torsten? This issue of the live system error caused a big issue between you and Alex. To the point where the relationship between the two of you had broken down. Alex probably fulfilled his work obligations by meeting with you whenever it was requested of him. But, I think he flatly refused to meet you privately to discuss how to resolve the outstanding issue, especially the apportionment of blame for the system problem. My guess is, other than work meetings in the office, you did not meet with Alex socially at all this year. Am I right?

[Pause]

TL: Yes.

JF: Good, now we are getting somewhere. So, next question, did you go to the pub quiz on Thursday and try to meet with Alex?

TL: Yes.

JF: At this point, I need you to say more than just 'yes'. If you want to clear your name, you are going to have to describe in detail what happened. So, you had tried unsuccessfully to get Alex to agree to meet you in the few weeks before?

TL: Yes. Alex would come to team meetings with other staff, but he would not attend any meetings with just me and him present. I tried booking a formal meeting through the work calendar system, but he didn't turn up. He sent me an email on second April; in it he explained he was considering his options, and until he had decided his course of action he believed it was best for both of us if we did not meet.

JF: And, you took advice on this from HR?

TL: No. I was under pressure from senior management to close the matter. Every week in the one-to-one meeting with my line manager, he asked me where my report was. He wanted clarity on what had happened, who was to blame and what mitigating actions I had implemented to make sure it would never happen again. I don't think HR were aware of the situation. I was finding it increasingly stressful, but Alex would not talk to me.

JF: I assume Alex claimed he had evidence that you were at fault for the system error?

TL: Yes. But, it would ruin my career. I pleaded with him for his help, hoping we could come to some compromise for the sake of the whole department.

JF: Why didn't you just say the cause of the problem was complex and your findings meant that blame could not be attributed to any one person?

TL: I'd already tried that. The company board had already labelled it 'the worst system outage in the company's history' and wanted to be able to report that appropriate action had been taken against the staff responsible. It was a key outstanding audit point and it needed to be closed off. My line manager had already wiped his hands of responsibility, so if the matter wasn't resolved to the board's satisfaction, I was most likely going to take the full blame as manager of the System Development department.

JF: We are not interested in whose fault it was, we are only interested in finding out who murdered Alex and the woman with him last Friday. But, a straight answer please to a straight question. Was the system problem your fault or his? If Alex was innocent, this information will go no further than this interview room.

[Pause]

TL: It was my fault. The system development issues went back to decisions I made in my former role before the promotion.

JF: Thank you. Honesty is always the best policy.

FM: Was Alex trying to blackmail you?

TL: No, it was nothing like that. He said he just wanted the truth to be known.

FM: But, this matter will be easier to close now, won't it?

TL: I can't believe you just said that.

FM: Well, it's true, isn't it?

TL: That hadn't even crossed my mind.

JF: Torsten, you can see why we are concerned. There appears to be clear motive, even if you claim you had nothing to do with Alex's murder. We need you to tell us exactly what happened last Thursday, the night of the pub quiz.

TL: That particular day had been stressful. I had tried numerous times to speak to Alex, but he had avoided me. I even called him from my office on the internal telephone system, but he refused to pick up. We work flexi-time and, as usual, he left early on the night of the pub quiz, about 16.30. I was left in the office feeling desperate. I called my wife, Kerstin (Lindberg), and we talked through the situation. She suggested I go to the pub quiz. She thought Alex would appreciate the effort I'd made, maybe I could even join his quiz team.

JF: But, it didn't work out as planned?

TL: No. I got there before the quiz started and approached him, but he didn't want to speak to me. I offered to join his team, but he also refused. He got quite animated, saying the pub quiz was one of his few pleasures in life and I had no right to intrude. He didn't exactly threaten me, but he made it clear he'd ask the manager to eject me if I stayed. Alex walked away and I appealed to George (Webb) who was standing close by. George just shrugged and walked away. I had no option but to leave the pub. I called Kerstin outside, but we agreed there was nothing else I could do. I went to the pub across the street for a quick beer because I was feeling low. Then I walked to the I. P. Pavlova metro station and travelled back to Chodov.

MB: Can you confirm the times please?

TL: The pub quiz starts at 20.30. I must have got there about forty-five minutes before, so about 19.45. I got on the metro about one hour later, say 20.45.

JF: We have CCTV footage from around the city area so we can easily check.

TL: What I have told you is correct.

JF: And, what did you do on Friday?

TL: It was again a difficult day at work. I tried talking to Alex all day, but he just blanked me. I wrote a long email explaining the situation and then called him, but he didn't respond. I even approached his desk in the morning and asked him if he wanted to grab a sandwich, but he told me he was going for lunch with Yulia (Ivanova). I gave up trying to talk to him in the afternoon. I thought I'd wait until the following week. Alex and Yulia left together at the end of the day. It looked like they were going on a date because she had an overnight bag with her. And, that was the last time I saw him.

JF: Hang on, when we spoke yesterday you gave us the impression you didn't really know the woman from the office design company. Now you know her name and are talking about her in a familiar way. Let me check the transcript. [Pause] Yes, during the interview yesterday we showed you a photograph of Yulia Ivanova and you said, and I quote 'I've seen her around the office'. It sounds to me like you knew her much better than that. [Pause]

JF: Torsten?

TL: I was feeling desperate. In truth, I've only talked to her once. She came over to introduce herself when she started working on our floor, measuring up and planning for the office changes. Then I noticed that Alex was flirting with her and they went for coffee a few times. I watched them and it was obvious she also liked him. I really didn't know what I was going to do, but I started to think I could somehow use the information against Alex. I had no clear plan, but I obviously knew he was still having a difficult time with Helena (Corbetová). I decided to try and find out what was going on between Alex and Yulia, that's all.

FM: You were going to blackmail Alex?

TL: No, no. I had no plan worked out. I just made sure I walked past when he was talking to her in the office and also watched them leave together on that Friday. I thought I'd watch and just see what happened; it was possible this might be useful to me. I know it was a stupid idea, but as I've already said, I was getting desperate.

JF: So, did you speak to Alex about it?

TL: No. The last time I saw Alex was when he left the office with Yulia on Friday evening.

JF: Had you followed them in the days before?

TL: No. I didn't know what I was going to do. As I've already said, I had no clear plan.

FM: Why did you lie to us?

TL: I was embarrassed, I suppose. I'm sorry.

JF: You have already told us you went to the pub after work on Friday evening after leaving the office. Did you go anywhere else?

TL: No. I was feeling quite depressed so I went down the local pub after work and stayed there. I got pretty drunk, lots of people will be able to tell you. I phoned Kerstin and she came to meet me and helped me get home.

MB: We have already established that you went to the pub on Friday. We will however now be re-checking this information to establish what time you left and whether your wife picked you up. We will also need to take fingerprint and DNA samples from you after this interview.

TL: Okay.

JF: I have no more questions at this stage, Torsten, but you'd better hope your story about staying at the pub in Chodov on Friday evening checks out. If not, you could be in big trouble.

TL: You won't mention this conversation to my company, will you?

FM: Mr Lindberg, you have weaved so many lies and half-truths. At this stage I can confirm nothing. I will need to consult with my colleagues before deciding on the next course of action. One of these next steps could be raising a warrant to search your home and/or your company office, including electronic equipment such as laptops and phones. Let's stop this interview now, there is no point in continuing.

MB: Interview terminated at 15.19.

28

The Seedy Side

Now, both Jonny and Mikeš were furious. Silence seemed the only option to prevent their anger from spilling over and souring the office atmosphere. Even Boukal was annoyed, shaking his head in frustration as he entered the Incident Room after completing the fingerprint and DNA tests with Torsten Lindberg.

"He's the worst type of person," Mikeš began, his voice trembling with contained rage. "He has made a mistake, but he won't admit it. Instead, he tries to blame it on another person who is innocent."

"Even worse," Jonny took up the mantle, "he then creates a web of lies to cover his tracks, leading to a total waste of police time."

"His wife sounds just as bad," Boukal added loudly, incensed. "They deserve each other!"

Never having seen Boukal angry before, Jonny and Mikeš glanced at each other, initially shocked, and burst out laughing in unison. Boukal appeared confused, looking between his boss and his mentor for clues to how his irritation with a witness had turned into a moment of hilarity.

Jonny put his arm around Boukal's shoulders and squeezed him with affection. "Marek, welcome to the Angry Detective Club."

Realising the joke, Boukal joined in the laughter. The

detectives sitting outside the Incident Room looked relieved.

"I needed that," Mikeš said, still chuckling to himself. "But, what shall we do with Torsten Lindberg?"

"I suggest we check out his story by confirming he was in the pub all Friday evening," Jonny proposed. "If he was as drunk as he says he was and was picked up by his wife, there's no way he could have got to the city centre and committed a double murder."

"Leave it to me," Boukal stated, now released from Jonny's caring grip. "I'll liaise with the HR Manager at his company and organise for some officers to go there to take more statements. I'll also check with the pub landlord; they may have CCTV."

***

After finishing his review of the other open serious crime cases, Mikeš was ready for the next step – Yulia Ivanova's ex-boyfriend, Mikhail Antonov. Boukal was needed at the station to lead the interview with an arrested suspect in a major burglary case, so Mikeš agreed to Jonny's request to walk to the Passion club just off Wenceslas Square.

Jonny had spent the intervening time alone in the Incident Room – peace and quiet to review all the existing links to the victims. He had hoped something new would jump out at him, but he'd come out scratching his head.

Even reviewing the phone and laptop records for Alex Corbet, as well as the newly arrived phone records for Yulia Ivanova, had revealed no new, potential leads. All contact to or from Alex was accounted for, including calls and messages from Torsten Lindberg. No contact from Daniela Nováková had been established, or from her husband, Jakub Novák. During the past month, Yulia had exchanged numerous calls and messages with Alex and her friend, Svetlana, also remaining in contact with her family in Russia, but all the other calls were related to her job with the office design company.

Although the situation wasn't yet desperate, he was aware their options were running out. The meeting with Mikhail Antonov was crucial; he was the only known person connected to the case they hadn't yet spoken to. If this also proved a dead end, they'd be back to square one.

Rather than following the well-trodden tourist route from Old Town Square to Wenceslas Square, Mikeš led them on a different course. He was setting his normal military pace as the last of the rain came down in fine, almost invisible droplets. They zigzagged the route of backstreets and cut-throughs, finally arriving in front of Jindřišská věž, showing in the guide books as Henry's Tower. The dark-stoned Gothic tower was imposing, the steeple standing tall and proud, the belfry clearly visible under the roof.

"The tallest freestanding bell tower in Prague," announced Mikeš, as if in tour guide mode. "We must have dinner at the top floor restaurant some time. Lovely food. The soup I had there was so good, it was like sex in a bowl."

Jonny recoiled at the information, unable to stop the laughter bubbling up inside him.

"You see," he stammered between fits of laughs, "you don't get that sort of vital information from your average city tour operator."

Enjoying their time together, they strolled the short distance to Wenceslas Square. The clouds were starting to clear, providing glimpses of blue sky behind, but the air still felt damp and cold after the earlier spring rain.

Traversing the mid-point of the square, they crossed to the seedy side of the new town, notorious for cabaret bars and sordid hostelries. An assortment of dubious-looking characters milled around the street, staggering from one venue to another, lured in by touts. Everything about the scene spelt 'undesirable'.

At the entrance to the club, Mikeš flashed his badge and strode purposefully through the heavy, velvet curtain without stopping. Jonny followed, showing his own badge and smiling, the bouncer showing no interest at all in the visitors.

Mikeš knew the drill and stood still in the middle of the club floor, waiting to be greeted. The unwritten rule, as Jonny was used to from London clubs, was not to make a scene, especially in front of the paying customers, and in return the club management would be co-operative. This trade was often useful in finding criminals hiding in the midst of the underworld. The police relied on the criminal fraternity's own law enforcement system more than it would ever care to admit.

All was dark inside the club, any natural light barred by the absence of windows. The bar area was painted silver and bordered by lighting, aiding waitresses carrying trays of drinks. The rest of the large space was black, pools of darkness around tables to provide privacy for customers to entertain the working ladies without prying eyes. A small stage was planted in the middle of the room, an uninterested young woman, not much older than Jonny's own daughter, dancing lazily to a pulsing dance beat whilst removing the top half of her bikini. Despite the flashing lights and loud music, the scene was tinged with sadness: the ladies not yet engaged sat together in the corner, scantily clad but looking bored and miserable, whilst the few paying customers feasted their eyes on the dancer as if they'd never seen a naked woman before.

Jonny stood by Mikeš' side, happy to be led. Whilst the scene was familiar from so many of his previous criminal investigations, he had no knowledge of the unwritten rules in this city, nor did he know the recent history between the club and the local police. He must have looked like an outsider because some of the girls were smiling suggestively at him, one beckoning him over with her curled index finger. Mikeš was receiving no such attention; his rigid stance, leaning forward on his cane with his hat still on, giving the clear statement that he was not there for any fun.

"Bosnian owners," Mikeš whispered to Jonny without turning his head. "We've been after them for years, but they're very clever. The club's ownership and working arrangements are wrapped up in multiple legal contracts, using every loophole in the book. We've tried raiding them a few times, but it just causes friction."

Jonny listened without acknowledging the words.

"The authorities don't give us much support either. They turn a blind eye because of all the money coming in from all the stag parties visiting Prague."

"Pane Mikeš!"

The booming voice from across the room was followed by a figure emerging from the gloom. The man was in his late thirties, short and robust, but presenting a suave image at odds with the club's interior. The club owners Jonny had met before usually conformed to the classic image of shaven head, black clothes, tattoos and heavy, gold jewellery. This man was far more sophisticated: well-groomed, with dark, wavy hair, he wore smart trousers and a pressed shirt, and gave off the impression of a financial adviser. His pleasure in seeing Mikeš appeared genuine, a smile on his face and his arm outstretched in a warm greeting.

Mikeš ignored the offered hand, instead opting to state his business in a terse manner. After a staccato exchange in Czech, Mikeš introduced Jonny.

"Ah, Mr Fox, pleased to meet you. I am Nedim Savić, but everyone calls me Ned. I must say, you are already becoming quite famous in this city. Please, just remember we are always here to help the police."

Ned's wide smile and dazzling teeth almost lit up the dark club. Jonny glanced across at Mikeš, but he remained unmoved.

"Now, gentlemen, please follow me," Ned added. "Mikhail has explained the nature of your visit. We can talk better through here."

He led them through a maze of dark corridors behind the stage. The tour of the club's inner sanctum took them past the open door to the women's changing rooms, through which female chatter and giggles could be heard.

Ned opened a door off the dark corridor to reveal a small room. The sole furniture inside was a sofa and two upright chairs, facing a large TV mounted on the wall with games consoles attached. The only occupant in the room was a tall and muscular, attractive man with dark hair and a thick-set jaw. He seemed edgy, having been pacing the room, his bulky physique making his nervous energy evident to see.

"Welcome to our chill-out room," Ned stated. "This is Mikhail. Gentlemen, please sit down and relax."

Mikhail Antonov silently acknowledged the visitors with a nod of his head and sat down first, clearly keen to get on with the meeting. His body was too big for the frame of the sofa, his knees uncomfortably above the level of the seat cushions. Jonny watched his movements carefully, his initial judgement being that Mikhail was approximately the same height and size as the disguised workman on the CCTV recordings.

Mikeš and Jonny took the chairs, both repositioning them away from the TV in order to face the sofa. Ned sat next to Mikhail and opened the discussion, keen to keep the atmosphere jovial. "Mikhail has asked me to sit in as a witness. Please ask your questions. I am only here for support if Mikhail needs it."

"Mikhail," Jonny started, "can you start by telling us what job you do here?"

The question was a planned check of sorts, an opener to test the ground and especially the relationship between the two men. As Jonny expected, Mikhail immediately turned to Ned for guidance.

"Mr Fox," Ned replied, "Mikhail has worked for me for about three years. He does general duties like security, box office and driving. He's a good worker. I would like him to work full-time, but he also has his life in Brno. So, our arrangement is that he comes to Prague to work for me at weekends, when the club is busy."

Mikhail's features remained deadpan, not even glancing at his boss. Jonny sensed he was playing the tough guy, an obvious first reaction given his size and build, but could see he was clearly uncomfortable in this company. Before Jonny had the chance to frame a question about Yulia to test his sensitivity, Mikhail blurted out his own question. "I don't know which one of you called me, but you said this was about Yulia. Is she okay?"

"I called you," Mikeš answered. "We found her murdered this week."

Mikhail's face dropped and he immediately brought his big hands up to cover his eyes.

"Was that the double murder in the news?" Ned asked.

Mikeš ignored the question.

Jonny had his answer; a tough-looking guy from the outside, but with a soft spot.

"Mikhail," Jonny restarted, "when was the last time you saw Yulia?"

The room remained silent whilst Mikhail composed himself. He eventually removed his hands from his pale face, the blood having drained away with the shock.

"I loved her."

"So, why did you beat her up?" Mikeš countered.

Mikhail's thick neck tensed in anger as he leaned forward on the sofa. "Don't listen to her stupid friend. Yes, we had one fight, but it was nothing. She actually hurt me more than I hurt her. I had a big scratch down my neck." Mikhail pulled his black t-shirt aside at the neck to show a fading, pink scar.

"So, why did Yulia move away from Brno?" Jonny asked with a gentler tone.

"That stupid friend—"

"Svetlana?"

"Yes, her. She was just jealous. She convinced Yulia that I was just a typical Russian man, beating his woman. She told Yulia it was only going to get worse. It is not true. I am not like that."

"Why didn't you chase Yulia?" Jonny prompted. "We understand you called her for a month after she moved away, but then stopped."

"My relationship with Yulia was fine. Her stupid friend was the problem. Yulia and I talked a lot on the phone after she moved. I respected her decision but asked for one more chance to prove myself. Mr Savić had offered me more hours, and my other work in Brno was going well. I am saving up to buy an

261

apartment in Brno. I told her I wanted to settle down and for her to move in with me, maybe get married later. I asked Yulia to meet me in the summer so I could show her how well I had done, to prove how I had changed. She agreed. I was going to call her next month to arrange when to meet."

"So, you hadn't seen her or talked to her since January?" Jonny probed.

"No. It was part of our agreement. I am an honourable man."

"Where were you last Friday and Saturday?"

"I was here all the time, apart from popping out for a walk and to get cigarettes on Saturday and Sunday afternoon," Mikhail confirmed. "I left Prague on Monday and went back to Brno."

"Because the weekends are so busy," Ned started explaining, "I ask all employees to sleep in. We provide beds and food, and even have a kitchen in the basement. Every room and corridor has CCTV so nobody can move without it being on camera."

Jonny looked at Mikeš, confused about the next move.

"Did you know Yulia was pregnant?" Mikeš blurted out.

Mikhail's bones seemed to collapse within his large frame, his muscles losing all strength as he fell back into the cushions on the sofa. He wiped at the uncontainable tears rolling down his cheeks, before suddenly breaking down completely, his whole body convulsing as the grief took over him.

29

Time for a New Plan

Leaving Mikhail Antonov crushed on the sofa, the sight of a large man sobbing uncontrollably being difficult on the eye, Mikeš and Jonny swiftly departed the room, and the club. Ned had walked them out, extolling Mikhail's work ethic and virtues all the way. Mikeš remained indifferent, making no response in return. At the exit door, he still refused to shake hands with the owner, using the opportunity to confirm arrangements for Boukal to collect the CCTV tapes, as well as handwriting, fingerprint and DNA samples from Mikhail Antonov.

Back on Wenceslas Square, Mikeš stopped abruptly and, with an almost natural reaction of his body, shook from head to toe. He took off his hat and cricked his neck in a final release of tension. "I hate those places," he explained. "They make me feel dirty. I can't wait to get out."

"I understand, Felix. But, I think you were a bit tough on him."

Mikeš shook his head in an animated fashion, his opinion clearly firmly set and not to be changed. "Honza, they are all scum. I know Mikhail Antonov loved Yulia and has aspirations to improve himself but, once a crook always a crook in my opinion."

Jonny couldn't argue. He felt compassion for people trying to improve themselves, but the reality was that only a small percentage pulled themselves out of the criminal world. Many sadly made a short-term change, only to find themselves pulled back into their former life, missing either the money or the buzz. It was only the young kids, pulled into a life of crime at a tender age, who could be truly saved. Kids were still impressionable; a respected family friend or community leader had a chance to help them pick up the pieces of their life.

The interview with Mikhail Antonov had, as Jonny feared, come to nothing. Mikhail's extreme reaction to the news of Yulia's murder had been sincere, and impossible to fake. Now, the pool of potential suspects had dried up. It was time for a new plan.

With an agreement to meet later and compare notes over a beer in the Black Cat pub, Mikeš headed off in earnest down the square, on his way back to the police station.

Jonny stood and watched him go, smiling as tourists parted on the pedestrian central reservation to allow the eccentric, elder gentleman to walk through, cane swishing in his hand. It was hard to comprehend how he'd developed such a strong friendship and affection for this man in the matter of only a few weeks.

Realising time was not on his side, Jonny strode in the opposite direction, up the square in the direction of the National Museum. He wanted to use the last daylight to revisit the streets around where the murder victims were found and test his powers of discovery to seek out potential places where the bodies could have been stored before being placed in the trenches.

Armed with a map marked with the position and timing of all the CCTV sightings, sent to his phone by Dvořáková, he marched off, turning right at the museum, in the direction of the burial site in Prague 2. His aim was to follow the marked route from the Červený lev pub, as taken by Alex Corbet and Yulia

Ivanova, but walk it in reverse. He wanted to see everything from a different perspective, to look at the puzzle another, less obvious, way.

The street Hluboká was again a mess, this time because of the police operation rather than the roadworks to lay new cabling. The plastic tenting was still erected over the pavement, covering the trenches, and access was protected by portable, chain-link fencing. Jonny flashed his police badge at an interested uniform officer and stood in the middle of the street to reconnect with the crime scene. His eyes scanned the buildings as he listened to the sounds of the area, and he breathed deeply, replaying in his mind the events of Wednesday evening when the bodies were found buried under the pavement – he wanted his senses stimulated for the task ahead.

First, he walked up the incline to the street entrance. The diversion was still in place, allowing access to residents only; the one-way street Sadová took traffic straight on as well as allowing the turn into Hluboká. He decided first to walk further down Sadová, following the one-way direction away from the route on the map. This was not the way Alex and Yulia would have walked, but Jonny wanted to check that their bodies hadn't been dragged to a nearby hiding place along the only other connecting street. After walking fifty metres, he stopped, having seen nothing unusual; the street was all residential buildings, on both sides, with no separate access to the areas behind the buildings, garages or openings to gardens.

He returned to the junction, checking the map, and began walking the opposite way down Sadová. He walked slowly, taking deliberate steps, scanning all around him. Whilst watching out for any unusual, parked vehicles, he looked for any alcoves, garages, gated gardens, alleyways or even recessed doorways –

secluded places where someone could hide something bulky for a couple of hours at night without being detected.

Following the street for approximately one hundred and seventy metres, he approached the corner of the street Polní, where Jakub Novák had met Alex and Yulia. Despite his studious search, he had still not seen anything that could be used for any storage, let alone two dead bodies. The terraced buildings were all connected to their neighbours on both sides, with no gaps or gated pathways. The only exit off the pavements was either into the main door entrances to the buildings, or through a select number of gated garages leading to parking areas behind or under the buildings. He had checked all the garage doors but all were only accessible by a physical key or by key card access.

He stopped at the corner where Jakub Novák and his dogs had met the victims before their tragic demise. Studying the routes highlighted on the map, he replayed the events: Novák had returned back down Polní after the altercation, with Alex and Yulia continuing along Sadová. Jonny scratched his head, confused. So, the victims must have been jumped along the portion of the pavement he had just walked, or at the top of the street Hluboká, where they were eventually found buried. He turned and walked back down the same stretch of pavement, moving even slower this time, taking photos with his phone, until he reached the turn into the Hluboká street.

Again, nothing.

Confused, he reconsidered the options. If there was no recess along the street in which to hide the bodies, where could they have been stored? They could have been thrown in the trench straight away, covered in plastic sheeting, and tidied up later. Or, maybe they were just laid on the pavement with plastic sheeting over them, passing them off as building material for later use.

266

The subsequent building work to refill the trenches after the weekend would then have removed any evidence. But, what about the blood? He moaned aloud, the frustration getting to him. There was nothing here; the killer was too clever. The only logical next step was to check the areas behind all the garage doors within a specified radius, but this would take time – time they didn't have.

Jonny had become notorious for these hunts in London, taking it upon himself to retrace the known routes taken by the victim(s) and/or the murderer(s). Most of his personal ventures ended up with some form of success, at least providing insight into the killer's thought process. But, unlike any previous foray, this retracing had provided no return; he understood nothing more than he had before. It was as if Alex Corbet and Yulia Ivanova had walked down the street after meeting Jakub Novák, turned into Hluboká and then miraculously ended up in a trench.

Feeling dejected, he decided to walk back to I. P. Pavlova, close to the pub. He followed the CCTV sightings on the map, the route being reasonably direct apart from where the maze of one-way streets forced a seemingly unnatural diversion. He crossed the busy main roads, full of early weekend traffic, and stopped at the metro station. Again, he had noticed nothing out of the ordinary. He suddenly felt alone; all around him people were boarding trams or rushing down the steps of the metro station, heading for their weekends.

The voice inside encouraged him to keep going, to keep asking questions. On a whim, he took out his phone and called George Webb. Somehow, Alex had got caught up in trouble that had proved fatal to him and Yulia, and Jonny needed to find out why. Luckily, George had just arrived home from work and was happy to see him.

Jonny powered over to Londýnská, keen to maintain momentum, and was greeted by George and Zuzana at the apartment door. They led him to the living room, leaving their daughter to continue with her homework at the kitchen table.

"Firstly, apologies for the short notice," Jonny started. "In truth, it was a bit of a last minute decision. I was passing close by and—"

"It is absolutely fine," George replied. "We had no plans tonight anyway."

"Thank you. At this point in the investigation we are struggling. Every lead we've had seems to have closed down. I just want to go back over a few points with you, just to make sure I haven't missed anything."

"We want to help, Mr Fox," Zuzana stated, echoing her husband.

"I'd like to talk again about Alex and Helena's relationship. It seems clear to me, and probably everyone, that Helena's mother is very domineering. Her interference has definitely caused problems between them. But, what I don't understand is why Helena didn't say something to her mother. She clearly still loved Alex. Why didn't she try to find a better balance so they could stay together, and her mother could still provide the financial support she and the family needed?"

"This is the difficult part," Zuzana began, sighing. "Unfortunately, neither of us will be able to give you a definitive answer. Families are complicated, and their family situation was more complicated than most. George and I enjoyed Alex and Helena's company immensely: our children were great together, we had lots of laughs, and we liked them all, including Daniela and Jakub. They just never totally opened up to us."

"Not even Alex?" Jonny prompted.

"Alex was a real gentleman, with old fashioned values," George added. "I really liked and respected that side of him. We both did." He glanced at his wife. "I asked him about it many times, but he would never tell me. He just said it was a matter for him and Helena to sort it out, and it wasn't right to involve us."

"I respect his approach as well," Jonny confirmed. "The more I find out about Alex, the more I like him. But, I am trying to catch the person who killed him and the woman he was with last Friday evening. I cannot go into details, but it is my view at the moment that this horrendous crime has more to do with him than her. Please think, is there anything else you can tell me about the triangular relationship between Alex, Helena and Helena's mother?"

George and Zuzana looked at each other. Jonny watched them intently, trying to determine if they were holding anything back, maybe protecting someone. There was nothing in their body or facial language indicating deceit.

"I think there are only two things I can say about the triangular relationship, as you call it," Zuzana started. "Firstly, Helena needed her mother more than she needed Alex. She could do without Alex, but she couldn't do without Daniela. In my view, this was the breaking point for Alex. As we have said, he was a gentleman, and he believed it was *his* role to support his wife, not her mother's. He would have accepted Daniela's help with money, or anything else, but he couldn't accept that he was the third person in the relationship."

"That makes perfect sense to me," Jonny concurred. "And, the second point?"

"Helena was ill. We never knew what was wrong with her, but she was always weak, tired and needing support. She was like the weak child; always too thin and not eating enough. I asked her about it on many occasions, but she always denied anything was wrong. In the end, I gave up asking her and just tried to enjoy our friendship. She is still a lovely person and my friend."

"I agree," Jonny declared. "She seems a very kind person, but maybe not in control of her own destiny."

"Mr Fox, Zuzana is being careful with her words, in respect of our friends," George summarised. "The second point is the reason for the first point. Alex loved Helena, but he knew, whatever the underlying issues, they would never have a conventional marriage. It was too complicated. And, too crowded."

"That is very useful." Jonny paused to write in his notepad. "Can I just ask a couple more things? Firstly, did Alex ever tell you he was being followed?"

"Yes, he did," George exclaimed. "You know, I'd forgotten."

"What can you remember?"

"Let me see," George paused, rubbing his chin. "I just remember he said he saw someone slightly suspicious when he came out of work on a few occasions, and then he also saw him again around where he lived."

"Was it someone in a dark coat and a trilby hat?" Jonny posed. "Dressed like a classic private detective."

"No, Alex said he wore a baseball cap. But, he did wonder if the man was a private detective hired by Daniela; he said it was the sort of thing she would do. Alex certainly wasn't worried about it, otherwise I'd have mentioned it to you when we spoke before. Alex just brushed it off, said it was nothing to worry about."

"Thank you. The final point is the note Alex received, the one that said 'LEAVE HER ALONE! I'M WARNING YOU'.

We discussed this last time we met. Can you remember anything else Alex told you about it?"

George paused again, a frown on his face, deep in thought.

"I'm sure I remember you telling me the note had been stuck to his apartment door, or something like that," Zuzana suggested.

"Yes, that's right," George exclaimed. "Alex was confused because he returned home from work and there was a sealed envelope stuck to his apartment door."

"That's a bit strange, isn't it?" Jonny asked.

"I think so," George answered. "I remember questioning him about it whilst at the pub quiz. In the end, he convinced himself the envelope had been stuck to the main building door and one of his neighbours had moved it, sticking it to his apartment door."

"And, was he worried about the note?"

"No." George shrugged. "I don't think so. If he was, he certainly didn't show it."

30

The Black Cat

Jonny left the apartment in need of enlightenment and refreshment. He sensed he was circling closer to the truth, but something important was missing. Revisiting the burial site, and talking to George and Zuzana again, had provided some insight into Alex Corbet's marriage, but no definite clues about how or why he and Yulia Ivanova had been murdered. The step forward was the endorsement that the motive for the murder was almost certainly centred upon Alex, not Yulia – he felt sure of it. This investigation needed clarity, and quickly, because the killer was still stepping ahead of them. And, he also needed a beer!

With a range of transport options available to get back to Old Town Square, Jonny still favoured travelling through the city centre on foot. It was almost as quick once time was added for waiting at the stop for the tram or metro, but it also cleared his head. With the daylight now fading, he was starting to feel the effects of the early start and the heavy schedule over the last few days. Unlike the other workers around him leaving their office, his weekend would provide no respite – this case had to be solved soon.

Checking his phone, he realised he'd missed an earlier message from Ivana.

Hi. Barbora called me, she's found something exciting! We've agreed to meet tonight for dinner. Come along – 20.00 at

Ivana's mood had lightened when Jonny had phoned earlier to tell her about uncovering the mystery of the stalker. He hadn't gone into details, only informing her there was no longer a threat, but he could hear the relief in her voice.

He quickly typed out a reply saying he'd be there.

Jonny's thoughts were now running with trepidation about what Barbora could have discovered so quickly. Maybe the search had uncovered a scandal, he thought, a saga that had made the newspapers and put a permanent cloud over the family name? Getting so close was playing with his nerves.

As he headed for the agreed rendezvous at the Black Cat pub, he called Mikeš to distract himself from his spiralling reflections. After being berated for being late, he used the opportunity to report his lack of success in finding any clue to where the victims had been murdered. Mikeš' frustration was evident, matching Jonny's irritated and edgy emotional state.

Just before reaching Old Town Square, he ducked through a passage under a building, reappearing in a small plaza hosting small, independent cafés and restaurants. The Černá kočka or Black Cat pub was tucked away in the corner. The frontage of black painted windows and dark, green tiles, under the shadow of the overhanging trees, provided a sense of mystique. A cut-out metal black cat took pride of place above the door, the pub name not visible anywhere. It had been Mikeš' favoured watering hole for years, partly because it was hidden and therefore hard to find, but also because it played to the tale of his surname; Mikeš was the name of the black cat in a famous set of children's books written by Josef Lada and read to children in the Czech Republic.

The pub was starting to get busy, people arriving to celebrate the weekend. Jonny spotted Mikeš immediately, sitting alone at the table in the corner, with his hat and cane hung up on the wall behind. Mikeš was shaking his head in rebuke and tapping his pocket watch impatiently as Jonny approached.

The table had a permanent 'Reserved' sign on it, being solely for regulars, some even having their own tankards stored in a dresser on the wall behind. The long, wooden table was sometimes exclusively for them, but other times they were joined by others, keen to discuss politics or the latest arts news. Jonny had initially been reticent to get involved, not having experienced such a cultural society before, and also not wanting to impose spoken English on the group, but he had been warmly embraced into the association and some of his most memorable evenings in Prague had been righting the world's wrongs in the Black Cat.

Although both Jonny and Mikeš felt dejected, the mood softened with the arrival of two, fresh Pilsner Urquell beers. They clinked their glasses, expressed the usual toast of "Na zdraví," and slugged their beers, both sighing with relief and foamed top lips.

"Honza, what do we do now?"

"Good question," Jonny replied, tired and all out of inspiration.

"Ella has confirmed she's finished checking the fibres found at the burial site," Mikeš reported. "One DNA sample matched with Jakub Novák, but I think we expected this after the earlier interview."

"Yes," Jonny mumbled.

"Unfortunately, none of the other samples match any DNA we have on record. She has isolated ten DNA samples in total, but one appeared a lot. My guess is it belongs to the killer – probably the person caught on the CCTV dressed as a building contractor. She has also confirmed that some of the fibres buried in the soil come from the type of fluorescent vest used by the building company. The only good news, I suppose, is that we'll have some evidence to prosecute if we can just catch this killer."

"That is good news," Jonny replied, half-heartedly.

"I had two other messages," Mikeš added. "Josef Liška is looking for you. He says he's found something interesting in Alex Corbet's apartment; he has it in the evidence room at the station. And, as predicted, Pavel Rosický is going mad following the warrant request. He's already left me five voicemails."

Jonny smiled briefly, the pleasure of angering Rosický dulled by the lack of progress on the case.

"I wonder what Josef has found," Jonny mused. "It felt all along that the family situation surrounding Alex and Helena was the key to unlocking the case, but I'm starting to doubt myself now. Alex is definitely the key."

"Why do you think the warning note was left on his apartment door?"

"I don't know," Jonny replied. "The security in the building is shocking. The person who left it, and probably stole it back, knew how easy it was to get in. But, why leave it on the door when he could have left it in the post? What message is it giving?"

"To scare him more?" Mikeš ventured.

"Maybe." Jonny paused, thinking through the scenario. "Felix, could you ask Lucie to send an officer over to Alex Corbet's building again? We should ask the neighbours if they saw someone leaving the note on Alex's door. My guess, it was probably in the week before he was murdered."

"Sure. Lucie called earlier and confirmed she has received all the TV coverage from the news channel who produced the outside broadcast. Her officers are going through it now."

"It does feel like the murderer has been watching us, always one step ahead. Maybe a camera has caught him trying to blend in with the crowd."

"Our options definitely seem to be running out," Mikeš exclaimed, taking another sip of his beer in consolation. "The only good news I've had today is that my date with Ella is back on for tonight. You and Ivana are welcome to join us for dinner."

"I'm sorry, Felix, but I'm already going for dinner with Ivana and a friend of hers."

Mikeš' face dropped in disappointment.

"Actually, I wanted to tell you about it," Jonny continued. "Ivana's friend helps find lost families. She is trying to find out about my mother's family in Prague. That was the important meeting I had to go to yesterday. I wanted to tell you, but—"

Mikeš put his hand up to stop Jonny in the tracks of his apology. "My friend, you have nothing to apologise for." He paused and smiled warmly. "You know I believe family is the number one priority. I hope your search is positive. To find relatives you didn't know you had would be incredible."

"Thank you, Felix."

The bar door opened and an imposing figure in dark coat and hat stood at the entrance, scanning the pub. They both recognised him immediately – Petr Řepka. Mikeš and Jonny exchanged a fleeting glance, both wondering the same thing. Spotting them in the corner, Řepka made his way over to the table and sat down, uninvited.

"Twice in one day, Petr," Mikeš stated. "What do you want?"

"Nice to see you too, gentlemen," Řepka replied smoothly, taking his hat off and making himself at home.

"How did you find us?" Mikeš asked.

"Felix, you've been coming to this pub for as long as I've known you." Řepka laughed. "And, you'll probably never change."

Mikeš shrugged his shoulders, accepting the facts.

"I have something for you," Řepka continued. "Something I think you'll find interesting."

"What is it?"

"Well, that's not very welcoming, Felix. How about a drink first?"

Without needing to ask, Mikeš ordered an extra beer and a whisky chaser. The table remained under strained silence, only Řepka making a passing comment about the weather forecast. Jonny felt out of his depth in the company of old friends and said nothing. The drinks were delivered to the table, Řepka taking his whisky and raising his glass, saying "Cheers," and downing the measure in one gulp. Whilst Řepka had his virtues and had clearly been a good detective in his day, it was evident to Jonny that his behaviour had become an irritant to his old friends and colleagues.

"And?" Mikeš prompted.

Řepka settled in his seat and took a sip of his beer. He clearly had something significant to tell, maybe important enough to restore his reputation with his old boss. And, he wasn't going to be rushed.

"Firstly, I'm sorry again for following Honza. I regret my actions and hope this doesn't affect our relationship going forward. Even though I left under a bit of a cloud, I like to think…"

"Petr, please," Mikeš interrupted, irritated now. "Save the excuses. We all know what happened: facts are facts. We have a double murder to solve and it is our only priority right now."

"Yes, Felix, I understand. But, I want your respect."

"Petr, it is not my role to be judge or jury. You made a mistake and paid for it. I can't do anything about it. I respect people for their actions now, not hold grudges for what they did in the past. Now, please tell us what you have come here to say."

"Thank you." Řepka nodded to his old boss in respect, knowing it was the closest to deliverance he was going to get. After taking another mouthful of beer, he settled in to tell his story.

"After we talked earlier I went home and had a sleep. In truth, I've been drinking too much lately. There have been too many late nights and it has affected my work. Honza's words were ringing around my head. How could I have missed the woman staying overnight with Alex Corbet earlier in the week? It is not acceptable. I made myself some promises to focus on the job, to not make the same mistakes again."

Jonny was watching Řepka intently, attempting to judge his sincerity and the truthfulness of the information to follow. The large mouthful of beer, following his recent swift whisky, made the claim seem a hollow promise.

"I started to think over everything I saw whilst following Alex Corbet. I looked over my notes and photos, copies of which I've handed over to Marek. Then, I remembered something. It was something I hadn't realised was odd before. As I told you earlier, I went to check inside the Červený lev pub when I realised the time, but Alex and the woman had already left. I rushed to try to catch them up but didn't see them anywhere. I went all the way to Alex's apartment, hung around outside for about ten minutes and then left. I stayed a while because the light was not on in his apartment, and even in the dark I could see the curtains were open and the light was off. I assumed they'd gone somewhere else,

278

maybe a late-night pub or club, and so I left. But, on the way to his apartment, I'd gone down the same street where you found the bodies, Hluboká. I remember the pavements had been dug up, it was a real mess. I entered at the top of the street and walked fast down the pavement as best I could. A little way down the street, I heard noises coming from inside a white van. The van was also rocking slightly. It was strange, not what you'd expect. It was enough to make me slow down and look."

"What sort of noises?" Jonny asked.

"Talking. And, I suppose, more like groaning. The van was also moving slightly. I remember smiling to myself, assuming there were some people inside having a bit of fun. But, now I think about it, maybe it wasn't—"

"Do you remember the registration of the van?" Jonny pushed.

"Sorry, no. But, it was definitely a small, white van and I remember the make and model." Řepka took a slip of paper from his jacket pocket and pushed it across the table.

"We need to get Marek to check this against the list of vehicles parked in the street on Wednesday night, when we found the bodies," Jonny stated, looking towards Mikeš. "We may have just got lucky and found where the victims were killed and held before they were buried."

31

Typical Czech Man

Jonny couldn't decide whether to get excited or not. Was the new information from Petr Řepka the slice of luck they needed, or was it too little too late? A number of unlikely events – with odds stacked against each of them – would need to happen to identify and find the vehicle. But Mikeš wasn't to be deterred. The new information, although sparse, had sparked him into life. He was immediately on the phone to Boukal, asking for the make and model of the white van to be cross-checked against any details taken down by any officer over the course of the murder investigation.

The first event was whether Boukal had seen and noted down the white van on Wednesday evening. Jonny remembered suggesting Boukal write down the registration number of all vehicles parked in the street, but at that time they'd only been looking for Alex Corbet's missing mobile phone. The state of the operation had escalated quickly once Mikeš had given the order for the exhumation, Jonny remembering only that some owners had moved their cars whilst the remaining vehicles had been towed away; the focus at the time had been solely on creating sufficient space to dig up the pavements. His time mentoring Boukal had included discussions on the importance of recording even the seemingly meaningless information – now was the time to see if the lesson had got through to his protégé.

Řepka had requested another beer and whisky chaser, implied as a reward of sorts, and Mikeš found it hard to refuse. Knowing it would be the last on offer, his time in the spotlight nearly over, Řepka began to reminisce about his and Mikeš' shared glories. "Felix, do you remember when we caught that serial killer?"

Mikeš smiled momentarily at the prompt from the past, enjoying the reminder but also not wanting to provoke a long journey down memory lane.

"Honza, I tell you," Řepka continued undeterred, "it was inspired. We had hardly any clues, but Felix remembered one of the victim's friends appearing a few times during the investigation. This man seemed to just pop up, eager to help with police searches, and Felix just had a hunch something wasn't right. Once we pulled him in, everything unravelled. He'd killed four women, but also had been closely tracking the police investigation."

"That's enough, Petr," Mikeš instructed.

Jonny looked impressed, but Mikeš shrugged it away, not prepared to be the centre of attention in Řepka's recollections.

Boukal's arrival signalled Řepka's time to leave. He finished the rest of his beer in one long glug and put the glass down loudly on the table. "Time to go. Good luck with the investigation." Řepka put on his coat, tipped his hat to his hosts in respect, before turning and walking out of the pub.

"Do you think he staged all of that?" Jonny asked.

"You think he might have known about the van all along?" Mikeš voiced the insinuation, then shook his head. "No, I don't think so. He always had failures in judgement, one fatal for his police career, but he was never a liar. I think it happened as he explained. If he'd had suspicions last Friday, on the night of the murder, he'd have noted down the registration number of the van."

Jonny nodded, trusting his friend's judgement fully.

Boukal sat down, having waved away the offer of a beer from one of the bar staff; his day wasn't finished, he still had work to do back at the station, as well as driving his boss around. "I checked my notes from Wednesday night. I wrote down the registration of all the vehicles on both sides of the street, as well as their make and model."

Jonny smiled to himself, pride rising within his chest.

"There was a white, unmarked van parked near the top of the street Hluboká," Boukal continued. "It was the fourth vehicle from the entrance into the street, parked alongside the pavement where the bodies were found buried. I remember it because it had a number of small dents in the driver-side front wing and sliding door. Because of the emergency on Wednesday night, we didn't have enough information to get in contact with the vehicle owners by telephone. Instead, we knocked on the building doors along the street and asked people to move their vehicles. There were six vehicles that weren't moved, including the white van, so all these were towed away and impounded. Checking with the traffic police, the van was picked up yesterday from the garage suppliers we use. But, no driver details were taken because no offence had been committed – the car was only moved because of a police operation. I drove back over to the street Hluboká on the way here, but the van wasn't parked there. I also checked the streets leading into Hluboká, but it wasn't there either."

Boukal handed Jonny and Mikeš each a single photocopy of a handwritten list on A4 paper.

"The van is marked on the list. I've put a call out to all units, with the registration details and a description of the van."

"Great work, Marek," Jonny stated. "Obviously, there is no guarantee that this white van is the same one that Petr Řepka saw. He saw it last Friday evening, whereas this van you are talking about was parked on the street when we were there this Wednesday. It would be odd for the murderer to leave the van there all the time. And, we don't even know if the van was used for the murder at all. Who is the owner?"

"The van is hired," Boukal replied. "I've tried contacting the hire company, but the office is closed now. I don't know what hours they are open over the weekend, but I've left a message on the answer machine for them to call me back urgently."

"At the moment, this van is the only lead we have," Mikeš declared. "We urgently need to find out who hired it and where they are living."

***

Ivana and Barbora were chatting intensely when Jonny arrived at the Hloupý Honza, closer to eight thirty p.m. than the agreed eight p.m. After greeting the bar owner, Jerry, his loyal barmaid, Monika, and saying "Dobrý večer" to the ever-present regular, Štefan, he hurried across to their table.

He'd just started with his profuse apologies when Štefan's small dog, Viky, spotted him and started barking, clearly unhappy at being left out of the welcoming party. The barking was so loud, Jonny's excuses couldn't be heard above the persistent, ear-piercing noise. When it was clear Viky was not going to stop, Jonny hopped out of his seat and satisfied the dog's desire, Viky dropping down on his haunches for a neck and back rub.

Barbora laughed when Jonny finally sat down in his seat, a

flustered look on his face. Viky barked again, seeking a repeat performance.

"You are very much in demand, I see," she said.

"I'm very sorry I'm late—"

"No kiss, Honza!" Ivana exclaimed, pouting her lips in mock umbrage. He leaned over and kissed her on the lips, lingering for effect and slipping his arm around her back.

"I'm so sorry," he began again. "This murder investigation is running us around in circles. We just got a new piece of information. I—"

"It smells like you've already been in the pub," Ivana retorted.

"Well, yes, I suppose so. I was with Felix." He could only smile naively.

Ivana turned to her friend, leaning forward over the table. "You see what I mean, Barbora. Honza is more Czech than he thinks. He'll be taking us on a pub crawl next."

They all laughed in unison. As he opened his arms innocently, he noticed how both Ivana and Barbora had dressed up for dinner: Ivana in a halter-neck blouse and jeans, her hair tied up; Barbora wore a more formal evening jacket, simple blouse and white trousers.

"And, I'm sorry I didn't get time to change," he explained. "I've come straight from work."

"The pub," Ivana corrected him. "Typical Czech man."

Jonny was just starting to think around Ivana's quip – either a backhanded insult or compliment, he couldn't decide – when Jerry walked over and put a beer down on the table in front of him. "You make quite an entrance these days," Jerry stated with a smile.

"Děkuju," Jonny replied, smiling innocently.

"Definitely one of the regulars now." Jerry winked at the ladies in jest before returning to the bar.

Having learnt not to argue with Ivana, Jonny raised his beer in toast. They all clinked glasses and settled back for the evening ahead.

"I've taken the liberty of ordering the food," Ivana said. "They make a great platter here with chicken wings, ribs, Czech sausage and Prague ham. I've ordered one to share plus potatoes and salad on the side."

"Perfect," echoed Jonny, realising how hungry he was after the mouth-watering description of the food.

Barbora took the opportunity to take a single sheet of paper out of her handbag, placing it in front of her on the table.

Jonny looked down at the paper, riveted by its innate power.

"I would like to be able to say it has taken me a long time to find this information," Barbora began, "but seeing as we only met yesterday you wouldn't believe me."

Jonny and Ivana were a picture, sitting across the table from Barbora. They had unconsciously huddled closer together, sitting perfectly still and holding hands, willing the story on. Both their mouths were slightly open in captivation. Jonny's mouth felt dry so he took a soothing mouthful of beer.

"Luckily, the information you provided me with yesterday led me straight to details of your mother's family. By using her old residence papers, I was able to cross-reference the address and her surname with the census records and the land archive records for the Prague area."

Ivana looked at Jonny and smiled. Jonny glanced back nervously, eager to get to the next part.

"I recognised the address from my previous work on family trees. There is a current street called Moskevská in Prague 10, but this is not the address where your mother lived."

"That's the street I walked to," he confirmed.

"The street Moskevská where your mother used to live is in what is now called Prague 5, near Anděl, or Angel as you would call it."

"Yes, I know where it is," he confirmed excitedly. "It is a station on the B Line of the metro."

"Yes, that's right," Barbora confirmed. "The metro station was opened in 1985 and was originally called Moskevská, named after the city of Moscow. As I explained yesterday, some streets and places were renamed in 1990 after the end of the communist era, and the station was one of them. Anděl is actually the name of the neighbourhood, in the central district of Smíchov."

"Wow, I didn't even know the metro station had a previous name," Ivana exclaimed.

"The street Moskevská where your mother lived was close to the metro station and was also renamed at the same time," Barbora continued. "Sadly, the building your mother lived in was knocked down in the late 1990s and replaced by an office block when the area was redeveloped. I can give you the address if you like, but I always advise people to be very careful returning to an old address when the building no longer exists. It can be quite upsetting to see a cold office block where your family used to live."

Jonny looked despondent and sipped his beer to hide his disappointment. Barbora smiled broadly, totally in control and knowing what information she had on the paper.

"I always like to give the bad news first," she explained, winking at Ivana. "I have found out that your mother's parents lived at the address of Moskevská 15 from 1945 to 1995. Your grandparent's names were Radek Vašek and Olga Vašeková.

Sadly, your grandparents died in the same year, 1995, aged seventy-five and seventy-three, respectively."

Jonny never imagined he would get emotional, but his body started to react without him even acknowledging the response. His eyes welled up and Ivana pulled him close. He never expected his grandparents to be alive, but the confirmation of the year they had died had a crushing, physical reaction on him. He had been promoted to his first detective role in London, aged thirty, in 1995.

"I have all the information here for you," Barbora said kindly.

"Thank you."

"Your mother had an elder sister. Your aunt's married name was Šárka Šimeková and she was born in 1940, three years before your mother. Sadly, the death records show she died in 2005, aged sixty-five. Her husband died before her. But, the exciting news is that she had two children, Erik and Lenka. I checked and a death certificate has not been filed for either of them. So, this means you hopefully have two cousins alive and living in the Czech Republic."

Jonny smiled, digesting the amazing but unexpected news. The built-up emotion of the situation suddenly became too much: his top lip quivered and heavy tears rolled down his cheeks. He hadn't felt joy at news like this since the birth of his daughter.

Enjoying the drama and happiness, Barbora promptly resumed the story of her findings. "By checking marriage certificates and again cross-checking against the more recent census data, Erik is fifty-two and is last recorded as married and living near Brno. He has two children. His sister, Lenka, is three years younger, so forty-nine, is also married and lives in Prague 6. She has one daughter who also appears to be living in Prague."

Barbora turned the paper in front of her and pushed it across the table to Jonny.

"These are the names of your cousins and what I believe are the names of their spouses and their respective children. Against each of them you will see their date of birth, date of marriage and previous surname, if relevant. I have also included the last known addresses, from the census records, but I would suggest sending a letter first. Just arriving at the door is not usually a good idea. Maybe Ivana can help prepare a letter in Czech for you to send?"

"Of course I will help," Ivana added, smiling, her arm around Jonny's back.

Jonny composed himself and looked at the names on the paper, digesting the information slowly. This was his Czech family. His eyes focused in on the bottom of the list. He glanced up at Barbora, confused, then back down at the list.

"Is something wrong, Honza?" Ivana asked.

Jonny looked down at the list again and shook his head softly, disbelieving. "This information can't be right."

32

Love Letters

Saturday, 17 April

When the alarm sounded, Jonny's eyes were already open despite the early hour. In fact, they'd been open for two hours. He'd struggled to get to sleep and then woken early, too many thoughts swimming around inside his head. At this critical crossroads of the investigation, searching for a gateway to prise open the murder hunt, his feelings were augmented by news of his family living in the Czech Republic. *And, what news!*

In quieter moments, before and after meeting Barbora, he had speculated about what the search for his mother's family would reveal. She had cautioned him about the potential for bad news: someone guilty of a heinous crime, or a family secret. He had mentally prepared himself for these possibilities, his police training equipping him to be primed for all eventualities. But, this was different. News about his grandparents had stirred emotions pushed deep down, the revelation of their names and the year in which they'd died bringing a flood of unexpected tears. His aunt also – someone he didn't even know existed. The news about his living relatives was mind-boggling, bordering on implausible. It wasn't bad news as such, he just couldn't get his head around it and its implications.

Ivana had been great, but she'd misunderstood his shock.

289

She'd seen his emotional response to Barbora's report and assumed it was just all too much for him to take in. She had pulled him close, shielding his face as the tears flowed, mouthing words of explanation across the table to her friend. Thankfully, the food had arrived soon after, breaking up the intense focus on him, although by then he'd lost his appetite. The evening had gone by in a blur, Jonny sitting back and letting the friends talk, only responding whenever asked for his opinion.

In truth, he had been desperately waiting for the evening to end, to provide some quiet time. Without attracting attention, he checked his watch frequently and, feigning tiredness, suggested they leave just after ten o'clock. He'd paid the bill, as promised, thanked Barbora profusely for her help, and suggested another meeting when he wasn't consumed by a murder investigation.

The closest he'd felt to the emotions he was now experiencing were during his separation and subsequent divorce. Even though the situation was irreconcilable, the emotional rollercoaster had caused him much heartache and many sleepless nights. Then, he'd simply taken the decision to accept whatever life threw at him and focus on taking care of the people close to him. And, of course, throw himself into his work. This situation felt the same. Whether he liked it or not, he had no control over what his Czech family search had uncovered and had to be prepared to accept all eventualities.

Deciding enough was enough, he sprung from the warm bed and hurried to the bathroom, his resolution to soldier on trumping any tiredness in his limbs. At the door, he glanced back to see Ivana sleeping soundly. The spray of the hot shower loosened the ageing cricks in his body and helped settle his anxieties. He felt as ready as he could be for the new day and everything it had to throw at him.

Jonny reached the police station before seven thirty a.m. his earliest arrival since starting his new role in Prague. After greeting the night duty officer, he trudged up the darkened inner stairwell and through the open plan office, the overhead lights coming on as the sensors detected movement. Once in the Incident Room, he slumped in a chair, not even taking off his jacket, and sat gazing up at the Murder Board.

Despite his good intentions, he found it difficult to shake off his sulky mood. The frustration and personal anxieties were reminiscent of his last year as a detective in London. He'd always taken unresolved murder investigations personally; it was his job after all, what he was paid for, and he blamed himself if he was failing. The case was consuming his thoughts, so much so that he'd unwittingly bypassed his normal, morning café stop, arriving at the station without having had breakfast.

Sitting in the chair, totally focused on the main characters of the double murder investigation, he failed to even sense Dvořáková ghosting into the room.

"Honza, are you okay?" she enquired gently, a look of disquiet on her face.

Jonny almost jumped out of his seat, his contorted face giving away his shock. "Lucie!"

"You look like you might need this." She placed a mug of coffee on the table in front of him.

Jonny rubbed his face, seeking some energy to enliven him.

"Thank you so much," he said, attempting to recover his composure. "Sorry, I wasn't expecting you."

"What do you mean?" She looked confused. "I'm always the

first person in, you should know that by now."

"Yes. Right. Sorry, of course."

Dvořáková looked him over with concerned eyes. "Well, you know where I am if you need me." She smiled warmly and turned to leave.

"Lucie?"

"Yes?"

"What time does Josef usually arrive?"

"He's definitely in today because he's still sorting out the evidence on the case." She looked at her watch. "Actually, he's probably here already. When Felix and he were a detective partnership they always arrived together at eight a.m. every day, like clockwork. It was the running joke, you could set your watch by it."

Jonny forced a chortle, trying to lighten the atmosphere. "Great, thanks. I'll pop down to see him."

The basement was eerily quiet. Classical music would normally be emitting from the hatch of the evidence room anytime during the day, Liška conducting the invisible orchestra behind the glass, a pen serving as his faithful baton. Without the usual, warm musical notes, the space felt cold and lonely, dominated by shelves of police manuals and reference materials. Only the loose collection of soft chairs provided any welcome, although officers preferred to book out any resources and take them upstairs to read, rather than review them under the poor artificial light.

Approaching the hatch, Jonny saw Liška through the glass window. He was standing in the middle of the office holding two CDs aloft, one in each hand. He held them lovingly: his index finger in the centre hole, his remaining fingers gently gripping the outside of the discs. He seemed to be in a state of confusion, his eyes moving from one CD to the other and back again.

Jonny rapped gently on the glass. Liška turned in response, a big smile enveloping his round, portly face as he shuffled across to the hatch and pulled back the glass.

"Honza, perfect timing," Liška exclaimed. "I can't decide which CD to play. The choice is between, firstly, the less well-known Johann Baptist Wanhal's Symphony in D minor, or a classic, Dvořák's String Quartet No. twelve, known as 'American'. Both are beautiful pieces of music by Czech composers. I can't decide. What do you think?"

Jonny smiled at Liška's eccentricity. It was not unlike that of Liška's former partner – his current boss and friend – Felix Mikeš.

"Tough decision, Josef. I have to be honest and confess I've never listened to either piece of music. But, I've never heard of Wanhal. It's always good to listen to something new."

"Great decision, Honza. Wanhal isn't well known but he had a big influence on Mozart's compositional style." He held up the winning CD in his left hand. "You'll love it... Actually, you'll love both of them."

Liška waddled over to the CD player and inserted the disc. He stood still, his conducting hands poised, as the first bars of music began. A big smile emerged on Jonny's face as he watched Liška become totally immersed in the music, helping to restore his positive disposition. He knew the feeling, having been totally absorbed in Bob Dylan's music so many times over his lifetime. A deep love for music, whatever the genre, seemed to lead to a natural kinship between people: the melody, harmony, or simply the words, taking them away to far-off places.

After allowing a respectful few minutes to pass, Liška seemingly having forgotten he was still there, Jonny coughed discreetly. Liška turned at the interruption, the spell broken, and toddled back to the hatch.

"Sorry, Honza. A beautiful melody is the heart of my life. I get lost in the music."

Jonny didn't answer, knowing it wasn't needed, nor did he have adequate words. They listened together as the rhythmic syncopation of the symphony rose and fell, dripping emotion at every note.

"Josef, I'm sorry to talk business, but Felix told me you found something at Alex Corbet's apartment."

"Yes, of course. I've put what I found in Room two. Here's the key, but I need you to sign the form to temporarily release the documents to you."

Liška pushed the key and form, along with a pair of plastic gloves, through the open hatch. Jonny signed and returned the form.

"I don't think what I found will help you solve the murder," Liška explained, "but it will definitely help you understand the family background."

"Interesting. Thanks, Josef."

Jonny walked the short corridor to Room two. The small number of rooms were rarely busy, only being used for purposes requiring total peace and quiet: study time, a disciplinary meeting or simply a space to compose oneself after an ordeal. Opening the door, Jonny saw an open shoe box on the table with a collection of loose papers inside. He put on the gloves, sat down and carefully took the handwritten pages out of the box.

It was immediately obvious they were letters. But, not just any old letters – love letters, from Alex Corbet to his wife, Helena Corbetová. The date of the letter on the top immediately struck a chord with Jonny, his thoughts going back to the stirring retelling of the couple's first meeting during the interview with Helena.

31 December 2009

  My dearest Helena,

  On this day eight years ago, I met the woman of my dreams. You and your friend's laughter lit up the pub, and you were the sparkle at the centre. That New Year's Eve was the most special day of my life and could never be bettered. The snow, the fireworks, and the significance of the date, were all perfect reasons to fall in love. And, I did. Head over heels...

Jonny read the rest of the crisp, well written letter; the words full of emotion. He couldn't help feeling further drawn to Alex Corbet and his values. But, why was the letter in the shoe box and not sent to Helena? Jonny turned to the next paper and got his answer.

10 January 2010

  My dearest Helena,

  I have to apologise. My last letter, on New Year's Eve, is the first I have ever written to you and not posted. I have tried to understand why, but it is too complicated to fully get my head round. I still love you, more than I believe I'll ever love anyone else. But, maybe my belief in us is failing. Despite sending you letters every week since I had to leave, not being able to stand the pressure from your mother any more, I see no glimmer of hope. I want 'us' to be together, man and wife, with our beautiful children, but I seem crowded out with no positive way forward...

The next four letters played on the same theme: a romantic man missing the love of his life, a forlorn and not improving marriage, frustration about the increasing influence of Helena's mother, and growing desperation about the future.

7 February 2010

Dearest Helena,

You have been the closest person to me since we met. I know you very well. I know you better than anyone else knows you, even your mother. You are ill again – it is as clear as day to me. However, when I said something to you today, after dropping back the children, you just blanked me. I love you, I want to take care of you, but you won't let me in. You have chosen your mother over me. Again! If this is really what you want, I have to accept it. But, surely you owe me the truth. I am your husband and the father of your children; the least you owe me is to tell me what is happening so that we can plan together. I want you to get better, and I know you want the same thing, so why am I left out? ...

Jonny slumped back in the chair, the missing part of the jigsaw in the family saga starting to take shape. He slowly read the rest of the letter. The key points were repeated, with increasing frustration and venom, Alex's worry and love for his wife shining through. The weekly letters continued, sometimes twice a week, short and sharp, but always repeating the same plea: demanding honesty and asking to be let back in to help his wife and family.

7 March 2010

Dearest Helena,

It is tearing me apart to see you ill again. I have told you over and over again that I want to help, but you will not even admit the situation. Why do you want me on the outside? We have two wonderful children and they deserve us both on the same side, fighting for your health and happiness.

I am here in this awful apartment only to provide you and the children with as much money as I can spare. But, why am I doing it when you treat me as an outsider? I have thought about it long and hard and I think I have no choice. Our children's futures are at stake here! My only option is legal and I've decided to contact Pavel. I'm sorry to do this, but you have left me with no choice.

I love you.

Alex x

The letters continued on a weekly basis, sometimes more frequent. A few were scrawled and hard to decipher, no doubt after returning from a night at the pub, but always clearly professing his love. Jonny had reached the bottom of the shoe box – the last letter.

4 April 2010

Dear Helena,

This letter is so hard for me to write; I have started and then stopped many times, screwing up the paper in anguish. Now, I have finally begun, maybe I will send it to you with all the other unsent letters.

The fact is I love you and will always love you. My first choice is to be with you and our children. But, if this is not your wish, I still offer you my full support. I will be there as much as you need me, to help you and look after our children as they grow.

The custody of our children if anything, God forbid, bad happens to you is still a contentious point. After Pavel refused to act further for me in a legal capacity, I consulted another solicitor. The will we both prepared is clear – I would get custody. I am sure your mother will push you to nullify our joint will, and prepare another one which would exclude me, but I believe I have strong grounds to contest. And, I would. The children should be with their father, not their grandmother. But, that is for a later day and one I hope never arrives.

I am also sorry I became angry a few times recently. I know you think I was wrong to move out, but I couldn't stand it any more. I wanted it to stimulate a reconciliation, for us to fall in love all over again, but I now see there was another matter that I was not privy to – your health. I think in hindsight, you will come to realise you were wrong to keep me on the outside; I knew you were ill again and raised it with you on numerous occasions, but you refused to talk about the situation. But, please do not ever berate yourself over it. I know who was to blame, and it wasn't you.

The final part of this letter is equally difficult. During our separation, I have remained faithful, thinking only of you and our family. But, with the realisation of the true situation, I naturally started to think about the future. And, I suppose it is fair to say that my eye started to wander. I have met a woman I like and we have seen each other a few times. I have no aspirations for an intense relationship at this time: you and the children are still my number one priority. But, I have to face facts and try to be happy. She makes me smile which I need at this point. This may be hard to read, and I apologise, but you must understand firstly, how hard I have tried and, secondly, that being with you will always be my first choice.

Forever yours
Alex x

Jonny placed the letters back in the box and replaced the lid. He sighed, the sadness of the broken marriage recalling his own previous intense emotions of blame and longing. Even sadder was the lost hope for the future, Alex Corbet's life having been cut short so young.

The confirmation of motive regarding the custody of the children could not be dismissed, but he still doubted Daniela Nováková would resort to organising a murder. Whilst the outcome of any legal challenge could not have been predicted, the power of her solicitor would have put every possible hurdle and delay in the way of her losing at least some involvement in raising her two grandchildren.

No, he knew he was still looking elsewhere for the murderer. But, sitting there looking at the secret shoe box of love letters, he vowed to himself to ensure the letters were given to Helena when the investigation was closed. It was his unspoken promise to Alex.

33

Compelled to Watch

The discovery of the letters had a more pronounced emotional impact on Jonny than he'd expected. He felt more fragile than normal; his new Czech family was bouncing around in his thoughts and they were no nearer to solving the double murder. Lack of sleep wasn't helping either.

Police work had hardened him over the years and he had grown immune to most of the grisly discoveries during murder investigations. But the pain of the victims and their families always touched him deeply, and he doubted that would ever change. The seemingly avoidable loss of love in this case, and the likelihood that the subsequent murder may not have happened at all if Alex and Helena hadn't separated, was almost too much to bear. Jonny felt every case had a cathartic moment, but it wasn't usually revealed until close to the end of the investigation.

Am I close to solving this case?

It certainly didn't feel like it. Returning the love letters to Helena would liberate her from some pain, but without catching the murderer, or at least having a prime suspect under interrogation, the gesture would be empty.

Having returned the letters to Liška, he went back to the Incident Room. He was so preoccupied, he missed greetings of "Honza" from two of the team already working away in the open floor office on their weekend shift. Tiredness had dulled his senses.

Boukal was already in the room, busily updating the Murder Board. "Ahoj, Honza," he said excitedly. "The van hire company have called back. Maybe, just maybe, we are finally getting somewhere."

"Right," Jonny muttered gruffly, sitting down heavily.

Boukal threw a swift glance at his mentor, clearly not expecting the apparent disinterest. Resisting the urge to say something, he quickly turned his attention back to the whiteboard to finish adding the new case information ahead of the update meeting.

Seeking a distraction, in need of something different to mull over, Jonny found himself assessing Boukal's scruffy suit jacket and trousers. The dark, blue material was so creased the thin white lines running down his leg appeared to be more of a zigzag pattern, rather than the intended straight, bold mark. He knew he'd promised to take Boukal shopping once the case had been solved, but he found himself mentally calculating the schedule of the day and if time would be available to get to the shops before they closed.

Dvořáková was next to arrive, carrying her usual bundle of papers. She sat down and looked across at Jonny. "Honza, you don't seem your usual self today."

"I'm sorry." He sighed. "I've just got a lot on my mind."

"Anything you want to talk about?"

He turned and smiled warmly at her. "Thanks, Lucie, but I'll be fine. I'll feel a lot better once we solve this case."

He knew a woman's intuition wasn't easily fooled and felt her eyes upon him. He wanted to open up and share his anxieties, but it wasn't the right time. Maybe later, he thought, when we've made some progress and my thoughts are clearer.

The commotion of Mikeš' arrival provided the distraction he sought. He could be heard from the other side of the office, greeting everyone in his team: rallying the troops with personal messages about their family, or the previous night's ice hockey results. It was a personal strength that Jonny admired greatly – being able to motivate his team on character alone. He had always been more of an introverted character, leading by example through respect and results gained over a sustained period of time.

"Dobré ráno," Mikeš boomed as he entered the room, full of early morning exuberance.

Matching his mood, Mikeš wore a bold yellow shirt and tie combination and a huge smile. He took off his wide-brimmed hat, placed it on the table with his cane, lovingly adjusted his tweed suit and sat down next to Jonny, slapping his colleague's thigh in welcome. "Emails done, telephone calls all returned," he related, smiling. "We just need to solve this case and it will be a good weekend."

Mikeš was about to clap his hands to start the meeting when he remembered something. He turned to face Jonny. "Honza, I forgot to ask, how did the dinner go? Did you find out anything interesting about your Czech family?"

All eyes were on Jonny now, exactly what he didn't want. "Yes, it was good." He paused, in thought. "It was also a bit emotional, I suppose. It's probably best if I tell you about it later."

Mikeš' eyes perked up in interest, willing more information. Jonny just shrugged in response, indicating that the subject was closed for now.

"No problem. Marek, let's get going," Mikeš bellowed. "Take us through where we are."

"To start, we have obtained a number of statements from

people who went to the pub in Chodov on the Friday night of the murders. We are still waiting for a few statements to come back, but at this stage it looks like Torsten Lindberg's story checks out. Other people at the pub remember that he was drunk and his wife came to pick him up after eleven p.m. Copies of the statements are in the folder. Also, Dr Králová has confirmed that his DNA does not match the samples found in the trenches."

"Thought that would be the case," Jonny remarked wearily.

"More importantly," Boukal continued quickly, "the van hire company returned my call early this morning. The van was hired two weeks ago, near the end of March. The hire period was one calendar month. The hire fee was paid for in cash up front, along with the required insurance and a deposit. The name of the person who hired the van is Henry Bialas."

"What sort of name is that?" exclaimed Mikeš.

"All we have at this stage is a copy of a residence document from Poland, and a copy of a recent electricity bill from a residence in Prague 4. He provided these as evidence of his identity and address to the hire company. Neither have a photo, but a team of detectives are on their way over to the address now. The mobile he gave is for a burner phone but it's switched off."

"Polish?" Jonny uttered, looking puzzled. "That explains the surname. But, Henry is a strange first name."

"He told the owner of the van hire company he was born in Canada, but has Polish heritage," Boukal explained. "We have checked the social media websites, but we haven't found any references to Henry Bialas at all. He is also not on our police database."

Dvořáková looked up from her mobile phone. "Bialas is a Polish surname which translates as 'White' in English. It's the same as 'Bílý' in Czech."

"All very odd," stated Mikeš. "Do we know anything more? If he is working here in Prague, or why he wanted to hire the van?"

"No," Boukal confirmed. "The hire company didn't ask for any more details. They told me most people hire the vans for moving apartments, or as a temporary replacement if a vehicle breaks down."

"Make sense," Jonny acknowledged. "What about CCTV at the office?"

"They run the business from home, just outside Prague. Unfortunately, they don't have any CCTV. But, they're coming to the station now to help put together a photo-fit description of the man. Let's hope they got a good look at the man because the description that Jakub Novák gave us of the workman from last Friday night was near useless."

"Yes, fingers crossed," Jonny stated. "Let us know as soon as we have information from the detectives visiting his address. We should definitely pull him in for interview if he is there."

"And, ask them to check if the white van is parked in the street or close by," Mikeš added.

"Yes, sir."

A gentle knock on the door caught everyone's attention. A detective from the office opened the door, and handed Boukal a paper, before nodding in respect to everyone and swiftly departing.

Boukal read the note carefully and shook his head in despair. "Henry Bialas moved out from the apartment stated on his electricity bill about five weeks ago. The current tenants don't know exactly when because there was a delay of a few days whilst the apartment was cleaned for them to move in. We are now contacting the landlord to confirm the precise dates."

"Damn!" Mikeš shouted. "We are not having any luck."

"There is no luck involved here," Jonny asserted. "No, in my opinion, this has all been carefully planned."

"I felt good this morning, but this killer is making me angry all over again," Mikeš proclaimed. "I want this man caught. Marek, please put his name, the van details, and the identity sketch when we have it, out to all units across the Czech Republic. And, also contact the Polish Police to find out if they have any information on him. It's possible he has returned over the border in the last few days."

"Yes, sir," Boukal replied. "I will also start contact with the Canadian and Polish Police, but this will not give us quick results."

Silence descended on the room as the further frustrating news sunk in.

"Don't forget," Jonny began solemnly, "there is still no definite connection between the person who hired the white van, Henry Bialas, and the murders. We definitely need to find him and interrogate him. But, at this stage, we only know that the van was parked in the street on the night the bodies were found and that Petr Řepka also saw a white van of the same make on the street the night of the murders."

"I think we might have a stronger connection than that," Dvořáková stated, handing out a wad of papers to each person.

"What have you found out, Lucie?" Jonny encouraged.

"This will take a bit of explaining, so please bear with me," she started. "We have now reviewed all the footage sent through by the TV news channel which produced the outside broadcast on Wednesday. Firstly, we reviewed the live reports broadcast on TV the night the victims were found, and any repeated in future evenings. There is some footage showing people in a small crowd behind the news reporter, but it is mostly teenagers messing around, waving at the camera. The images of the people are not clear and there certainly doesn't seem to be anyone in the crowd looking like our disguised workman."

"Remember, he may have been wearing different clothes than on the CCTV recordings," Jonny clarified. "The exhumation was five days after the murders."

"We did consider that point," she replied, slight irritation in her voice. "We checked carefully and there is definitely nobody on the film matching the height and build of the man we are looking for."

Jonny chided himself for his harsh tone and nodded respectfully back at Dvořáková.

"But, we did find something," she continued, pride in her voice. "The TV news channel also sent us all the digital film they have from the outside broadcast. It seems they keep all their film for a period of time in case they get challenged about the accuracy or bias of their reporting. The film is mostly made up of practice reports, before the reporter goes on air, and also background filming to use during the live broadcasts, when the reporter talks over the images of the scene. Now, because the street Hluboká is in a residential area, some people needed access to or from their apartments whilst the police operation was ongoing. We had blocked off the bottom end of the street and set up an entrance post as part of the police cordon at the top of the street, close to where the TV camera crew was based. My officers were checking the ID of any person wanting to go through the checkpoint. If the person didn't have ID on them, they were escorted to their building by an officer where they had to show proof they lived there. The recorded film shows a few people arriving and being let through the checkpoint, or being escorted to their building, as I have just explained."

"Lucie, I'm sorry but I'm starting to lose track of this," Mikeš said, a perplexed frown on his face.

"I've nearly finished, sir. The key point is that we never thought to check the ID of the people wanting to exit. We assumed any people wanting to leave through the checkpoint were going to work, maybe to a nightshift or something similar. The recorded film catches a few people leaving like this. And, if you look at the photos marked one to five in your pack, you will see a man, who I believe is our disguised workman, leaving through the checkpoint at 9.47 p.m. The man is not wearing the fluorescent vest, but he's all dressed in black with a cap on. It is difficult to see the features of his face because he is in the distance on the video, but the height and build of the man in the film look the same as the workman on the CCTV."

Mikeš suddenly realised the importance of the information. He turned his head in an exaggerated manner to look directly at Jonny. "He was there whilst we were digging up the two people he'd murdered. I can't believe it!"

"The last photo in your pack is the best blown-up image we could get from the film," Dvořáková added. "It's not good enough to issue to the press, but maybe we could combine it with the photo-fit description we get from the owners of the van hire company."

Jonny lowered his head to study the photos, taking time to consider the options.

"Does he live there?" he mumbled aloud. "Or maybe he was visiting someone?"

"I think it was neither of those options," Dvořáková answered quickly, "but I need a few more minutes to explain."

Jonny, Mikeš and Boukal remained silent, totally captivated, flicking ahead to look at the remaining photos in the pack.

"Along with copies of the live recordings and the digital film, the TV news channel also sent us all the mobile footage they'd received from the public. If you remember, lots of local residents were watching the operation out of their windows, and some must have taken videos and photos on their phones and emailed them to the TV news channel. In the end, none of them were used on TV, but I still looked through them. Most are from high up, floors two or above, where residents had a good vantage point. But, there was one that caught my attention. This mobile video was taken from inside a vehicle parked on the street. To be precise, the video is taken through the front windscreen of the vehicle. See photos six to twelve in your pack. The video lasts about two minutes and mostly shows police officers moving around as part of the operation, going in or out of the tent we had erected. In the middle of the video, the camera zooms in on Honza, Marek and you, sir, as you walk across the street."

"The front of the vehicle is visible in the video," Jonny added, "and—"

"It's the white van!" Boukal cried out, excitedly.

Mikeš looked at Jonny again, eyes wide in alarm.

"He's been watching our every move," Jonny attested, no emotion in his voice.

"Sick bastard!" Mikeš snapped.

"And, he is revelling in it." Jonny paused to check his words. "These people are usually on some sort of mission or crusade. Whatever it is, it means a lot to him, more than anything else in his life. He is compelled to watch. Even if he tries, he cannot leave. That's why I think he is still here, in Prague. And I bet he's still watching us."

34

A Game of Chase

The update meeting had finished swiftly and with no consensus on the next steps. Mikeš had started to rant and rave, his frustration with the case starting to boil over. Jonny's customary role in the relationship was a calming influence, soothing the highs and lows of his colleague's emotions, but this time he let Mikeš vent his anger unhindered.

Mikeš had eventually stormed out of the room, insisting Boukal follow him. Ignoring the habitual briefing with his detective team, he declared he was indignant at chasing around a criminal to their own tune and instead was going to close down some of the other serious crime cases. Jonny knew Mikeš would return to his senses in a few hours and re-join the murder hunt, full of renewed enthusiasm, but for now he was happy to push on alone.

In a way, Jonny had found it soothing; Mikeš' vented anger echoed his own frustrations. The thunder had taken the heat out of the situation and allowed him to see the murder investigation for what it was – a game of chase. Granted, it was complicated, with the odds stacked against the pursuer, but it was a game, nonetheless. The positive news from the meeting was the identification of the man who had hired the van and the subsequent link to the night when the victims' bodies had been found buried under the pavement. With the new evidence providing some light at the end of the tunnel, he felt strangely renewed, a conviction returning to catch the cold-blooded killer still on the loose.

"Great work, Lucie. That was inspired police work."

Dvořáková appeared unconvinced as she collected up the papers, some having been strewn on the floor during the commotion.

"Really, I mean it," he insisted. "There are not many sergeants I've worked with who would have thought to check the extra film footage provided by the TV news channel, let alone the mobile videos. And, by the way, some of the sergeants I'm thinking of went on to make top detectives."

Dvořáková stopped gathering the papers. "Thank you, Honza. That means a lot to me."

He stooped to pick up the last paper laying under the desk. "I also noticed there were a few more papers in the pack you handed out. But, you didn't get a chance to report them."

"Yes," she replied, idly tidying up the layout of the displaced table and chairs. "The information is mostly about Yulia Ivanova. We finally had a full report from the local police in Hradec Králové, including a summary of her family in Russia. Her parents and brother still live there, but there's no report of anything suspicious: no family feud or angry ex-husband. After you met Mikhail Antonov yesterday, I also called Svetlana Lebedev. She admitted to exaggerating the fights between Yulia and Mikhail, but is adamant Yulia wanted to get away from him, hence why they moved away from Brno. Something doesn't quite add up, but I suppose we will never know."

"Probably right," he sighed. "Was there anything else?"

"Only about Mikhail Antonov. His handwriting came back negative; the graphologist said it definitely wasn't a match. Jakub

Novák also did not recognise his headshot. And finally, Dr Králová has confirmed that his DNA does not match the samples found at the burial site. But, I think we expected these outcomes."

"Yes, but it's important to be thorough."

Dvořáková walked towards the door of the meeting room and turned. "I'm going back to my desk. Let me know if you need anything."

"Are you busy now?" he asked.

"Well," she replied, looking at her watch, "I have a few things to check on. I asked one of my officers to start searching through the CCTV recordings from Thursday and Friday afternoon around the street Hluboká. As you suggested, I thought we should examine if the man posing as the building contractor undertook any reconnaissance before the murders were committed. She's also looking for the white van. The officer won't be finished yet, but I need to check on her progress."

"I think it's definitely worth checking. This murderer doesn't seem the type to make a mistake, but if he's on CCTV exploring the area beforehand it might be the only way we will find out what he looks like."

"Apart from that, I just need to follow up on the progress of a few other cases. Why?"

"I was thinking maybe you could come with me to talk to Alex Corbet's parents. They were on the early flight from London and are staying at a hotel close by."

"Yes, sure. But, I'll have to let Felix know. Give me thirty minutes or so and I'll join you."

"Great, thanks, Lucie."

Jonny stayed in the Incident Room whilst Dvořáková returned to her post. He paced the room for a while, thinking through everything that had happened since the bodies were found on Wednesday evening. The knowledge that the murderer was watching them added a new, slightly odd dimension to his evaluation. Everything told him this was the pivotal point in the investigation; they were getting closer, but the murderer was still ahead of them. Their next steps had to be right.

He sat down, closed his eyes and breathed deeply. Distilling his thoughts, he came to two, clear conclusions: firstly, he felt sure the motive was centred on Alex Corbet, and, secondly, the murders were almost certainly committed by the man who had hired the white van. Linking the two strands at this stage was difficult, but he knew the best chance of uncovering the murderer's identity was to find out why Alex was the target.

His deliberations turned to why the mystery man, assumed to be Henry Bialas, would want to follow the investigation so closely. He thought through the possibility that the murderer wanted to be caught, gaining notoriety in the process, or maybe even fancied himself in a head-to-head dual with the renowned detectives. Whilst both were possible, neither felt right because the murders were personal, and messy; not cold-blooded.

No, there must be a deep personal connection in the murderer's mind to Alex – enough to kill him.

Jonny's time in the Metropolitan Police had brought him face-to-face with many criminals fitting the profile of this man. Bill Sutherland, the serial killer, had left the most lasting impression, but he'd also led the pursuit of villains with a delusional disorder or psychosis in other high profile cases. These people had mental health issues and were characterised by holding idiosyncratic beliefs that contradicted reality. He learned that murderers with this condition didn't run off, away from the scene of the crime. Instead, the personal connection made them stay close, wanting to be involved or follow the progress of the investigation – like Mikeš' serial killer. But, because of their commitment to the cause, they planned every move meticulously, lowering the chance of catching them because of an oversight or mistake.

The more he thought about the case, the more Jonny convinced himself the murderer must have been following Alex Corbet during the last month. Given the high level of planning involved, the murderer would definitely have needed to undertake a significant amount of reconnaissance work. It was probably also the reason why Petr Řepka thought he was being followed. Whilst Jonny was no nearer understanding the motive for the murders, it was clear that everyone involved, including the police, was a pawn in someone's sick chess game.

Feeling increasingly sure Alex Corbet had always been the target, Jonny pulled out his notepad. He quickly drew the spider-like diagram from the whiteboard, circling the names of people connected to Alex. George Webb had already provided confirmation that Alex knew he was being followed. But, the most important part of the revelation to Jonny was that Alex had played down the seriousness of the situation to protect others. He'd only been able to stir George Webb's memories of what Alex had said about being followed and the delivery of the warning note after talking to him for a second time. Jonny checked his watch. The next scheduled job was to talk to Alex Corbet's parents, but there was still time left in the day to organise another interview with Torsten Lindberg. He knew he should also talk to Tanya Murray again, to test what confidences Alex Corbet might have shared with her over coffees and lunches. He felt he probably had everything from George Webb but noted down a potential visit to the Červený lev pub later to speak to the manager and some of the locals.

First stop, though, was Helena Corbetová. Although they hadn't been speaking much, as her statements and the unposted letters had already attested, she knew Alex very well, probably better than anyone. He decided to call, knowing another face-to-face audience with Helena was probably already barred by her mother unless their solicitor was present; maybe he could catch Helena alone at her apartment before Daniela arrived.

Jonny's call was answered after three rings.

"Daniela Nováková."

He sighed – too late.

"Mrs Nováková, Jonathan Fox here. I have a couple of simple questions I would like to ask Helena. It will just take a few minutes. Can I please speak to her?"

"No."

"But, this is important to the investigation. It could be vital to catching her husband's murderer."

"No. And, especially not after the stunt you pulled yesterday, hauling my husband down the station for questioning. Speak to my solicitor if you want to arrange any further interviews. You know how to contact him."

The phone line went dead.

Not to be deterred, he decided to try Helena's sister. He dialled the London telephone number for Kristýna Davies and, to his surprise, she picked up after two rings.

"Kristýna Davies."

"Hello, Ms Davies. It's Jonathan Fox again. Please don't hang up. Can you just hear me out for one minute? If you still don't want to talk then I will leave you alone. But, I hope you might listen to my question because I think you might be able to help me find the person who killed Alex Corbet."

"My family had nothing to do with his murder."

"I know."

"So, why are you calling me?"

"Will you at least just listen to what I have to say?"

"Okay, but just one minute."

"Thank you. Firstly, it's nice to see someone else working on a Saturday. I assume you are working on a big case like me."

There was no answer, just an audible sigh on the other end of the line.

"Secondly, I know your family were not involved in the murder of Alex and the woman he was with last Friday. Mind you, Jakub could have made it easier for us—"

"What do you mean?"

"He met Alex and the woman murdered with him when walking his dogs about thirty minutes before we believe they were killed. But, he conveniently forgets to tell us. Anyway, I think you'd best speak to your mother about that."

Again, silence.

"The last and final point is part statement and part question. We know Alex was being followed. Your mother hired a private detective which we know about."

"Mr Fox—"

"It's true, ask her. But, I'm not interested in this. I believe Alex was also being followed by someone else. Someone who eventually killed him. My question is this: did Alex say anything to you about being followed? Anything he said to you, maybe something you thought was odd, could prove vital to the investigation."

There was a long pause. Jonny waited patiently.

"That was actually the reason Alex was calling me. He thought my mother had organised someone to follow him. He wanted me to speak to her, to ask her to stop it. I told my mother, but she flatly denied it."

"But, why did Alex call you five times in as many days?"

"Because he claimed lots of things were happening, something almost every day. I can't remember exactly, but one day his post was taken, another day a note was stuck to his door, then a pizza was delivered he hadn't ordered. He claimed it was my mother trying to spook him, putting pressure on him to back off."

"How did he know his post was taken?"

"Again, I'm not exactly sure. He said something about the post boxes in the entrance hall having small windows in the front. He saw there was post when he came in from work but left it because he had his hands full. When he came back down later in the evening, the post had gone from the box. And, he claimed it then reappeared the next day."

"And, Alex hadn't seen any one strange in the building where he was living?"

"I asked him that. He said that he'd talked to some people living in other apartments, but none of them had seen anyone unusual in the building."

"Finally, did Alex tell you he was also being followed outside the building?"

"No, he didn't say anything about that to me."

"Mrs Davies, I know it may not appear much, but this information has been really useful. I know you were at odds with Alex, but once this is all over I strongly suggest you speak to your sister about what really happened. Thank you again. And, I hope your case goes well."

"Thank you, Mr Fox."

Jonny finished the call and punched the air.

35

Deeply Shocked

Feeling buoyed by a small chink of light at the end of the tunnel, Jonny was already less tense when Dvořáková returned to the Incident Room. His appetite was also returning, hunger pains starting to increase in frequency and volume; he'd grabbed an instant coffee after speaking to Kristýna Davies by phone, but still hadn't eaten all day.

"You look better," she remarked, casually. She was fitting on her police hat, ready to venture outside the station.

"Yes. Sorry about earlier. I can't stand it when a murder investigation stalls. I take it personally and usually have to hide myself away to take a fresh look at all the evidence."

"Is this one of your secrets? The reason you've been such a successful detective?"

He tilted his head to the side, considering the question. "I suppose I consider everyone to be different. What works for one person may not work at all for another. Most successful detectives I've known have had quirky ways of working, but it helps them see possibilities other people cannot see. Sure, it's important to follow all the leads, but you need a technique to get through the block when it comes – and I can assure you, it comes a lot. I'm not easy to be around when it happens to me; I need personal space to go back through every bit of evidence until I find a link to work on."

"And, there's no special technique?"

"I'm afraid not. I suggest you follow your own personality traits – be yourself, basically. The more eccentric the better."

"Great!" She rolled her eyes. "So, I'm going to have to be like you or Felix if I want to be a successful detective."

"Very likely." He laughed.

"By the way, I phoned ahead to the hotel and Alex Corbet's parents have arrived."

"Great," he replied. "Shall we get going?"

The hotel was a short walk from the police station, nestled amongst the cobbled streets of the old town, close to the river. The boutique hotel was not what Jonny thought would be first choice for such a distressing trip, but he knew not to judge harshly decisions made under stress. Perhaps the hotel was their preferred place to stay when visiting Alex, Helena and their grandchildren over recent years.

Jonny and Dvořáková walked in comfortable silence under the brightening skies as they crossed Old Town Square and entered the warren of cobbled streets, following Karlova through its many twists and turns. Walking alongside someone was always an enlightening experience: the sequencing of steps, body movement and head turning telling so much about a person that simple conversation could not convey. His walks alongside Mikeš were now well established, and a source of considerable pleasure. But outside of the station he'd only spent time alone with Dvořáková in a car. Long drives were good for finding a middle ground in any relationship, but the freedom of walking opened up so much more in the physical connection between two people.

He broke the silence as they strode across the cobbles. "The good news is I think I found a link in the case this morning."

She turned her head to him, looking interested. "What did you find?"

"Well, I went back over every step of the investigation so far and came to the simple conclusion that Alex Corbet was the original target all along. Finding out Petr Řepka was following Alex initially threw me off the scent. Whoever killed Alex and Yulia must have been following Alex for a while, and they possibly even started before Řepka. This man, Henry Bialas or whoever he is, had a big issue with Alex and tried to unnerve him. We know about the warning note, which George Webb has now told us was stuck to Alex's apartment door. And, earlier, I called Helena's sister in London. When Alex spoke to her in the week before he was murdered, he claimed someone was playing games with him: moving his post, ordering pizzas, that sort of thing. I'm convinced the motive for the murders is connected to this bizarre behaviour."

"But, why would the killer play these games?"

"I'm still not sure yet. But, I want to talk to Torsten Lindberg and his wife later. Also, Tanya Murray. Maybe even some of Alex's friends at the pub: people he spoke to regularly. Someone knows something that could unlock this case completely, probably something they don't even realise is important."

Turning left, now deep in the historic, old town, they approached the Prague Crossroads, otherwise known as St. Anne's Church. The newly restored public venue had appealed to Jonny from the first time he'd read about it. Vaclav Havel, the world renowned Czech statesman and writer, and last president of Czechoslovakia, had restored the church and opened it with his wife as an international spiritual centre.

He stopped abruptly at the large noticeboard outside the steps to the church and scanned the programme.

"Are you thinking of going to an event, Honza?" she asked, stopping alongside him.

"Yes, I would like to take Ivana."

"The interior is amazing. I've only been to one event, but I'd love to go again."

Jonny took a leaflet and put it into his jacket pocket, restarting the walk. Dvořáková stepped in alongside him.

"You seem much better now," she suggested. "I was worried about you earlier. I know this murder investigation is causing all sorts of headaches, but you didn't seem like your normal self."

He glanced across at her as they approached the hotel. "Yes, much better thanks. But, it would be good to talk. Shall we grab a coffee after this meeting?"

"I'd like that."

The foyer of the hotel was busy. Dvořáková approached reception to announce their arrival whilst he loitered around the central fountain feature, reading the inscription explaining the history of the building. His attention was drawn to a middle-aged couple in their mid-fifties, sitting in a corner with a pot of tea on the table in front of them. The woman was crying softly into a handkerchief whilst her husband attempted to calm her. Jonny's experience told him immediately they were Alex's parents and he approached them respectfully.

"Mr and Mrs Corbet?"

"Yes," Mr Corbet replied.

"Hello. My name is Jonathan Fox, I'm a consultant working with the Czech Police. My colleague, Sergeant Dvořáková, is just at reception, but I thought I'd introduce myself."

"Please sit down."

Dvořáková walked over, introduced herself to the Corbet's and sat down.

"Mr and Mrs Corbet," Jonny began, "we know how difficult this is for you. I'm sure you are keen to see Helena and your grandchildren as soon as possible. The sergeant can also arrange for you to see your son's body if you wish."

"Yes, please," Mrs Corbet answered, slightly breathless. "I need to see my son."

"How about three p.m. this afternoon?" Dvořáková proposed, receiving nods in response. "I will arrange a car to pick you up and then return you to the hotel."

"Thank you," Mr Corbet said, pulling his wife close.

"I also want to assure you," Jonny continued, "we are doing everything we can to find out who murdered Alex. I just have a couple of questions. Any information you can provide could really help us understand what happened to him in the last few weeks."

Mr Corbet nodded his acceptance whilst his wife lowered her head and continued weeping.

"Firstly, Alex believed Helena was ill. Do you have any information to help us understand what had happened?"

Mrs Corbet shot a knowing look at her husband.

"We last visited Prague in December," Mr Corbet started to explain. "We were delivering Christmas presents. It was very difficult because Alex had recently left the marital home. We came away very upset, but my wife said then that Helena was ill again. We asked Alex about it, but he refused to say what was happening."

"Again?" Jonny questioned.

"Helena had leukaemia when she was a child…" Mrs Corbet blurted out, unable to finish what she planned to say.

"We were told she had fully recovered when she was a young teenager," Mr Corbet took over the explanation. "We were naturally worried about it when Alex and Helena initially told us, including the potential of the disease being genetic and passing on to the grandchildren. Helena was always slim, fragile-looking. But, over the past few years we were becoming increasingly worried she was getting weaker, especially since their second child was born."

"I suppose you were better placed to see the changes in her health," Jonny suggested.

"Yes. We came to Prague three or four times a year, so we could clearly see how much weaker she was becoming. We mentioned it to Alex on numerous occasions, but he always dismissed it and said she was fine."

"So, Alex didn't even tell you recently that Helena was ill again?"

"No," Mr Corbet confirmed, "but he probably didn't want to worry us."

"Yes, of course," Jonny answered. "Thank you, I think I understand now."

"Does it have anything to do with why he was murdered?" Mr Corbet asked.

"No, I don't think so. It was an unexplained thread of the investigation, something I didn't understand."

"Daniela is so controlling," Mrs Corbet snapped. "We tried telling Alex."

An awkward silence descended. Jonny consulted his notepad.

"I have only one other question," he restarted. "Did Alex say anything to you about being followed in the past week or so?"

Mr Corbet cleared the emotion from his throat. "Alex never wanted to worry us. He knew living in a different country brought us some anxiety, especially as he was our only son. He was always positive, painting a happy picture for us so we wouldn't worry. But it was different in the last month or so. I could tell he was getting stressed and anxious, so I finally convinced him to open up to us. That's when he told us he was being followed."

"Did he say who he thought was following him?" Jonny asked gently.

"Well, this is the part that confused us," Mr Corbet continued. "In the last two weeks, we had numerous phone conversations with him. Some days he was fine, but other days he was quite disturbed, almost paranoid. The situation at work was definitely getting tense, and some days he was convinced his boss, Torsten Lindberg, was following him and trying to mess with his head. Alex claimed Torsten wanted to blackmail him and force him to resign from the company. On other days, Alex thought Daniela, Helena's mother, was having him followed, although we never fully understood why. In truth, we didn't really know what to make of it."

"We've spoken to Alex's friends and work colleagues about this," Jonny confirmed. "The slightly odd aspect is that he didn't seem stressed by what was happening to him. George Webb, who I'm sure you know, told me Alex didn't seem worried."

"Alex was always like that, protecting others. We know our son and he was always thinking of other people ahead of himself. He was initially doing the same with us, pretending everything was fine. But, we knew something wasn't right. It took a few pleas from us before he finally started to open up, and when he did, well…" Mr Corbet glanced at his wife. "Well, we were deeply shocked and concerned."

36

Once Removed

Sitting in the café with Dvořáková, waiting for their coffees, Jonny couldn't help feeling on edge. The revelation of Alex Corbet's concerns about being followed in the weeks before his murder had only served to strengthen the sensation, looming larger by the minute, that he'd initially missed something during the first few days of the investigation. Coming from Alex's parents, the disclosure carried more weight because they had no connection to their son's company in Prague; they had been at arm's length, in a different country, and were only repeating the information Alex had told them over the phone.

The resentment from the parents towards Helena's family was expected; they would naturally side with their son, worrying about the effect on their grandchildren, blaming Helena, and especially her mother, for the separation. The added information about Helena's childhood illness had closed the loop for Jonny on this particular sad strand of the investigation.

He found his thoughts spiralling around the connections with Alex's work. Torsten Lindberg seemed such a weak character to him, not capable of such a callous crime. He also seemed to have a solid alibi. Maybe someone else connected to him, such as his wife, had taken matters into their own hands. *Could it be an organised killing after all?*

As he sat replaying words and body language from the

previous interviews in his head, Dvořáková was busy on the phone. Liaising with her team back at the station, she was arranging a further interview with Torsten Lindberg, this time with his wife present, and a visit to Tanya Murray.

They'd felt guilty leaving Alex's parents bereft in the hotel foyer, but time was of the essence and they needed to act. After establishing that Mr and Mrs Corbet were going to be staying in Prague for the foreseeable future, Jonny's only concession was to promise to update them as soon as he had any material updates on the case.

"Right, Honza," she began. "Tanya Murray is at her apartment and will wait for us before going out. Torsten Lindberg was more difficult. He wanted to know what the meeting was about and tried to delay it until Monday. My guess is that he doesn't want the whole situation discussed in front of his wife."

"I think you're right."

"In the end, I just told him we'd be visiting him at two p.m. and advised him and his wife to be in at this time, otherwise we would send a marked police car with flashing lights to pick both of them up."

"I like your style, Lucie," he said, chuckling to himself.

"I also tried to get hold of Felix, but he didn't answer. I've left him a voicemail to say I'm going with you on the interviews, but I'm not sure he's going to be happy. I know it's the weekend, but there are still outstanding tasks on some of the ongoing investigations to oversee."

"Don't worry," he replied. "I'll also send him a message. This is my decision and he'll have to take it out on me if he doesn't like it."

Dvořáková had clearly been impressed by being invited into the inner sanctum of Jonny and Mikeš' hideaway café. Jonny knew she was burning to become a detective and used every opportunity to quiz him on his thoughts and practices. Her girlish glances gave away how privileged she was to be offered a seat at the top table, despite Jonny's protests that it was just a simple, but welcoming café.

Luka had also been clearly captivated by Dvořáková, winking at Jonny and pulling an impressed face when she turned her back on her way over to the corner table. Despite being in uniform, without makeup and with her hair tied up under her police hat, she still struck an attractive figure: a typical Slavic appearance of fair hair, light skin, blue eyes, a straight but not prominent nose, matched with a tall, slim frame and good posture. Jonny had found himself suddenly becoming protective, shaking his head in a fatherly way to rebuke Luka.

"There we are," Luka said cheerfully. "Honza's usual cappuccino with chocolate, and a single shot skinny cappuccino with cinnamon for you. And, two baguettes: one tuna, one cheese."

Luka stood back, smiling at Dvořáková and waiting to be introduced.

"Luka, this is Sergeant Dvořáková," Jonny began, enjoying the role of introducing people in his adopted city. "She is the one who organises both Felix and I. And, to be truthful, we'd be lost without her."

"Please call me Lucie," Dvořáková stated quickly, holding out her hand in greeting.

"Hi, Lucie, really pleased to meet you. I'm Luka. I opened this café about nine months ago. It's small, but I'm building a loyal set of customers, including Honza and Felix: the dynamic duo and my best customers."

Dvořáková laughed at the reference.

"Please pop in anytime," he continued, "I like to think I make a mean cappuccino."

"I would like that," she replied, demurely lowering her eyes.

Jonny coughed gently with a serious face, interrupting the flirtation but secretly laughing inside – he was acting part-boss, part-mentor and part-protector.

"Sorry, Honza. I know you probably have plenty to discuss," Luka apologised. "I'm over there if you need me. And, Lucie, really nice to meet you."

"Nice to meet you too, Luka."

Luka smiled generously and withdrew to his faithful counter.

"I think he likes you," Jonny whispered when Luka was out of hearing distance.

"It's just the uniform," she replied, chuckling. "It has that effect on men."

Jonny lifted his mug to his mouth and sipped his coffee. Now was the right time. Well, maybe not the perfect time, seeing as they were in the middle of a murder investigation, but he knew he had to talk about it with someone and she was definitely the right person.

"Lucie, there was something I wanted to talk to you about."

She only smiled in return, indicating he had milk froth from the cappuccino on his top lip. He wiped the froth away and smiled.

With the ice broken, he began again, "I'm not sure if you know, but I decided to search for my mother's Czech family."

"Yes, Felix mentioned it."

"Did he? Why would he do that?" Jonny looked confused.

"Honza, he cares for you," she paused, letting her statement sink in. "Families are not easy. He probably told Marek and I because he thought you might need some support; he knows we have a better understanding of the computer data now available."

"That makes sense," he replied. "Thank you. That means a

lot to me."

"Honza, I think you'd best just tell me what you want to say. I will help any way I can."

He paused, composing himself before continuing.

"My mother was the only family I had for most of my life. My father ran off when I was young and he never returned to see me, not that I wanted him to. She was Czech, born in Prague, but she never wanted to talk about her past life before coming to the UK. I am sure she thought about it, but she would never talk about it. She had no photos and had no contact with her family in the Czech Republic – it was just me and her. It made me who I am, quite insular, but also able to operate on my own. She was an extraordinarily strong woman, fulfilling everything I needed as a child. I used to think I was unlucky, but later in life I realised how lucky I actually was to have her looking after me."

"It seems to me she did a great job raising you on her own."

"Thank you. It wasn't always an easy relationship, but I loved her dearly. I suppose it's the same with any close relationship: you laugh, you fight, but you're always there for each other. She sadly died a few years ago without returning to Prague. When I left the Metropolitan Police I thought I needed to take a total break, but pretty quickly I was looking for things to do. Before I knew it, I'd booked a three month trip to Prague off the back of buying tickets for a Bob Dylan concert due here in June."

"Felix says it was fate."

"I never used to believe in all that stuff, but now I'm not so sure."

He took a sip of his coffee to steady his nerves.

"When I arrived in Prague, everything seemed to happen so fast. I met Ivana, got pulled into a fantastic detective team by Felix, and then helped solve a murder."

"Honza, *you* solved the Old Town Square Murder!"

"Well, it doesn't really matter. The point is I felt at home. Everyone, including you, has been so nice to me, it was like the extended family I never had. I'd worked in the police in London for years, but nothing had felt like this. It was strange as well. I always thought I would honour my mother's wishes and leave her family in the past. But, then I realised I wanted to search the family tree for myself, not for her. It was a big moment for me, and I debated it long and hard, but it just felt right."

"I think I would do the same," she said gently, providing encouragement.

"Ivana has a friend who works in the government department for registrations. I met with her and gave her the only documents I still have from my mother. There was only an old passport and residence papers, but it was enough. Within one day she had tracked down her old address, her parents, her siblings and their children. It was amazing."

"Wow, that's fantastic."

"Yes, but this is where it gets a bit weird. Ivana and I met her for dinner last night and she gave me the family tree: the names, dates of their births, recorded dates of death, and where each of the living family members lives, according to the last census records. The big shock was that your name was on the bottom of the list."

Dvořáková laughed nervously, slightly uncomfortable. "Honza, it's a popular surname because of the famous composer."

"Yes, I realise that. But, I remember you telling me you live in Prague 6 and I also know your birthday is in November."

She looked at him with a blank expression.

"Is your date of birth the twenty-ninth of November 1983?" he asked gently.

"Yes," she muttered, hardly audible.

"Is your mother's first name Lenka?"

"Yes."

"And was her maiden name Šimeková?"

"Yes."

He took a paper out of his jacket pocket and placed it on the table. She pulled the paper towards her, glancing at him, and proceeded to study the list closely.

He watched her face intently. All his training in reading facial expressions amounted to nothing in that moment, his panic overrunning his sense of rationale. Time seemed to stop. His heart was beating so fast and hard, he thought his chest was going to explode.

Placing the paper back on the table, she turned to him with the biggest, most endearing smile he'd received since his daughter's first ever smile.

"Honza, we're related!" she exclaimed loudly. "I can't wait to tell my mother."

She half stood, shuffled around the bench of their corner table, and launched herself at him. As he held her close, thoughts of introducing her to his daughter crept up on him, tears of joy and relief rolled down his cheeks.

When she finally pulled back she also had tears in her eyes but was smiling. "So, you and my mother are cousins?" she managed, wiping her watery eyes.

"Yes. And, in English we say you are my first cousin once-removed."

She shook her head in disbelief and grabbed him for another family cuddle.

37

Neat Freak

The process of revealing their family connection had been emotionally draining, but also therapeutic. Jonny had never wanted to change anything in his small world, knowing how lucky he had been, but he'd suffered from a lonely existence since his mother had died. His daughter was a joy to him but having no other known family member led to solitude, especially at birthdays and festive holidays. But, now he had an extended family – in Prague!

He wasn't religious, but he felt his mother smiling down on him. Whatever had happened to her before she left Prague was in the past. Now, he could look forward to enjoying quality time with the next generation of her family.

Once the initial celebration was over, his sensible side started to take over and he became conscious of time; they had responsibilities, and this was a vital phase of the murder investigation. If they didn't find the link to the man disguised as a building contractor soon, the chances of successfully concluding the investigation would start to narrow considerably.

"Lucie, your reaction to this news has made me so happy. Thank you. I'm so looking forward to meeting the rest of your family. And, I can't wait to introduce you to Charlotte when she comes over in the summer."

"Me too, Honza. It's amazing news."

He looked at his watch again. "But, we need to get going. Time is running out to catch this murderer."

"Yes, cousin," she said jokingly, with an accompanying laugh. "I mean, yes, sir."

Jonny paid Luka at the counter, leaving an extra generous tip.

"Is everything okay?" Luka enquired. "There was quite a lot of emotion going on over there."

"Yes, fine," Jonny reassured him. "Actually, more than fine – life is great! I'll tell you all about it when I pop in next time."

"You always say that," Luka retorted. "Some crazy things seem to happen to you, Honza, many of them in this café. But, you never explain what's going on."

"I will, Luka, I will. Just let me solve this case and I'll tell you everything." Jonny patted Luka's forearm across the counter in a fatherly fashion.

"And, Luka, I can promise you I will be back here very soon," Dvořáková stated emphatically. "This place is very special to me already and, well, I love the coffee."

"See what I mean?" Luka said, pleased at her promise, but looking confused. "Everyone talks in riddles and I never know what's going on."

"You will, Luka," Jonny repeated. "Patience, my friend, patience."

They hurried back to the police station and picked up her unmarked police car. Jonny knew time was against them and wanted to get to Tanya Murray's apartment as soon as possible; going into the station would only bring distractions and slow them down.

Conversation became subdued as Dvořáková drove through the midday traffic towards Chodov. She glanced across at him a few times, always smiling or chuckling to herself, shaking her head in disbelief at the heart-warming news. Her mood was infectious, and he found it hard to stop smiling as he sat in the passenger seat, watching the beautiful city – his city – drift past the window.

Checking his mobile, he'd missed calls from both Ivana and Mikeš. Dvořáková confirmed she'd also had two missed calls from Mikeš. Seizing the situation, Jonny fired off a message to buy them some time and privacy to conduct the next interview alone.

Felix, just going into an interview. Sorry we haven't been in touch. Will call you when finished. Honza.

He knew Ivana was also worried about him after his emotional reaction to the news from Barbora the previous evening.

Hi Ivana. I'm fine, thanks. But I have a crazy story to tell you later. You will definitely believe in fate then! H x

By the time he'd read Ivana's quick and excited reply, Dvořáková was pulling up outside an apartment building. After parking the car, she led him across the wide pavement to the entrance door and pressed the buzzer for Tanya Murray's apartment. Tanya was waiting for them at the open door of her apartment.

"Mr Fox, good to see you again."

"Hello Tanya, this is Sergeant Dvořáková. We won't take up much of your time. We just have a couple of follow-up questions we'd like to ask you."

"No problem. Please come in."

Tanya led them through to her small living room, beckoning them towards the sofa, all the time making profuse apologies for the mess. Jonny's assessment was the complete opposite: the apartment appeared meticulously clean and tidy, not one item seemingly out of place.

Tanya was also dressed smartly, as if going out for dinner or a party: she wore an elegant but fashionable red, knee-length dress with embroidered shoulder straps and matching shoes. Her makeup was also complete, and her dark brown hair was pulled away from her face and clipped at the back.

While Tanya sat in a chair facing them, smoothing down her dress to avoid creases, Jonny stole a glance at Dvořáková. Her raised eyebrows made it clear the spotlessness of the apartment was as much of a surprise to her as him.

After politely declining the offer of a cup of tea, Jonny opened, "Tanya, thank you for seeing us again at such short notice. I realise it is Saturday and I'm sure you have plans."

"Yes, I'm meeting friends a little later. That's why I'm dressed up. I like to be prepared, get ready early."

"I understand," he replied, his warm tone intended to put her at ease. "We won't keep you long. I just have a couple of more detailed questions about what Alex said to you when you met in the last few weeks."

"Sure. Are you any closer to finding out who did this to Alex and that woman?"

"Well, we're currently following up on some new lines of enquiry. That's why we've come to see you."

"Good. I hope you catch them soon. It's horrible when something like this happens to someone you know."

Jonny opened his notepad and flicked through the pages. "Tanya, when we spoke on Thursday, you said you saw Alex once or twice a week. You also said you'd started meeting him for coffee in October. So, am I right to think he confided in you?"

"Yes, I like to think so. As I told you, I was trying to get him interested in me, so I kept the momentum of our communication going. I sent him messages, some of which his wife probably saw, and tried to meet up with him whenever he had time."

"And, what type of information did he tell you?" he asked.

"I tried to be his confidante, I suppose," Tanya admitted. "I thought if he opened up to me, we would get closer and… well, you know already because I told you last time. He told me about his marriage and the difficulties with his mother-in-law. It was clear to me back in October he was still in love with his wife, but he seemed to give up hope as the months went on."

"Did he tell you about any troubles at work?"

"Yes, he did. At first, he didn't want to get me involved just in case I got into trouble. But, after a while he opened up and showed me all the evidence he had against his boss. He had put together a dossier about the system problem and it seemed quite comprehensive to me."

"Did Alex ever tell you, or maybe imply, he was being followed by someone?"

"He said that his boss was hounding him, trying to get him to attend meetings to talk about the system problem. I've never met his boss, I only know him by sight. Alex said his boss was scared of losing his job if the evidence in the dossier was presented. His boss' wife even contacted Alex in secret, to see if she could convince him to agree to a deal of some sort."

"Interesting," Jonny remarked. "Do you know when this was?"

"I think it was the weekend before Alex went missing. I think she called him and they spoke over the phone. But, I don't think they actually met."

"Very useful, we didn't know that. Do you know where the dossier is?"

"No," she confirmed. "Alex told me he stored it electronically. He also said he had it backed up."

"Would you recognise some documents from it?"

"Yes, maybe. He showed me the complete file one day on his laptop."

"But, he didn't mention anyone following him around?" Jonny repeated.

"You mean, like a stalker?" She looked startled.

"More like someone following him to get some information," he clarified. "Maybe about the dossier."

"No, I don't remember him telling me anything like that. He told me his mother-in-law was a dragon and wanted some dirt on him to stop him seeing his children. But, I don't recall him saying he was being followed."

"Thank you."

Dvořáková leaned forward in her seat. "Tanya, when we spoke on the phone two days ago, you acknowledged you made a call to the central police line last year about being followed yourself."

"Yes, I did," Tanya responded hesitantly, glancing at Jonny. "But, what has that got to do with Alex? It was nine months ago now and I didn't even know Alex then. I just phoned the police line to ask for some information."

Jonny glanced across at Dvořáková, slightly confused at the relevance. He decided to remain quiet, allowing her space to ask the questions she probably wanted for the case file.

"I completely understand," Dvořáková replied. "But, just so we have a complete picture of everything that has happened to people close to Alex Corbet, could you please explain what caused you to call the police."

"I was in a relationship for close to a year. It started well, we were both very similar and had shared interests. I'm not the easiest person to be with because I'm a bit of a neat freak; everything has to be clean and in the right place. My ex-boyfriend was the same so we matched. We had a lovely time over the first six months or so, but he grew increasingly clingy, not wanting me to go out with my friends and insisting I got back at a certain time. He got extremely jealous if he saw me talking to any other men and caused a scene on a few occasions, dragging me away, which was very embarrassing. In summer last year, he followed me when I went out and we had a big argument, the end result being he hit me. That was the final straw for me and I broke off the relationship. Luckily, we'd never moved in together, so I had the locks changed and thought I wouldn't see him again. But, he kept following me. He would be outside my apartment sometimes in the morning and then follow me to work. The same in the evening, even sometimes when I went out with my friends. It all got too much and that's when I called the police to get some guidance."

"In the end, you didn't actually file a harassment report against him," Dvořáková stated. "Why was that?"

"I confronted him and told him to back off, otherwise I was going to take it further. Then I had my summer holiday; I went back to the States for three weeks. When I came back the situation had calmed down. I still saw him hanging around, more than normal, but it was nothing compared to what it was like before. I knew he wasn't going to do anything to me, so it was tolerable. And, I knew I could go to the police again if the situation escalated."

Jonny had also edged forward in his seat. "Tanya, what is your ex-boyfriend's name?"

"Harry White."

Jonny glanced at Dvořáková, his eyes wide in alarm.

"Tanya, what happened in the following months?" Dvořáková encouraged.

"He found ways of bumping into me, trying to be nice. He sent me letters, flowers, cuddly toys, to both home and work. I told him firmly our relationship was over, but he wouldn't listen. He just kept telling me he loved me and that we were supposed to be together."

"Why did he think you were made for each other?" Jonny probed.

"Well, you just have to look around to see I'm borderline OCD. He was the same, but worse. It's hard being intimate with someone when you have this condition. We understood each other at the beginning; I thought we had a good chance of getting married. But, his behaviour became extreme and I couldn't tolerate it. I could never accept violence of any sort. I'd rather live on my own for the rest of my life."

Jonny and Dvořáková shared a look.

"Tanya, you talk about all this in the past," he stated. "I assume he has stopped harassing you now?"

"Yes, thank goodness."

"How did you get him to stop?"

"I told him I was in a relationship with someone from work."

"Alex?" he suggested.

"No. I didn't give a name. I just said I'd started seeing someone from my office. I told Harry it was definitely all over between us and he should move on. Since then, I've only seen him around a few times."

"Tanya, have you still got any of the letters he sent to you?" Jonny asked.

"Yes. I kept everything he sent to me just in case I ever

needed to show it to the police. Wait a minute." Tanya almost skipped out of the room, pleased to have a test of her organisation and filing system. Sounds could be heard of cupboards being opened.

Jonny turned to Dvořáková, his face grave with concern. "Harry is short for Henry in English speaking countries. Like Prince Harry."

"And, the surname is the same, just translated into English," Dvořáková confirmed.

Tanya returned carrying a large box which she placed on the floor in front of the sofa.

"What nationality is Harry?" Jonny asked.

"He's Canadian. He's a mature student in Prague, probably in the last year of his degree now." She searched in the box. "Yes, here we are."

Tanya handed Jonny a big wad of letters and cards, bound together by a thick elastic band. He pulled aside the elastic and took the top letter out carefully. Unfolding the page, he saw the letter was written in capital letters. Unlocking his mobile phone, he found the photo of the warning note received by Alex Corbet and held it up side-by-side with the letter.

"It looks like a match to me," he whispered to Dvořáková.

He handed the letter and his phone over to her, and she nodded her agreement after studying both carefully.

"A match with what?" Tanya asked, a confused look on her face.

Jonny ignored the question. He took back the letter and studied it closely. "Tanya, did Harry always write in capitals?"

"Yes," she stated, looking confused. "He didn't like writing in lowercase; he said it was messy. He said he preferred the structure and neatness of capital letters. As I told you before, he was more OCD than me."

"Have you got a photo of Harry?"

"I threw away most of the photos, but I definitely still have a couple."

She searched around the edge of the box. "Yes, here we are. I kept this photo because it reminds me of our good times together. The photo was taken at Prague Castle. It was our favourite place, we walked there most weekends. We loved the old buildings on Golden Lane." She held the photo up to the light and sighed in disappointment. "He told me he loved me there. That photo was our favourite, I used to keep it on my fridge."

Jonny took the photo from Tanya and looked at it. His eyes slowly enlarged as he studied the photo, transfixed by the face staring back at him.

"We've been looking in the wrong places," he muttered. "I've seen this man before."

38

Homage to the Murder Investigation

Once she'd realised the enormity of the situation, Tanya had collapsed in the chair, crying uncontrollably. A welcome opportunity to entertain guests and showcase her proud home had turned into a nightmare from her past.

The last question to seal the theory developing in Jonny's mind concerned Harry White's address. Tanya couldn't remember the building number, but the street name was a match with the address given by Henry Bialas to the van hire company. Not having visited him there for nine months, she also had no idea if Harry was still living there or where he may have moved to.

Dvořáková was stunned when Jonny leaned in and whispered where he had seen Harry White before. Seizing the initiative, she called Boukal immediately to arrange the rendezvous and then kick-start the process to mobilise her uniformed officers. Jonny reminded her he still had the keys to Alex Corbet's apartment, but the landlord would need to be contacted to obtain information on the other residents and spare keys to all the apartments in the building.

Whilst Dvořáková was busy on the phone, Jonny used the opportunity to talk to Tanya. "I completely understand why you are upset. But, and this is really important, you need to know you have done nothing wrong."

"But, I told him I was seeing someone at work."

"Tanya, it is not your fault," he quickly replied, keen to get his point across. "I can see you are a good person and I know you wouldn't harm any one. Unrequited love and break-ups are life situations that people have to deal with. If Harry did this, and we are still not totally sure, it is nothing, I repeat *nothing* to do with you."

Tanya grabbed more tissues from a laced box holder on the side table. Whilst she was upset, Jonny could see she was listening.

"Do you mind if we take this box of letters and photos?" he asked.

"Take it! I don't want them in my apartment... In fact, I never want to see those letters or photos again."

Jonny flicked through the remaining few photos of Harry and Tanya; they were all the same, smiley photos kept as a reminder of happy times together. Identifying the deeper personal meaning of the photo at Prague Castle, he placed the photo in his jacket pocket. Collecting up the rest of the letters and photos, he placed them back in the box and closed the lid.

"Tanya, we need to go now," Jonny explained, "but if you see Harry hanging around I want you to call us immediately."

Dvořáková handed over her card. Tanya nodded, her eyes watery and puffy.

With the box in hand, they returned to the car. Dvořáková drove off at speed towards Prague 2. The start of the journey was silent; their shared concern being that Harry White or Henry Bialas, whatever his real name was, had fled the city.

Dvořáková caught Jonny smiling at her. "What, Honza?"

"I am just proud, I suppose. Asking Tanya Murray about the harassment was inspired. What made the connection in your mind?"

"Well, I wasn't sure," she replied slowly, choosing her words carefully. "As I looked around her living room, the words from Dr Králová's autopsy report kept coming back to me. The report was in Czech, so maybe you missed the nuance of the wording. It said that, in her opinion, the bodies were buried very precisely, laid out in a head to head position, because of either some kind of ritual, possibly remorse on the part of the killer, or by someone with an excessive compulsion to wanting everything neat and tidy."

"She said something similar to both Felix and I at the autopsy. I hadn't made the connection, though."

"But, you recognised him from the photo," she quickly responded.

"Yes, but only because he has been hanging around, wanting to see me and talk to me."

"Let's agree on teamwork," she said with a wide grin.

"Teamwork," he repeated, returning her smile.

As she drove, Jonny called Mikeš to brief him. Then, on impulse, he dialled the same UK number he had called earlier. The call was answered almost immediately.

"Kristýna Davies."

"Hello Ms Davies. I'm sorry to bother you again, it's Jonathan Fox. I believe we might have found out who murdered Alex Corbet. But, to check, can I ask you just one question? It will only take thirty seconds."

"Sure."

"When Alex was telling you about the strange things happening to him at his apartment, did he mention anything about his bike?"

"Yes, he did. He said his bike was stolen twice, but both

times it reappeared the next day. The bike was put back in exactly the same position Alex had left it. He couldn't understand it and he was quite shaken up by it. I must admit, I did wonder if he was making it up for attention."

"Thank you, Ms Davies, that's all I needed to know. And, I can confirm that he definitely wasn't making it up."

"I'm glad I could help."

"By the way," he added, hesitantly, "I found some things amongst Alex's possessions to prove he still loved your sister. I will give them to Helena when I can. I think your view of Alex might change when you read them."

"Thank you, Mr Fox."

"My pleasure. Goodbye, Ms Davies."

Jonny finished the call and sat looking at the phone.

"Who was that?" Dvořáková asked.

"It was Helena's sister. I've spoken to her a few times, trying to get some background information. But, now I definitely know Harry White is the same man I met the first time I looked around Alex Corbet's apartment."

"Even before we found the bodies buried?" she gasped.

"Yes. He's been watching us since he first killed Alex and Yulia. It's the compulsive behaviour."

"Wow!" she exclaimed, shaking her head, eyes firmly on the road.

Mikeš and Boukal were waiting outside when they pulled up. A marked police car was blocking the entrance to the one-way street, two uniformed officers waving cars straight on in diversion. Boukal was talking to another man: the landlord, Jonny presumed.

"Right, the warrant is served and I have the keys," Boukal reported. "Henry Bialas had rented an apartment in the building:

it's on the third floor."

Boukal opened the entrance door to the building and they all started to ascend the concrete stairs. The landlord followed them in, looking stressed, and stood waiting at the bottom of the stairs.

"So, he moved into the building to keep watch on Alex Corbet," Mikeš stated.

"Yes," Jonny confirmed. "It gave him a sense of control. Harry White was better able to start playing games with Alex from inside the building. He stole his post, his bike, ordered unwanted pizzas, and left the warning note stuck to Alex's apartment door – all to torment him. The trigger point was when Tanya told Harry she'd started seeing someone at work. He must have spied on her and seen her with Alex in the canteen or going for a drink together in Chodov. Tanya's life became easier, but only because Harry's fixation had transferred to Alex."

"What do you think he was trying to achieve?" Mikeš asked.

"It probably started with the sole focus of getting Tanya back. But from there it escalated, spiralling out of control. We know his obsession with Tanya led to violence, so the same has sadly happened with Alex. And, poor Yulia got caught up in something she and Alex knew nothing about."

"And, he spoke to you?"

"Yes. He magically appeared both times I visited Alex's apartment. First time, I met him on the stairs after leaving the apartment, when it was still a missing person case. The following day, I came back when Josef realised the apartment had been broken into overnight. He was leaving the building when I was studying the lock on the main building door. By then, we had found the bodies, but he knew that because he'd been watching us."

"Sir," Dvořáková interrupted, "I've just checked the social

media websites for Harry White. All the posts portray him and Tanya as a couple – as if they are still together."

"It's his fantasy," Jonny corroborated. "But, sadly the fantasy is also his reality. And, he'll do anything to protect their love because he believes they are destined to be together forever."

When they had reached the second floor landing, Jonny stopped. His heightened instinct drove him to step down the corridor to check on Alex Corbet's apartment. Mikeš followed. The police tape was still in place across the door with a police warning notice in Czech. A gleaming new, industrial-strength bolt-lock system was in place, securing the door, but the lock was scratched where forced entry had been attempted. A piece of paper with the word 'LOSERS!' was taped to the door.

"He obviously wanted to get into Alex's apartment again," Jonny observed. "This note is a sign of frustration."

"It's a good job Josef organised extra security," Mikeš noted.

They re-joined the others and climbed the last flight of stairs. Boukal stepped forward and opened the front door with the keys. Jonny immediately put his arm in front of Boukal to prevent him entering. "Let me go first," he commanded. "It's possible he's set up a trap of some sort: maybe an explosion. I know the signs."

Boukal and Dvořáková looked towards Mikeš for confirmation.

"Let him lead," Mikeš stated. "But, Honza, I don't want you taking any unnecessary risks. This madman is not worth it."

Jonny nodded and started inching into the apartment. The room was dark even though it was only early afternoon, the light shut out by the drawn, heavy curtains. Rather than risk turning on the lights, he shuffled across the middle of the apartment floor using the light on his mobile phone as a guide, past the sofa, towards the window. The apartment was the same size and layout as Alex Corbet's studio, cramped and dingy, only facing out onto the garden and parked cars at the back of the building rather than the street. He remembered Alex's flat painted white to create the illusion of space, but, although he couldn't see clearly in the poor light, the walls in this apartment seemed to be decorated in a dark pattern.

Reaching the window, he checked around the curtains and windowsill, looking for wires. Seeing nothing suspicious, he pulled back an inch of material, followed slowly by both curtains. Turning around to face into the room, he froze. Looking towards the doorway, he could see Mikeš, Boukal and Dvořáková all standing just inside the doorway, also staring at the walls, mouths open in amazement.

Almost every part of available wall, from the kitchen area to the window, was pasted with photos, newspaper cuttings and print-outs of internet pages. The mosaic pattern was compelling, hard to look away from, and distinctly creepy.

The wall next to the apartment door was a montage of photos of Tanya Murray. The centrepiece was a large A3 close-up print of her face, the other photos circling around it in a haphazard pattern. Some of the photos were clearly taken when they had been together, but many were from when she had been followed from a distance. Under each photo was a label, written in capital letters, ranging from 'HAPPY', 'SAD', to 'LATE FOR WORK', and even 'BITCH'.

The remaining collages paid homage to the murder investigation.

The first group of photos featured Alex Corbet, including a few recent snapshots of him with Yulia Ivanova. The photos showed Alex undertaking various mundane activities, all taken from a safe distance, a zoom lens capturing him having lunch with Tanya in the office canteen. The collection also included photos of Helena and the children, where they lived, the pub quiz in full swing with an animated Alex at the centre of proceedings, inside Alex's apartment, a hand holding Alex's toothbrush, even Alex's bike – it was, basically, a photo album of Alex's day-to-day life.

The second mosaic was the largest, taking up the whole wall opposite the apartment door. Newspaper and online reports of the murder case were pasted in a carefully planned pattern to create a timeline from when the two bodies were found buried. The reports were marked with emoji symbols and comments on labels, again in capital letters: 'CATCH ME IF YOU CAN', 'WHAT A JOKE', 'DUMB DETECTIVES', and 'HA-HA'.

The final group of photos was all about the police, centred on Jonny. Still photos from the mobile video taken from the van, as sent to the TV news channel, showed Jonny, Mikeš and Boukal walking to the tent where the exhumation was taking place. These were surrounded by photos of Jonny at the pub quiz, entering and leaving the apartment building, visiting Helena, standing on the Náměstí Míru square with Ivana, and entering the Black Cat pub. A photo even showed Jonny and Mikeš in deep conversation with Petr Řepka in the pub the previous evening.

Apart from the decorated walls, the room was empty of possessions, and spotless, cleaned to an almost professional standard. All the surfaces were sparkling clean, no dust in sight. There was no trace of anyone having lived there in the past few months, let alone the last few days. The contrast between the frenzy of the collages on the wall and the sterile room was stark.

"I've never seen anything like this," Mikeš ventured, shaking his head in disbelief.

"Now you get a glimpse inside the mind of the man we are looking for," Jonny answered, his voice grave.

Working carefully around the studio apartment, including the small bathroom, Jonny checked for signs of a booby trap. He opened the single wardrobe and a few drawers on the side table, but all were clean and empty. "All clear," he finally declared.

The waiting entourage walked into the room, studying different portions of the collages on the walls. Boukal and Dvořáková were studying the newspaper cuttings, trying to decipher something meaningful from the timeline. Mikeš was particularly animated. He kept calling Jonny over, keen to show him a particular photo of them together, clearly disturbed that this man had also been present to capture what should have been a private moment.

Jonny was deep in contemplation and didn't respond. He stood still in the middle of the room, thinking hard. He knew they were being led. Again. It had been the same all the way through the investigation, from the original missing person case.

He slowly turned around on the spot, studying the photos, clippings and handwritten labels on the walls. The apartment was spotlessly clean, but the walls had been left. Although Jonny couldn't see the detail of every item pasted to the wall from his position in the middle of the room, he needed to understand the patterns.

He considered each pattern in turn, working backwards in time. The media reports, timeline and the photos of Jonny and the team were the most recent; this was Harry White's compulsive behaviour, compelled to follow the investigation, enjoying the missed clues and dead ends. The photos of Alex Corbet and Yulia Ivanova were all part of the planning phase; these photos were history, the justification for why Alex Corbet had to be killed. He stopped turning when he came to the photos of Tanya Murray. This collection of photos was still living and breathing, and had a story to finish; Tanya was still alive, and Harry White loved her and wanted them to be together – but, at what cost?

Jonny stepped across the room to stand in front of the photos of Tanya. There were at least one hundred photos, but he was only interested in the ones from when they were still together. He carefully studied all the older photos: shared laughs on nights out, Tanya posing on weekend walks, selfies on the sofa. Some of the photos were the same as the photos Tanya had kept in the box. He put his hand into his jacket and pulled out the photo of them at Prague Castle. Despite it being on the top of Tanya's pile of photos, having a deep held meaning for both of them, this photo was not on the wall. He looked closely again, and then spotted a space where a photo had been pulled off. The glue was visible behind, but the vacated space was half obscured by a handwritten label. He held the photo in his hand up to the space in the collage, and whilst he had no way of understanding the mind that had created the pattern, it just seemed to fit.

"Honza, have a look at this," Dvořáková shouted across the room.

Jonny walked over to the kitchen area and was joined by Mikeš and Boukal. A small, white envelope was laying on the work surface marked 'JONATHAN FOX'. Jonny took the plastic gloves handed to him and carefully peeled back the seal and tipped the contents onto the work surface.

It was a handwritten letter and a car key.

MR FOX
 I WOULD BE GRATEFUL IF YOU CAN KINDLY RETURN

THE VAN.
IT IS PARKED IN THE NEXT STREET.
THANK YOU
HARRY WHITE

"What does it mean?" Mikeš asked.

"I think it means exactly what it says," Jonny replied with a frustrated sigh. "We will probably find the van parked in the next street, and it will have been cleaned thoroughly. This kind of compulsive mind is less able to play mind games. He wants us to think he is a good guy by cleaning the apartment and the car. Even the photos on the wall are a type of tribute to us and his love for Tanya. It's his excuse, his way of saying sorry."

"The van wasn't near here this morning," Boukal stated for clarity. "We've had a patrol car driving around the whole area every morning and evening."

"Don't worry, Marek," Jonny stated. "This guy probably hid the van somewhere after it was cleaned. He's brought it back today so he can leave it for us."

"But, what now?" Mikeš asked, a deep frown on his face.

"We need to find a way of getting ahead of him," Jonny declared.

He walked back to the photos of Tanya on the wall, the others crowding around him. He held up the photo in his hand. "Tanya told us that this photo was their favourite. Whilst their relationship ended badly, it is her best memory of their time together. And, I think Harry White feels the same. I was looking for the photo in the collage, but I couldn't find it. Then, I spotted this space where a photo has been torn down."

Jonny held the photo up against the space in the collage for everyone to see. "What would Harry's next step be?" he posed

351

for the crowd.

"Run?" Boukal suggested. "Maybe he's heading for the airport."

"Possible. But, I think he has unfinished business."

"He's going to see Tanya," Dvořáková declared.

"Yes, I agree," boomed Mikeš. "Let's get over there quick."

"Hang on!" Jonny said firmly, putting his hand up.

The tension in the silent room was close to bursting.

"This is exactly what he wants," he continued. "He's been one step ahead of us all the way through this investigation. I believe he knew we were coming here and he's used the time to capture Tanya and take her to Prague Castle."

"What's he going to do?" Mikeš questioned.

"My guess? A double suicide. If Harry can't have Tanya, he'll want their love to die with both of them."

Jonny watched as the blood drained from their faces and silence filled the room.

39

Golden Lane

Time was of the essence, so Jonny was pleased Boukal would be driving. If his gut instinct was right, Harry White would have been watching them leave Tanya Murray's apartment less than an hour earlier, knowing where they were headed and ready to put his plans into action. Capturing Tanya, maybe rendering her unconscious in the process, and then transporting her to Prague Castle would take some time, but Jonny still had the feeling Harry White was ahead of them.

Boukal roared the black Skoda Superb into life, turned on the flashing police lights, and accelerated away before Jonny had even fully closed the back door. Mikeš turned in the front passenger seat to ask Jonny a question, appearing composed and relaxed, seemingly immune to the violent motion. Jonny could hardly focus on the blurred shape in front of him, let alone hear anything. His body was being thrown about without the harness of a seat belt, lurching forwards and backwards in the seat as the car bounced at speed over the cobble-stoned streets towards the main road. His hand finally found the safety of the hand strap after grappling in mid-air for a few gravity-defying moments.

"Sorry Felix, what did you say?" he finally managed to reply, having clipped the belt and regained some composure.

"I said, what's the plan?" Mikeš repeated.

"To tell you the truth, I don't know. I'm convinced Harry

White is taking Tanya back to the castle, but other than that I have no idea."

"Will he be armed?"

"He's going to need the threat of a weapon to scare her and stop her screaming. So, yes, I think he will be armed. Maybe a gun, or more probably a knife."

"Let me have a look at the photo again," Mikeš requested.

Jonny took the photo out of his jacket pocket with his free hand, the other still gripping tightly to the hand strap, and passed it to Mikeš between the front seats. Mikeš held the photo up to the window for extra light.

"We have one advantage on him," Jonny continued. "I believe he now knows we've worked out it was him who murdered Alex Corbet and Yulia Ivanova; the follow-up visit to Tanya's apartment would have sealed it for him. But, importantly, he will not be aware we've made the connection about Prague Castle. Remember, the photo was missing from the collage on the wall so he took it with him. It's only my deduction that it was the same photo as this one, but I'm pretty sure about it because of what Tanya told me – it held a deep meaning for both of them."

"I hope you're right, Honza. It means we'll be able to surprise him."

Mikeš continued studying the photo closely.

Boukal swung the car onto the main road, not waiting for a gap in the traffic. Angry drivers beeped their horns as they swerved out of the way. Unmoved, total focus on the road, he accelerated down the hill towards the river.

"It looks to me like the photo was taken outside St. George's Basilica, in the corner of the castle's main courtyard," Mikeš shouted over the engine. "Someone else obviously took the photo. Behind them is the Great South Tower of the St. Vitus Cathedral."

"Where is Golden Lane in relation to where the photo was taken?" Jonny shouted back.

"It would be behind them, past the Rosenberg Palace."

Jonny nodded to himself, starting to understand. "So, they'd probably just been to Golden Lane, where Harry had pronounced his love for her. Then they'd strolled through to the main courtyard."

"How does that help?" Mikeš looked confused. "Prague Castle has the largest surrounding grounds of any castle in the world. They could be anywhere."

Jonny took back the photo and studied it again, looking for another clue.

"We don't want another chase up a tower," he finally said. "I suggest we secure the Cathedral and the entrance to the Great South Tower. Actually, it's probably best to close all the attractions, including the toilets. It will be much easier to track them if he and Tanya are outside."

"I agree," Mikeš echoed his approval. "I'll get Lucie on it."

"And, tell the backup police cars to have no sirens or lights on when approaching the castle. We don't want him knowing we are onto him."

Mikeš called Dvořáková immediately. She had stayed back at the apartment to secure the crime scene. She'd also taken the role of designated liaison point, with Mikeš and Boukal controlling the deployment of police officers in support of the operation. A police car had been despatched immediately to Tanya Murray's apartment even before Boukal had driven off in haste.

Boukal slowed the car as they approached the bottom of the

main road Žitná, weaving between vehicles aware of the flashing lights, then swung right off Karlovo Náměstí square towards the old town. The centre was still busy with people shopping at the weekend, but Boukal was circumventing potential delays by following the tram lines. As they hit the busy road Národní, Boukal swerved around a turning tram and in front of another tram crossing from the other direction, accelerating straight over onto Na Perštýně. Jonny missed most of the slick manoeuvre because his eyes were closed tight. He'd listened to the close metal-on-metal sound of tram wheels on track, one squealing as it rounded the bend, and, fearing the worst, had only opened his eyes when the sound had disappeared completely. *I could never get used to this.* Whilst Boukal's prowess as a driver was buying them invaluable minutes, it was painful to endure.

The rest of the journey was less eventful by comparison, as Boukal turned off the flashing lights and steered the car across the river on Mánesův most. The relative calm even allowed Jonny to try calling Tanya Murray again, but each attempt went straight to voicemail.

Across the bridge, Boukal followed the street Klárov uphill, winding past the Government Office building. Just past the Malostranská tram stop and metro station. Boukal swung the car sharp left onto Na Opyši, a narrow, steep approach to the east wing of the castle. As he pulled up and stopped the car, Mikeš was still talking to Dvořáková on the phone.

"Right," Mikeš stated, after finishing the call. "Lucie has confirmed that Tanya Murray is not at her apartment. One of the neighbours heard her leaving with a man, but nobody saw them."

"It must be Harry White," Jonny murmured.

"And," Mikeš continued, "a police car is in position at the northerly moat bridge and also at the pedestrian entrance from the Hradčanské Náměstí square. These are the main exits. All the historic buildings are also now closed and visitors have been asked to leave. Unfortunately, we don't have police radios, so I've told the uniform officers to keep watch and wait for an instruction from me, which I'll need to relay via Lucie."

They got out of the car, Mikeš grabbing his hat and cane, and hurried up the pathway to the castle entrance. The afternoon brightness was holding, the last sun fighting back against the brooding clouds.

"We should split up," Mikeš suggested. "Otherwise, we'll be too conspicuous."

"Agreed," Jonny replied. "Felix, I suggest you and I head for the main courtyard, but we should split up and walk around different sides of the wall. We can communicate by hand signals."

"I'll take the Cathedral side," Mikeš confirmed. "I want to check with the guards to make sure it has been closed and nobody is inside."

"And, Marek," Jonny said to Boukal, "I suggest you hang back, outside the courtyard, just in case he runs for it."

"Sure. I'll find a place to keep watch."

Jonny and Mikeš walked quickly along the walkway between the historic castle buildings, until the main courtyard opened up at St. George's Basilica. With a nod for good luck, Mikeš went right, following the perimeter of the inner wall, in the direction of the Cathedral. Jonny steered left, following the opposite wall towards the Old Royal Palace.

The crowd in the courtyard was expansive and dense. The vivid colours reflected people at leisure, most on holiday. With the castle attractions closed, the visitors were standing around in the spring weather, enjoying the sight of the impressive

Cathedral. As Jonny walked the perimeter of the wall, he gazed across the blurred mass of heads. The location was certainly not ideal for trying to identify a wanted person, especially a criminal who had kidnapped someone and could be armed.

Halting at the Old Royal Palace, Jonny confirmed the building entrance was closed. He then backed up against the wall to gain a protected vantage point. Craning his neck, he started to scan the courtyard. The umbrellas and flags of tourist guides made the task more difficult. Objects masked his view, forcing him to backtrack and start again.

He suddenly caught sight of a tall, dark-haired man and woman, close together in the middle of the crowd. Their heads were turned away, but touching, their bodies moving together. As their heads separated and joined together, he realised they were kissing, lost in the happiness of young love – definitely not Harry White and Tanya Murray.

He looked for Mikeš and saw him standing in front of the Cathedral entrance, unmistakable in his unconventional suit and hat. Mikeš' eyes locked on Jonny and he raised his cane to indicate he was going to walk further around the Cathedral perimeter.

Jonny moved along the wall a few metres to get a different perspective and started his scan again. The crowd was still thick, swollen by the increased number of visitors milling around the courtyard; it was now almost impossible to distinguish faces clearly. Giving up on the scan, he raised his line of sight and started to look around for an elevated position where he'd be better able to identify faces in the swarm of people.

He froze, hearing a man's angry shout, closely followed by a woman's terrified shriek. Not a normal sound for a sightseeing crowd.

Raising himself on tiptoes and shuffling along the wall, he strained his neck to see. Then he heard another cry of "Hey!" and his eyes caught a swift movement in the crowd.

Jonny moved in, weaving slowly between the tourists. As he snaked around bodies, he kept his eye on a man's head that seemed to be moving unnaturally. As the crowd moved randomly, he suddenly got a clear glimpse of Harry White's side profile: tall and dark, he stood out from those around him, even though he was dressed casually in sweatshirt, jeans and trainers. Tanya was pulled close to him, wearing a thin coat over the same dress she'd been wearing earlier. As they moved with the crowd, Jonny could see him, holding her left arm tightly whilst his right hand was pushed hard into her back.

Jonny pushed on into the crowd, moving quicker. He was now seven or eight metres from them, moving parallel to their slow, shuffling progress. Tanya was stumbling as Harry pushed her along.

Trusting his instinct to protect the public around, he waited until some space had developed around them and shouted, "Stop! Police."

As he'd expected, the people close by panicked but started to spread apart. Within seconds, there was clear space around Harry and Tanya. The space extended as the crowd continued separating and Jonny moved forward towards them. He was now four metres away from them with clear sight through the parted crowd. "Harry, stop. All the exits are blocked."

Harry White halted, jerking Tanya upright, close to him. He turned to Jonny with a contemptuous, frustrated look, angry that his plan had been thwarted. Tanya's eyes, by contrast, were pleading for help.

Jonny saw Mikeš on the far wall, directly behind Harry. He

was shuffling forward slowly, trying not to make any noise.

"Harry, you are surrounded!" Jonny shouted.

Harry heard a footstep behind him and swivelled around to see Mikeš approaching. "Tell him to stop now," he shouted at Jonny. "Or I'll kill her!"

"Felix!" Jonny shouted, putting his hand up in a stop signal.

Mikeš stopped. But, when Harry turned his attention back to Jonny, Mikeš made a hand gesture indicating a knife.

The pincer movement had worked. They'd surprised Harry White in the castle courtyard by getting one step ahead of him, and he was now cornered. Tanya was also alive, and they'd identified the weapon he was carrying. Jonny knew the immediate priority had to be keeping Tanya alive at all costs.

The crowd was slowly dispersing. No visitors were within ten metres of the unfolding drama. They were heading for the exits as quickly as they could. Two uniform officers were now inside the courtyard, ready to provide backup if instructed by Mikeš.

"Harry, I know you don't want to kill Tanya," Jonny began calmly. "You love her. Put the knife down."

"She told me she loved me," Harry shouted back. "But she lied!"

"Harry, I think she still loves you," Jonny lied.

"No, she doesn't. The only way to end this is for us to die… together!"

"She does love you," Jonny repeated the lie. "She kept all the letters you sent her."

Harry pulled Tanya's head roughly to face him. "Did you?"

Tears were rolling down her cheeks. "Yes," she mumbled, hardly audible. She nodded, a frightened look in her eyes.

Harry pulled her head hard again. She screamed in pain.

"Why did you start seeing Alex Corbet?"

Jonny knew he had to take control of the dialogue and push the narrative in a certain direction. "Harry, listen to me. Tanya liked Alex and wanted him to like her. But, they were just friends. She kissed him once when drunk at the Christmas party, but they never went out on a single date and were definitely never intimate."

"I don't believe you," Harry replied firmly. "I saw them together almost every day, having coffee or lunch. She was always touching him across the table."

"Alex was a nice guy," Jonny confirmed, "but there was no relationship. He had his eye on Yulia, not Tanya."

"You're lying!" Harry shouted back.

"Harry, you know how difficult it is to have a close relationship with the condition you both have," Jonny stated calmly. "Ask Tanya."

"It's all true," Tanya cried out, still sobbing.

"So, we could still have been together," Harry said flatly, no emotion in his voice, the full realisation of the situation hitting him.

"You can still be together," Jonny lied again. "Harry, we can work this out."

Harry looked at Jonny with sad, tired eyes. "I thought it was a message for me, like a test, that I needed to kill Alex to keep our love alive. I thought it was the only way we could stay together."

"Harry, listen. Tanya didn't want you to kill anyone. But, it's okay, it's all over now. The most important thing is that both of you are still alive. Let's stop this. Put down the knife and let her go."

Harry stared hard at Jonny, clearly considering everything

he'd just been told. He turned his attention to Tanya, pulling her face to him, searching for the truth in her eyes. He looked a broken man. Everything he believed in, the reasons for his actions, had been shattered into pieces. He let go of her and she collapsed to the floor, sobbing. His arms fell to his sides, the knife hanging limply in his hand.

A noise behind him suddenly brought Harry back to life. He twisted his head to see Mikeš moving forward. Harry started to run, the knife thrusting forward with his pumping arm movements. He headed diagonally across the courtyard, back the way Jonny and Mikeš had entered. Jonny set off in pursuit. Mikeš beckoned over the two police officers, indicating they should take care of Tanya, and followed the chase.

Harry White was tall and fit, his big strides allowing him to pull away from Jonny. Members of the public still walking towards the Cathedral jumped out of the way to let the chasing trio through. Some women screamed when they saw the swinging blade.

Instead of heading for the exit at the east wing of the castle, Harry veered left at the Rosenberg Palace, ducking down an alleyway. Jonny heard Mikeš' footsteps closing behind him, his previous experience as an amateur runner giving him greater agility over the cobble stones.

"He's heading for Golden Lane," Mikeš yelled from behind.

Heavy footsteps were the overriding noise as they chased Harry down the alleyway. A family slammed their backs against an inner castle wall as Harry weaved through the narrow passage. At the end of the alley, he turned right, leading the pursuit into Golden Lane. Tourists enjoying their tour of the sixteenth century dwellings saw the oncoming chase and panicked, ducking into souvenir shops for safety.

Halfway down the lane, Mikeš caught up with Jonny. Harry was now fifteen metres ahead. The pathway in front of him was clear as he charged towards the north-east castle exit. Jonny and Mikeš glanced at each other, silently weighing up their options and knowing the younger man had the legs on them.

Powering on, but blowing hard and feeling the strain, Jonny looked ahead and saw Boukal standing in the middle of the path at the end of Golden Lane. His feet were planted wide, legs tensed. The message of the stance was clear – he was not going to be passed. Harry also saw him and slowed slightly. After a slight hesitation, Harry roared like a battle soldier and continued running directly at Boukal, pumping his arms hard with the blade flashing in front of him.

Boukal had taken off his suit jacket and had it wrapped around his left forearm. Harry slowed as he approached, raising the knife as a deterrent. Boukal didn't move; he stood motionless, eyes focused, not even blinking, assessing the potential moves available. Jonny and Mikeš speeded up, knowing they were going to be needed.

Harry stuck out the knife, aiming straight at Boukal. As their bodies came together, Harry's body was turned and lurched upwards, before both men fell to the floor. Harry fought back, putting all his energy into twisting and turning like a wrestling animal. The entwined bodies continued to heave and reel, resistant forces in competition. Harry had the strength, but Boukal had the technique. Boukal twisted his arms down and upward, raising Harry's arm behind his back and pushing into the middle of his shoulder blades. The arm lock was firm. Harry tried to move one more time but could only groan loudly as his body fell limp.

Jonny and Mikeš arrived in a burst of panting, both

363

struggling to breathe. Mikeš was quicker to assess the scene, moving around the grappling bodies to put the full sole of his shoe on the side of Harry's head – a simple but effective, old-style move. A loud grunt was heard from under his shoe, followed by a scream of pain.

"Marek, are you okay?" Jonny finally managed.

Boukal slowly raised himself up, panting hard but keeping his hands and knees in position to apply downward pressure on the assailant. The knife was lying free next to the bodies and there was no evident blood. Boukal released one hand to grab the handcuffs from his belt, swiftly pulling both of Harry's wrists behind his back and clipping the metal cuffs.

Two different uniform officers arrived, stepping in to take over from Boukal. Mikeš reluctantly lifted his shoe and the officers lifted Harry up into a kneeling position, taking one arm each.

"You bastard," Harry spat at Mikeš.

"You don't deserve words, scumbag." Was Mikeš' venomous retort. "But, try these! You are being arrested for the suspected murder of Alex Corbet and Yulia Ivanova, plus the kidnapping of Tanya Murray against her will. You have the right to remain silent. Anything you say can and will be used against you in a court of law. You have the right to speak to a lawyer and to have a lawyer present during any questioning."

Two more officers arrived to help secure the situation, Mikeš barking orders. As one of the officers read Harry his rights again in Czech, Mikeš turned to Boukal, putting his hand on his shoulder in a fatherly fashion. "Great work, Marek. But, please don't ever do that again."

"I suppose you were a junior martial arts champion, as well as a racing car champion," Jonny added, still breathing hard.

Boukal grinned. He unrolled the suit jacket from around his forearm, holding it up for all to see. The suit material was more screwed up than ever before, but the back of the jacket was also slashed, deep knife cuts exposing light through the material.

"We definitely need to get you a new suit now," Jonny added, laughing.

40

Cathartic Action

Jonny's involvement in the Old Town Square Murder had been simpler: he'd worked out the identity of the murderer, helped the Czech Police catch them, and then swiftly left the scene. This time was different. He was now a core part of Mikeš' team – an experienced consultant and being paid for it – so he stayed with his boss and Boukal until Harry White had been cautioned, trounced back across the castle courtyard, and bundled into the back of a police van.

Boukal had also received a modest cut to his forearm. Initially not noticed in the jubilation of apprehending the wanted villain, his arm was treated by the first aid team at the castle. He came out smiling, proudly showing off his butterfly stitches under a gauze bandage.

Jonny spent his time with Tanya Murray. Like Alex Corbet, and Yulia Ivanova, she was a victim, an innocent party to the crime, the only difference being she'd lived to tell the tale. She was naturally distraught, crying uncontrollably until he managed to calm her down. He suggested counselling as a way to come to terms with her relationship with Harry White and the horrific events that had followed.

Helping Tanya to the police car waiting to escort her home, he had promised to call her in a week. He also made a mental note to call the HR Manager at her company; the post-trauma care would need to be carefully constructed if Tanya wasn't to quit immediately and return to her home country. He wanted to promise more help, to be involved in her rehabilitation in some way, but he knew that new serious crime investigations had to be his focus. That was the nature of detective police work.

Once back at the police station, Jonny headed straight for the basement, leaving Mikeš and Boukal to process the necessary reporting and paperwork. Liška was waiting for him with a big smile, the glass hatch of the evidence room wide open and classical music playing.

"Congratulations, Honza, another master class in detective work."

"Thank you, Josef, but this was truly a team effort. Lucie showed exceptional talent recognising the link to Tanya's ex-boyfriend, and Marek again showed talents I never imagined he would have. And, Felix was Felix, leading from the front with bravado."

Liška laughed heartily, his big frame rising and falling with his weighty breaths.

"I recognise this piece of music," Jonny stated, trying to place it.

"It is perhaps the most famous piece of Czech classical music ever made, now renowned the world over. It is Dvořák's Slavonic Dance No. eight. Near perfection, in my opinion."

Jonny listened, recognising the rhythmic patterns and structures of traditional folk dances.

"You know, it's funny," Liška continued. "I played this music to Felix when we solved our first case together back in the mid- '80s. It has become a bit of a ritual for me since. I now play it every time the team at this station solves a major case."

"I think that's lovely, Josef. Maintaining traditions is so

important."

The pair remained silent in honour as the music continued for a few precious minutes.

"By the way, here are the documents you wanted," Liška said finally. "I've taken photocopies of them all and put them into the evidence filing system. I just need you to sign this form for me."

"Thanks, Josef," he said, taking the form, signing it and returning it through the hatch.

"Good luck, Honza. I'll see you at the pub later."

"Definitely. I need a beer, it's been a tough few days."

***

Braced with the documents, Jonny pressed the buzzer on the intercom for Helena Corbetová's apartment. After a brief wait, the call was answered by her mother.

"Dobrý den."

"Dobrý večer, Mrs Nováková. It is Jonathan Fox."

There was a momentary silence followed by a muffled shout as Daniela informed her daughter who it was, her hand probably held over the receiver.

"Mr Fox, as I told you this morning, I would rather our solicitor, Pavel Rosický, is present when you talk to us again."

"Mrs Nováková, we have apprehended the person who killed Alex Corbet. I have come to inform his wife as the next of kin."

He heard a heavy sigh, followed eventually by the click of the door latch being released.

Exiting the lift on the third floor, he found Daniela waiting for him. He could hear the children playing, the boisterous play noise carrying through the open apartment door and down the corridor.

"Mr Fox, my daughter is very delicate at the moment and I don't want her upset."

"I am just doing my job, Mrs Nováková," he replied firmly. "I think she deserves to be informed in person by the police, rather than read about it in the newspaper over the coming days. Don't you agree?"

Daniela stood her ground, staring directly into his eyes. He returned her gaze, unfazed, with the audacity of knowing he was acting right and correct.

"There will be no further questions from me," he added. "I already have all the information I need. I will only stay ten minutes."

The impasse continued for twenty seconds, before she turned abruptly and walked back down the corridor. He followed at his own pace, closing the apartment door behind him.

Helena was in the living room, laying on the sofa under a thin blanket. Daniela cajoled the children into the kitchen; she was clearly giving him the requested ten minutes, but he knew she would re-emerge with menace if he overstayed his welcome.

"Mr Fox, nice to see you. Please sit down." Helena swung her legs into a sitting position and beckoned to the armchair he had sat in before on his previous visits.

"Thank you."

"Mummy mentioned you have some news about the investigation."

"Yes," he confirmed. "I wanted to come and tell you in person. But I'm on a timer so I will not stay long."

Helena smiled weakly, conveying her silent understanding.

"A few hours ago we caught the man who murdered Alex and the woman he was with last Friday night. I am limited in

369

what I can say because of the prosecution case that will follow. What I can say, however, is that Alex was a totally innocent party. Someone connected to a person working at the same office as Alex wrongly thought he'd done something and took a sick sort of revenge. But, and this is really important, Alex didn't do anything wrong at all. In fact, he knew nothing about it. Also, it is important for me to stress that his boss, Torsten Lindberg, and the ongoing matter about the recent live system error, which I'm sure you know about, was also not connected to what happened."

"But, Mr Fox," she said, pausing, a confused look on her face. "Why was he killed?"

"The man we have detained thought Alex was in a relationship with his ex-girlfriend—"

"Tanya?"

"Yes. But, Alex wasn't in a relationship with her at any time. The person who did this to your husband misunderstood something he was told, and then fabricated his own reality to act out his perverse revenge. Sadly, I don't think anyone could have predicted, or stopped, what subsequently happened."

Helena lowered her head, dabbing the flowing tears with her handkerchief.

"And, Helena, I want to tell you something about Alex. From the early part of this investigation, when we thought he was missing, I have had to ask a lot of questions about him. It is my job. I'll be truthful and say that I expected to find some secret he had; maybe the affair you believed he was having, or something else which got him into trouble. But, I found nothing like this at all. In fact, the more I found out about him, the more I liked him. He was a gentleman, as you know, and principled. And, as far as I can see, he acted correctly at every stage since you separated."

"Mr Fox—"

"I am sorry to interrupt you, but I need to finish. Otherwise, I will run out of time. Alex was not having an affair with Tanya. She wanted it, and chased him, including the messages you saw, but he never reciprocated. He was still in love with you."

"So, who was the woman he was with? The woman who was murdered with him, Yulia I think her name was."

"I am not here to defend Alex, but I want you to know the truth. Yulia was the first woman Alex started to see in the months since you had separated. You may still think this action was wrong of him, but before you judge him I would just ask that you read these."

Jonny opened up the shoe box he had placed on the floor and passed it to her.

"Mr Fox, what are these?"

"Letters from Alex to you. We found them in his apartment. The first one is dated New Year's Eve last year. For some reason he never posted them, but I think they will provide every answer you need."

Helena carefully held the box and flicked through the letters. "I still have all the letters he ever sent me. I keep them in a shoe box at the bottom of my wardrobe."

"That is exactly where we found these, at the bottom of Alex's wardrobe."

Tears rolled down her cheeks, splashing on the box and the letters.

"When Alex left, he started writing letters to me," she blubbered. "They were lovely, like the letters he used to write to me when we first met. But, then the letters just stopped."

"These letters will explain everything," Jonny reassured her.

The kitchen door opened and Daniela emerged, bustling into the living room with purpose. "Time's up, Mr Fox."

Jonny didn't turn around. His focus remained solely on Helena. "Helena, I also know about your illness. I hope the treatment is having a positive effect."

"Thank you," she replied, glancing briefly at her mother. "My chemotherapy starts next week."

"Well, I wish you all the best fighting your illness. You deserve some luck and a swift recovery."

Jonny smiled at Helena and rose from the armchair.

"Finally, I would just like to say I totally appreciate how important it is to have a strong family at times like these. But, Helena, there are also other family and friends who want to help you, if you'd only open up to them. Alex wanted to help you, and you know it. He is not here now, but maybe instead his parents can play some role in supporting you and their grandchildren. Let them in. Fight this illness together."

Helena continued crying into her handkerchief as her children ran over to her. She embraced them tightly, kissing the tops of their heads.

"I will show myself out. Good luck, Helena."

Jonny turned and left the apartment, without even a glance at Daniela.

41

Suited and Booted

Despite vehement protests, Jonny finally forced Boukal out of the police station to go clothes shopping. The resistance cited was the outstanding case paperwork and the need for preparation ahead of the next day's formal interview with Harry White. When Mikeš had intervened in the conversation, informing Boukal that these tasks could wait, he then began bemoaning the fact he was going to miss the celebration drink. In the end, Mikeš had told Boukal plainly he couldn't wear the slashed suit to work any more, and if he didn't have an alternative he'd have to stay off work until he could buy a new one.

So it was that a sulking Boukal was being manhandled by the tailor, measuring his chest and neck size, arm length and finally, waist and inside leg. Jonny sat watching the proceedings, chuckling to himself, seeing Boukal go through his own version of hell.

As he sat watching Boukal picking out colours and styles of suit to try on, Jonny had the first opportunity in days to sit in peace and reflect. The realisation dawned on him that he felt more needed and cared for than at any other time in his working life. This obviously discounted his mother, who was special beyond words and would always be with him. But, now he had family working closely with him, as well as an exceptionally close and rewarding friendship with Mikeš. It was easy to discount Boukal, but the truth was he also felt extremely proud and protective of him; like the son he'd never had. With his relationship with Ivana added into the mix, he knew he was lucky, having landed in the warmest nest possible.

"What do you think, Honza?"

Jonny's cogitations were interrupted by a smiling Boukal, standing in front of him, having stepped out from the changing cubicle. Boukal turned clockwise slowly, his neck craned to see the back of the suit in the long mirror. The suit was simple but effective, providing Boukal with a much needed fresh image; the dark blue, single breasted jacket was complemented by a gleaming new, white shirt and a dark green, woven tie.

"Marek, you look like a new man." Jonny laughed. "You're going to give Felix a run for his money."

"I'll take it," Boukal said, repeating the statement in Czech for the tailor.

"We'll take two suits the same," Jonny stated. "Plus, five white shirts in total. And, Marek can choose four other matching ties."

The tailor looked at Boukal for confirmation. After a moment's consideration, he nodded, appearing reluctant but clearly pleased with the result.

"And, I'm paying," Jonny added firmly.

"No way!"

"Fifty-fifty, then. That's my final offer."

Boukal shook his head in genuine disbelief and stepped forward to shake Jonny's outstretched hand. "Thank you, Honza."

***

When Boukal entered the Black Cat pub, suited and booted, he was greeted by wolf whistles from the collected detectives and uniform officers. He proudly strutted around the open, wooden bar floor to applause and shouts of approval. Even his shiny new, black shoes – a last minute purchase at Jonny's insistence – were getting noticed.

Mikeš stepped forward and looked Boukal up and down, a big cat-like grin spreading across his face. He held his deputy at arm's length, taking in the new look. Releasing him, Mikeš adjusted the knot of Boukal's tie in a fatherly fashion and slapped him on the arm, finally enveloping him into a warm embrace.

Jonny and Dvořáková joined them in the middle of the bar, holding two beers each.

"It looks like I have competition," Mikeš remarked to Jonny, amusement in his voice as he took his beer.

Mikeš immediately spun around to address his captive audience. "Dámy a pánové. Gratulujeme. Skvělá práce pro každého!"

The gathered team members broke out into a crescendo of applause, the clapping rising and falling in waves, with accompanying whoops of joy. Jonny had been immediately taken by the celebration ritual when he'd first experienced it, now believing it to be the best possible endorsement of a team job well done; everyone was involved, playing their own part, the outcome creating a swell of energy and happy faces all round.

Mikeš then shouted, "Na zdraví," in salute. Everyone raised their glass, repeated the toast and took a long swig of their drink. Jonny spotted Liška in the crowd and raised his beer glass towards him in celebration.

Once the noise had faded, Mikeš grabbed Jonny and pulled him aside, beckoning Boukal and Dvořáková over to join them.

"Honza, I just said congratulations to everyone for a great job."

"Yes, I understood," Jonny replied, smiling at his friend.

Mikeš put on a face of mock surprise. "You are learning fast, my friend. I'd better be careful what I say in front of you."

The four of them laughed and clinked glasses.

"Actually," Mikeš continued, "I have a few more announcements to make." He paused for dramatic effect, looking around the small group, locking eyes with each of his core team.

"Firstly, because of Marek's courage in capturing Harry White, risking his own life in the process, I have put him forward for a bravery award. The Police Commissioner has agreed with me and the recommendation will be submitted to the High Commission next month."

Jonny was first to shake his protégé's hand. "And, you have a great, new suit to wear at the ceremony now."

Dvořáková wrapped Boukal up in a big, congratulatory hug.

"Secondly," Mikeš continued, "I have submitted a written report to the Police Commissioner explaining Lucie's crucial role in linking Harry White to the double murders. This I have submitted with a glowing endorsement from Honza. The report states that Harry White would possibly have escaped, and Tanya Murray may also have been killed, without Lucie's timely intervention. Sadly, there will be no bravery award, Lucie, but today I have finally got around to opening my post and I have had notification you have been put forward for your detective exam in June."

Dvořáková's hands went up to her face in shock.

"Congratulations, Lucie," Boukal exclaimed.

This time it was Jonny's turn to step forward and embrace her. "You deserve it, Lucie. And, I know you will make a top detective."

"Sadly, Honza," Mikeš concluded, "I have no awards, but you have my heartfelt thanks for helping us all. You are the best detective I've ever known, and it is a pleasure to work with you every day and be your friend."

Mikeš and Jonny shook hands respectfully across the group.

"Actually," Jonny said, "I have an announcement of my own."

"You're getting married," Mikeš bellowed. "I knew it—"

"No, Felix, no." Jonny shook his head, alarmed at the suggestion. "Not even close."

Mikeš held his arms out in innocence.

"As you all know," Jonny restarted, "I have been looking for my Czech family here in Prague. This week brought some amazing, but initially confusing news. To tell you the truth, it's been a bit of a shock. I was bracing myself for bad news, preparing for the worst, but instead the news is wonderful. I am pleased to announce that Lucie's mother is my cousin."

Mikeš looked at Jonny, slowly across at Dvořáková, and back again.

"Yes, Lucie and I are family," Jonny confirmed.

Jonny put his arm around Dvořáková and pulled her into him proudly.

Mikeš remained open-mouthed, his finger wagging hesitantly in mid-air between them.

Boukal was beaming in pleasure at the news, the drama of the day now all making sense.

"Well, well, well," Mikeš finally said, shaking his head in incredulity. "Now, it's totally clear where Lucie gets her detective pedigree from."

42

Family Album

Sunday, 18th April

Jonny kept telling himself it was no big deal, just a Sunday lunch with family. But, his trembling knees were giving him away, involuntarily jumping to their own nervous beat. He could also feel sweat building along the nape of his neck and down his spine.

Ivana had been a rock, encouraging him when he had second thoughts during the morning. When he'd claimed he was too tired and suggested postponing, especially after the heavy night of celebration, she'd simply played the fate card back to him, telling him it was meant to be this way. Coming from a smaller family herself, having just one living sister she hardly saw, she empathised with his apprehension about an extended family.

Dvořáková and her father, Miloš, had met them at the front door. The introductions were warm, but polite, something Ivana had warned Jonny to expect – the guard would be held high until mutual confidences were shared and a personal bond established. But, this caution had dissipated the moment Lenka, his newly found cousin, entered the living room. She brought with her the emotion of the saved up family saga over more than five decades, bursting into tears of happiness as, unable to speak, she took him deep in her arms.

Tea was organised by Miloš and his daughter in the kitchen whilst pleasantries were exchanged. Jonny sat in the middle of the sofa, Ivana on one side, her hand supportively on his back, and Lenka holding both his hands on the other. Human touch alone was starting to bridge the gap of years not knowing each other.

Lenka's English was adequate but rusty, so Ivana helped her with the words forgotten without regular use. She told Jonny how lucky and relieved she felt, never believing the family would all be together again.

All Jonny could think about was how much Lenka looked like his mother: the eyes, the hairline and the shape of the face that he knew so well from his childhood seemed to be miraculously staring back at him. He had tried to explain, with Ivana's help, but he knew words could not do justice to what he was seeing. Only the photo in his wallet, taken at a police awards ceremony, would prove the similarity. But, he was keen to be patient and not thrust his history on the meeting – the family album would come in time.

Dvořáková kneeled down on the carpet in front of the sofa, reaching out to hold hands with both Jonny and Lenka.

"Honza, after I left the pub last night, I came straight to see my mother and father. I told my mother about what you had found in your family tree search and I showed her the document with all the family names, dates of birth and last known addresses. Naturally, she was shocked but also overjoyed. Later in the evening, my mother started crying and was quite upset. I didn't know what was wrong, but once she had calmed down she told me a story that I had never heard before. Because her English is not great, she has asked me to tell you this story now."

Lenka smiled at Jonny and squeezed his hand, nodding at her daughter in encouragement.

"When my grandmother was dying, she wanted to tell my mother all the family stories so they could be passed down through the generations. My mother thought she had heard all these stories many times before, but there was one story, saved until last, that she did not know. When my grandmother was young she got married early and had a son – my uncle – Erik. But, the pregnancy was difficult and she nearly died. After her son was born, she was told by the doctors that she couldn't have any more children."

Jonny looked at Lenka confused. She waved on her daughter, wanting to get to the end before any questions were asked.

"Three years later, your mother also got pregnant. However, she wasn't married and the father ran off, never to be traced. Rather than face a family embarrassment, her father, your grandfather, insisted that when the child was born it would be raised by your mother's sister – my grandmother. This was because she was married and already had a child. So, the sisters were hidden inside the house for months, until the baby was born. That child was my mother. Your mother was so angry with the family for what they had forced on her, she ran away to the UK, cutting off all contact."

"So," Jonny stuttered, "your mother is my sister?"

"I think you say half-sister. But, yes, that is correct."

Now, it was Jonny's turn to be overcome with emotion. His body reflex took over, his chest heaving in uncontrollable judders. He buried his head in Lenka's shoulder, the tears flooding as the heightened emotion drained out of him.

Minutes passed before he could raise his head. He kissed Lenka on the cheek and embraced her properly, speaking the words, "Moje sestra," softly for them both to hear.

My sister.